DEBBIE MACOMBER

This Time for Keeps

MIRA

ISBN 1-55166-474-7

THIS TIME FOR KEEPS
Copyright © 2003 by MIRA Books.

THE MATCHMAKERS
Copyright © 1986 by Debbie Macomber.

THE FORGETFUL BRIDE
Copyright © 1991 by Debbie Macomber.

Visit us at www.mirabooks.com

Printed in U.S.A.

CONTENTS

THE MATCHMAKERS

One

"Danny, hurry up and eat your cereal," Dori Robertson pleaded as she rushed from the bathroom to the bedroom. Quickly pulling on a tweed skirt and a shell-knit sweater, she slipped her feet into black leather pumps and hurried into the kitchen.

"Aren't you going to eat, Mom?"

"No time." As fast as her fingers would cooperate, Dori spread peanut butter and jelly across bread for a sandwich, then opened the refrigerator door and took out an orange. She stuffed both items in a brown paper sack with a cartoon cat on the front. Lifting the lid of the cookie jar, she dug around and came up with only a handful of crumbs. Graham crackers would have to do.

"How come we're always so rushed in the mornings?" eleven-year-old Danny wanted to know.

Dori paused and laughed. The sound was low and sweetly musical. There'd been a time in her life when everything had fitted into place. But not anymore. "Because your mother has trouble getting out of bed."

"Were you always late when Dad was here?"

Turning, Dori leaned against the kitchen counter and crossed her arms. "No. Your father used to bring me a cup of coffee in bed." Brad had had his own special way of waking her with coffee and kisses. But now Brad was gone and, except for their son, she faced the world alone. Admittedly the rushed mornings were much easier to accept than the long lonely nights.

"Would you like me to bring you coffee? I could," Danny offered seriously. "I've seen you make it lots of times."

A surge of love for her son constricted the muscles of her throat, and Dori tried to swallow the dry lump. Every day Danny grew more like his father. Tenderly she looked down at his sparkling blue eyes and the broad band of freckles that danced across his nose. Brad's eyes had been exactly that shade of bottomless blue, though the freckles were all hers. Pinching her lips together, she turned back to the counter, picked up a cup and took her first sip of lukewarm coffee. "That's very thoughtful of you," she said.

"Then I can?"

"Sure. It might help." Anything would be better than this infernal rushing every morning. "Now brush your teeth and get your coat."

When Danny moved down the hallway, Dori carried his empty cereal bowl to the sink. The morning paper was open, and she quickly folded it and set it aside. There had once been a time when Danny had pored over the sports section, but recently he'd been reading the want ads. He hadn't asked for anything in particular lately, and she couldn't imagine what he found so fascinating in the classified section. Kids! At his age, she remembered, her only interest in the newspaper had been the comics and Dear Abby. Come to think of it, she didn't read much more than that now.

Danny joined her in the kitchen and together they went out the door and into the garage. While Dori backed the Dodge onto the narrow driveway, Danny stood by and waited to pull the garage door closed.

"One of these days," she grumbled as her son climbed into the front seat, "I'm going to get an automatic garage-door opener."

Danny tossed her a curious look. "Why? You've got me."

A smile worked its way across Dori's face. "Why, indeed?"

Several minutes followed while Danny said nothing. That was unusual, and twice Dori's gaze sought his eager young face. His look was troubled, but she didn't pry, knowing her son would speak when he was ready.

"Say, Mom, I've been wanting to ask you something," Danny began haltingly, then paused.

"What?" Dori said, thinking that the Seattle traffic got worse every morning. Or maybe it wasn't that the traffic got thicker, just that she got later.

"I've been thinking."

"Did it hurt?" That was an old joke of theirs, but Danny didn't have an immediate comeback the way he usually did.

"Hey, kid, this is serious, isn't it?"

Danny shrugged one shoulder in an offhand manner. "Well, I know you loved Dad and everything, but I think it's time you found me another dad."

Dori slammed on her brakes. The car came to a screeching halt at the red light as she turned to her son, her dark eyes rounded in shock. "Time I did what?" she asked incredulously.

"It's been five years, Mom. Dad wouldn't have wanted you to mope through the rest of your life. Next year I'm going to junior high and a kid needs a dad at that age."

Dori opened her mouth searching for words of wisdom that didn't come.

"I can make coffee in the mornings and all that, but you need a husband. And I need a dad."

"This is all rather sudden, isn't it?" Her voice was little more than a husky murmur.

"No, I've been thinking about it for a long time." Danny swiveled his head over his shoulder and pointed behind him. "Say, Mom, you just missed the school."

"Damn." She flipped on her turn signal and moved into the right lane with only a fleeting glance in her rearview mirror.

"Mom...watch out!" Danny shrieked just as her rear bumper barely missed the front end of an expensive foreign car. Dori swerved out of the path, narrowly avoiding a collision.

The driver of the other car blared his horn angrily and followed her when she pulled into a side street that would lead her back to the grade school.

"The guy you almost hit is following you, Mom and, boy, does he look mad."

"Great." Dori's fingers tightened around the steering wheel. This day was quickly going from bad to worse.

With his head turned around, Danny continued his commentary. "Now it looks like he's writing down your license plate number."

"Wonderful. What does he plan to do? Make a citizen's arrest?"

"He can do that?" Danny returned his attention to his flustered mother.

"Yup, and he looks like the type who would." The uncompromising, hard face that briefly met hers in the rearview mirror looked capable of just about anything. The deeply set dark eyes had narrowed into points of steel. The thick, equally dark hair was styled away from his face, revealing the harsh contours of his craggy features. He wasn't what could be called handsome, but his masculinity was blatant and forceful. "A man's man" was the term that came to mind.

"I recognize him," Danny said thoughtfully. "At least I think I do."

"Who is he?" Dori took a right-hand turn and eased to a stop in front of Cascade View Elementary. The man in the Audi 5000 pulled to a stop directly behind her and got out of his car.

"He looks familiar," Danny commented a second time, his wide brow furrowed in concentration, "but I don't know from where."

Squaring her shoulders, Dori reluctantly opened the car door and climbed out. Absently she brushed a thick swatch of auburn hair off her shoulder as she walked back to meet the tall formidable man waiting for her. Dressed in an impeccable three-piece suit and expensive leather shoes, he was all the more intimidating. His dark eyes followed her movements. They were interesting and arresting eyes in a face that looked capable of forging an empire—or at least slicing her to ribbons—with one arch of a brow. Dori was determined not to let him unnerve her. She indicated with her hand that Danny should stay by the car, but he seemed to think she'd need him for protection. She didn't, but couldn't take the time to argue with him.

"I don't appreciate being followed." She decided her best defense was an offense.

"And I don't appreciate being driven off the road."

"I apologize for that, but you were in my blind spot and when I went to change lanes—"

"You didn't so much as look."

"I most certainly did," Dori stated evenly, her voice gaining volume. For the first time she noticed a large brown stain on his suit jacket. The beginnings of a smile edged up the corners of her mouth.

"Just what do you find so amusing?" he demanded harshly.

Dori cast her eyes to the pavement. "I'm sorry. I didn't mean to be rude."

"The most polite thing you can do, lady, is to stay off the roads."

Hands on her hips, her hazel eyes sparking fire, Dori advanced one step. "In case you weren't aware, there's a law in Washington state against drinking any beverage while driving. You can't blame me if you spilled your coffee. You shouldn't have had it in the car with you in the first place." She prayed the righteous indignation in her tone would be enough to assure him she knew what she was talking about.

"You damned near caused an accident." He, too, advanced a step and a tremor ran through her at the stark anger in his eyes.

"I've already apologized for that," Dori said, knowing that if this confrontation continued she would come out the loser. Discretion was the better part of valor—at least that was what her father always claimed, and for once Dori was willing to follow his advice. "If it will smooth your ruffled feathers any, I'll pay the cleaning cost for your suit."

The school bell rang, and Danny hurried back to the car for his books and his lunch. "I've got to go, Mom."

Dori was digging around the bottom of her purse looking for a business card. "Okay, have a good day." She hoped one of them would; hers certainly didn't look promising.

"Don't forget I've got soccer practice after school," he reminded her, walking backward toward the front steps of the school.

"I won't."

"And Mom?"

"Yes, Danny," she answered irritably, the tight rein on her patience quickly slackening.

"Do you promise to think about what I said?"

Dori glanced up at him blankly.

"You know, about getting me another dad?"

Dori could feel the hot color creep up her neck and invade her pale face. Diverting her gaze from the unpleasant man standing beside her, she expelled her breath in a low groan. "I'll think about it."

A boyish grin brightened Danny's face as he turned and ran toward his classmates.

Searching for a business card helped lessen some of Dori's acute embarrassment. Another man would have said something to ease her chagrin, but not this one. "I'm sure I've got a card in here someplace."

"Forget it," the man said gruffly.

"No," she argued. "I'm responsible, so I'll pay."

Unable to find what she wanted, Dori wrote her name and address on the back of her grocery list. "Here," she said, handing him the long narrow slip of paper.

He examined it briefly and stuck it into his suit pocket. "Thank you, Mrs. Robertson."

"It was my fault."

"I believe you've already admitted as much." Nothing seemed capable of cracking the granite facade this man wore like armor.

"I'll be waiting for the bill, Mr...?"

"Parker," he completed grudgingly. "Gavin Parker." He turned and retreated toward his car.

The name was strangely familiar to Dori, but she couldn't recall where she'd heard it. Odd. Danny had seemed to recognize him, too.

"Mr. Parker," Dori called out and raised her finger.

"Yes?" Irritably he turned to face her again.

"Excuse me, but I wonder if I could have another look at the paper I gave you."

The set of his mouth tightened into an impatient line as he removed the slip from his pocket and handed it back to her.

Quickly her eyes scanned the grocery list, hoping to commit it to memory. "Thanks. I just wanted to be sure I remembered everything."

The cold raking gaze of his eyes unsettled her, and by the time Dori was in her car and heading for the insurance office, she had forgotten every item. What an unnerving man! Just the memory of the look in his eyes was enough to cause a chill to race up her spine. His mouth had been interesting, though. Not that she usually noticed men's mouths. But his had been firm with that chiseled effect so many women liked. There was a hard-muscled grace to him...Dori put a bridle on her thoughts. How ridiculous she was being. She refused to give one extra minute's thought to that unpleasant character.

The employee parking lot was full when she arrived and she was forced to look for a place on the street, which was nearly impossible at this time of morning. Luckily, she found a narrow space three blocks from the insurance company where she was employed as an underwriter for homeowner policies.

By the time she arrived at her desk, she was irritated, exhausted and ten minutes late.

"You're late." Sandy Champoux announced as Dori rolled back her chair.

"I hadn't noticed," Dori returned sarcastically, dropping her purse in a bottom drawer and pretending an all-consuming interest in the file on her desk as her boss, Mr. Sandstorm, sauntered past.

"You always seem to make it to your desk on time," Sandy said, ignoring the sarcasm. "What happened this morning?"

"You mean other than a near car accident with a nasty man in a three-piece suit or Danny telling me the time has come to find him a new father?"

"The kid's right, you know."

Purposely being obtuse, Dori batted her thick lashes at her friend and smiled coyly. "Who's right? Danny or the man in the three-piece suit?"

"Danny! You *should* think about getting married again. It's time you joined the world of the living."

"Ah—" Dori pointed her index finger at the ceiling "—you misunderstand the problem. Danny wants a father in the same way he wanted a ten-speed bike.

He's not interested in a husband for me..." She paused and bit the her bottom lip as a thought flashed into her mind. "That's it." Her eyes lit up.

"What's it?" Sandy demanded.

"The ten-speed."

"You're going to bribe your son with another bicycle so he'll forget his need for a father?" Sandy was giving Dori the look she usually reserved for people showing off pictures of their children.

"No, Sandy," Dori groaned, slowly shaking her head from side to side. "You don't want to know."

Her brow marred with a disgruntled frown, Sandy reached for a new policy from her basket. "If you say so."

Despite its troubled beginnings, the day passed quickly and without further incident. Dori was waiting to speak to her son when he trooped into the house at five-thirty, his soccer shoes looped around his neck.

"Hi, Mom, what's there to eat?"

"Dinner. Soon."

"But I'm starved now."

"Good, set the table." Dori waited until Danny had washed his hands and placed two dinner plates on the round oak table before she spoke. "I've been thinking about what you said this morning."

"Did it hurt?" Danny questioned and gave her a roguish grin, creating twin dimples in his freckled face. "What did you decide?"

"Well..." Dori paid an inordinate amount of attention to the cube steak she was frying, then said, "I'll admit I wasn't exactly thrilled with the idea. At least not right away."

"And now?" Danny stood at the table and studied her keenly.

She paused, gathering her resolve. "The more I thought about it," she said at last, "the more I realized you may have a valid point."

"Then we can start looking?" His young voice vibrated with eagerness. "I've had my eye on lots of neat guys. There's one who helps the coach with the soccer team who would do real good, but I don't think he's old enough. Is nineteen too young?"

This was worse than Dori had thought. "Not so fast," she said, stalling for time. "We need to go about this methodically."

"Oh, great," Danny mumbled and heaved a disgusted sigh. "I know what that means."

"It means we'll wait until after the dinner dishes are done and make up a list just like we did when we got your bike."

Danny brightened. "Hey, that's a great idea."

Dori wasn't nearly so sure as Danny rushed through his dinner in record time. The minute the dishes were washed and put away, the boy produced a large writing tablet.

"You ready?" he asked, pausing to chew on the tip of the eraser.

"Sure."

"First we should get someone as old as you."

"At least thirty," Dori agreed, pulling out a chair.

"And tall, because Dad was tall and it'd look funny if we got a really short guy. I don't want to end up being taller than my new dad."

"That makes sense." Again Dori was impressed by how seriously her son was taking this.

"He should like sports because I like sports. You try, Mom, but I'd really like someone who can throw a football better than you."

That was one duty Dori would relinquish gladly. "I think that's a good idea."

"And I think it would be neat if he knew karate."

"Why not?" Dori agreed amicably.

Danny's pencil worked furiously over the paper as he added this latest specification to the growing list. "And most important—" the blues eyes grew sober "—my new dad should love you."

"That would be nice," Dori murmured in a wavering breath. Brad had loved her. So much that for a while she'd thought she'd die without him. Even after all these years, the capacity to love another man with such intensity seemed beyond her.

"Now what?" Danny looked up at her expectantly.

"Now," she said and sucked in a giant breath. "Now that we know what we're looking for, all we need to do is wait for the right man to come along."

Danny looked doubtful. "That could take a long time."

"Not with both of us looking." She took Danny's list and placed it on the refrigerator with a large strawberry magnet. "Isn't it time for your bath, young man?"

Danny stood with obvious reluctance, shoved the pad and pencil into the kitchen drawer and headed down the hall that led to his bedroom.

Dori retired to the living room, took out her needlepoint and turned on the television. Maybe Danny was right. There had to be more to life than work, cooking and needlepoint. It wasn't that she hadn't tried to date. She had. Sandy had fixed her up with a friend of a friend at the beginning of summer. The evening had turned out to be a disaster, and Dori had refused her friend's attempts to match her up again. Besides, there hadn't been any reason to date. She was fairly content and suffered only occasionally from bouts of loneliness, usually late at night. Danny managed to fill her life. He loved sports and she loved watching him play.

But Danny was right. He did need a father figure, especially now as he moved into adolescence. Deep down Dori wondered how anyone could replace Brad. Danny had been too young to remember much about his father, as Brad had died when Danny was only six. Her own memories of that age were vague and distant, and she wondered how much she would have remembered of her father if she'd been in Danny's place.

The house was unusually quiet. Danny was normally in and out of the bath so quickly that she often wondered if he'd even given himself the chance to get completely wet.

Just as she was about to investigate, Danny ran into the room, clutching a handful of bubble gum cards. "Mom, that was Gavin Parker you nearly ran into today!"

Dori glanced up from her needlepoint. "I know."

"Mom—" the young voice was filled with awe "—why didn't you say something? I want his autograph."

"His autograph?" Suddenly things were beginning to add up. "Why would you want that?"

"Why?" Danny gasped. "He's only the greatest athlete in the whole world."

Dori decided to ignore her son's exaggeration.

Gavin Parker might be a talented sportsman, but he was also rude and arrogant. He was one man she instinctively wanted to avoid.

"Here, look." Danny shoved a football card under her nose.

Indeed, the name was the same, but the features were much younger, smoother, more subdued somehow. The dark piercing eyes in the picture only hinted at the capacity for aggression. Gavin Parker's appearance had altered over the years and the changes in him were due to more than age. The photo that glared back at her was of an intense young man, filled with an enthusiasm and energy for life. The man she'd met today was angry and bitter, disillusioned. Of course the circumstances of their meeting hadn't exactly been conducive to a friendly conversation.

The back of the card listed his height, weight and position—quarterback. According to the information, Gavin had played for the Oakland Raiders, leading his team to two Super Bowl championships. In the year he'd retired, Gavin had been given the Most Valuable Player award.

"How did you know who he was?" Dori questioned in a light tone of surprise. "It says here that he quit playing football six years ago."

"Mom, Gavin Parker was one of the greatest players to ever throw a football. Everyone knows about him. Besides, he does the commentary for the Vikings' games on Sundays."

Every Sunday afternoon, Dori and Danny joined her parents for dinner. Vaguely, Dori recalled the games that had captured the attention of the two men in her life: her father and her son. Football had never interested her very much.

"Can we ask him for his autograph?" Danny asked hopefully.

"Danny," Dori said with a sigh, sticking the needle forcefully through the thick linen fabric, "I sincerely doubt that we'll ever see Mr. Parker again."

The young shoulders sagged with defeat. "Darn. Now the guys won't believe me when I tell them my mom nearly drove Gavin Parker off the road."

"I know you may find this hard to believe," Dori admitted softly, "but I'd rather not have the world know about our little mishap this morning, anyway."

"Aw, Mom."

"Haven't you got homework?"

"Aw, Mom."

Her lips curved and her resolve not to smile vanished. "The room seems to have developed an echo recently."

His head drooping, Danny returned to his bedroom.

The following morning in the early dawn light, Dori was awakened by a loud knock on her bedroom door. Struggling to lift herself up on one elbow, she brushed the wild array of springy auburn curls from her face.

"Yes?" The one word was all she could manage.

Already dressed in jeans, Danny entered the bedroom, a steaming cup of coffee in his hand.

"Morning, Mom."

"My eyes are deceiving me," she mumbled, leaning back against the pillow. "I thought I saw an angel bearing me tidings of joy and a cup of java."

"Nope," Danny said with a smile. "This is coffee."

"Bless you, my child."

"Mom?"

"Hmm?" Still fighting off the urge to bury her face in the pillow and sleep, Dori forced her eyes open.

"Do…I mean, do you always look like this when you wake up?"

Dori blinked self-consciously and again smoothed the unruly mass of curls from her face. "Why?"

Clearly uneasy, Danny shuffled his feet and stared at the top of his tennis shoes. "If someone were to see you with your hair sticking out like that, I might never get a new dad."

"I'll try to improve," she grumbled, somewhat piqued.

"Thanks." Appeased, Danny left, giving Dori the opportunity to pout in private. Muttering to herself, she threw back the sheets and climbed out of bed. A glance in the bathroom mirror confirmed what Danny had said. And her hair wasn't the only thing that needed a change.

By the time Dori arrived in the kitchen, she'd managed to transform herself from the Wicked Witch of the West to something quite presentably feminine.

One look at his mother and Danny beamed her a radiant smile of approval. "You look real pretty now."

"Thanks." She refilled her cup with coffee and tried to hide her grimace at its bitterness. Later, with the utmost tact and diplomacy, she'd show Danny exactly how much ground coffee to use. If she drank any more of this brew, she thought, she wouldn't need perms to curl her hair.

"Do you think we might see Gavin Parker on the

way to school?'' her son asked brightly as they pulled out of the driveway.

''I doubt it,'' Dori answered. ''In fact, I doubt that Mr. Parker lives in Seattle. He was probably just visiting.''

''Darn. Do you really think so?''

''Well, keep your eyes peeled. You never know.''

For the remainder of the ride to the school, Danny was subdued, studying the traffic. Dori was grateful he didn't catch a glimpse of Gavin Parker. If he had, she wasn't sure what Danny would have expected her to do. Running him off the road again was out of the question. She felt lucky to have come away unscathed after the encounter the day before.

Danny didn't mention Gavin again that day or the next, and Dori was convinced she had heard the last about ''the world's greatest athlete.'' But the first of the week she was surprised when a cleaning bill arrived in the mail.

The envelope was typed, and fleetingly Dori wondered if Mr. Gavin Parker had instructed his secretary to mail the bill. In addition to the receipt from a downtown dry cleaner, Gavin had returned her grocery list. Hot color blossomed in Dori's cheeks as she turned the paper over and saw the bold handwriting. At the bottom of her list Gavin had added ''Driving lessons.'' Dori crumpled the paper and tossed it into the garbage.

The sooner she ended her dealings with this audacious man the better. She had just finished writing the check when Danny sauntered into the room.

''What can I have for a snack?'' he asked as he looked over her shoulder.

''An apple.''

"Can I have some cookies, too?"

"All right, as long as you promise to eat a decent dinner." Not that there was much worry. Danny had developed a perpetual appetite of late. The refrigerator door opened behind her.

"Hey, Mom, what's this?"

Dori tossed a look over her shoulder at the yellow nylon bag Danny was holding up, pinched between forefinger and thumb. "Tulip bulbs. For heaven's sake, don't eat one."

Her son ignored her attempt at humor. "How long are they going to be in here?"

Dori flushed slightly, recalling that she'd bought them on special six weeks earlier. "I'll plant them soon," she promised.

With a loud crunch from a crisp red apple, Danny pulled up the chair across from her. "What are you doing?"

"Paying a bill." Guiltily she diverted her gaze to her checkbook, deciding to leave well enough alone and not mention to whom she was sending money. Another one of her discretion-and-valor decisions.

On the following Saturday morning, Dori came out of her bedroom and sleepily tied the sash of her housecoat. The sound of cartoons blaring from the living room assured her that Danny was already up. An empty cereal bowl on the table was further testimony. The coffee was made, and with a soft smile she poured a cup and diluted it with milk.

"You're up." Danny strolled into the kitchen and grinned approvingly when he noticed she'd combed her hair.

"Don't get hooked on those cartoons," she warned. "I want us to get some yard work done today."

"I've got a soccer game." Danny's protest was immediate.

"Not until eleven-thirty."

"Aw, Mom, I hate yard work."

"So do I," she said, although planting the tulip bulbs was a matter of pride to her. Otherwise they'd sit for another year in the vegetable bin of the refrigerator.

Twenty minutes later, dressed in washed-out jeans and a faded sweatshirt that had seen better days, Dori got the hand trowel from the garage.

The day was glorious. The sun had broken through and splashed the earth with a flood of golden light. The weather was unseasonably warm for October, and the last days of an Indian summer graced Seattle.

Danny was content to rake the leaves that had fallen from the giant maple tree onto the boulevard, and Dori was surprised to hear herself humming softly. The scarf that held her hair away from her face slipped down and she pushed it back with one hand, smearing a thin layer of mud across her cheek.

She was muttering in annoyance when Danny went into peals of excitement.

"You came, you came!" Danny cried enthusiastically.

Who came? Stripping off her gloves, Dori rose reluctantly to find Gavin Parker staring at her from across the yard.

"This damned well better be important," he said as he advanced toward her.

Two

"Important?" Dori repeated, not understanding. "What?"

"This." Impatiently Gavin shoved a slip of paper under her nose.

Not bothering to read the message, Dori shrugged. "I didn't send you anything more than the check."

His young face reddening, Danny stepped forward, the bamboo rake in his hand. "You didn't, Mom, but I...I did."

Dori's response was instinctive and instant. "What?" She jerked the paper from Gavin's fingers. "I MUST TALK TO YOU AT ONCE—D. ROBERTSON" was typed in perfect capital letters.

"You see," Danny went on to explain in a rushed voice, "Mom said we would probably never see you again and I wanted your autograph. So when Mom put the envelope on the counter to go in the mail, I opened it and stuck the note inside. I really want your autograph, Mr. Parker. You were the greatest quarterback ever!"

If Gavin felt any pleasure in Danny's profession of undying loyalty, none was revealed in the uncompromising line of his mouth. From the corner of her eye, Dori caught a glimpse of a blonde fidgeting in the front seat of his car, which was parked on the boulevard. Obviously Gavin Parker had other things on his mind.

Placing a protective arm around her son's shoulders, Dori met Gavin's unflinching gaze. "I apologize for any inconvenience my son has caused you. I can assure you it won't ever happen again."

Taking his cue from the barely restrained anger vibrating in his mother's voice, Danny dropped his head and kicked at the fallen leaves with the toe of his tennis shoe. "I'm sorry, too. I just wanted your autograph to prove to the guys that Mom really did almost drive you off the road."

A car door slammed and Dori's attention was diverted to the boulevard. Surprise mingled with disbelief. It wasn't a woman with Gavin Parker, but a young girl. No more than thirteen and quite pretty, but desperately trying to hide her femininity.

"What's taking so long?" The girl sauntered up in faded blue jeans and a Seahawk football jersey. The long blond hair was pulled tightly away from her face and tied at her nape. A few curls had worked themselves free and she raised a disgruntled hand to her head, obviously displeased with the way the natural curls had sprung loose.

A smile lit her eyes as she noticed that Danny was wearing a football jersey identical to her own. "Hey, do you like the Seahawks?"

"You bet I do. We're gonna make it to the playoffs this year," Danny boasted confidently.

"I think so, too. My dad used to play pro ball and he says that the Hawks have got a good chance."

Approving dimples appeared on Danny's freckled face.

"Get back to the car, Melissa." Gavin's tone brooked no argument.

"But, Dad, it's hot in there and I'm thirsty."

"Would you like a glass of orange juice?" Danny offered enthusiastically. "Gosh, I didn't think girls liked football."

"I know everything there is to know about it and I throw a good pass, too. Just ask my dad."

Before either Gavin or Dori could object, Melissa and Danny were walking toward the house.

A delicate brow lifted in questioning. "I'll trade you one cup of coffee for an autograph," said Dori resignedly. A cup of Danny's coffee was poetic justice, and a smile hovered at the edge of her mouth.

For the first time since their dubious beginning, Gavin smiled. The change the simple movement of his mouth made in his austere expression was remarkable. Deep lines fanned out from his eyes and grooves bracketed his mouth. But the transformation didn't stop with his face. Somehow, in some way, the thick armor he wore had cracked as she was given a rare dazzling smile.

Unfortunately his good humor didn't last long, and by the time he'd followed her into the house the facade was back in place.

Melissa and Danny were at the kitchen table, sipping from tall glasses filled with orange juice.

"Dad—" Melissa looked up eagerly "—can Danny go to the Puyallup Fair with us? It's not any fun to go on the rides by myself and you hate that kind of stuff."

"I'm afraid Danny's got a soccer game this afternoon."

"I'm the center striker," Danny inserted proudly. "Would you like to come and watch me play?"

"Could we, Dad? You know how I love soccer. When the game's over we could go to the fair." Melissa immediately worked out their scheduling.

It was all happening so fast that Dori didn't know what to think.

"Mrs. Robertson?" Gavin deferred to her for a decision.

"What time would Danny be home tonight?" Dori asked, stalling for time. Gavin Parker might be a famous football player, but he was a stranger and she wasn't about to release her child to someone she didn't know. If she had to come up with an excuse, she could always use church the following morning and their weekly dinner with her parents.

"You have to come, too," Melissa insisted. "Dad would be bored to tears with Danny and me going on all the rides."

"Could we? Oh, Mom, could we?"

Needing some kind of confirmation, Dori sought Gavin's eyes.

Gavin said quietly, "It would make Melissa happy."

But not him. It didn't take much for Dori to tell that Gavin wasn't overly pleased with this turn of events. Not that she blamed him. The idea of spending an afternoon with two children and a dirt-smudged mom wouldn't thrill her, either.

Apparently seeing the indecision in her eyes, Gavin added, "It would solve several problems for me."

"Oh, Mom, could we?" repeated Danny, who seemed to have become a human pogo stick, bouncing around the kitchen.

"Who could refuse, faced with such unabashed enthusiasm?" Dori surrendered, wondering what she was letting herself in for. She gave Gavin the address of the nearby park where the game was to be played and arranged to meet him and Melissa there.

Granted a new audience, Danny was in top form for his soccer game. With boundless energy he ran up and down the field while Dori answered a multitide of questions from Melissa. No, Dori explained patiently, she wasn't divorced. Yes, her husband was dead. Yes, Danny and she lived alone. Danny was eleven and in the sixth grade.

Then Melissa explained that her parents were divorced and her dad had custody of her. She attended a boarding school in Seattle because her dad traveled so much. As the vice president in charge of sales in the whole northwest for a large computer company, her dad was real busy. In addition, he did some television commentaries for pro football games on Sunday afternoons, and she couldn't always travel with him.

Standing on the other side of his daughter, Gavin flashed her a look that silenced the girl immediately. But her father's censure apparently didn't intimidate Melissa for long, and a few minutes later she was prodding Dori with more questions.

Danny kicked two of his team's three goals and beamed proudly when Gavin complimented him on a fine game. A couple of the boys followed the small group back to the car, hoping one or the other would get up enough courage to ask Gavin for his autograph.

Since even the discouraging look he gave them wasn't enough to dissuade the young boys, Gavin spent the next five minutes scribbling his name across a variety of slips of paper, hurriedly scrounged from jacket pockets.

The small party stopped at the house so that Danny could take another of his world-record-speed baths and change clothes. While they were waiting, Melissa watched Dori freshen her makeup. When Dori asked the girl if she'd like to use her cologne, Melissa looked at her as though she'd suggested dabbing car grease behind her ears.

"Not on your life. No one's going to get me to use that garbage. That's for sissies."

"Thanks, anyway," Gavin murmured on the way out to the car.

"For what?"

"I've been trying for months to turn this kid into a girl. She's got the strongest will of any female I've yet to meet."

Dori couldn't imagine Gavin losing any argument and was quick to conceal her surprise that his daughter had won this battle.

The Puyallup Fair was the largest agricultural fair in Washington state. Situated in a small farming community thirty miles southwest of Seattle, the fair attracted millions of visitors from all over western Washington and presented top Hollywood entertainment.

As a native Seattlite, Dori had been to the fair several times in the past and loved the thrill and excitement of the midway. The exhibits were some of the best in the nation. And the food was fabulous. Since Gavin had paid for their gate tickets, Dori treated everyone to hush puppies and cotton candy.

"Can we go to the rides now?" Melissa asked eagerly, her arms swinging excitedly at her side.

The crowds were thick, especially in the area of the midway, giving Dori reason for concern.

"I think I'd rather look at some of the exhibits before you two run loose," she said, looking at Gavin. His stoic expression told her he didn't care either way.

If Melissa was disappointed at having to wait, she didn't show it. Spiritedly she ran ahead, pointing out the displays she and Danny wanted to see first.

Together they viewed the rabbits, goats and pigs. Despite herself, Dori laughed at the way Melissa and Danny ran through the cow barn holding their noses. Gavin, too, seemed to be loosening up a little, and his comments regarding Melissa's and Danny's behavior were quite amusing, to Dori's surprise.

"Dad, look." Melissa grabbed her father's arm as they strolled into the chicken area and led him to an incubator where a dozen eggs were set under a warm light. A tiny beak was pecking its way through the white shell, enthralling everyone who watched.

The bee farm, its queen bee marked with a blue dot on her back, was another hit. Fascinated, Danny and Melissa watched the inner workings of a hive for several minutes. On their way out, Dori stopped to hear a ten-minute lecture from a wildlife group. Gavin and the kids weren't nearly as interested, but they all stood and listened to the plight of the American bald eagle.

From the animals' barns, they drifted to the 4-H displays and finally to the agricultural center.

Two hours later, Dori and Gavin sat drinking coffee at a picnic table on the outskirts of the midway while the two youngsters scurried for the rides.

"You don't like me much, do you?" Gavin's direct approach caught Dori by surprise.

It wasn't that she actually disliked him. In fact she had discovered she enjoyed his sharp wit. But Dori didn't try to fool herself with the belief that Gavin had actively sought her company. Having her and Danny along today simply made this time with his daughter less complicated.

"I haven't made up my mind yet." She decided to answer as straightforwardly as he'd asked.

"At least you're honest."

"I can give you a lot more honesty if you want it."

A slow smile crinkled around his eyes. "I have a feeling my ears would burn for a week."

"You're right."

A wary light was reflected in Gavin's gaze. "I've attracted a lot of gold diggers in my day. I want you to understand right now that I have no intention of remarrying."

What incredible conceit! The blood pounded angrily through Dori's veins. "I don't recall proposing marriage," she snapped.

"I didn't want you to get the wrong idea. You're a nice lady and you're doing a good job of raising your son. But he's looking for a father, so he's said, and you're looking for a husband. Just don't try to include me in your rosy little future."

Dori's hand tightened around the cup of coffee. Her eyes widened as she fought back the urge to empty the contents over his head.

The beginning of a smile worked its way across his face. "You have the most expressive eyes. No one need ever doubt when you're angry."

"You wouldn't be smiling if you knew what I was thinking."

"Temper, temper, Mrs. Robertson."

"Far be it from me to force myself on you, Mr. Parker." The derision in her voice was restrained to a bare minimum. Dori was amazed she'd managed that much control. Standing, she deposited her half-full coffee cup into a nearby bin. "Shall we synchronize our watches?"

He stared at her blankly.

"Three hours. I'll meet you back here then."

With his attitude, she'd enjoy herself far more alone. There were still a lot of exhibits to see. Remaining with Gavin was out of the question now. Undoubtedly he'd spend the entire time worrying that she was going to jab a ring through his nose.

Standing hastily, Gavin followed her, a perplexed look narrowing his eyes. "Where are you going?"

"To enjoy myself. And that's any place you're not."

Stopping in his tracks, Gavin looked stunned. "Wait a minute."

Dori jerked the strap of her purse over her shoulder. "Never." Rarely had a man evoked so much emotion in her. The worst part, Dori realized, was that given the least bit of encouragement, she could come to like Gavin Parker. He was a mystery and she always enjoyed a challenge. Melissa was an impressionable young girl, desperately in need of some feminine guidance. It was obvious the girl was more than Gavin could handle. From their conversation during Danny's soccer game, Dori had learned that Melissa spent only an occasional weekend with her father. Dori could only speculate as to the whereabouts of the girl's mother, since Melissa hadn't mentioned her. And Dori didn't want to pry openly.

"You know what your problem is, Gavin Parker?" Dori stormed, causing several people to turn and stare curiously.

Gavin cleared his throat and glanced around self-consciously. "No, but I have a feeling you're going to tell me."

Having worked herself up to a fever pitch, Dori hardly heard him. "You've got a chip on your shoulder the size of a California redwood."

"Would it help if I apologize?"

"It might."

"All right, I'm sorry I said anything. I thought it was important that you understand my position. I don't want you to go home smelling orange blossoms and humming 'The Wedding March.'"

"That's an apology?" Dori yelped.

People were edging around them as they stood, hands on their hips, facing each other, their eyes locked in a fierce duel.

"It's about the best I can do!" Gavin shouted, losing his composure for the first time.

A vendor who was selling trinkets from a nearby stand apparently didn't appreciate their bringing their argument his way. "Hey, you two, kiss and make up. You're driving away business."

Gavin tucked her arm in his and led her away from the milling crowd. "Come on," he said and inhaled a steady breath. "Let's start again." He held out his hand for her to shake. "Hello, Dori, my name is Gavin."

"I prefer Mrs. Robertson." She accepted his hand with reluctance.

"You're making this difficult."

"Now you know how I feel." She bestowed her most chilling glare on him. "I hope you realize that I have no designs on your single status."

"As long as we understand each other."

Dori was incredulous. If he weren't so insulting, she would have laughed.

"Well?" He was waiting for some kind of response.

"I'm going to look at the farm equipment. You're welcome to join me if you like; otherwise, I'll meet you back here in three hours." It simply wasn't a real fair to Dori if she didn't take the time to look at the latest in farm gear. It was a penchant that was a throwback to her heritage. Her grandfather had owned an apple orchard in the fertile Yakima Valley—often called the apple capital of the world.

Gavin brushed the side of his clean-shaven face and a fleeting smile touched the corners of his sensuous mouth. "Farm equipment?"

"Right." If she told him why, he'd probably laugh and she wasn't making herself vulnerable to any more attacks from this irritating male.

As it turned out, they worked their way from one end of the grounds to the other. Several times people stopped to stare curiously at Gavin. If he was aware of their scrutiny, he gave no indication. But no one approached him and they continued their leisurely stroll undisturbed. Dori assumed the reason was that no one would expect the great Gavin Parker to be with someone as ordinary as she. Someone over thirty, yet.

At the arcade, Dori battled to restrain her smile that hovered on the edge of laughter as Gavin tried to pitch a ball and knock over three milk bottles. With his pride on the line, the ex-football hero was determined to win the stuffed lion. An appropriate prize, Dori felt, although he could have purchased two for all he spent to win the one.

"You find this humorous, do you?" he questioned, carrying the huge stuffed beast under his arm.

"Hilarious," she admitted.

"Well, here." He handed the lion to her. "It's yours. I feel ridiculous carrying this around."

Feigning shock, Dori placed a hand over her heart. "My dear Mr. Parker, what could this mean?"

"Just take the stupid thing, will you?"

"One would assume," Dori said as she stroked the orange mane, "that an ex-quarterback could aim a little better than that."

"Ouch." He put out his hands and batted off invisible barbs. "That, Mrs. Robertson, hit below the belt."

She paused and bought some cotton candy, sharing its sticky pink sweetness with him. "Now you know what 'smelling orange blossoms and humming "The Wedding March"' felt like."

Masculine fingers curved around the back of her neck as his eyes smiled into hers. "I guess that did sound a little arrogant, didn't it?"

Smiling up at him, Dori chuckled. "Only a bit."

The sky was alight with stars and a crescent moon in full display before they headed out of the fair grounds and back to Seattle. The Audi's cushioned seats bore a wide variety of accumulated prizes, hats and leftover goodies. Both Danny and Melissa were asleep by the time they located the freeway, exhausted from eight solid hours of recreation.

Forty minutes later, Gavin parked the Audi in front of Dori's small house. Suppressing a yawn, she offered him a warm smile. "Thank you for today."

Their eyes met above the lion's thick mane. He released her gaze by lowering his attention to her softly parted lips, then quickly glancing up.

Flushed and a little self-conscious, Dori directed her attention to her purse, withdrawing her house keys.

"I had fun." Gavin's voice was low and relaxed. "Don't act so surprised."

At the sound of their voices, Danny stirred. Sitting upright, he rubbed the sleep from his eyes. "Are we home?" Not waiting for an answer, he began gathering up his treasures: a mirrored image of his favorite pop star and the multicolored sand sculpture he'd built with Melissa.

Undisturbed, Gavin's daughter slept soundly.

"I had a great time, Mr. Parker." The sleepy edge remained in Danny's voice.

With her keys in one hand and the stuffed lion clutched in the other, Dori opened the car door and helped Danny out of the back seat. "Thanks again," she whispered, bending forward. "Tell Melissa goodbye for me."

"I will." Gavin leaned across the front seat so that his eyes could meet Danny's. "Good night, Danny."

"'Night." The boy turned and waved, but was unsuccessful in his attempt to hold back a huge yawn.

Dori noted that Gavin didn't pull away until they

were safely inside the house. Automatically, Danny moved into his bedroom, not waiting for his mother. Dori set the stuffed lion on the carpet and moved to the window to watch the taillights fade as Gavin disappeared silently into the night. She doubted she'd ever see him again. Which was just as well. At least that was what she told herself.

"Time to get up, Mom." The sound of a loud knock against her bedroom door was followed by Danny's cheerful voice.

Dori groaned and propped open one eye to give her son a desultory glance. Mondays were always the worst. "It can't be morning already," she moaned, blindly reaching out to turn off the alarm before she realized it wasn't ringing.

"I brought your coffee."

"Thanks." Danny's coffee could raise the dead. "Set it on my nightstand."

Danny did as she requested, but instead of leaving as he usually did, he sat on the edge of the mattress. "You know, I've been thinking."

"Oh, no," Dori moaned. She wasn't up to more of Danny's budding insights. "Now what?"

"It's been a whole week now and we still haven't found me a new dad."

After spending the entire Sunday afternoon arguing that Gavin Parker wasn't husband material, Dori didn't feel ready for another such conversation. Someone like her wasn't going to interest Gavin. In addition, he'd made his views on marriage quite plain.

"These things take time," she murmured, raising

herself up on one elbow. "Give me a minute to wake up before we do battle. Okay?"

"Okay."

Dori grimaced at her first sip of strong coffee, but the jolt of caffeine started her heart pumping again. She rubbed a hand over her weary eyes.

"Can we talk now?"

"Now?" Whatever was troubling her son appeared to be important. "All right."

"It's been a week already and other than Mr. Parker we haven't met a single prospective father."

"Danny." Dori placed a hand on his shoulder. "This is serious business. We can't rush something as important as a new father."

"But I thought we should add bait."

"Bait?"

"Yeah, like when Grandpa and I go fishing."

Another sip of coffee confirmed that she was indeed awake and not in the midst of a nightmare. "And just exactly what did you have in mind?"

"You."

"Me?" Now she knew what the worm felt like.

"You're a real neat mom, but you don't look anything like Christie Brinkley."

Falling back against the thick pillows, Dori shook her head. "I've heard enough of this conversation."

"Mom."

"I'm going to take a shower. Scoot."

"But there's more." Danny looked crestfallen.

"Not this morning, there's not."

His young face sagged with discouragement as he moved off the bed. "Will you think about exercising?"

"Exercising? Whatever for? I'm in great shape." She patted her flat stomach as proof. She could perhaps afford to lose a few pounds, but she wouldn't be ashamed to be seen in a bikini. Well, maybe a one-piece.

Huge doubting eyes raked her from head to foot. "If you're sure."

After scrutiny like that, Dori was anything but confident. But she was never at her best in the mornings. Danny knew that and had attacked when she was weakest.

As the shower spurted warm water, Dori's nylon gown slipped to the floor. She lifted her breasts and tightened her stomach as she examined herself sideways in the full-length mirror on the back of the bathroom door. At five-three she was a little shorter than average, but no pixie. Her breasts were full and she arched her back to display them to their best advantage. A bent knee completed her pose. All right, *Sports Illustrated* wasn't going to contact her for their swimsuit issue. But she didn't look that bad for an old lady of thirty. Did she?

By the time Dori arrived at the office, her mood hadn't improved. She was working at her desk and had begun to attack the latest files when Sandy walked in, holding a white sack emblazoned with McDonald's golden arches.

"Morning," her friend greeted cheerfully.

"What's good about Mondays?" Dori demanded, not meaning to sound as abrupt as she did. When she glanced up to apologize, Sandy was at her side, depositing a cup of coffee and a Danish on her desk. "What's this?"

"A reason to face the day," Sandy replied.

"Thanks, but I'll skip the Danish. Danny informed me this morning that I don't look anything like Christie Brinkley."

"Who does?" Sandy laughed and sat on the edge of Dori's desk, dangling one foot. "There are the beautiful people in this world and then there are the rest of us."

"Try to tell Danny that." Dori pushed back her chair and peeled the protective lid from the plastic cup. "I'm telling you, Sandy, I don't know when I've seen this child more serious. He wants a father and he's driving me crazy with these loony ideas of his."

The beginnings of a smile lifted the corners of Sandy's mouth. "What's the little monster want now?"

"Danny's not a monster." Dori felt obliged to defend her son.

"All kids are monsters."

Sandy's dislike of children was well-known. More than once, she had stated emphatically that the last thing she wanted was a baby. Dori couldn't understand such an attitude, but Sandy and her husband were entitled to their own feelings. Unless a child was wanted and loved, Dori couldn't see the point of bringing one into the world.

"Danny thinks I need to develop an exercise program and whip myself into shape," she said, her hands circling the coffee cup as she leaned back in her chair. A slow smile grew on her face. "I believe his exact words were that I was to be the bait."

"That kid's smarter than I give him credit for." Sandy finished off her Danish and reached for Dori's.

Dori had yet to figure out how anyone could eat so much and stay so thin. Sandy had an enormous appetite, but managed to remain svelte no matter how much she ate.

"I suppose you're going to give in?" Sandy asked, wiping the crumbs from her mouth.

"I suppose," Dori muttered. "In some ways he's right. I couldn't run a mile to save my soul. But what jogging has to do with finding him a father is beyond me."

"Are you honestly going to do it?"

"What?"

"Remarry to satisfy your kid?"

Dori's fingers toyed nervously with the rim of the coffee cup. "I don't know. But if I do marry again it won't be just for Danny. It'll be for both of us."

"Jeff's brother is going to be in town next weekend. We can make arrangements to get together, if you want."

Dori had met Greg once before. Divorced and bitter, Greg didn't make for stimulating company. As she recalled, the entire time had been spent discussing the mercenary proclivities of lawyers and the antifather prejudices of the court. But Dori was willing to listen to another episode of *Divorce Court* if it would help. Danny would see that she was at least making an effort, which should appease him for a while, anyway.

"Sure," Dori said with an abrupt nod of her head. "Let's get together."

Sandy didn't bother to hide her surprise. "Danny may be serious about this, but so are you. It's about time."

Dori regretted agreeing to the date almost from the

minute the words slipped from her lips. No one was more shocked than she was that she'd fallen in with Sandy's latest scheme.

That afternoon when Dori returned home, her mood had yet to improve.

"Hi, Mom." Danny kissed her on the cheek. "I put the casserole in the oven like you asked."

In only a few more years, Danny would be reluctant to demonstrate his affection for her with a kiss. The thought produced a twinge of regret. All too soon, Danny would be gone and she'd be alone. The twinge became an ache in the area of her heart. Nothing could be worse than being alone. The word seemed to echo around her.

"Are you tired?" Danny asked, following her into her bedroom where she kicked off her shoes.

"No more than usual."

"Oh." Danny's lanky frame was at the doorway.

"But I've got enough energy to go jogging for a while before dinner."

"Really, Mom?" His blue eyes lit up like sparklers.

"As long as you're willing to go with me. I'll need a coach." She wasn't about to tackle the streets of Seattle without him. No doubt Danny could run circles around her, but so what? She wasn't competing with him.

Dori changed out of her blue linen business suit and dug out an old pair of jeans and a faded T-shirt.

Danny was running in place when she came into the kitchen. Dori groaned inwardly at her son's display of energy.

As soon as he noticed her appearance, Danny stopped. "You're not going like that, are you?"

"What's wrong now?" Dori added a sweatband around her forehead.

"Those are old clothes."

"Danny," she groaned. "I'm not going to jog in a prom dress." Apparently he had envisioned her in a skintight leotard and multicolored leg warmers.

"All right," he mumbled, but he didn't look pleased.

The first two blocks were murder. Danny set the pace, his knobby knees lifting with lightning speed as he sprinted down the sidewalk. With a lot of pride at stake, Dori managed to meet his stride. Her lungs hurt almost immediately. The muscles at the back of her calves protested such vigorous exercise, but she managed to move one foot in front of the other without too much difficulty. However, by the end of the sixth block, Dori realized she was either going to have to give it up or collapse and play dead.

"Danny," she gasped, stumbling to a halt. Her breath was coming in huge gulps that made talking impossible. Leaning forward, she rested her hands on her knees and drew in deep breaths of oxygen. "I don't...think...I...should...overdo it...the first... day."

"You're not tired are you?"

She felt close to dying. "Just...a little." Straightening, she placed a hand over her heart. "I think I might have a blister on my heel." She was silently begging God for an excuse to stop. The last time she'd breathed this deeply, she'd been in labor.

Perspiration ran in rivulets down the valley between her breasts. It took all the energy she had in the world to wipe the moisture from her face. Women weren't supposed to sweat like this. On second thought, maybe those were tears of agony wetting her cheeks. "I think we should walk back."

"Yeah, the coach always makes us cool down."

Dori made a mental note to give Danny's soccer coach a rum cake for Christmas.

Still eager to display his remarkable agility, Danny continued to jog backward in front of Dori. For good measure she decided to add a slight limp to her gait.

"I'm positive I've got a blister," she mumbled, shaking her head for emphasis. "These tennis shoes are my new ones. I haven't broken 'em in yet." In all honesty she couldn't tell whether she had a blister or not. Her feet didn't ache any more than her legs did, or her lungs.

The closer they came to the house, the more real her limp became.

"Are you sure you're all right, Mom?" Danny had the grace to show a little concern.

"I'm fine." She offered him a feeble smile. The sweatband slipped loose and fell across one eye, but Dori hadn't the energy to secure it.

"Let me help you, Mom." Danny came to her side and placed an arm around her waist. He stared at her flushed and burning face, his brows knit. "You don't look so good."

Dori didn't know what she looked like, but she felt on the verge of throwing up. She'd been a complete idiot to try to maintain Danny's pace. Those six blocks might as well have been six miles.

They were within a half block of the house when Danny hesitated. "Hey, Mom, look. It's Mr. Parker."

Before Dori was able to stop him, Danny shouted and waved.

Standing in the middle of the sidewalk, hands on his hips, stood Gavin Parker. He didn't bother to disguise his amusement.

Three

"Are you all right?" Gavin inquired with mock solicitude, battling back a snicker.

"Get that smirk off your face," Dori threatened. She was in no mood to exchange witticisms with him. Not when every muscle in her body was screaming for mercy.

"It's my fault," Danny confessed, concerned now. "I thought she'd attract more men if they could see how athletic she is."

"The only thing I'm attracting is flies." She ripped the sweatband from her hair; the disobedient curls sprang out from her head. "What can I do for you, Mr. Parker?"

"My, my, she gets a bit testy now and then, doesn't she?" Gavin directed his question to Danny.

"Only sometimes." At least Danny made a half-hearted attempt to be loyal.

There was no need for Gavin to look so pleased with himself. His smug grin resembled that of a cat with a defenseless mouse trapped under its paws.

"Aren't you going to invite me in?" he asked dryly.

Clenching her jaw, Dori gave him a chilly stare. "Don't press your luck, Parker," she whispered for his ears only. Hobbling to the front door, she struggled to retrieve her house key from the tight pocket of her jeans.

"Need help?" Gavin offered.

The glare she flashed him assured him she didn't.

With a mocking smile Gavin raised his arms. "I was just asking."

The front door clicked open and Danny forged ahead, running to the kitchen and opening the refrigerator. He stood at the entrance, waiting for Dori to limp in—closely followed by Gavin—and handed her a cold can of root beer.

With a hand massaging her lower back, Dori led the way to the kitchen table.

"Do you want one, Mr. Parker?" Danny held up another can of soda.

"No, thanks," Gavin said, pulling out a chair for Dori. "You might want to soak out some of those aches and pains in a long hot bath."

It was on the tip of her tongue to remind him that good manners forbade her to seek comfort in a hot bath while he still sat at her kitchen table. She couldn't very well abandon him.

Danny snapped open the aluminum can and guzzled down a long swig. Dori restrained herself to a ladylike sip, although her throat felt parched and scratchy.

"I found Danny's jacket in the back seat of the car the other day and thought he might need it." Gavin explained the reason for his impromptu visit. He handed Danny the keys. "Would you bring it in for me?"

"Sure." Danny was off like a rocket blast, eager to obey.

The front screen slammed and Gavin turned his attention to Dori. "What's this business about jogging to make you more attractive to men?"

Some of the numbness was beginning to leave Dori's limbs and her heartbeat had finally returned to normal. "Just that bee Danny's got in his bonnet lately about me remarrying. Rest assured you're out of the running."

"I'm glad to hear it. I'm rotten husband material."

A laughing sigh escaped as Dori's eyes met his. "I'd already determined that."

"I hung the jacket in my room," Danny explained to his mother, obviously wanting to please her. "It was real nice of you to bring it back, Mr. Parker."

For the first time, Dori wondered if the jacket had been left intentionally so Gavin would have an excuse to return. She wouldn't put it past her son.

Gavin held out his palm to collect the key chain.

"How come Melissa isn't here?" Danny wanted to know. "She's all right for a girl. She wasn't afraid to go on any of the rides. She even went on the Hammer with me. Mom never would." A thoughtful look came over Danny as if he were weighing the pros and cons of being friends with a girl. "She did scream a lot, though."

"She's at school." Gavin stood up to leave, the scrape of his chair loud in the quiet kitchen. "She thought you were all right, too…for a boy." He exchanged teasing smiles with Danny.

"Can we do something together again?" Danny asked as he followed Gavin into the living room. Dori hobbled at a safe distance behind them, pressing her hand to the ache at the small of her back. Who would have believed a little run could be this incapacitating?

"Perhaps." Gavin paused in front of the television and lifted an ornate wooden frame that held a family portrait taken a year before Brad's death. It was the only picture of Brad that Dori kept out. After a silent study, he replaced the portrait and stooped to pat the stuffed lion, now guarding the front window. "I'll get Melissa to give you a call the next weekend she's not at school."

"Not at school?" Danny repeated incredulously. "You mean she has to go to school on Saturdays, too?"

"No," Gavin explained. "She attends boarding school and spends the weekends with me if I'm not broadcasting a game. Things get hectic this time of year, though. I'll have her give you a call."

"Danny would like that," Dori said and smiled sweetly, assured that Gavin had understood her subtle message. Having Melissa call Danny was fine, but Dori didn't want anything to do with Gavin.

As Gavin had suggested, a leisurely soak in hot water went a long way toward relieving her aching muscles. Her parting shot to him had been childish, and Dori regretted it. She drew in a deep breath and eased down farther in the steaming water. Her toe toyed with the faucet. It felt sinful to be so lazy, so relaxed.

"The table's set and the timer for the oven rang," Danny called.

With her hair pinned up and her lithe—but abused—body draped in a thick housecoat, Dori ambled into the kitchen. Danny was standing in front of the refrigerator rereading the list of prerequisites for a new father.

"Dinner smells good. I'll bet you're hungry after all that exercise."

Danny ignored her obvious attempt to divert his attention. That kid was getting wise to her ways.

"Did you realize Mr. Parker knows karate? I asked him about it."

"That's nice," Dori hoped to play down the information. "I'll take out the casserole and we should be ready to eat."

"He's tall and athletic and Melissa said he's thirty-six—"

"Danny," she snapped impatiently, "no! We went over this yesterday. I have veto power, remember?"

"Mr. Parker would make a great dad," he argued.

Her glass made a sharp clang as it hit the table. "But not yours."

To his credit Danny didn't bring up Gavin Parker's name again. Apparently the message had sunk in, although Dori realized her son genuinely liked Gavin and Melissa. As for herself, she still hadn't made up her mind about Gavin. Melissa was a sweet child but her father presented another picture. No one exasperated Dori more than he did. Gavin Parker was arrogant, conceited and altogether maddening.

Another week passed and Danny marked off the days on the calendar, reminding Dori daily of his need for a new father. Even the promise of a puppy wasn't enough to dissuade him. Twice he interrupted her while they did the weekly shopping to point out men in the grocery store. He actually wanted her to introduce herself.

The date with Sandy's brother-in-law, Greg, did more harm than good. Not only was she forced to listen to an updated version of *Divorce Court*, but Danny drilled her with questions the following morning until she threatened to drop the new father issue entirely.

The next few days, her son was unusually subdued. But Dori knew the boy well enough to realize that although she had won this first battle, he was out to win the war. The situation was weighing on her so heavily that she had a nightmare about waking up and discovering a stranger in her bed who claimed Danny had sent him.

Monday evening, when Danny was supposed to be doing homework, she found him shaking money from his piggy bank onto the top of his mattress. She'd purposely given him a bank that wouldn't open so that he'd learn to save his money. He dodged her questions about the need to rob from it, telling her he was planning a surprise.

"That kid's got something up his sleeve," Dori told Sandy the following day.

"Didn't you ask?"

"He said he was buying me a present." This morning Dori had brought in the coffee and Danishes and she set a paper sack on Sandy's desk.

"Knowing Danny, I'd say it's probably a jar of wrinkle cream."

"Probably," she murmured and took a bite of the Danish.

"I thought you were on a diet."

"Are you kidding? With all the calisthenics and jogging Danny's got me doing, I'm practically wasting away."

Sandy crossed one shapely leg over the other. "And people wonder why I don't want kids."

The phone was ringing when Dori let herself into the house that evening. She tossed her purse onto the kitchen table and hurried to answer it, thinking that the caller was probably her mother.

"Hello."

"I'm calling about your ad in the paper."

Dori brushed an errant curl from her forehead. "I'm sorry, but you've got a wrong number." The man on the other end of the line wanted to argue, but Dori replaced the receiver, cutting him off. He sounded quite unpleasant, and as far as she was concerned, there was nothing more to discuss.

Danny was at soccer practice at the local park, six blocks from the house. The days were growing shorter, the sun setting at just about the time practice was over. On impulse, Dori decided to bicycle to the field and ride home with him. Of course, she wouldn't let him know the reason she'd come. He'd hate it if he thought his mother had come to escort him home.

When they entered the house twenty minutes later, the phone was ringing again.

"I'll get it," Danny shouted, racing across the kitchen floor.

Dori didn't pay much attention when he stretched the cord around the corner and walked into the hall closet, seeking privacy. He did that sometimes when he didn't want her to listen in on the conversation. The last time that had happened, it was because a girl from school had phoned.

Feeling lazy and not in a mood to fuss with dinner, Dori opened a package of fish sticks and dumped them on a cookie sheet, tossing them under the broiler with some French fries. She was chopping a head of cabbage for cole slaw when Danny reappeared. He gave her a sheepish look as he hung up the phone.

"Was that Erica again?"

Danny ignored her question. "Are you going to keep on wearing those old clothes?"

Dori glanced down over her washed-out denims and Irish cable-knit sweater. "What's wrong with this?" Actually, this was one of her better pairs of jeans.

"I just thought that you'd like to wear a dress for dinner or something."

"Danny—" she released an exasperated sigh "—we're having fish sticks, not filet mignon."

"Oh." He stuck his hands in his pockets and yanked them out again as the phone rang. "I'll get it."

Before Dori knew what was happening, he was back in the closet, the phone cord stretched to its farthest extreme. Within minutes, he was out again.

"What's going on?"

"Nothin'."

The phone rang and the doorbell chimed simultaneously. "I'll get it," Danny hollered, jerking his head from one direction to the other.

Drying her hands on a dish towel, Dori gestured toward the living room. "I'll get the door."

Gavin Parker stood on the other side of screen, the morning paper tucked under his arm.

"Gavin." Dori was too surprised to utter more than his name.

Laugh lines fanned out from his eyes as if he found something highly amusing. He had that cat-with-the-trapped-mouse look again. "Phone been ringing a lot lately?"

"Yes. How'd you know? It's been driving me crazy." Unlatching the screen door, she opened it, silently inviting him inside. What a strange man Gavin was. She hadn't expected to see him again and here he was on her doorstep, looking inexplicably amused about something.

Gavin sauntered in and sat on the deep, cushioned sofa. "I don't suppose you've read the morning paper?"

Dori had, at least the sections she always did. Dear Abby, the comics, Mike Mailway and the front page, in that order. "Yes. Why?"

Making a show of it, Gavin pulled out the classified section and folded it open, laying it across the coffee table. Idly, he moved his index finger down the narrow column of the personal ads until he located what he wanted.

A sick feeling attacked the pit of Dori's stomach, weakening her knees so that she had to lower herself into the maple rocking chair across from him.

"Are you in any way related to the person who ran this ad? 'Need dad. Tall, athletic, knows karate. Mom pretty. 555-5818.'"

It was worse, far worse, than anything Dori could ever have dreamed. Mortified and angry, she supported her elbows on the arms of the rocker and buried her face in the palms of her hands. A low husky sound slipped from her throat as hot flashes of color invaded her neck, her cheeks, her ears, not stopping until her eyes brimmed with tears of embarrassment.

"Daniel Bradley Robertson, get in here this minute.'' Rarely did she use that tone with her son. Whenever she did, Danny came running.

The closet door opened a crack and Danny's head appeared. ''Just a minute, Mom, I'm on the phone.'' He paused, noticing Gavin for the first time. ''Oh, hi, Mr. Parker.''

''Hello, Daniel Bradley Robertson.'' Gavin stood up and took the receiver out of the boy's hand. ''I think your mother would like to talk to you. I'll take care of whoever's on the phone.''

''Yeah, Mom?'' A picture of innocence, Danny met Dori's fierce gaze without wavering. ''Is something wrong?''

Her scheming son became a watery blur as Dori shook her head, not knowing how to explain the embarrassment he'd caused her.

''Mom?'' Danny knelt in front of her. ''What's wrong? Why are you crying?''

Her answer was a sniffle and a finger pointed in the direction of the bathroom. Danny seemed to understand her watery charades and leaped to his feet, returning a moment later with a box of tissues.

''Do you people always use the hall closet to talk on the phone?''

Gavin was back and Danny gave his visitor a searching look. ''What's the matter with Mom? All she does is cry.''

The phone pealed again and Dori sucked in a hysterical sob that sounded more like a strangled cry of pain.

''I'll take care of it,'' Gavin assured her, quickly taking control. ''Danny, come with me into the kitchen. Your mother needs a few minutes alone.''

For a moment it looked as though Danny didn't know what to do. Indecision played across his freckled face. His mother was crying and there was a man with an authoritative voice barking orders at him. With a weak gesture of her hand, Dori dismissed her son.

In the next hour the phone rang another twenty times. With every ring, Dori flinched. Gavin and Danny remained in the kitchen and dealt with each call. Dori didn't move. The gentle sway of the rocker was her only solace. Danny ventured into the living room only once, to announce that dinner was ready if she wanted to eat. Profusely shaking her head, she assured him she didn't.

After a while the panic abated somewhat and she decided not to sell the house, pack up her belongings and seek refuge at the other end of the world. A less drastic approach gradually came to mind. The first thing she had to do was get that horrible ad out of the personals. Then she'd have her phone number changed.

More in control of herself now, Dori blew her nose and washed her tear-streaked face in the bathroom off the hall. When she moved into the kitchen, she was shocked to discover Gavin and Danny busy with the dinner dishes. Gavin stood at the sink, the sleeves of his expensive business shirt rolled up past his elbows. Danny was standing beside him, a dish towel in his hand.

"Hi, Mom." His chagrined eyes didn't quite meet hers. "Mr. Parker explained that what I did wasn't really a very good idea."

"No, it wasn't." The scratchy high sound that slid from her throat barely resembled her voice.

"Would you like some dinner now? Mr. Parker and I saved you some."

She shook her head, then asked, "What's been happening in here?"

In response the phone rang, its jangle almost deafening—or so it seemed to Dori, who tucked in her chin and cringed.

Not hesitating at all, Gavin dried his hands and walked across the kitchen toward the wall phone.

"Listen to him," Danny whispered with a giggle. "Mr. Parker figured out a way to answer the phone without having to argue. He's a real smart man."

Catching Dori's eye, Gavin winked reassuringly and picked up the receiver. After a momentary pause, he mocked the phone company recording. "The number you have reached has been disconnected," he droned.

For the first time that evening, the tight line of Dori's mouth cracked with the hint of a smile. Once again, she was forced to admire the cleverness of Gavin Parker.

Grinning smugly, he hung up the phone and sat in the chair next to Dori's. "Are you feeling okay now?"

She managed a nod, her jaw clenched. The confusion and anger she'd experienced earlier had only been made worse by Gavin's gloating. But now she felt grateful that he'd stepped in and taken charge of a very awkward situation. Dori wasn't sure what would have happened otherwise.

A finger under her chin tilted her face upward. "I don't believe you're fine at all. You're as pale as a sheet." A rush of unexpected pleasure shot through her at the impersonal contact of his finger against her soft skin.

His index finger ventured over the smooth line of her jaw in an exploratory caress. The action was meant to soothe and reassure, but his touch was oddly sensual and highly arousing. Bewildered, Dori raised her gaze to his. Their eyes met and held as his hand slipped to her neck, his fingers tangling with the auburn softness of her shoulder-length hair. Dori could see the gentle rise and fall of his chest and noted that the movement increased slightly, as if he too had been caught unawares by these emotions. His eyes narrowed as he withdrew his hand. "You need a drink. Where...?"

With a limp arm, Dori gestured toward the cupboard that held her small stock of liquor. As he poured a shot of brandy into a glass, Gavin demanded quietly, "Danny, haven't you got some homework that needs to be done?"

"No." Danny shook his head then hurriedly placed his fingers over his mouth. "Oh...I get it. You want to talk to my mom alone."

"Right." Gavin exchanged a conspiratorial wink with the boy.

As Danny left the room, Gavin deposited the brandy in front of Dori and sat beside her again. "No arguments. Drink."

"You like giving orders, don't you?" Whatever had passed between them was gone as quickly as it had come.

Gavin ignored the censure in her voice. "I have an idea that could benefit both of us."

Dori took a swallow of the brandy, which burned a passage down her throat and brought fresh tears to her eyes. "What?" was all she could manage.

"It's obvious Danny is serious about this new father

business and to be truthful, Melissa would like me to remarry so she won't have to board at the school anymore. She hates all the restrictions.''

Dori sympathized with the young girl. Melissa was at an age when she should be testing her wings and that included experimenting with makeup and wearing the latest fashions. Nuns probably wouldn't encourage that type of behavior. Being cooped up in a convent school was obviously squelching Melissa's enthusiasm for adventure.

''You're not humming 'The Wedding March,' are you?'' Dori asked.

Gavin gave her a look that threatened bodily harm, and she couldn't contain a soft laugh. She loved turning the tables on this impudent male.

''I've already explained that I have no intention of remarrying. Once was enough to cure me for a lifetime. But I am willing to compromise if it will help let up on the pressure from Melissa.''

''How do Danny and I fit into this rosy picture?''

Eager now, Gavin shifted to the edge of his seat and leaned forward. ''If the two of us were to start going out together on a steady basis, then Melissa and Danny would assume we're involved with each other.''

Dori drew in a slow trembling breath. As much as she hated to admit it, the idea showed promise. Melissa needed a woman's influence, and all Danny really cared about was having a man who would participate in the things she couldn't. Dori realized her son was already worried about the father-son soccer game scheduled for the end of the season. For years his grandfather had volunteered for such events, but her dad was close to retirement and playing soccer these days would put a strain on him.

"We could start this weekend. We'll go to dinner Friday night and then on Sunday I'll take Danny to the Seahawks game if you'll take Melissa shopping." His mouth slanted sideways in a coaxing smile.

Dori recognized the crooked grin as the one he probably used on gullible young women whenever he wanted to get his own way. Nibbling her lower lip, Dori refused to play that game. She wasn't stupid; he was willing to tie up Fridays and Sundays, but he wanted his Saturday nights free. Why not? She didn't care what he did.

"Well?" Gavin didn't look nearly as confident as he had earlier, and that pleased Dori. There wasn't any need for him to think she'd fall in with his plans so easily.

"I think you may have stumbled on to something."

His slanted smile returned. "Which, translated, means you doubt that I have more than an occasional original thought."

"Perhaps." He had been kind and helpful tonight. The least she could do, then, was to be just a little more accommodating. "All right, I agree."

"Great." A boyish grin not unlike Danny's lit up his face. "I'll see you Friday night about seven, then."

"Fine." Standing, she joined her hands behind her back. "And, Gavin, thank you for stepping in and helping tonight. I do appreciate it. I'll phone the paper first thing in the morning to make sure the ad doesn't appear again and contact the telephone company to have my number changed."

"You know how to handle any more calls that come in tonight?"

Dori plugged her nose and in a high-pitched voice imitated the telephone company recording.

The laugh lines around his eyes became prominent as he grinned. "We can have a good time, Dori. Just don't fall in love with me."

So he was back on that theme. "Believe me, there's no chance of that," she snapped. "If you want the truth, I think you may be the—"

She wasn't allowed to finish as he suddenly hauled her into his arms and kissed her soundly, stealing her breath and tipping her off balance. With her hands pushing forcefully against his chest, Dori was able to break off the unexpected attack.

"Shh," Gavin whispered in her ear. "Danny's right outside the door."

"So?" She still wasn't free from his embrace.

"I didn't want him to hear you. If we're going to convince either of those kids, we've got to make this look real."

A pale pink spot appeared on each cheek. "Give me some warning next time."

Gently Gavin eased her away, studying the heightened color of her face. "I didn't hurt you, did I?"

"No," she assured him, thinking the worst thing about being a redhead was her pale coloring. The slightest sign of embarrassment was more pronounced because she was naturally pallid.

"Well, how'd I do?"

"On what?"

"The kiss." He shook his head as though he expected her to know what he was talking about. "How would you rate the kiss?"

This, Dori was going to enjoy. "On a scale of one to ten?" She allowed a lengthy pause to follow as she folded her arms and quirked her head thoughtfully at the ceiling. The time had come for someone to put this overconfident male in his place. "If I take into consideration that you are an ex-quarterback, I'd say a low five."

The corners of his mouth twitched briefly upward. "I was expecting you to be a little less cruel."

"And from everything you say, I don't expect your technique to improve with time."

"It might," he chuckled, "but I doubt it."

Danny wandered into the kitchen, whistling. "I'm not interrupting anything, am I?"

"You don't mind if I take your mom out to dinner Friday night, do you, sport?"

"Really, Mom?" Dori would willingly have given her son double his allowance not to have been quite so eager.

"I suppose," Dori said dryly. Gavin ignored her lack of enthusiasm.

"But I thought you said Mr. Parker was a—"

"Never mind that now," she whispered pointedly, as another flood of color cascaded into her cheeks.

"I'll see you at seven on Friday." Gavin rolled down the sleeves of his shirt and rebuttoned them at the wrist.

"It's a date."

Rarely had Dori seen Danny more pleased about anything. He quizzed her Friday from the very moment she walked in the door after work. As she drove him to her parents' place—they were more than happy to have their grandson for the night—he wanted to know what dress she was going to wear, what kind of perfume, which earrings, which shoes. He gave her advice and bombarded her with football statistics.

"Danny," she breathed irritably, "I don't think Gavin Parker expects me to know that much about football."

"But, Mom, it'll impress him," his singsong voice pleaded.

"But, Danny." Her twangy voice echoed his.

Back at her own house, an exhausted Dori soaked in the tub, then hurriedly dried herself, applied some makeup—why was she doing it with such care, she wondered—and dressed. She wasn't surprised when Gavin was fifteen minutes late, nor did she take offense. The extra time was well spent adding the last coat of pale pink polish to her long nails.

Gavin looked rushed and slightly out of breath as he climbed the porch steps. Dori saw him coming and opened the front door, careful not to smear the wet polish. "Hi." She didn't mention the fact that he was late.

Gavin's smile was wry. "Where's Danny?"

"My mom and dad's."

"Oh." He paused and raked his fingers through his hair, mussing the carefully styled effect. "Listen, tonight isn't going exactly the way I'd planned. I promised a friend a favor. It shouldn't interfere with our date if you don't let it."

"I'm not going to worry about it," Dori murmured and cautiously slipped her arms into the coat Gavin held for her. She hadn't the faintest idea what he had in mind, but knowing Gavin Parker, it wasn't moon-light and roses.

"Do you mean that?" Already he had his car keys out and was fiddling with them, his gaze lowered. "I ran into some minor complications at the office so I'm a bit late."

"I'm not concerned. It isn't like we're madly in love with each other." Dori was grateful Danny wasn't there to witness her "hot date." With Gavin she used the term "hot" very loosely.

While she locked the front door, Gavin sprinted down the porch steps and started the car engine. Dori released an exasperated sigh as he leaned across the front seat and opened the car door for her. With a forced smile on her lips, she slid inside. So much for gallantry and romance.

It wouldn't have shocked her if there were another woman waiting for him somewhere. What did surprise her was that he pulled into a local fast-food drive-in, helped her out of the car and seated her, then ordered hamburgers and milk shakes. She didn't know what he had up his sleeve or if he expected a reaction, but she didn't as much as blink.

"I did promise you dinner."

"That you did," she returned sweetly.

"Whatever else happens tonight, just remember I did feed you."

"And I'm grateful." She had difficulty keeping the sarcasm out of her voice. Good grief, where could he be taking her?

"The thing is, when I asked you to dinner I forgot about a...previous commitment."

"Gavin, don't worry about it. For that matter you

can take me back to my house; it's not that big a deal. In fact, if there's another woman involved it would save us both a lot of embarrassment.'' Not him, but the two women.

Gavin polished off the last of his hamburger and crumpled up the paper. ''There isn't another woman.'' He looked shocked that she'd even suggest such a thing. ''If you don't mind coming, I don't mind bringing you. As it is, I had one hell of a time getting an extra ticket.''

''I'm game for just about anything.'' Fleetingly Dori wondered what she was getting herself in for, but learning that it involved a ticket was encouraging.

''Except that sometimes these things can go on quite late.''

Now her curiosity was piqued. ''Not to worry. Danny's staying the night with my parents.''

''Great.'' He flashed her a brilliant smile. ''As Danny would say, for a girl, you're all right.''

He made it sound exactly like her son. ''I'm glad you think so.''

After dumping their leftovers in the garbage, Gavin escorted her to the car and pulled out of the parking space. He took the freeway toward Tacoma. Dori wasn't sure what he had in mind, but she wasn't turning back now.

Several other cars were parked outside a dimly lit part of the downtown area of Tacoma. Gavin stepped out of the car and glanced at his wristwatch. He hurried around the front of the car to help her out of the passenger side. His hand grasped her elbow as he led her toward a square gray building. The streetlight was too dim for Dori to read the sign over the door, not that Gavin would have given her time. They were obviously late.

They entered a large hall and were greeted by shouts and cheers. The room was so thick with smoke that Dori had to strain to see. The automatic smile died on her lips as she turned furiously to Gavin.

"I promised a friend I'd take a look at his latest prodigy," he explained, studying her reaction.

"You mean to tell me that you brought me to the Friday-night fights?"

Four

"Is that such a problem?" Gavin asked defensively, his gaze challenging hers.

Dori couldn't believe this was her "hot date" with the handsome and popular Gavin Parker. She'd never been to a boxing match in her life, nor had she ever wanted to. But then, sports in general had never interested her very much. Despite that, her "No, I guess not," was spoken with a certain amount of honesty. Danny would be thrilled. Little else would convince the eleven-year-old that Gavin was serious about her.

Following Gavin into the auditorium and down the wide aisle, Dori was surprised when he ushered her into a seat only a few rows from the ring. Whatever was about to happen she would see in graphic detail.

Apparently Gavin was a familiar patron at these matches. He introduced Dori to several men whose names floated past her so quickly that she could never hope to remember them. Glancing around, Dori noted that there were only a few other women present. In her gray-and-black crepe dress with its Peter Pan collar and the thin silk tie, she was decidedly overdressed. Cringing, Dori huddled down in her seat while Gavin carried on a friendly conversation with the man sitting in the row in front of them.

"You want some peanuts?" He bent his head close to hers as he asked.

"No thanks." Her hands lay in her lap, clutching her purse and an unread program she'd received at the door. People didn't eat while they watched this kind of physical exhibition, did they?

Gavin shrugged and stood up, reaching for some loose change in his pocket. He paused and turned back to her. "You're not mad, are you?"

Dori was convinced that was exactly what he expected her to be. Perhaps it was even what he wanted. Her anger would be just the proof he needed that all women were alike. Based on everything that had happened between them, Dori realized Gavin didn't particularly want to like her. Any real relationship would be dangerous to him, she suspected—even one founded on friendship and mutual respect.

"No." She gave him a forced but cheerful smile. "This should be very interesting." Already her mind was fashioning a subtle revenge. Next time they went out, she'd have Gavin take her to an opera—one performed in Italian.

"I'll be back in a minute." He left his seat and clambered over the two men closest to the aisle.

Feeling self-conscious and completely out of her element, Dori sat with her shoulders stiff and squared against the back of the folding wooden seat. She was mentally bracing herself for the ordeal.

"So you're Dori." The man who'd been talking to Gavin turned to her.

They'd been introduced, but she couldn't recall his name. "Yes." Her smile was shy as she searched her memory.

"This is the first time Gavin's ever brought a woman to the fights."

Dori guessed that was a compliment. "I'm honored."

"He was seeing that blond beauty for a while. A lot of the guys were worried he was going to marry her."

A blonde! Dori's curiosity was piqued. "Is that so?" Gavin hadn't mentioned any blonde to her. If he was going to continue to see someone else regularly it would ruin their agreement. Gavin took her to the Friday-night fights, while he probably wined and dined some dizzy blonde on the sly. Terrific.

"Yeah," the nameless man continued. "He was seeing her real regular. For a while he wasn't even coming to the fights."

Obviously Gavin and this blonde had a serious relationship going. "She must have been really something for Gavin to miss the fights." Smiling encouragingly, Dori hoped the man would tell her more.

"He doesn't come every week, you understand."

Dori nodded, pretending she did.

"Fact is, during football season we're lucky to see him once a month."

Dori was beginning to wonder just how "lucky" she was. The man grinned and glanced toward the aisle. Dori's gaze followed his and she saw Gavin returning down the crowded center aisle, carrying a large bag of peanuts.

As soon as he sat down, Dori absently helped herself to a handful.

"I thought you said you didn't want any," Gavin said, giving her the sack.

"I don't," she mumbled, cracking one open with her teeth. "I don't even like peanuts."

"Then why did you grab them out of my hand the minute I sat down?"

"I did?" When she was agitated or upset, often the first thing Dori did was reach for something to eat. "Sorry," she said, returning the paper sack. "I didn't realize what I was doing."

"Is something bothering you?" Gavin's disturbed gaze was studying her. His eyes darkened as if he were expecting an argument.

Dori hated being so readable. She'd thought that sometime during the evening she'd casually bring up his liaison with this…this other woman who was jeopardizing their tentative agreement.

"Nothing's bothering me," she answered. "Not really."

His glittering eyes mocked her.

"It's just that your friend—" she gestured with her hand toward the row in front of them "—was explaining that you were seeing a blonde and…"

"And you jumped to conclusions?"

"Yes, well…it isn't exactly in our agreement." What bothered Dori most was that it mattered to her if Gavin was seeing another woman. She had no right to feel anything for him…except as far as their agreement was concerned. But her pride was on the line. If Danny heard about this other woman, she might slip in her own son's estimation.

"Well, you needn't worry. I'm not seeing her anymore."

"What's the matter," Dori taunted in a low whisper, "was she unfortunate enough to smell orange blossoms?"

"No." He pursed his lips and reached for a peanut, cracking it open with a vengeance. "Every time she opened her mouth, her brain leaked."

Dori successfully hid a smile. "I'd have thought that type was the best kind."

"I'm beginning to have the same feeling myself," he said dryly, his gaze inscrutable.

Feeling a growing sense of triumph, Dori relaxed and didn't say another word.

Soon cheers and loud hoots rose from the auditorium as the young boxers paraded into the room with an entourage of managers and assistants.

The announcer waited until the two men had parted the thick ropes and positioned themselves in their appropriate corners. Glancing at her program, Dori read that these first two were in the lightweight division.

Pulling down a microphone that seemed to come from nowhere, the announcer shouted in a clear, distinct voice. "Ladies and gentlemen, welcome to the Tacoma Friday-night fights. Wearing white trunks and weighing 130 awesome pounds is Boom Boom Bronson."

The sound echoed forcefully around the room. Immediate cheers and whistles followed. Boom Boom hopped into the middle of the ring and punched at a few shadows, to the delight of the audience, before he returned to his corner. Even when he was in a stationary position, his hands braced against the ropes, Boom Boom's feet refused to stop moving.

Then the other boxer, Tucker Wallace, was introduced. Tucker hopped in and out of the middle ring, punching all the way. The crowd went crazy. The man beside Dori stormed to his feet, placed two fingers in his mouth and pierced the air with a shrill whistle. Dori reached for another handful of peanuts.

The two fighters met briefly with the announcer and spoke with the referee before returning to their respective corners. The entourages formed again around each fighter. Probably to decide a strategy, Dori mused.

The bell clanged and the two men came out swinging. Dori blinked twice, stunned at the fierce aggression between the men. They may have been listed in the lightweight division, but the corded muscles of their abdomens and backs assured her that their stature had little to do with their strength or determination.

Gavin had shifted to the edge of his seat by the end of round one. The bell brought a humming silence to the room.

Dori knew next to nothing about boxing. She hated fighting, but the fierce competition between Boom Boom and Tucker seemed exaggerated and somehow theatrical. Despite her dislike of violence, Dori found herself cheering for Boom Boom. When he was slammed to the ground by Tucker's powerful right hand, Dori jumped to her feet to see if he was all right and could continue fighting.

"Oh, goodness," she wailed, covering her forehead with one hand as she sank back into her seat. "He's bleeding."

Gavin was looking at her, his compelling dark eyes studying her flushed, excited face as if he couldn't quite believe what he saw.

"Is something wrong?" Boldly her gaze met his

and a shiver of unexpected sensual awareness danced over her skin. "I'm cheering too loud?" She'd become so engrossed in what was happening between the two boxers that she'd embarrassed him with her vocal enthusiasm.

"No," he countered quickly, shaking his head. "I guess I'm surprised you like it."

"Well, to be honest," she admitted. "I didn't think I would. But these guys are good."

"Yes." He gave her a dazzling smile. "They are."

The adrenaline pumped through Dori's limbs as Boom Boom fought on to win the match in a unanimous decision. At the end of three bouts the evening was over and Gavin helped her on with her thick woolen coat. The night had turned rainy and cold, and Dori shivered as they walked to the car.

The moment they were settled, Gavin turned on the heater. "You'll be warm in a minute."

Dori stuck her bare hands deep in her pockets. "If it gets much colder, it'll probably snow."

"It won't," Gavin stated confidently. "It was warm in the auditorium, that's all." He paused to snap his seat belt into place. Dori averted her face to check the heavy flow of traffic. They wouldn't be able to get out of their parking spot for several minutes, but there wasn't any need to rush. As much as she hated to admit it, she'd enjoyed the evening. Being taken to the fights was the last thing she'd expected, but Dori was quickly learning that Gavin was a man of surprises.

"Here," Gavin said, half leaning across her. "Buckle up." Before Dori could free her hand to reach for the seat belt, Gavin had pulled it across her waist. He hesitated, his eyes meeting hers. Their

mouths were close, so close; only a hair's breadth separated them. Dori swallowed convulsively. Her trai-
torous heart skipped a beat, then hammered wildly.
She stared at him, hardly able to believe what she saw
in his warm eyes or the feelings that stirred in her own
breast. A strange, inexplicable sensation came over
her. At that moment, she felt as though she and Gavin
were good friends, two people who shared a special
bond of companionship. She liked him, respected him,
enjoyed his company.

She knew when he dipped his head that he was
going to kiss her, but instead of drawing away, she
met him halfway, shocked at how much she wanted
him to do exactly this. His mouth fit easily, expertly,
over hers in a tender, undemanding caress. A hand
smoothed the hair from her temple as he lifted his
mouth from hers and brushed his lips over her troubled
brow.

"Warmer?" he asked in a husky murmur.

Her body was suffused by an unexpected rush of
inner heat, her blood vigorously pounding through her
veins. Unable to find her voice, she nodded.

"Good." He clicked her seat belt into place, and
with utter nonchalance, checked the rearview mirror
before pulling onto the street.

Silently Dori thanked God for the cover of night.
Her face burned at her own imprudence. Gavin had
kissed her and she'd let him. Worse, she'd enjoyed it.
So much that she'd been sorry when he'd stopped.

"I give you a six, maybe a low seven," she challenged evenly, struggling to disguise his effect on her.

"What?"

"The kiss," she returned coolly, but there was a

brittle edge to her airy reply. Her greatest fear was that he might be secretly amused by the ardor of her response.

"I'm pleased to know I'm improving. As I recall, the last kiss was a mere five." He merged with the moving traffic that led to the main arterial, halted at a stoplight and chuckled. "A seven," he repeated. "I'd have rated it more of an eight."

"Maybe." Dori relaxed and a light laugh tickled her throat. "No, it was definitely a low seven."

"You're a hard woman, Dori Robertson."

Her laugh would no longer be denied. "So I've been told."

Instead of heading for the freeway as she expected, Gavin took several turns that led indirectly to the waterfront.

"Where are we going?"

"For something to eat. I thought you might be hungry."

Dori had to stop and think about it before deciding that yes, she probably could eat something. "One thing."

"Yeah?" Gavin's eyes momentarily left the road.

"Not another hamburger. That's all Danny ever wants when we go out."

"Don't worry, I have something else in mind."

Gavin's "something else" turned out to be The Lobster Shop, an elegant restaurant overlooking the busy Tacoma harbor. Dori had often heard about the restaurant but had never been there. It was the kind of place where reservations were required several days in advance.

"You were planning this all along," she stated as

he drove into the parking lot in front of the restaurant. Her warm gaze studied the strong, broad face, with its thick brows and silver wings fanning out from the temples.

"I thought I might have to appease you after taking you to the fights."

"I enjoyed myself."

His soft chuckle filled the car. "I know. You surprised the hell out of me, especially when you flew to your feet and kissed Boom Boom."

"It's so different from seeing it on television. And I blew him a kiss," she said on a note of righteous indignation. "That's an entirely different matter from flying to my feet and kissing him. I was happy he won the bout, that's all."

"I could tell. However, next time you feel like kissing any athletes, you might want to try me."

"You must be joking!" She placed her hand over her heart and feigned deep shock. "You might rate me."

Gavin was still chuckling when he left the car and came around to her side. There was a glint of admiration in his eyes as he escorted her into the restaurant.

The food was as good as Dori had expected. They both had lobster and an excellent white wine, and following their meal, they sat and talked over cups of strong, hot coffee.

"To be truthful," Dori said, staring into the dark depths of her drink, "I didn't have much hope for our 'date.'"

"You didn't?" A crooked smile slid across Gavin's sensuous mouth.

"To my utter amazement, I've really enjoyed myself. The best part of this evening is not having to worry about making any real commitment or analyzing our relationship. So we can just enjoy spending this time together. We both know where we stand and that's comfortable. I like it.''

"I do, too," Gavin agreed softly, finishing his coffee. He smiled absently at the waitress when she collected the money for their bill.

Dori knew it was time to think about leaving, but she felt content and surprisingly at ease. When another waitress refilled their cups, neither objected.

"How long have you been a widow?" Gavin asked.

"Five years." Dori's fingers curved around the cup as she lowered her gaze. "Even after all this time I still have trouble accepting that Brad is gone. It seems so unreal. Maybe if he'd had a lingering illness, it would have been easier to accept. It happened so fast. He went to work one morning and was gone the next. A year later I was still reeling from the shock. I've thought about that day a thousand times. Had I known it was going to be our last morning together, there would have been so many things to say. As it was, I didn't ever get a chance to thank him for the wonderful years we shared."

"What happened?" Gavin reached for her hand. "Listen, if this is painful, we can drop it."

"No," she whispered and offered him a reassuring smile. "It's only natural for you to be curious. It was a freak accident. To this day I'm not sure exactly what happened. Brad was a bricklayer and he was working on a project downtown. The scaffolding gave out and a half ton of bricks fell on him. He was gone by the time they could free his body." She swallowed to relieve the tightness in her throat. "I was three months pregnant at the time. We'd planned this baby so carefully, building up our savings so I could quit my job. Everything seemed to come crashing in all at once. A week after Brad's funeral, I lost the baby."

Gavin's fingers tightened over hers and he squeezed them as if to lend her strength. "You're a strong woman to have survived those years."

Dori felt her throat muscles constrict and she nodded sadly. "I didn't have any choice. There was Danny, and his world had been turned upside down with mine. We clung to each other, and after a while we were able to pick up the pieces of our lives. I'm not saying it was easy, but there really wasn't any choice. We were alive, and we couldn't stay buried with Brad."

"When Danny asked for a new father it really must have thrown you."

"That certainly came out of left field." Her eyes sparkled with silent laughter. "That boy thinks up the craziest notions sometimes."

"You mean like the want ad?"

Dori groaned and slowly shook her head. "That has to be the most embarrassing moment of my life. You'll never know how grateful I am that you stepped in when you did."

"If you can persuade Melissa to buy a dress, I'll be forever in your debt."

"Consider it done."

Strangely, her answer didn't appear to please him. He gulped down the last of his coffee, then scraped back his chair and rose to his feet. "You women have ways of getting exactly what you want, don't you?"

Dori bit back an angry retort. She hadn't done anything to deserve this attack. But fine, let him act like that. She didn't care.

As he held open the car door for her, he hesitated. "I didn't mean to snap at you back there."

An apology! From Gavin Parker! Dori stared at him in shock. "Accepted," she murmured, hiding her stunned reaction as she concentrated on getting into the car.

On the return drive to Seattle, Dori rested her head against the seat and closed her eyes. It had been a long difficult week and she was tired. When Gavin stopped in front of her house, she straightened and tried unsuccessfully to hide a yawn.

"Thank you, Gavin. I had a good time. Really."

"Thank you." He left the engine running as he came around to her side of the car to help her out. Dori experienced an odd mixture of regret and relief. She'd toyed with the idea of inviting him in for coffee. But knowing Gavin, he'd probably assume the invitation meant more. Obviously, since he'd left the engine running, he was ready to be on his way. Dori found she was disappointed that their time together was coming to an end.

With a guiding hand at her elbow, Gavin walked her to the front porch. She fumbled momentarily in her purse for her key, wondering if she should say anything. It hadn't slipped her notice that he'd asked her about Brad yet hadn't offered any information regarding his ex-wife. Dori was filled with questions she didn't want to ask.

She hesitated, her house key in her hand. "Thanks again." She didn't think he was going to kiss her, but she wouldn't object if he tried. The kiss they'd shared earlier had been pleasant, more than pleasant—exciting and stirring. Even now the taste of his mouth clung to hers. Oh no, what was happening to her? Dori's mind whirled. It must have been the wine that was giving her this lightheaded feeling, she decided frantically. It couldn't have been his kiss. Not Gavin Parker. Oh, please, don't let it be Gavin.

He was standing so close that all she had to do was sway slightly and she'd be in his arms. Stubbornly, Dori stood rigid; staying exactly where she was. His finger traced the delicate line of her chin as his eyes met hers in the darkness. Dori's smile was weak and trembling as she realized that he wanted to kiss her but wouldn't. It was almost as though he were challenging her to make the first move—so he could blame her for enticing him.

Dori lowered her gaze. She wouldn't play his game. "Good night," she said softly.

"Good night, Dori." But neither of them moved and he added, "I'll be by to pick up Danny about noon on Sunday."

"Fine." Her voice was low and slightly breathless. "He'll be ready." Knowing Danny, he was ready now. Her quavering smile was touched by her amusement at the thought.

"I'll bring Melissa at the same time," Gavin murmured, and his gaze shifted from the key clenched in her hand to her upturned face.

"That'll be fine." She moistened her lips. Not for anything would she make this easy for him. If they were going to kiss, he'd be the initiator.

He took a step in retreat. "I'll see you Sunday then."

"Sunday," she repeated, purposefully turning around and inserting the key in her lock. The door opened and she looked back at him over her shoulder. "Good night, Gavin."

"Good night." His voice was deep and smooth. She recognized the look in his eyes, and her heart responded while her nerve endings screamed a warning. Hurrying now, Dori walked into the house and closed the door. He hadn't kissed her, but the look he'd given her as he stepped off the porch was more powerful than a mere kiss.

The next morning the front door slammed shut as Danny burst into the house. "Mom! How did it go? Did Mr. Parker ask you any football questions? Did he try to kiss you good-night? Did you let him?"

Dori sat at the kitchen table, dressed in her old bathrobe with the ragged hem; her feet rested on the opposite chair. Glancing up from the morning paper, she held out her arms for Danny's hug. "Where's Grandma?"

"She has a meeting with her garden club. She wanted me to tell you that she'd talk to you later." Pulling out a chair, Danny straddled it backward, like a cowboy riding a wild bronco. "Well, how'd it go?"

"Fine."

Danny cocked his head to one side. "Just fine? Nothing *happened*?" Disappointment caused his voice to dip dramatically.

"What did you think we were going to do?" Amusement twitched at the edges of her mouth, and her eyes twinkled. "Honey, it was just a date. Our first one, at that. These things need time."

"But how long?" Danny demanded. "I thought I'd have a new dad by Christmas, and Thanksgiving will be here soon."

Dori set the newspaper aside. "Danny, listen to me. We're dealing with some important issues here. Remember when we got your bike? We shopped around and got the best price possible. We need to be even more careful with a new father."

"Yeah, but I remember that we went back and bought my bike at the very first store we looked at. Mom, Mr. Parker will make a perfect dad." His arm curled around the back of the chair. "I like him a lot."

"I like him, too," Dori admitted, "but that doesn't mean we're ready for marriage. Understand?"

Danny's mouth drooped and his shoulders hunched forward. "You looked so pretty last night."

"Thank you."

"Did Mr. Parker notice how pretty you looked?"

Dori had to think that one over. To be honest, she wasn't sure Gavin was the type to be impressed by a new dress or the fact that she was wearing an expensive perfume. "Do you want to hear what we did?"

"Yeah." Danny's spirits were instantly buoyed and he didn't seem to notice that she hadn't answered his question.

"First we had hamburgers and fries."

"Wow."

Dori knew that would carry weight with her son. "But that wasn't the best part. Later we went to a boxing match in Tacoma."

Danny's eyes rounded with excitement.

"If you bring me my purse, I'll show you the program."

He bounded into the other room and grabbed her handbag. "Mom—" he hesitated before passing it to her, staring pointedly at her feet "—you didn't let Mr. Parker know that you sometimes sleep with socks on, did you?"

Dori could feel the frustration building inside her in turbulent waves. "No," she said, keeping her gaze level with the morning paper. "The subject never came up."

"Good." The relief in his voice was evident.

"Gavin wants you to be ready tomorrow at noon. He's taking you to the Seahawks football game."

"Really?" Danny's eyes grew to saucer size. "Wow. Will I get to meet any players?"

"I don't know, but don't ask him about it. All right? That would be impolite."

"I won't, Mom. I promise."

Danny was dressed and ready for the game hours before Gavin arrived on Sunday morning. He stood waiting at the living room window, fidgeting anxiously. But the minute he spotted the car, Danny was galvanized into action, leaping out the front door and down the stairs.

Dori followed and stood on the porch steps, her arms wrapping her middle to ward off the November chill. She watched as Melissa and Gavin climbed out of the Audi. A smile fanned fine lines around her eyes at the way Danny and Melissa greeted each other. Like conquering heroes on a playing field, they ran to the middle of the lawn, then jumped up and slapped their raised hands in midair in a gesture of triumph.

"What's with those two?" Gavin asked, sauntering toward Dori.

"I think they're pleased about...you know, our agreement."

"Ah, yes." A dark frown puckered his brow as he gave her a disgruntled look and walked past her into the house.

Dori's good mood did a nosedive, but she turned and followed him inside. "Listen, if this is too much of an inconvenience we can do it another time." Somehow she had to find a way to appease Danny. The last thing she wanted was for Gavin to view his agreement to spend this time with her son as an annoying obligation. For that matter, she could easily take Danny and Melissa to a movie if Gavin needed some time alone. She was about to suggest doing just that when Danny and Melissa entered the house.

"Hi, Mr. Parker," Danny greeted cheerfully. "Boy, I'm really excited about you taking me to the game. It's the neatest thing that's ever happened to me."

Gavin's austere expression relaxed. "Hi, Danny."

"Mom packed us a lunch."

"That was nice of your mom." Briefly, Gavin's gaze slid to Dori. Although he offered her a quick smile, she wasn't fooled. Something was bothering him.

"Yeah, and she's a really great cook. I bet she's probably one of the best cooks in the world."

"Danny," Dori warned in a low breath, flashing her son an admonishing look.

"Want a chocolate chip cookie?" Danny directed

his attention to Melissa. "Mom baked them yesterday."

"Sure." Gavin's daughter followed Danny into the kitchen.

Dori turned her attention to Gavin. "Listen, you don't have to do this. I'll take Danny and Melissa to a movie or something. You look worn out."

"I am." He jammed his hands deep inside his pants pockets and marched to the other side of the room.

"What's wrong?"

"Women."

Dori recognized the low murmuring that drifted out from the kitchen as the sound of Melissa talking nonstop and with great urgency. Whatever was wrong involved Gavin's daughter.

"In the plural?" Dori couldn't hide a knowing grin as she glanced toward the children.

"These are probably the very best cookies I've ever had in my whole life," Melissa's voice sang out from the kitchen.

Shaking her head, Dori broke into a soft laugh. "Those two couldn't be any more obvious if they tried."

"No, I suppose not." Gavin shifted his gaze and frowned anew. "Melissa and I had an argument last night. She hasn't spoken to me since. I'd appreciate it if you could smooth things over for me."

"Sure, I'll be happy to."

Gavin lapsed into a pensive silence, then stooped to pat the stuffed lion he'd won for her at the fair. "Don't you want to know what we fought over?"

"I know already."

As he straightened, Gavin's dark eyes lit with amused speculation. "Is that a fact?"

"Yes."

"All right, Ms Know-It-All, you tell me."

Dori crossed the living room and stopped an inch in front of him. "The next time you go out with another woman, you might want to be a bit more discreet." Deftly she lifted a long blond hair from his shoulder.

Five

"It wasn't my fault," Gavin declared righteously. "Lainey showed up last night uninvited."

Dori's eyebrows arched expressively. How like a man to blame the woman. From the very beginning of time, this was the way it had been. It had started in the Garden of Eden when Adam blamed Eve for enticing him to partake of the forbidden fruit, Dori thought, and it was still going on. "Uninvited, but apparently not unwelcome," she murmured, doing her best to hide a smile.

Gavin rubbed the back of his neck in an agitated movement. "Don't you start in on me, too." His angry response sliced the air.

"Me!" It was all she could do to keep from laughing outright.

"No doubt I'm sentenced to a fifteen-minute lecture from you, as well."

Feigning utter nonchalance, Dori moved to the other side of the room and sat on the sofa arm. With relaxed grace she crossed her legs. "It wouldn't be fair for me to lecture you. Besides, I have a pretty good idea of what happened."

"You do?" He eyed her speculatively.

"Sure. This gorgeous blonde showed up..." She

paused to stroke the side of her face as if giving the matter deep thought. "Probably with two tickets to something she knew you really wanted to see."

"Not tickets but—" He stopped abruptly. "Okay. You're right, but I was only gone an hour and Melissa acted like I'd just committed adultery or worse." His defensiveness quickly returned. Stalking over to stand by the television set, he whirled around, asking, "Are you mad at me, too?"

"No." Amused was more the word.

Gavin expelled his breath forcefully and looked visibly relieved. "Thank God. I swear this arrangement is sometimes as bad as being married."

"Even if I were upset, Melissa has scolded you far more effectively than I ever could."

The beginning of a smile touched his eyes, revealing tiny lines of laughter at their outer corners. "That girl's got more of her mother in her than I thought."

"One thing, Gavin."

"Yes?" His gaze met hers.

"Is this Lainey the one whose brain leaks?"

"Yeah, she's the one."

"So you went out with her again although you claimed you weren't going to?" She wanted to prove to him that he wasn't as stouthearted or strong willed as he'd wanted her to believe.

A narrowed look surveyed her calmly. "That's right."

"Then what does that make you?" Dori hated to admit how much she was enjoying this.

His level gaze was locked on her face. "I knew you'd get back at me one way or another."

Blinking her thick lashes wickedly, Dori gave him

her brightest smile. It was obvious that Gavin was more angry with himself than with anyone else and that he didn't like his susceptibility to the charms of this blond bombshell. And to be honest, Dori wasn't exactly pleased by it, either, although she'd rather have choked than let him know.

"Don't worry, all's forgiven," she said with a heavy tone of martyrhood. "I'll be generous and overlook your faults. It's easy, since I have so few of my own."

"I hadn't asked for your pardon," he returned dryly.

"Not to worry, I saved you the trouble."

A barely suppressed smile passed over his face. "I can't remember Melissa ever being so angry."

"Don't worry, I'll talk to her."

"What are you going to say?"

Not for the first time, Dori noticed how deeply resonant his voice was. She shrugged one shoulder and glanced out the window. "I'm not sure, but I'll think of something," she assured him.

"I know what will help."

"What?" She raised her eyes to his.

He strode over to her and glanced into the kitchen. "Danny, are you about ready?" Before Danny had a chance to answer, Gavin pulled Dori to her feet, enfolded her in his arms and drew her so close that the outline of his masculine body was imprinted on her much softer one.

"Ready, Mr. Parker," Danny said as he flew into the living room with Melissa following sluggishly behind. Before Dori could say anything, Gavin's warm mouth claimed hers, moving sensuously over her tender lips, robbing her of clear thought. Instinctively her arms circled his neck as his fiery kiss burned away her objections.

"Gavin." The words vibrated from the emotion-charged tenseness of her throat. Somehow she managed to break the contact and, bracing her hands against his chest, eased her body from his. She was too stunned to say more than his name. The kiss had been so unexpected—so good—that she could only stare up at him with wide disturbed eyes.

"Danny and I should be back about five. If you like, we can all go to dinner afterward."

Mutely, Dori nodded her head. If he'd asked her to swim across Puget Sound naked, she would have agreed. Her mind was befuddled, her senses numb.

"Good." Gavin buried his mouth in the curve of her neck and Dori's bewildered eyes again widened with surprise. As he released her, she caught a glimpse of Melissa and Danny smiling proudly at each other. Dori had to smother an angry groan.

"See you at five." With a thoughtful frown, Gavin paused and ran his index finger down the side of her face.

"Bye, Mom," Danny interrupted.

"Bye." Dori shook her head to free her muddled thoughts and calm her reactions. "Have a good time."

"We will," Gavin promised. He hesitated, studying his daughter. "Be good, Melissa."

The brilliant smile she gave him forced Dori and Gavin to hide a tiny, shared laugh.

"Okay, Dad, see you later."

Gavin's astonished eyes sought Dori's and he winked boldly. Parents could do their own form of manipulating. Again, Dori had difficulty concealing her laughter.

The front door closed and Melissa plopped down on the sofa and firmly crossed her arms. "Dad told you about 'her,' didn't he?"

"He mentioned Lainey, if that's who you mean."

"And you're not mad?" The young girl leaned forward and cupped her face in her hands, supporting her elbows on her knees. "I thought you'd be furious. I was. I didn't know Dad could be so dumb. Even I could see that she's a real phony. Miss Peroxide was so gushy-goo last night I almost threw up."

Dori sat beside the girl and took the same pose as Melissa, placing her bent elbows on her knees. "Your dad doesn't need either of us to be angry with him."

"But..." Melissa turned to scrutinize Dori, her smooth brow furrowed in confusion. "I think we should both be mad. He shouldn't have gone out with her. Not when he's seeing you."

Throwing an arm around the girl's shoulders, Dori searched for the right words. Explaining his actions could get her into trouble. "Your father was more angry at himself than either of us could be. Let's show him that we can overlook his weaknesses and...love him in spite of them." Immediately Dori realized she'd used the wrong word.

"You love Dad?"

A shudder trembled through Dori. "Well, that word may have been a little too strong."

"I think he's falling in love with you," Melissa said fervently. "He hardly talks about you, and that's a sure sign."

Dori was unconvinced. If he didn't talk about her,

it was because he wasn't thinking about her—which was just as well. She wasn't going to fool herself with any unwarranted emotions. She and Gavin had a dating agreement and she wasn't looking for anything more than a way of satisfying Danny's sudden need for a father. Just as Gavin was hoping to appease his daughter.

"That's nice," Dori said, reaching for the Sunday paper. "What would you like to do today?" Absently she flipped the pages of the sales tabloids that came with the paper.

The young girl shrugged and reclined against the back of the sofa. "I don't know. What would you like to do?"

"Well," Dori eased herself into a comfortable position and pretended to give the matter some thought. "I could do some shopping, but I don't want to drag you along if you'd find it boring."

"What are you going to buy?"

Remembering the way Melissa had watched her put on her makeup sparked an idea. "I thought I'd stop in at Northgage plaza and sample a few perfumes at The Bon. You can help me decide which scent your father would like best."

"Yeah, I'd like that."

Two hours later, before she was even aware of Dori's scheme, Melissa owned her first cosmetics, a new dress and shoes. Once Dori had persuaded the girl that it was time to experiment with some light makeup, progressing to a dress and shoes had been relatively easy.

Back at the house Melissa used Dori's bedroom to try on the new outfit. Shyly she paraded before Dori, her intense eyes lowered to the carpet as she walked. The dress was a lovely pink floral print with lace collar and cuffs. The T-strap dress shoes were white and Melissa was wearing her first pair of nylons. Self-consciously she held out her leg to Dori. "Did I put them on right?"

"Perfect." A sense of pride and happiness shone in Dori's bright eyes. Folding her hands together, she said softly, "Oh, Melissa, you're so pretty."

"Really?" Disbelief caused her voice to rise half an octave.

"Really!" The transformation was astonishing. The girl standing before her was no longer a defiant tomboy but a budding young woman. Dori's heart swelled with emotion. Gavin would hardly recognize his own daughter. "Come look." Dori led her into the bathroom and closed the door so Melissa could see for herself in the full-length mirror.

The girl breathed a long sigh. "It's beautiful," she said in a low, shaking voice. "Thank you." Impulsively she gave Dori a hug. "Oh, I wish you were my mother. I really, really wish you were."

Dori hugged her back, surprised at the emotion that surged through her. "I'd consider myself very lucky to have you for a daughter."

Melissa stepped back for another look at herself. "You know, at first I was really hoping Dad would marry Lainey." She pursed her lips and tilted her head mockingly. "That's how really desperate I am to get out of that school. It's not that the nuns are mean or anything. Everyone's been really nice. But I really want a family and a regular, ordinary life."

Dori hid a smile. *Really* was obviously Melissa's word for the day.

"But the more I thought about it, the more I realized Lainey would probably keep me in that stupid school until I was twenty-nine. She doesn't want me hanging around. If Dad marries her, I don't know what I'd do."

"Your father isn't going to marry anyone..." Dori faltered momentarily. "Not someone you don't like, anyway."

"I hope not," Melissa said heatedly. Turning sideways, she viewed her profile. "You know something else I'd really like to do?"

"Name it." The day had gone so well that Dori was ready to be obliging.

"Can I bake something?"

"Anything you like."

The spicy aroma of fresh-baked apple pie filled the house by the time Danny burst in the front door. "Mom!" he screamed as if the very demons of hell were in pursuit. "The Seahawks won. The score was 14 to 7."

Dori had been so busy that she hadn't thought of turning on the television. "Did you have a good time?"

"Mr. Parker bought me a hot dog and a soda pop and some peanuts."

Dori cast an accusing glare at Gavin, who gestured dismissively with his hands and grinned sheepishly.

"What about the lunch I packed you?"

"We didn't eat it. Mr. Parker says it's more fun to buy stuff at the game."

"Oh, he did, did he?" Amused, Dori found her laughing eyes meeting Gavin's.

The bedroom door opened a crack. "Can I come out yet?"

Guiltily Dori's gaze swung to the hallway. "Oh goodness, I nearly forgot. Sit down, you two. Melissa and I have a surprise."

Gavin and Danny obediently took a seat. "Ready," Dori called over her shoulder. The bedroom door opened wide and Melissa started down the hallway. Halting her progress for a moment, Dori announced, "While you two were at the game, Melissa and I were just as busy shopping."

Confident now, none of her earlier coyness evident, Melissa strolled into the room and gracefully modeled the dress, turning as she came to a stop in front of the sofa. Smiling, she curtsied and demurely lowered her lashes. Then she rose, contentedly folding her hands in front of her, ready to receive their lavish praise.

"You look like a girl," Danny said, unable to disguise his lack of enthusiasm. At the disapproving look Dori flashed him, he quickly amended his hastily spoken words. "You look real pretty though—for a girl."

Dori studied Gavin's reaction and felt her tension build at the pride that shone from his eyes. A myriad of emotions were revealed in the strong, often stern features. "This can't be my little girl. Not Melissa Jane Parker, my daughter."

Melissa giggled happily. "Really, Dad, who else could it be?"

Gavin stroked his chin as if he still couldn't believe his eyes. Slowly he shook his head, apparently speechless. "I don't know who's wearing that dress, but I can hardly believe I've got a daughter this pretty."

"I made you a surprise, too," Melissa added eagerly. "Something to eat."

"Something to eat?" He echoed her words and looked at Dori, who shrugged innocently.

Tugging at his hand, Melissa urged her father off the couch and led him into the kitchen. "Dori helped me."

"Not all that much. She did most of the work herself."

"A pie?" Gavin's gaze fell to the cooling masterpiece that rested on the kitchen countertop.

"Apple," Melissa boasted proudly, "your favorite."

Later that night, Dori lay in bed gazing at the darkened ceiling, her clasped hands supporting the back of her head. The day had been wonderful. There wasn't a better word to describe it. She'd enjoyed shopping with Melissa, particularly because the girl had been so responsive to all Dori's suggestions. Dori didn't like to think about the baby she'd lost after Brad's death. She'd so hoped for a daughter. Today it was almost as if Melissa had been hers. Dori felt such enthusiasm, such joy, in sharing little things, like shopping with Melissa. She loved Danny beyond reason, but there were certain things he'd never appreciate. Shopping was one. But Melissa had enjoyed it as much as Dori had.

Danny's day had been wonderful, too. All evening he'd talked nonstop about the football game and had obviously had the time of his life. Long after Gavin and Melissa had left, Danny continued to recount the highlights of the game, recalling plays with a vivid memory for every minute detail. Either the two children had superlative—and hitherto unsuspected—acting abilities, or their reactions had been genuine. Dori found it difficult to believe that the whole thing had been a charade. To be honest, she'd had her suspicions when Gavin first suggested this agreement, but now she believed that it could be the best thing to have happened to her in a long time—the best thing for all of them.

The following morning Sandy looked up from her work when Dori entered the office.

"Morning," Dori said absently as she pulled out the bottom drawer of her desk and routinely deposited her purse. When Sandy didn't immediately respond, Dori glanced up. Sandy was eyeing her speculatively, her head cocked slightly. "What's with the funny, bug-eyed look?" Dori demanded.

"There's something different about you."

"Me?"

"You and this football hero went out Friday night, didn't you?"

Dori couldn't help but chuckle. "Yes, to the fights, if you can believe it."

"I don't."

"Well, do, because it's the truth. But first he took me out for a four-star meal of hamburgers, French fries and a chocolate shake."

"And he's living to tell about it?"

Dori relaxed in her chair and crossed her arms, letting the memory of that night amuse her anew. "Yup."

"From that dreamy look in your eyes I'd say you had a good time."

Dreamy look! Dori stiffened and reached for her pen. "Oh, hardly. You just like to tease, that's all."

Sandy gave her a measured look and returned her attention to her desk. "If you say so, but you might want to watch where you walk, with all those stars blinding your eyes."

At about eleven o'clock the phone buzzed. Usually Sandy and Dori took turns answering, but Sandy was away from her desk and Dori automatically reached for the receiver.

"Underwriting," she announced.

"Dori?"

"Gavin?" Her heart responded, pounding like a jackhammer gone wild. "Hi."

"What time are you free for lunch?" he asked without preamble.

"Noon." From the sound of his voice, something was troubling him. "Is something wrong?" Dori probed gently.

"No, not really. I just think we need to talk."

They agreed on an attractive seafood restaurant beside Lake Union. Gavin was already seated at one of the linen-covered tables when Dori arrived. She noticed that his eyes were veiled and thoughtful as he watched the maître d' lead her to his table.

"This is a pleasant surprise," she said to Gavin, smiling appreciatively at the waiter who held out a chair for her.

"Yes, well, I don't usually take this type of lunch break." There seemed to be a hidden meaning in the statement.

Gavin always managed to throw her off base one way or another. Just when she felt she understood him, he would say or do something that made her realize she hardly knew this man. Her intuition told her it was about to happen again. Mentally she braced herself, and a small sigh of dread quivered in her throat.

To mask her fears, Dori lifted the menu and studied it with unseeing eyes. The restaurant was known for its wide variety of seafood, and Dori was toying with the idea of ordering a Crab Louis when Gavin spoke. "Melissa had a good time yesterday."

"I enjoyed her, too. She's a wonderful child, Gavin." Dori set the menu aside, having decided on a shrimp salad.

"Once we got off the subject of you, Danny and I had a great time ourselves."

Dori groaned inwardly at the thought of Danny endlessly extolling her virtues. Gavin must have been thoroughly sick of hearing about her. She'd make a point of saying something to Danny later.

"Danny certainly enjoyed himself."

Gavin laid the menu alongside his plate and stared at her in thoughtful, nerve-racking silence.

Instinctively, Dori stiffened. "But there's a problem, right?" she asked with deliberate softness, fighting off a sense of unease.

"Yes. I think you might have laid on this motherhood bit a little too thick, don't you? Melissa drove me crazy last night. First Danny and now my own daughter."

Anger raged within Dori and it was all she could do not to bolt out of the restaurant. To Gavin's twisted way of thinking, she had intentionally set out to convince his daughter that she would be the perfect wife and mother. On the basis of nothing more than her visit with Melissa the day before, Gavin had cynically concluded that she was already checking out engagement rings and choosing a china pattern. "You know, I was thinking the same thing myself," she announced casually, surprised at how unemotional she sounded.

Gavin studied her with amused indifference. "I thought you might be."

His sarcastic tone was her undoing. "Yes, the more I think about it, the more I realize that our well-plotted scheme may be working all *too* well. If you're tired of listening to my praises sung, then you should hear it from my end of things."

"Yes, I imagine—"

"That's exactly your problem, Gavin Parker," she cut in, her voice sharp and brittle. "The reason Melissa responded to me yesterday was because that child has a heart full of love and no one who seems to want it." Dori fixed her gaze on the water glass as she battled back the rising swell of anger that threatened to choke her. "I feel sorry for you. Your thinking is so twisted that you don't know what's genuine and what isn't. You're so afraid of revealing your emotions that your heart has become like granite."

"I suppose you think you're just the woman to free me from these despicable shackles?" he taunted.

Dori ignored the derision and the question. "For Melissa's sake I hope you find what you're looking for soon." She tilted her head back and raised her eyes enough to look full into his face with haughty disdain. "For my part, I want out." She had to go before she became so attached to Melissa that severing the relationship would harm them both. And before she made the fatal mistake of giving Gavin Parker her heart.

His eyes glittered as cold and dark as the Arctic Sea. "Are you saying you want to cancel our agreement?"

Calmly, Dori placed the linen napkin on top of her unused plate and stood, "I swear the man's a marvel," she murmured sarcastically. "It was nice knowing you, Gavin Parker. You have a delightful daughter. Thank you for giving Danny the thrill of his life."

"What are you doing?" he hissed under his breath. "Sit back down and let's discuss this like adults."

Still standing, Dori boldly met Gavin's angry eyes. Sick at heart and so miserable that given any provocation she would have cried, she slowly shook her head. "I'm sorry, Gavin, really sorry, but even a phony arrangement can't work with us. We're too different."

"We're not different at all," he argued heatedly, then paused to glower at the people whose attention his raised voice had attracted.

"Careful, Gavin," she mocked, "someone might think you're coming on a bit too—"

"Melissa's mother phoned me this morning," he announced starkly, and for the first time Dori noted the deep lines of worry that marred his face.

"What?" she repeated, her heartbeat accelerating at an alarming rate. She sat down again, her eyes wide and fearful at the apprehension in Gavin's expression.

"Our conversation was less than congenial. I need to talk to someone. I apologize if I came at you like a kamikaze pilot."

If, Dori mused flippantly. He'd invited her because he wanted someone to talk to and then he'd tried to sabotage their lunch. "What happened?"

"The usual. Deirdre's living in New York and is

divorcing her third or fourth husband, I forget which, and wants Melissa to come and live with her.''

Dori sucked in a shocked breath. She knew nothing about this woman. Until today she hadn't even known her name. But Dori was privy to the pain this woman had wreaked in Gavin's life. ''Does she have a chance of getting her?'' Already her heart was pounding at the thought of Gavin's losing his daughter to a woman he so obviously detested.

Gavin's laugh was bitter. ''Hardly, but that won't stop her from trying. She does this at the end of every marriage. She has an attack of guilt and wants to play mommy for a while.''

''How does Melissa feel about Deirdre? Does she ever see her mother?'' She didn't mean to pry and she didn't want him to reveal anything he wasn't comfortable sharing. But the thought of this young girl being forced into an uncomfortable situation tore at her heart.

''Melissa spends a month every summer. Last year she phoned me three days after she arrived and begged me to let her come home. At the time Deirdre was just as glad to be rid of her. I don't know what happened, but Melissa made me promise that I wouldn't send her there alone again.''

''I realize you're upset, but the courts aren't going to listen—''

''I know,'' Gavin interrupted abruptly. ''I just needed to vent my frustrations and anger on someone. Melissa and I have gone through this before and we can weather another of Deirdre's whims.'' Gavin's hand gently touched hers. ''I owe you an apology for the way I behaved earlier.''

"It's forgotten." What wasn't forgotten was that he'd sought her out. Somehow, in some way, she'd reached Gavin Parker—and now they were on dangerous ground. This charade was becoming more real every time they saw each other. They'd thought they could keep their emotions detached and they were failing. More and more, Gavin dominated her thoughts, and despite herself, she found excuses to imagine them together. It wasn't supposed to work like this.

"You told me about Brad. I think it's only fair to let you know about Deirdre."

A feeling of gladness raced through Dori. Not because Gavin was telling her about his ex-wife. To be truthful, Dori wasn't even sure she wanted to hear the gory details of his marriage breakdown. But the fact that Gavin was telling her was a measure of his trust in her. He felt safe enough with her to divulge his deepest pain—as she had with him. "It isn't necessary," she said softly, their gazes holding.

"It's only fair that you know." His hand gripped the water glass, apparently oblivious to the cold that must be seeping up his arm. "I don't even know where to begin. We married young, too young I suppose. We were in our last year of college and I was on top of the world. The pros were already scouting me out. I'd been seeing Deirdre, but so had a lot of other guys. She came from a wealthy family and had been spoiled by an indulgent father. I liked him; he was a terrific guy, even if he did cater too much to his daughter— but he really loved her. When she told me she was pregnant and I was the baby's father, I offered to marry her. I have no difficulty believing that if I hadn't, she would have had an abortion. I went into the marriage with a lot of expectations. I think I was even glad she was pregnant. The idea of being a father pleased me—proof of my manhood and all that garbage.'' He paused and focused his gaze on the table-top.

Dori realized how difficult this must be for him, and her first instinct was to tell him to stop. It wasn't necessary for him to reveal this pain. But even stronger was the feeling that he needed to talk—to get this out of his system.

''Usually people can say when they felt their marriage going bad. Ours went bad on the wedding day. Deirdre hated being pregnant, but worse, I believe she hated me. From the moment Melissa was born, she didn't want to have anything to do with her. Later I learned that she hated being pregnant so much that she had herself sterilized so there would never be any more children. She didn't even bother to tell me. Melissa was given to a nanny and within weeks Deirdre was making the rounds, if you know what I mean. I don't think I need to put it any more clearly.''

''No.'' Dori's voice was low and trembling. She'd never known anyone like that and found it impossible to imagine a woman who could put such selfish, shallow pleasures ahead of her own child's needs.

''God knows I tried to make the marriage work. More for her father's sake than Deirdre's. But after he died I couldn't pretend any longer. She didn't want custody of Melissa then, and I'm not about to give up my daughter now.''

''How long ago was that?''

''Melissa was three when we got divorced.''

Three! The girl had never really known her mother.

Dori's heart ached for this child who had never experienced a mother's love.

"I thought you should know," he concluded.

"Thank you for telling me." Instinctively Gavin had come to her with his doubts and worries. He was reaching out to her, however reluctantly at first. But he'd made a beginning, and Dori was convinced it was the right one for them.

That same week, Dori saw Gavin two more times. They went to a movie Wednesday evening, sat in the back row and argued over the popcorn. Telling Dori about Deirdre seemed to have freed him. On Friday he phoned her at the office again, and they met for lunch at the same restaurant they'd gone to the previous Monday. He told her he was going to be away for the weekend, broadcasting a game.

By the following Monday, Dori was worried. She had trouble keeping her thoughts on her work. Every time she tried to concentrate, she wondered if she was falling in love with Gavin. It didn't seem possible that she could grow to care about him this quickly. The physical response to his touch was a pleasant surprise. But it had been years since a man had held her the way he did, so Dori had more or less expected and compensated for the physical impact of his lovemaking. The emotional response was what overwhelmed her. She cared about him. Worried about him. Thought about him to the exclusion of all else. They were in trouble, deep trouble. But Gavin had failed to recognize it. If they were going to react sensibly, the impetus would have to come from her.

Dori's thoughts were still troubled when she

stopped at the soccer field to pick up Danny after work that Monday night. She pulled into the parking lot at the park and walked across the thick lawn to the field. The boys were playing a scrimmage game and she stood by the sidelines, proudly watching Danny weave his way through the defenders.

"You're Danny's mother, aren't you?"

Dori's attention was diverted to the lanky, thin man at her side. She recognized him as Jon Schaeffer's dad. Jon and Danny had recently become the best of friends and had spent the night at each other's houses two or three times since the beginning of the school year. From what she understood, Jon's parents were separated. "Yes, you're Jon's father, right?"

"Right." He crossed his arms and watched the boys running back and forth across the long field. "Danny's a good player."

"Thank you. So is Jon."

"Yeah, I'm real proud of him." The conversation was stilted and Dori felt a little uneasy.

"I hope you won't think I'm being too bold, but did you put an ad in the paper?"

Dori felt waves of color flood her face. "Well, actually Danny did."

"I thought he might have." He chuckled and held out his hand. "My name's Tom, by the way."

Less embarrassed, Dori shook it. "Dori," she introduced herself.

"I read the ad and thought about calling. As much as I'd hoped, it doesn't look like Paula and I are going to get back together and I was so damned lonely, I thought about giving you a call."

"How'd you know the number was mine?"

"I didn't," he was quick to amend. "I wrote it down on a slip of paper and set it by the phone, trying to work up enough courage. Jon spent last weekend with me and saw it and wanted to know how come I had Danny's phone number."

"Oh." Color blossomed anew. "I've had the number changed since."

"I think Jon mentioned that. So Danny put the ad in the paper?"

"All on his own. It was the first time I've ever regretted being a mother." Involuntarily her voice rose with remembered embarrassment.

"Did you get many responses?"

He was so serious that Dori was forced to conceal a smile. "You wouldn't believe the number of calls that came the first night."

"I thought as much."

They lapsed into a companionable silence. "You and your husband split up?"

Tom had a clear-cut view of life, it seemed, and a blunt manner. The question came out of nowhere. "No, I'm a widow."

"Hey, listen, I'm sorry. I didn't mean to be nosy. It's none of my business."

"Don't worry about it," Dori reassured him softly.

Tom wasn't like most of the men she'd known. He was obviously a hard worker, frank, a little rough around the edges. Dori sensed that he was still in love with his wife and she silently hoped they'd get back together again.

"Jon and Danny are good friends, aren't they?"

"They certainly see enough of each other."

"Could you tolerate a little more togetherness?" His gaze didn't leave the field.

"How do you mean?"

"Could I take you and Danny to dinner with Jon and me?" He looked as awkward as a teenager asking a girl out for the first time.

Dori's immediate inclination was to politely refuse. The last thing she wanted to do was alienate Jon's mother. On the other hand, Dori needed to sort through her own feelings for Gavin, and seeing someone else was bound to help.

"Yes, we'd enjoy that. Thank you."

The smile he beamed at her was bright enough to rival the streetlight. "The pleasure's all mine."

Six

"Mom," Danny pleaded, following her into the bathroom and frantically waving his hand in front of his face while she deftly applied hair spray to her pinned-up curls.

"What?" Dori answered irritably. She'd been arguing with Danny from the minute he'd learned she was going out with Tom Schaeffer.

"Mr. Parker could phone."

"I know, but it's unlikely." Gavin hadn't been in touch with her since their Monday lunch. If he expected her to sit around and wait for his calls, then he was in for a surprise.

Danny's disgruntled look and defiantly crossed arms made her hesitate. "If he does phone, tell him I'm out for the evening and I'll return his call when I get home."

"But I thought you and Mr. Parker were good friends...real good friends. You even kissed him!"

"We are friends," she answered, feigning indifference as she tucked in a stray hair and examined her profile in the mirror. With a sigh of disgust she tightened her stomach—and wondered how long she could go without breathing.

"Mom," Danny protested anew, "I don't like this and I don't think Mr. Parker will, either."

"He won't care," she stated with more aplomb than she was feeling. Danny assumed that because she was going out on a weeknight, this must be some "hot date." It wasn't. Tom had invited her after their dinner with the boys and Dori had accepted because she realized that what he really wanted was a sympathetic ear. He was lonely and still deeply in love with his wife. She couldn't have picked a safer date, but Danny wouldn't understand that and she didn't try to explain.

"If you're such good friends with Mr. Parker, how come you're wearing perfume for Jon's dad?"

"Moms sometimes do that for no special reason."

"But tonight's special. You're going out with Mr. Schaeffer."

Dori placed her hands on her son's shoulders and studied him closely. The young face was pinched, and the deep blue eyes intense. "Don't you like Mr. Schaeffer?"

"He's all right, I guess."

"But I thought you had a good time when we went out to dinner Monday night."

"That was different. Jon and I were with you."

Dori knew that Danny wasn't terribly pleased that a high school girl from the neighborhood was coming to sit with him. He was at that awkward age—too young to be left completely alone, especially for an evening, but old enough to resent a baby-sitter, particularly when she was one of his own neighbors.

"I'll be home early—probably before your bedtime," Dori promised, ruffling his hair.

Danny impatiently brushed her hand aside. "But

why are you going, Mom? That's what I don't understand.''

Dori didn't know how she could explain something she didn't completely comprehend herself. She was worried that her emotions were becoming involved with Gavin. Tom was insurance. With Tom there wasn't any fear of falling in love or being hurt. Every time she saw Gavin her emotions became more entangled; she cared about him and Melissa. But as far as Gavin was concerned, the minute her heart was involved would be the end of their relationship. He'd made it abundantly clear that he didn't want any kind of real involvement. He had no plans to remarry, and the minute she revealed any emotional commitment he wouldn't hesitate to reject her as he had rejected others. Oh, she might hold on to him for a time, the way Lainey was trying to. But Gavin wasn't a man easily fooled—and Dori wasn't a fool.

The doorbell chimed and the sixteen-year-old who lived across the street came in with an armful of books.

''Hello, Mrs. Robertson.''

''Hi, Jody.'' Out of the corner of her eye Dori noted that Danny had plopped down in front of the television. She wasn't deceived by his indifference. Her son was not happy that she was dating Tom Schaeffer. Dori ignored him and continued her instructions to the sitter. ''The phone number for the restaurant is in the kitchen. I shouldn't be much later than nine-thirty, maybe ten.'' The front doorbell chimed again and Danny answered it this time, opening the door for Tom, who smiled appreciatively when he saw Dori.

"Be good," Dori whispered and kissed Danny on the cheek.

He rubbed the place she'd kissed and examined the palm of his hand for any lipstick. "Okay," he agreed with a sad little smile calculated to tug at a mother's heart. "But I'm waiting up for you." He gave her the soulful look of a lost puppy, his deep blue eyes crying out at the injustice of being left at the fickle mercy of a sixteen-year-old girl. The emphasis being, of course, on the word "girl."

If Dori didn't leave soon, he might well win this unspoken battle and she couldn't allow that. "We'll talk when I get back," she promised softly.

Tom, dressed in a three-piece suit, placed a guiding hand at the small of her back as they left the house. "Is there a problem with Danny?"

Dori cast a speculative glance over her shoulder. She felt guilty and depressed, although there was no reason she should. Now she realized how Melissa had made Gavin feel when he'd gone out with Lainey that Saturday night. No wonder he'd been upset on Sunday. Neither of them were accustomed to this type of adolescent censorship. And she didn't like it any more than Gavin had.

"Danny's unhappy about being left with a baby-sitter," she answered Tom half-truthfully.

With such an ominous beginning, Dori realized that the evening was doomed before it even began. They shared a quiet dinner and talked over coffee, but the conversation was one-sided and when the clock struck nine, Dori fought not to glance at her wristwatch every five minutes.

On the drive home, she felt obliged to apologize.

"I'm *really* sorry…" She paused, then remembered how often Melissa used that word and, in spite of herself, broke into a full laugh.

Tom's bewildered gaze caught hers. "What's so amusing?"

"It's a long story. A friend of mine has a daughter who alternates 'really' with every other word. I caught myself saying it just now and…"

"It suddenly seemed funny."

"Exactly." She was still smiling when Tom turned into the street that led to her house. The muscles of her face tightened, and the amusement drained from her eyes when she noticed a car parked in front. Gavin's car. Damn, damn, damn! She clenched her fist tightly and drew several deep breaths to calm her nerves. There was no telling what kind of confrontation awaited her.

As politely as possible, Dori thanked Tom for the dinner and apologized for not inviting him in for coffee.

When she opened the door a pair of accusing male eyes met hers. "Hello, Gavin," Dori said on a cheerful note, "this is a pleasant surprise."

"Dori." The glittering harshness of his gaze told her he wasn't pleased. "Did you have a good time?"

"Wonderful," she lied. "We went to a Greek restaurant and naturally everything was Greek to me. I finally decided what to eat by asking myself what Anthony Quinn would order." Dori hated the way she was rambling like a guilty schoolgirl. Her mouth felt dry and her throat scratchy.

Danny faked a wide yawn. "I think I'll go to bed now. It's bedtime already."

"Not so fast, young man." Dori stopped him. Her son had played a part in this uncomfortable showdown with Gavin. The least he could do was explain. "Is there something you want to tell me?"

Danny eyed the carpet with unusual interest while his cheeks flushed with telltale color. "No."

Dori was convinced that Danny had phoned Gavin, but she'd handle that later with a week's grounding. "I'll talk to you in the morning."

"'Night, Mr. Parker." Like a rabbit unexpectedly freed from a trap, Danny bolted down the hallway to his bedroom.

It didn't escape Dori's notice that he hadn't wished her good-night. Hanging her coat in the hall closet gave Dori precious moments to collect her thoughts and resolve to ignore the distressing heat that warmed her blood. When she finally turned to face Gavin, she saw that a cynical smile had quirked up the corners of his stern mouth.

"Don't look so guilty," he challenged.

Dori's cheeks burned, but she boldly met his hard eyes, sparks flashing defiantly from hers. "I'm not." She walked into the kitchen and prepared a pot of coffee. Gavin followed her and she automatically took two mugs from the cupboard. Turning, her back pressed against the counter, Dori confronted his gaze squarely. "What happened? Did Danny phone you?"

"I thought we had an agreement."

Involuntarily, Dori flinched at the harshness of his voice. "We do," she replied calmly, watching the coffee drip into the glass pot.

"Then what were you doing out with a man? A married one, at that."

"Exactly what has Danny been telling you? Tom and his wife are separated. For heaven's sake, we didn't even hold hands." She studiously avoided meeting his fiery glare, angry now that she'd bothered to explain. "Good grief, you went out with Lainey. I don't see the difference."

"At least I felt guilty."

"So did I! Does that make you feel any better?"

"Yes!" he shouted.

Furious, she whirled around, tired of playing mouse to his cat. Her hand shook as she poured hot coffee into the mugs.

"Are we going to fight about it?" she asked as she placed his mug on the kitchen table.

"That depends on whether you plan to see him again." His face was impassive, as if the question were of no importance. Dori marveled at his self-control. The hard eyes that stared back at her were frosted with challenge, daring her to say she would be seeing Tom again.

"I don't know." She sat in the chair opposite him. "Does it matter?"

His mouth twisted in a faintly ironic smile. "It could. I don't particularly relish another frantic phone call from your son informing me that I'd better do something quick."

"Believe me, that won't happen again," Dori insisted, furious with Danny and more furious with herself. She should have known that Danny would do something like this and taken measures before she went out.

"So you felt guilty." His low, drawling voice was tinged with amused mockery.

"I didn't like it any more than you did." She expelled her breath and folded her arms in a defensive gesture. "I don't know, Gavin, our agreement is working much too well." With an impatient gesture she reached for the sugar bowl in the middle of the table and stirred a teaspoon into her coffee. "Before we know it, those two kids are going to have us married and living in a house with a white picket fence."

"You needn't worry about that."

"Oh, no—" she waved her hands in the air helplessly "—of course that wouldn't concern you. Mr. Macho here can handle everything, right? Well, you admitted that Melissa made you miserable when you saw Lainey. Danny did the same thing to me. I think we should bow gracefully out of this agreement while we can." Although Dori offered the suggestion, she hoped Gavin would refuse; she needed to know that the attraction was mutual.

"Is that what you want?" Deftly he turned the tables on her.

In a flash of irritation, Dori pushed back her chair and walked quickly to the sink where she deposited her mug. She gave a sharp sigh of frustration and returned to the table. "No, unfortunately I don't. Darn it, Parker, in spite of your arrogant ways, I've discovered I like you. That's what scares me."

"Don't sound so shocked. I'm a great guy. Just ask Danny. Of course, it could be my virility that you find so alluring, in which case we're in deep trouble." Chuckling, he rolled lazily to his feet and delivered his empty cup to the sink.

"Don't fret," she muttered sarcastically, "your masculinity hasn't overpowered me yet."

"That's probably the best thing we've got going for us. Don't fall in love with me, Dori," he warned, the amusement gone from his eyes. "I'd only end up hurting you."

Her pulse rocketed with alarm. He was right. The problem was that she was already halfway there. And she was standing on dangerously thin ice, struggling to hold back her feelings.

"I think you've got things twisted here," she told him dryly, "I'm more concerned about you falling for me. I'm not your usual type, Gavin. The danger could well be of your own making."

Her appraisal didn't appear to please him. "There's little worry of that happening. One woman's already brought me to my knees and I'm not about to let that happen again."

Dori forced back the words of protest, the assertion that a real woman didn't want a man on his knees. She wanted him at her side as friend, lover and confidant.

"There's another problem coming up I think we should discuss," he continued.

"What?"

He ignored her worried look and casually leaned a hip against the counter. "Melissa and I are going to San Francisco over Thanksgiving weekend. I'm doing the play-by-play of the Forty-niners game that Saturday. For weeks, Melissa's been asking me if you and Danny can come with us."

"But why? This should be a special time between the two of you."

"Unfortunately, Melissa doesn't see it that way. She'll be left in the hotel room alone on the Saturday because I'll be in the broadcast booth and I don't want her attending the game by herself. It *is* Thanksgiving weekend, as Melissa keeps pointing out. But I hate to admit that my daughter knows exactly which buttons to push to make me feel guilty.''

''I don't know, Gavin,'' Dori hedged. She had planned to spend the holiday with her parents, but she loved San Francisco. Her mind was buzzing. She'd visited the Bay area as a teenager and had always wanted to return. This would be like a vacation and she hadn't been on one in years.

''The way I see it,'' Gavin went on, ''this may even suit our needs. The kids are likely to overdose on each other if they spend that much time together. Maybe after three or four days in each other's company, they'll face a few truths about this whole thing.''

Dori was skeptical. ''It could backfire.''

''I doubt it. What do you say?''

The temptation was so strong that she had to close her eyes to fight back an immediate yes. ''Let...let me think on it.''

''Fine,'' he answered calmly.

Dori pulled out a chair and sat down. ''Have you heard anything more from Deirdre?''

''No, and I won't.''

''How can you be so sure?''

The hard line of his mouth curved upward in a mirthless smile. ''I have my ways.''

Just the manner in which he said it made Dori's blood run cold. Undoubtedly Gavin knew Deirdre's weaknesses and knew how to attack his ex-wife.

''There's no way on this earth that I'll hand my daughter over to that bitch.''

Until then, Dori had never seen a man's eyes look more frigid or harsh. "If there's anything I can do to help…" She let the rest fade. Gavin wouldn't need anything from her.

"As a matter of fact, there is." He contradicted her thoughts. "I'm broadcasting a game this Sunday in Kansas City, which means Melissa has to spend the weekend at the school. Saturday and Sunday alone at the school are the worst, or so she claims."

"She could stay with us. I'd enjoy it immensely." There wasn't anything special planned. Saturday she did errands and bought the week's groceries, and Danny had a soccer game in the afternoon, but Melissa would enjoy that.

"I was thinking more like one afternoon," Gavin said with some reluctance. "As it is, you'll hear twenty-four hours of my limitless virtues. Why ask for more?"

"Let her stay the whole weekend," Dori requested softly. "Didn't you just say we should try to 'overdose' the kids?"

Gavin's warning proved to be prophetic. From the moment Dori picked up Melissa at the Eastside Convent School on Mercer Island, the girl chattered nonstop, extolling her father's apparently limitless virtues—just as he'd predicted.

"Did you know that my father has a whole room full of trophies he won playing sports?"

"Wow," Danny answered, his voice unnaturally high. "Remember our list, Mom? I think it's important that my new dad be athletic."

"What else was on the list?" Melissa asked, then

listened attentively as Danny explained each requirement. She continued to comment, presenting Gavin as
the ideal father and husband in every respect. However, it hadn't escaped Dori's notice that Melissa
didn't mention the last stipulation, that Danny's new
father love Dori. Instinctively Melissa recognized it
would be overstepping the bounds. Dori appreciated
the girl's honesty.

As Melissa continued her bragging about Gavin,
Dori had to bite her tongue to keep from laughing.
Given the chance, she'd teach those two something
about subtlety—later. For now, they were far too
amusing. In an effort to restrain her merriment, she
centered her concentration on the heavy traffic that
moved at a snail's pace over the floating bridge. Friday
afternoons were a nightmare for commuters.

The chatter stopped and judging by the sounds she
heard coming from the back seat, Dori guessed that
Danny and Melissa were having a heated discussion
under their breaths. Dori thought she heard Tom's
name but let it pass. With all the problems it caused,
she doubted she'd be seeing him again. For his part,
Tom was hoping to settle things with his wife and
move back home for the holidays. Dori knew that Jon
would be pleased to have his father back, and she
prayed Tom's wife would be as willing.

Following the Saturday expedition to the grocery
store, the three attended Danny's soccer game. To Melissa's delight, Danny scored two goals and was
cheered as a hero when he ran off the field at the end
of the game. Luckily they arrived back home before
it started to rain. Dori popped the corn and the two
children watched a late-afternoon movie on television.

The phone rang just as Dori was finishing the dinner dishes. She reached for it and glanced at Danny and Melissa who were playing a game of Risk in the living room.

"Hello," she answered absently.

"Dori, it's Gavin. How are things going?" The long-distance echo sounded in her ear.

"Fine," she returned smoothly, unreasonably pleased that he'd phoned. "They've had their first spat but rebounded remarkably well."

"What happened?"

"Melissa wanted to try on some of my makeup and Danny was thoroughly disgusted to see her behaving like a real girl."

"Did you tell him the time will come when he'll appreciate girls?"

"No." Her hand tightened around the receiver. Gavin was a thousand miles from Seattle. The sudden warmth she felt at hearing his voice made her thankful he wasn't there to witness the effect he had on her. "He wouldn't have believed it, coming from me."

"I'll tell him. He'll believe me."

Danny would. If there was anything wrong with this relationship, it was that Danny idealized Gavin. One day, Gavin would fall off Danny's pedestal. No man could continue to breathe comfortably so high up, in such a rarefied atmosphere. Dori only hoped that when the crash came, her son wouldn't be hurt. "Are you having a good time with your cronies?" she asked, leaning against the kitchen wall.

He chuckled and the sound produced a tingling rush of pleasure. "Aren't you afraid I've got a woman in the room with me?"

"Not in the least," she answered honestly. "You'd hardly phone here if you did."

"You're too smart for your own good," he chided affectionately. He paused, and Dori's blood raced through her veins. "You're going to San Francisco with us, aren't you?"

"Yes," she answered softly.

"Good." No word had ever sounded more sensuous to Dori.

She straightened quickly, frightened by the intensity of her emotions. "Would you like to talk to Melissa?"

"How's she behaving?"

Dori chuckled. "As predicted."

"I told you she would. Do you want me to say something?"

Gavin was obviously pleased that his daughter's behavior was running true to form. "No, Danny will undoubtedly list my virtues for hours the next time you have him."

"I'll look forward to that."

"I'll bet." Hiding her mirth, Dori set the phone aside and called Melissa, who hurried into the kitchen and picked up the receiver. Overflowing with enthusiasm, she relayed the events of the day, with Danny motioning dramatically in the background, instructing Melissa to tell Gavin about the goals he'd scored that afternoon. Eventually Danny got a chance to report the great news himself. When the children had finished talking, Dori took the receiver back.

"Have they worn your ear off yet?"

"Just about. By the way, I might be able to catch an early flight out of here on Sunday, after the game."

She hadn't seen Gavin since her date with Tom, and

much as she hated to admit it, she wanted to spend some time with him before they left for San Francisco. "Do you need me to pick you up at the airport?"

"If you could."

"I'll see if I can manage it."

Before ending the conversation, Dori wrote down Gavin's flight number and his time of arrival.

Late the following afternoon, the three of them were sitting in the molded plastic chairs at the Sea-Tac International. They'd arrived early enough to watch Gavin's plane land, and Dori frequently found herself checking her watch, less out of curiosity about the time than out of an unexpected nervousness. She felt she was behaving almost like a love-struck teenager. Even choosing her outfit had been an inordinately difficult task; she'd debated between a wool skirt with knee-high black leather boots and something less formal. In the end she chose mauve corduroy slacks and a thick pullover sweater the color of winter wheat.

"That's Dad's plane now." Melissa bounded to her feet, ran to the floor-to-ceiling window and pointed to the 727 taxiing toward the building.

Dori brushed an imaginary piece of lint from her slacks and cursed her foolish heart for being so glad Gavin was home and safe. With the children standing at either side, her hands resting lightly on their shoulders, she forced a strained smile to her lips. A telltale warmth invaded her face and Dori raised a self-conscious hand to brush the hair from her temple. Gavin was the third passenger off the plane.

"Dad." Melissa broke formation and ran to Gavin, hugging him fiercely. Danny followed shyly and offered Gavin his hand to shake. "Welcome back, Mr. Parker," he said politely.

"Thank you, Danny." Gavin shook the boy's hand with all the seriousness of a man closing a million-dollar deal.

"How was the flight?" Dori stepped forward, striving to keep her arms obediently at her side, battling the impulse to greet him as Melissa had done.

His raincoat was draped over one arm and he carried a briefcase with the other hand. Dark smudges under his eyes told her that he was exhausted. Nonetheless he gave her a warm smile. "The flight was fine."

"I thought you said he'd kiss her," Danny whispered indignantly to Melissa. The two children stood to one side of Dori and Gavin.

"It's too public...I think." Melissa whispered back and turned accusing eyes on her father.

Arching two thick brows, Gavin held out an arm to Dori. "We'd best not disappoint them," he murmured. "We're liable not to hear the end of it for the entire week."

One hand was all the invitation Dori needed. No step had ever seemed so far—or so close. Relentlessly, Gavin held her gaze as she walked into the shelter of his outstretched arm. His hand slipped around the back of her neck, bringing her closer. Long fingers slid into her soft auburn hair as his mouth made a slow, unhurried descent to her parted lips. As the distance lessened, Dori closed her eyes, more eager for this than she had any right to be. Her heart was doing a drumroll and she moistened her suddenly dry lips. She heard Gavin softly suck in his breath as his mouth claimed hers in a slow, provocative exploration.

Of their own accord, her hands moved over the taut muscles of his chest and shoulders until her fingers linked behind his neck. In the next instant, his mouth hardened, his touch firm and experienced and unbelievably warm. The pressure of his hand at the back of her neck lifted her onto the tips of her toes, forcing the full length of her body intimately close to the unyielding strength of his. The sound of Gavin's briefcase hitting the floor barely registered to her numbed senses. Nor did she resist when he wrapped both arms around her so tightly that she could barely breathe. All she could taste, feel, smell, was Gavin. She felt as if she had come home after a long time away. He'd kissed her before, but it had never been like this, like a hundred shooting stars blazing a trail across an ebony sky.

Dori struggled not to give in to the magnificent light show, not to respond with every facet of her being. She had to resist. Otherwise, Gavin would know everything.

The grip of his hand at the back of her neck was painful, but Dori didn't object. If Gavin was experiencing the same overwhelming emotion as she was, he'd be just as confused and disarmed. He broke the contact and buried his face in her hair, mussing it as he rubbed his jaw over it several times.

"That kiss has to be a ten," he muttered thickly, unevenly.

"A nine," she insisted, her voice weak. "When we get to ten, we're in real trouble."

"Especially if we're in an airport."

Gavin's hold relaxed, but he slipped his hand

around her waist, bringing her closer to his side. "Well, kids, are you happy now?"

"You dropped your suitcase, Mr. Parker." Danny held it out to him and eyed Melissa gleefully. He beamed from ear to ear.

"So I did," Gavin said, taking the briefcase. "Thanks for picking it up for me."

"Dori put a roast in the oven," Melissa informed him, "just in case you were hungry. I told her how starved you are when you get home from these things and how much you hate airplane food."

"Your father's tired, Melissa. I'll have you both over for dinner another time."

"I appreciate the thought," Gavin told Dori, his gaze caressing her. "But I *have* been up for the past thirty hours."

A small involuntary smile crept up the corners of Dori's mouth. She hadn't been married all those years to Brad without having some idea of the way a man thought and behaved away from home.

Gavin's eyes darkened briefly as if he expected a sarcastic reply. "No comment?"

"No comment," she echoed cheerfully.

"You're not worried about who I was with?"

"I know, or at least I think I do," she amended.

Gavin hesitated, his eyes disbelieving. "You think you do," he said with a sarcastic smile.

"Well, not for a fact, but I have a pretty good hunch of what you were up to."

"This I've got to hear." His hand tightened perceptibly around her trim waist. "Well?"

Both Danny and Melissa looked concerned. They were clearly disappointed that Dori wasn't showing signs of jealousy. Obviously, the two assumed Gavin had been with another woman. Dori doubted it. If he had, he wouldn't be so blatant about it with her. Nor would he mention it in front of the children.

"I'd guess that you were with some football friends, drinking beer, eating pretzels and probably playing a hot game of poker."

The smug expression slowly faded as a puzzled frown drew his brows together and hooded his dark eyes. "That's exactly where I was."

Disguising her pride at guessing correctly was nearly impossible. "Honestly, Gavin, think about it. I'm two months away from being thirty. I've been married. I know the way a man thinks."

"And men are all alike," he taunted.

"No," she said, trying desperately to keep a straight face. "But I'm beginning to know you. When you quit asking me if I'm concerned who you were with, then I'll worry."

"You think you're pretty smart, don't you?"

"No," she was forced to disagree. "Men I can understand. It's children that baffle me."

He continued to hold her close as they walked down the long concourse. Melissa and Danny skipped ahead.

"Were they a burden this weekend?" Gavin inclined his head toward the two youngsters.

"Nothing I couldn't handle."

"I have the feeling there's very little you can't handle."

Self-conscious now, Dori looked away. There was so much she didn't know, so much that worried her.

And the main object of her fears was walking beside her, holding her as if it were the most natural thing in the world—as if he meant to hold on to her for a lifetime. But Dori knew better.

Seven

The discordant clanging bell of the cable car sounded as Dori, Melissa, Danny and Gavin clung precariously to the side. A low-lying fog was slowly dissipating under the cheerful rays of the early afternoon sun.

"When are we going to Ghiradelli's?" Melissa wanted to know, her voice carried by the soft breeze. "I love chocolate."

"Me too," Danny chimed in eagerly.

"Soon," Gavin promised, "but I told Dori we'd see Fisherman's Wharf first."

"Sorry, kids." Although Dori was apologizing, there was no regret in the shining brightness of her eyes. The lovely City of Saint Francis was everything she remembered, and more. The steep, narrow streets, brightly painted gingerbread houses, San Francisco Bay and the Golden Gate Bridge. Dori doubted that she'd ever tire of the subtle grace and beauty of this magnificent city.

They'd arrived Thanksgiving Day and gone directly to a plush downtown hotel. Gavin had reserved a large suite with two bedrooms that were connected to an immense central room. After a leisurely dinner of turkey with all the traditional trimmings, they'd gone to bed, Gavin and Danny in one room, Dori and Melissa in the other, all eager to explore the city the following morning.

After a full day of viewing Golden Gate Park, driving down Lombard Street with its famous ninety-degree curves, and strolling the water's edge at Fisherman's Wharf, they returned to their hotel suite.

Melissa sat in the wing backed chair and rubbed her sore feet. "I've got an enormous blister," she complained loudly. "I don't think I've ever walked so much in my life. There's nothing I want more than to watch television for a while and then go straight to bed." She gave an exaggerated sigh and looked toward Danny, who stared back blankly. When he didn't immediately respond, Melissa hissed something at him that Dori couldn't understand, then jabbed him in the ribs with her elbow.

"Oh. Me too," Danny agreed abruptly. "All I want is dinner and bed."

"You two will have to go on without us," Melissa continued with a look Joan of Arc would have envied. "As much as we'd like to join you, it's probably best we stay here."

Gavin caught Dori's gaze and rolled his eyes toward the ceiling. Dori had difficulty containing her own amusement. The two little matchmakers were up to their tricks again. "But we couldn't possibly leave you alone and without dinner," Dori said in a concerned voice.

"I'm not all that hungry." For the first time Danny looked unsure. He'd never gone without dinner in his life and lately his herculean appetite seemed likely to bankrupt her budget. For Danny to offer to go without a meal was the ultimate sacrifice.

"Don't worry about us—we can order room service," Melissa said with the casual ease of a seasoned traveler. "You two go on alone. We insist. Right, Danny?"

"Right."

By the time Dori had showered and dressed, Danny and Melissa were poring over the room-service menu like two people who hadn't eaten a decent meal in weeks. Gavin appeared to be taking the children's rather transparent scheme in his stride, but Dori wasn't so confident. They'd had two wonderful days together. Gavin had once lived in San Francisco and he gave them the tour of a lifetime. If Gavin had hoped that Melissa and Danny would overdose on each other's company, his plan was failing miserably. The two had never gotten along better.

After checking the contents of her purse, Dori sat on the end of the bed and slipped on her imported leather pumps. Then she stood and smoothed her skirt. Her pulse was beating madly and she paused to place her hand over her heart and inhale a deep, soothing breath. She felt chilled and warm, excited and apprehensive, all in one. Remembering how unemotional she'd been about their first dinner date only made her fret more. That had been the night of the fights, and she recalled how she hadn't really cared what she wore. Ten minutes before Gavin was due to pick her up, she'd added the final coat of polish to her nails. Tonight, she was as nervous as she'd ever been in her life. Twenty times in as many minutes she'd worried about her dress. This pink-and-gray outfit with its pleated front bodice and long sleeves ending in delicate French cuffs was her finest, but it wasn't an evening gown. Gavin was accustomed to women far more worldly and sophisticated than she could ever hope to be. Bolstering her confidence, Dori put on her gold earrings and freshened her lipstick. With fingers clutching the bathroom sink, she forced a smile to her stiff lips and exhaled a ragged breath. Dear heavens, she was falling in love with Gavin Parker. Nothing could be worse. Nothing could be more wonderful, her heart responded.

When she reentered the suite's sitting room, Melissa and Danny were sprawled across the thick carpet in front of the television. Danny gave her a casual look and glanced away, but Melissa did an automatic double take.

"Wow!" the young girl murmured in a low breath and immediately straightened. Her eyes widened appreciatively. "You're—"

"Lovely." Gavin finished for his daughter, his eyes caressing Dori, roving slowly from her lips to the swell of her breasts and downward. "An angel couldn't look any lovelier."

"Thank you." Dori's voice died to a whisper. She wanted to drown in his eyes. She wanted to be in his arms. A long silence ran between them and purposely Dori looked away, her heart racing.

"Don't worry about us," Melissa said confidently.

"We'll be downstairs if you need anything," Gavin murmured, taking Dori by the elbow.

"Be good, Danny."

"I will," he answered without glancing up from the television screen.

"And no leaving the hotel room for any reason," she warned.

"What about a fire?"

"You know what we mean," Gavin answered for Dori.

"Don't hurry back on our account," Melissa said, propping up her chin with one hand as she lay sprawled on the carpet. "Danny and I'll probably be asleep within the hour."

Danny opened his mouth to protest, but closed it at one fierce glare from Melissa.

Gavin opened the door and Dori tossed a smile over her shoulder. "Have fun, you two."

"We will," they chimed merrily.

The door closed and Dori thought she heard them give a shout of triumph.

Gavin chuckled and slid a hand around her trim waist, guiding her to the elevator. "I swear those two have all the finesse of a runaway roller coaster."

"They do seem to be a bit obvious."

"Just a bit. However, this is one time that I don't mind being alone with you." His hand spread across the hollow of her back, lightly caressing the silken material of her dress. Slowly his hand moved upward to rub her shoulder. His head was so close that Dori could feel his breath against the sensitized skin of her neck. She didn't know what kind of game Gavin was playing, but her heart was a far too willing participant.

At the whirring sound of the approaching elevator, Gavin straightened. The hand at her back directed her inside, and he pushed the appropriate button.

Inside the restaurant, the maître d' led them to a linen-covered table in the middle of the spacious room and held out Dori's chair for her. Smiling her appreciation, she sat, accepted the menu and scanned the variety of dishes offered. Her mouth felt dry, and judging by the way her nerves were acting, Dori doubted she'd find anything that sounded appetizing.

No sooner were they seated and comfortable than the wine steward, wearing a crisp red jacket, approached their table. "Are you Mr. Parker?" he asked in a deep resonant voice.

"Yes." Gavin looked up from the oblong menu.

The red-coated man snapped his fingers and almost immediately a polished silver bucket was delivered to the table. Cradled in a bed of ice was a bottle of French champagne.

"I didn't order this." His brow was marred by lines of bewilderment.

"Yes, sir. This is compliments of Melissa and Danny in room 1423." Deftly he removed the bottle from the silver bucket and held it out for Gavin's inspection. As he read the label, Gavin raised his thick eyebrows expressively.

"An excellent choice," he murmured.

"Indeed," the steward agreed. With amazing dexterity he removed the cork and poured a sample into Gavin's glass. After receiving approval from Gavin, he filled both their glasses and left.

Gavin held up his glass for a toast. "To Melissa and Danny."

"To our children." Dori's answering comment was far more intimate than she'd meant it to be.

The champagne slid smoothly down Dori's throat and eased her tenseness. She closed her eyes and savored the bubbly tartness. "This is wonderful," she whispered, setting her glass aside. "How did Melissa and Danny know how to order such an exquisite label?''

"They didn't. I have a strong feeling they simply asked for the best available.''

Dori's hand tightened around the stem of her glass. "Oh, my goodness, this must have cost a fortune.'' Color flooded her face, blossoming in her pale cheeks. "Listen, let me pay half. I'm sure Danny played a part in this and he knows that I love champagne. It's my greatest weakness.''

"You're not paying for anything,'' Gavin insisted with mock sternness. "The champagne is a gift and if you mention it again, you'll offend me.''

"But Gavin this bottle could well cost a hundred dollars and I can't—''

"Are we going to argue?'' His voice was low and warm.

Dori felt a throb of excitement in her veins at the way he was studying her. "No,'' she answered finally. "I'll agree not to argue, but under protest.''

"Do you have any other weaknesses I don't know about?'' he inquired smoothly.

You! her mind tossed out unexpectedly. Struggling to maintain her composure, she shrugged and dipped her gaze to the bubbling gold liquid. "Bouillabaisse.''

Something close to a smile quirked his mouth as he motioned for the waiter and ordered the fish stew that was cooked with a minimum of eight different types of seafood. In addition, Gavin ordered hearts-of-palm salad, another uncommon delicacy. Taking their menus, the waiter left the table and soon afterward the steward returned to replenish their champagne.

Relaxing in her chair, Dori propped her elbows on

the table. Already the champagne was going to her head. She felt a warm glow seeping through her, heating her blood.

The bouillabaisse was as good as any Dori had ever tasted; the wine Gavin had ordered with their meal was mellow and smooth.

While they lingered over cups of strong black coffee, Gavin spoke freely about himself for the first time. He told her of his position with the computer company and the extensive traveling it sometimes involved. The job was perfect for him since it gave him the freedom to continue broadcasting during the football season. Setting his own hours was a benefit of being part-owner of the computer firm. He spoke of his goals for the future and his love for his daughter; he spoke of the dreams he had for Melissa.

His look was poignant in a way she had never expected to see in Gavin. A longing showed there that was deep and intense, a longing for the well-being and future happiness of those he loved. He didn't mention the past or the glories he'd achieved on the football field. Nor did he mention his marriage to Deirdre. No comment was necessary; his reactions to his ex-wife had said it all.

Every part of Dori was conscious of Gavin, every nerve, every cell. Dori had never thought to experience such a spiritual closeness with another human being again. She saw in him a tenderness and a vulnerability he rarely exposed. So often in the past, just when Dori felt she was beginning to understand Gavin, he'd withdrawn behind a hard shell, where he kept his feelings hidden most of the time. The fact that he was sharing these confidences with Dori told her he'd come to trust and respect her, and she rejoiced in it.

The waiter approached with a pot of coffee and Dori shook her head, indicating that she didn't want any more.

Gavin glanced at his watch. "Do we dare go back to the suite? We've only been gone two hours."

The way she was feeling, there wasn't any place safe for her with Gavin tonight. She wanted to be in his arms so badly that she was almost anticipating the softness of his touch. She cast about for an excuse to stay. "They'd be terribly disappointed if we showed up so soon."

"There's a band playing in the lounge," he suggested smoothly. "Would you care to go dancing?"

"Yes." Her voice trembled slightly with renewed awareness. "I'd like that."

Gavin didn't look for a table when they entered the lounge. A soft, melodious ballad was playing and he guided her directly to the dance floor and turned her into his arms.

Dori released a long sigh. She linked her fingers at the back of his neck and pressed the side of her face against the firm line of his jaw. Their bodies were intimately close until Dori could feel the uneven rhythm of his heartbeat and recognized that her own was just as erratic. They made only the pretense of dancing, holding each other so tight that for a moment even breathing was impossible. Dragging air into her constricted lungs, Dori closed her eyes to the fullness of emotion that surged through her. For weeks she'd been battling her feelings for Gavin. She didn't want to fall in love with him. Now, in these few brief moments since he'd taken her in his arms, Dori knew that it was too late. Her heart was already committed. She loved him. Completely and utterly. But admitting her love now would only intimidate him. Her intuition told her that Gavin wasn't ready to accept her feelings yet or acknowledge his own. Pursuing this tiny spark could well extinguish it before it ever had a chance to flicker and flame.

"Dori." The raw emotion in his voice melted her heart. "Let's get out of here."

"Yes," she whispered, unable to force her voice any higher or make it any stronger.

Gavin led her off the tiny floor and out of the lounge and through the bustling lobby. He hesitated momentarily, as if undecided about where they should go.

"The children will be in bed," she reminded him softly.

The elevator was empty and just as soon as the heavy doors closed, Gavin wrapped his arms around her.

Shamelessly yearning for his kiss, Dori tilted her head back and smiled up at him boldly. She saw his eyes darken with passion as he lowered his head. Leaning toward him, she met his lips with all the eager longing that this evening had evoked. Gavin kissed her with a fierce tenderness until their breaths became mingled gasps and the elevator slowed to a stop.

Sighing deeply, Gavin tightened his hold, bringing her even closer. "If you were to kiss me like this every time we entered an elevator, I swear we'd never get off."

"That's my own fear," she murmured and looked deeply into his eyes.

He was silent for a long moment. "Then perhaps we should leave now, while we still can." His grip relaxed slightly as they stepped off the elevator.

No light shone from under the door of their suite, but Dori doubted that they would have any real privacy in the room. Undoubtedly Melissa and Danny were just inside the bedroom doors, eager to document the most intimate exchanges between their parents.

Gavin quietly opened the door. The room was dark; what little light there was came from a bright crescent moon that shone in through the windows. They walked into the suite, Gavin's arm around her waist. He turned, closed the door and pressed the full length of her body against it, his gaze holding hers in the pale moonlight.

"I shouldn't kiss you here," he murmured huskily as if he wanted her to refuse.

Dori could find no words to dissuade him—she wanted him so badly. The moment seemed to stretch out. Then, very slowly, she raised her hands to explore the underside of his tense jaw. Her fingertips slid into the dark fullness of his hair and she raised herself onto the tips of her toes to gently place her lips over his. The pressure was so light that their lips merely touched and their breath mingled.

Gradually his mobile mouth eased over hers in exquisite exploration, moving delicately from one side of her lips to the other. The complete sensuality of the kiss quivered through Dori and she experienced a heady sweep of warmth. A sigh of breathless wonder slid from the tightening muscles of her throat. The low groan was quickly followed by another as Gavin's mouth rocked over hers in an eruption of passion and desire that was all too new and sudden. She'd thought these feelings, these very sensations, had died with Brad. She wanted Gavin. She couldn't have stopped him if he'd lifted her in his arms and carried her to the bedroom. The realization shocked her.

His hands stroked the curves of her shoulders as he nibbled at her lips, taking small, sensuous bites. His long fingers tangled themselves in the soft strands of her hair, and he dragged his mouth over her cheek to her eyes and nose and grazed her jaw. She felt him shudder and held his head close as she took in huge gulps of oxygen, trying to control her growing desire. The need to experience the intimate touch of his hands and mouth flowered deep within her. Her breasts ached to be held and kissed. Yet he restrained himself with what Dori believed was a great effort.

"If you rate that kiss a ten, then we're in real trouble," he muttered thickly, close to her ear.

"We're in real trouble."

"I thought as much." But he didn't release her.

"Knowing Danny, I'd guess he's probably video-taped this little exchange." The delicious languor slowly left her limbs.

"And knowing Melissa, I'd say she undoubtedly supplied him with the tapes." Gradually, his arms relaxed their hold.

"Do you think they'll try to blackmail us?" she said, hoping to end the evening in a lighter vein.

"I doubt it," Gavin whispered confidently. "In any case, I have the perfect defense. I believe we can attribute tonight to expensive champagne and an excellent meal, don't you?"

No, she didn't. Dori was forced to swallow an argument. She knew that this feeling between them had been there from the time they'd boarded the plane in Seattle. Gavin had wanted to be alone with her tonight, just as she'd longed to be with him. Even the kissing was a natural consequence of this awakened discovery.

Deciding that giving no answer was better than telling a lie, Dori faked an exaggerated yawn and murmured, "I'd better think about bed; it's been a long day."

"Yes," Gavin agreed far too easily. "And tomorrow will be just as busy."

They parted in the center of the room, going in the opposite directions, toward their respective rooms. Dori undressed in the dark, not wanting to wake Melissa—if indeed Melissa was asleep. Even if she wasn't, Dori didn't feel up to answering the young girl's questions.

Gently lifting back the covers of the twin bed, Dori slipped between the sheets and settled into a comfortable position. She watched the flickering shadows playing against the opposite wall, tormenting herself with doubts and recriminations. Gavin attributed this overwhelming attraction to the champagne. Briefly she wondered what he'd say if it happened again. And it would. They'd come too far to go back now.

The following afternoon, Melissa, Danny and Dori sat in front of the television set to watch the San Francisco Forty-niners play the Denver Broncos. Dori was not particularly interested in football and knew very little about it. But she had never before watched a game that Gavin was broadcasting. Now she listened proudly and attentively to his comments, appreciating for the first time his expertise in the area of sports.

Frank Gifford, another ex-football player, was Gavin's announcing partner and the two exchanged witticisms and bantered freely. During halftime, the television camera crew showed the two men sitting in the broadcast booth. Gavin held up a pad with a note that said, "Hi, Melissa and Danny."

The kids went into peals of delight and Dori looked on happily. This four-day weekend was one she wouldn't forget. Everything had been perfect—perhaps too perfect.

Gavin returned to the hotel several hours after the end of the game. His broad shoulders were slightly hunched and he rubbed a hand over his eyes. His gaze avoided Dori's as he greeted the children and sank heavily into a chair.

"You were great," Danny said with unabashed enthusiasm.

"Yeah, Dad." The pride in Melissa's voice was evident.

"You're just saying that because the Forty-niners won and you were both rooting for them." Gavin's smile didn't quite reach his eyes.

"Can I get you something, Gavin?" Dori offered quietly, taking the chair across from him. "You look exhausted."

"I am." His gaze met hers for the first time since he'd returned. The expression that leaped into his eyes made her catch her breath, but just as quickly an invisible shutter fell to hide it. Without a word, he turned his head to the side. "I don't need anything, thanks." The way he said it forced Dori to wonder if he was referring to her. That morning, he'd been cool and efficient, but Dori had attributed his behavior to the football game. Naturally he would be preoccupied. She hadn't expected him to take her in his arms and wasn't disappointed when he didn't. Or so she told herself.

Melissa sat on the carpet by Gavin's feet. "Danny and I knew you'd be tired so we ordered a pepperoni pizza. That way, you and Dori can go out again tonight and be alone." The faint stress placed on the last word caused telltale color to suffuse Dori's face.

She opened her mouth to protest, then closed it. She certainly wasn't ready for a repeat performance of their last meal together, but she wanted to hear what Gavin thought. His gaze clashed with hers and narrowed fractionally as he challenged her to accept or decline.

"No," Dori protested quickly, her voice low and grave. "I'm sure your dad's much too tired. We'll have pizza tonight."

"Okay." Melissa shot to her feet, willing to cooperate with Dori's decision. "Danny and I'll go get it. The pizza place is only a couple of blocks from here."

"I'll go with you," Dori offered, not wanting the two children walking the streets by themselves after dark.

A hand stopped her, and Dori turned to find Gavin studying her. His mouth twisted wryly; his eyes were chilling. "What's the matter?"

She searched his face to find a reason for the subtle challenge in his question. "Nothing," she returned smoothly, calmly. "You didn't want to go out, did you?"

"No."

"Then why are you looking at me like I'd committed some serious faux pas?" Dori tipped her head to one side, not understanding the change in him.

"You're angry because I didn't hold up your name with the kids' this afternoon."

Dori's mouth dropped open in shock. "Of course not. That's crazy." Gavin couldn't honestly believe something that trivial would bother her.

But apparently he did. He released her arm and leaned back in the cushioned chair. "You women are all alike. You want attention, and national attention is all the better. Right?"

"Wrong!" She took a step in retreat, stunned by his harshness. Words failed her. She didn't know how to react to Gavin when he was in this mood and from the look of things, she expected it wasn't about to change.

Dori's thoughts were prophetic. Gavin seemed withdrawn and unnaturally quiet on the flight home early the next morning. He didn't phone her in the days that followed. Over the past few weeks, he'd taken the time to call her twice and sometimes three times a week. Now there was silence—deafening silence that echoed through the canyons of emptiness he'd exposed in her life. Worse than the intolerable silence was the fact that she found herself sitting by the phone, eagerly waiting for his call. Her own reaction angered her more than Gavin's silence. And yet, Dori thought she understood why he didn't contact her. And with further reasoning, she realized that she mustn't contact him. Maybe he thought she would; maybe he even wanted her to, but Dori wouldn't, couldn't. For Gavin was fighting his feelings for her. He knew that what had happened between them that evening in San Francisco couldn't be blamed on the champagne, and it scared the living hell out of him. He couldn't see her, afraid of what he'd say or do. It was simpler to invent some trumped-up grievance, blame her for some imaginary wrong.

Friday morning, after a week of silence, Dori sat at her desk, staring into space.

"Are you and Gavin going out this weekend?" Sandy asked, with a quizzical slant of one delicate brow.

Dori returned her attention to the homeowner's insurance policy on her desk. "Not this weekend."

"Is Gavin announcing another football game?"

"I don't know," she responded without changing her expression.

"Did you two have a fight or something?"

"Or something," Dori muttered dryly.

"Dori." Sandy's eyes became serious. "You haven't ruined this relationship, have you? Gavin Parker is perfect for you. Whatever's happened, make it right. This fish is much too rich and good-looking to toss back for another fisherman. Reel him in very carefully, Dori, dear."

A hot retort trembled on the tip of her tongue, but Dori swallowed it. Not once had she thought of Gavin as a big fish, and she didn't like the cynical suggestion that she should carefully reel him in or risk losing him. Their relationship had never existed on those terms. Neither of them was looking for anything permanent—at least not in the beginning.

Dori's mood wasn't much better by the time she returned home.

Danny was draped over the sofa, his feet propped up against the back, his head touching the floor. "Hi, Mom."

"Hi." She unwound the scarf from around her neck and unbuttoned her coat with barely repressed anger. Stuffing her scarf in the sleeve, she reached for a hanger.

"Aren't you going to ask me about school?"

"How was school?" For the first time in years, she didn't care. A long soak in a hot bath interested her far more. This lackadaisical mood infuriated her.

"Good."

Dori closed the hall closet door. "What's good?"

Danny untangled his arms and legs from the sofa and sat up to stare at her. "School is." He cocked his head and gave her a perplexed look. "You feeling sick?"

It was so easy to stretch the truth. She was sick at heart, disillusioned and filled with doubts. She never wanted to see Gavin Parker again, and she was dying for a word from him. Anything. A Christmas card would have elated her, a business card left on her doorstep, a chain letter. Anything. "I'm a little under the weather."

"Do you want me to cook dinner tonight?"

"Sure." Her willingness to let Danny loose in the kitchen was a measure of how miserable she felt. Last week at this time they'd been flying to San Francisco and Gavin had been sitting in the seat beside hers. A sad smile touched her mouth as she remembered how Gavin had reached for her hand when the plane sped down the runway ready for takeoff. When she'd objected that she wasn't afraid of flying, he'd smiled brightly into her eyes, brushed his lips over her cheek and told her that *he* was afraid and that she should humor him. What a difference one week could make.

"You want me to cook?" Danny was giving her a puzzled look again.

"There might be a TV dinner in the freezer. Put that in the oven."

"What about you?"

Dori hesitated before heading down the long hallway to her room. "I'm not hungry." There wasn't enough chocolate in the world to get her through another week of not hearing from Gavin.

"Not hungry? You must really be sick."

Dori's appetite had always been healthy and Danny knew it. "I must be," she said softly, and went into the bathroom to run hot water into the tub. On impulse she added some bath-oil beads. While the water was running, she stepped into her room to get her pajamas, the faded blue housecoat with the ripped hem and a pair of thick socks.

Just as she was sliding into the fragrant mass of bubbles, Danny knocked anxiously on the bathroom door.

"Go away," she murmured irritably.

Danny hesitated. "But, Mom—"

"Danny, please," she cried. "I'm miserable. Give me a few minutes to soak before hitting me with all your questions." She could hear him shuffling his feet outside the door. "Listen, honey, if there are any cookies left in the cookie jar, they're yours. Eat them in good health and don't disturb me for thirty minutes. Understand?"

Dori knew she should feel guilty, but she was willing to bend the rules this once if it brought peace and quiet.

"You're sure, Mom?"

"Danny, I want to take a nice, hot, uninterrupted bath. Got that?"

He hesitated again. "Okay, Mom."

Dori soaked in the bath until all the bubbles had disappeared and the hot water had turned lukewarm. This lethargy was ridiculous, she decided, nudging up the plug with her big toe. The ends of her auburn curls were wet, but after brushing it, Dori left it free to hang limply around her face. The housecoat should have been discarded long ago, but it suited Dori's mood. The socks came up to her knees and she slipped her feet into rabbit-shaped slippers that Danny had given her for Christmas two years before. She seldom wore them but felt she owed her son an apology for repeatedly snapping at him. The slippers had long floppy ears that dragged on the ground and pink powder-puff tails that tickled her ankles. They were easily the most absurd-looking things she owned, but wearing them was her way of apologizing.

"Hi, Mom…" Danny hesitated when she stepped into the living room, concern creasing his young face. "You look terrible."

Dori didn't doubt it, with her limp hair, old ragged housecoat and rabbit slippers.

"Mr. Parker's never seen you look so awful."

"He won't, so don't worry."

"But, Mom," Danny protested loudly. "He'll be here any minute."

Eight

For a wild instant, Dori resisted the panic. "He's not coming." She'd waited all week for him to call and heard nothing. And now he was about to appear on her doorstep, and she didn't want to see him. She couldn't face him, looking and feeling the way she did. In her heart she was pleading with her son to say that Gavin wasn't really coming. "I'm sure Gavin would phone first." He'd better!

"He did, Mom." Danny gave her a look of pure innocence.

"When?" Dori shouted, her voice shaking.

"While you were running your bathwater. I told him you'd had a bad day and wanted to soak."

"Why didn't you tell me?" she cried, giving way to alarm.

The doorbell chimed and Dori swung around to glare at it accusingly. Gripping her son by the shoulders, she had the irrational urge to hide behind Danny. "Get rid of him, Danny. Understand?"

"But, Mom—"

"I don't care what you have to tell him." She must be crazy to make an offer like that, Dori realized.

The doorbell continued to ring in short, impatient peals. Before either mother or son could move, the front door opened and Gavin sauntered in. "What's the problem with you two? Couldn't you see..." His words faded to a whisper as his gaze collided with Dori's. "Has anyone called the doctor? You look terrible."

"So everyone's been telling me," she snapped, clenching her fists at her sides. All week she'd been dying for a word or a glance, anything, from Gavin and now that he was here, she wanted to throw him out of her house. Whirling, she stalked into the kitchen. "Go away."

Gavin followed her there and stood with his feet braced as if he expected a confrontation. "I want to talk to you."

Dori opened the refrigerator door and set a carton of eggs on the counter, ignoring him. She wasn't hungry, but scrambling eggs would give her mind something to concentrate on and her hands something to do.

"Did you hear me?" Gavin demanded.

"Yes, but I'm hoping that if I ignore you, you'll go away."

Whistling a carefree tune, Danny strolled into the room, pulled out a kitchen chair and sat down. His eager gaze went from his mother to Gavin and again to Dori, and they both stared back at him warningly.

"You two want some privacy, right?"

"Right," Gavin answered.

"Before I go, I want you to know, Mr. Parker, that Mom doesn't normally look like...this bad."

"I realize that."

"Good. I was worried because..."

"Danny," Dori hissed. "You're doing more harm than good."

The chair scraped against the linoleum floor as he pushed it away from the table. "Don't worry," he said, gesturing with his hands. "I get the picture."

Dori wondered how her son could claim to know what was going on between her and Gavin when even she didn't have the slightest idea. For that matter, she suspected Gavin didn't, either.

Taking a small bowl from the cupboard, she cracked two eggs against the side.

"How was your week?" Gavin wanted to know.

Dori squeezed her eyes shut and mentally counted to five. "Wonderful."

"Mine too."

"Great." She couldn't hide the sarcasm in her voice.

"I suppose you wondered why I didn't phone?" Gavin said next.

Dori already knew, but she wanted to hear it from him. "It had crossed my mind once or twice," she said flippantly, as she whipped the eggs with a vengeance such that they threatened to slosh out of the small bowl.

"Dori, for heaven's sake, would you turn around and look at me?"

"No!" A limp strand of hair fell across her cheekbone and she jerked it aside.

"Please." His voice was so soft and caressing that Dori felt her resistance melt away.

With her chin tucked against her collarbone, she battled down a mental image of herself with limp, lifeless hair, a ragged housecoat and silly slippers. She turned toward him, her fingers clenching the counter as she leaned against it for support.

Gavin moved until he stood directly in front of her and placed his hands on her shoulders. Absurd as it was, Dori noticed that his shoes were shined. Worse, they were probably Italian leather, expensive and perfect. A finger lifted her chin, but her eyes refused to meet his.

"I've missed you this week," he whispered, and she could feel his heated gaze resting on her mouth. It took all Dori's strength not to moisten her lips and invite his kiss. She felt starved for the taste of him. A week had never seemed so long. "A hundred times I picked up the phone to call you," he continued.

"But you didn't."

"No." He sighed unhappily and slowly shook his head. "Believe it or not, I was afraid."

His unexpected honesty allowed her to meet his gaze openly. "Afraid?"

"Things are getting a little thick between us, don't you think?" His voice rose with the urgency of his admission.

"And heaven forbid that you have any feelings for a thirty-year-old woman," she drew a sharp breath and held out a lifeless strand of auburn hair. "A woman who is about to discover her first gray hair, no less."

"Dori, that has nothing to do with it."

"Of course it does," she argued angrily. "If you're going to become involved with anyone, you'd prefer a twenty-year-old with a perfect body and flawless skin."

"Would you stop!" He shook her shoulders lightly. "What's the matter with you tonight?"

"Maybe this week has given me time to think. Maybe I know you better than you know yourself. You're absolutely right. You *are* afraid of me and the feelings I can arouse in you, and with damn good reason. You're attracted to me and it shocks you. If it hadn't been for the kids last weekend, who knows what would have happened between us?" At his narrowed look, she took another deep breath and continued her tirade. "Don't try to deny it, Gavin. *I* can figure a few things out for myself—that's the problem when you start seeing a woman whose brain doesn't leak. I've got a few live brain cells left in this ancient mind and I know darned well what's going on here. I also know what you're about to suggest."

"I doubt that." His brow furrowed with displeasure.

"It's either one of two things," she continued undaunted.

"Oh?" He took a step in retreat, defiantly crossed his arms and leaned against the kitchen table. His gaze was burning her, but Dori ignored the heat.

"Either you want to completely abandon this charade and never see each other again. This, however, would leave you with a disgruntled daughter who is persistent enough to have you seek out a similar arrangement with another woman. Knowing the way you think, I'd say that you probably toyed with this idea for a while. However, since you're here, it's my guess that you decided another mature woman would only cause you more trouble, given time. You're so irresistible that she's likely to fall in love with you. It's best to deal with the enemy you know—namely me."

His mouth was so tight that white lines appeared at the corners of his lips. "Go on."

"Option number two," she continued on a wobbly breath. "This one, I'll tell you right now, is completely unacceptable and I deplore you for even thinking it."

"What hideous crime have I committed in my thought-life now?" he inquired on a heavy note of sarcasm.

All week the prospect of his "invitation" had been going through her mind. Oh, he'd undoubtedly deny it, but the intention was there; she'd stake a month's salary on it. "You are about to suggest that we both abandon everything we think of as moral to sample marriage."

"Believe me—" he snickered loudly "—marriage is the last thing on my mind."

"I know that. I said *sample*, not actually commit the act. You were about to suggest that Danny and I move in with you. This, of course, would only be a trial run to see if things go smoothly. Then you'd call it off when things got complicated or life was disrupted in any way. My advice to you on that one is don't even bother suggesting it. I'd never agree and I'll think less of you for asking."

"Less than you already do," he finished for her. "Be assured the thought never entered my mind."

Dori could have misjudged him, but she doubted it. "Take a good look at me," she said and held out the sides of her ragged terry-cloth housecoat. Its tattered blue hem dragged on the kitchen floor. "Because what you see is what you get."

Gavin might not have been angry when he arrived, but he was now. "What I can see is that having any kind of rational discussion with you is out of the question.''

Lowering her gaze, Dori released a jagged sigh. ''As you may have guessed, I'm not the best of company tonight. I…I didn't mean to come at you with my fingers in the claw position.'' The apology stuck in her throat. She wished he'd leave so she could indulge her misery in private.

''I'll admit to having seen you in better moods.''

She decided to ignore that. ''As I said, it's been a rough week.''

A long moment passed before Gaving spoke again and when he did, Dori could tell that he'd gained control of his anger. ''There's a Neil Simon play at the 5th Avenue. Do you think you'll feel well enough to go tomorrow night?''

The invitation was so unexpected that it stunned Dori. The muscles of her throat seemed paralyzed, so she merely gave an abrupt nod.

''I'll pick you up around seven-fifteen. Okay?''

Again, all Dori could manage was a nod.

He turned to leave, then paused in the doorway. ''Take care of yourself.''

''I will.''

Dori heard the living room door close, and she shuddered in horror at herself. What was the matter with her? She'd come at Gavin like a madwoman. Even now, she didn't know what he'd actually intended to say.

The recriminations and self-doubts remained with her the following afternoon. Perhaps because of them she splurged and had her hair styled at the local beauty parlor, a rare treat. Dori wanted to tell her stylist to do something new and exciting that would disguise her years and make five pounds instantly disappear. But she decided not to bother—the woman did hair, not magic tricks.

Dori couldn't recall any other date that had involved so much planning, not even her high school prom. She bought a fashionable jumpsuit that came with a fancy title: "Rhapsody in Purple." The label said it was sophisticated, dynamic and designed for the free-spirited woman, and for tonight, those were all the things she wanted to be. Reminding herself that it was the season to be generous and that she deserved some generosity herself, Dori plunked down her credit card, praying the purchase wouldn't take her over her credit limit.

At home, she hung the outfit on the back of her bedroom door and studied it. The soft, pale lavender jumpsuit had pleats, pads and puffs, and for what she'd paid, it should have been fashioned out of pure gold. The deep V in the back made it the most daring outfit she owned.

Dori had delivered Danny to her parents' house earlier that afternoon, so she was dressed and ready at seven. While she waited for Gavin, she searched the newspaper, looking for an advertisement for the play. He had told her it was a Neil Simon comedy, but he hadn't mentioned which one. A full-page blurb announced the title: *The Odd Couple*. Dori nearly laughed out loud; the description so aptly fitted her and Gavin. She certainly didn't know any odder couple.

Gavin was right on time, a minor surprise, and did a double take when Dori opened the door.

"Hi," she said almost shyly, holding her head high.

Her dangling gold earrings brushed the curve of her shoulders.

"Hello…" For the first time in recent memory, Gavin seemed at a loss for words. He let himself into the living room, his gaze never leaving hers. "For a woman with dying brain cells and wrinkled skin, you look surprisingly good."

"I'll take that as a compliment," she said, priding herself on not rising to the bait. Any reaction from Gavin was good, she felt, and a positive one was worth every penny of the jumpsuit. "You don't look so bad yourself."

He straightened his tie and gave her another of his dazzling smiles. "So my innumerable female companions tell me."

That was another loaded comment best ignored. Dori reached for her handbag, an antique one beaded with a thousand minute pearls. She tucked it under her arm and smiled brightly, eager to leave. From past experience, Dori knew that they'd have trouble finding a parking space if they dallied over drinks.

Gavin hesitated as if he expected her at least to offer something, but she felt suddenly ill-at-ease, anxious to get to the theater and into neutral territory. "We should probably leave, don't you think?" she asked flatly.

Gavin frowned and looked toward her hall closet. "What about your coat?" he said in a lightly mocking voice.

"I don't need one." A woman didn't wear "Rhapsody in Purple" with a full-length navy blue coat. This jumpsuit was created for minks and ermine, not wool.

"Dori, don't be ridiculous. It's just above freezing out there. You can't go outside without a coat."

"I'll be fine," she argued. "I'm naturally warm-blooded."

"You'll freeze," he replied.

Grudgingly, Dori stomped across the room, yanked open the hall closet and threw on her winter coat. "Satisfied?"

"Yes," he breathed irritably, burying his hands deep within the pockets of his dark overcoat. Dori suspected he was resisting the urge to throttle her.

"I'll have you know I'm ruining my image," she muttered with ill grace, stalking past him and out the front door.

The seats for the play were excellent and the performers had received enthusiastic reviews. But Dori had trouble concentrating on the characters and the plot. Although Gavin sat beside her, they could have been strangers, for all the notice he gave her. He didn't touch her, hold her hand or indicate in any way that he was aware of her closeness. Nor did he laugh at the appropriate times. His mind seemed to be elsewhere—which pleased Dori immensely. Of course, her own concentration wasn't much better.

During the intermission, it became her goal to make him aware of her. After all, she'd spent a lot of time, money and effort to attract his attention. And she intended to get it.

Her plan was subtle. When the curtain rose for the second act, Dori crossed her legs and allowed the strap of her sandal to fall loose. With her heel exposed, she pretended to inadvertently nudge his knee. She knew she'd succeeded when he crossed his legs to avoid her touch. Part two of her plan was to place her hand on the common arm between their seats. Before he was aware of it, she'd managed to curl her fingers around the crook of his elbow. Almost immediately she could feel the tension drain out of him, as though he'd craved her touch, hungered for it. But that couldn't be. If that was how he felt, why hadn't he simply taken her hand? Gavin was anything but shy. This reluctance to touch her shattered her preconceived ideas about him and why he'd asked her out. When he'd admitted the night before that he was frightened, he hadn't been overstating his feelings. The revelation must have cost him a great deal, and she'd carelessly tossed it back in his face and then hurled her own accusations at him. He wanted to be with her, enjoyed her company, perhaps even loved her. Earlier he'd admitted that he'd missed her that week, and she'd cut him off with her fiery tirade. Now she wanted to groan and cry at her own stupidity.

Dori wanted to take him in her arms and humbly ask him to forgive her. She wanted to drop to her knees and plead with him to tell her what he'd really come to say. Regret, doubt and uncertainty all collided in her mind, drowning out the performers on the stage.

Oh, dear heaven! Could Gavin have realized that he loved her? Maybe. Even if he wasn't ready to act on his feelings, he had at least reached the point of discussing them. And she'd blown it. She'd taunted him in her outraged presumptions of a trial marriage, condemning him before he'd even spoken. Dori closed her eyes at the agony of her own thoughtlessness.

In that moment, when all the doubts crashed together in her mind, Gavin lifted his hand and closed it over hers, holding her slender fingers in his warm grasp.

Dori couldn't breathe; she couldn't move. An eternity passed before she could turn her face to him and see for herself the wonder she knew would be waiting for her. What she found nearly brought her to tears. His eyes were gentle and yielding in their dark depths, his look potent enough to bring her to her knees.

The play ended without either of them noticing and they applauded politely only because those surrounding them did. When the audience came to its feet, Gavin and Dori rose, but his hand continued to grip hers as if he didn't ever want to let her go.

Dori had never felt such deep communication with another person. If he admitted to being frightened, then so was she. Dori hadn't expected Gavin to come to her so easily. She loved him but had assumed it would take him far longer to acknowledge his feelings.

"The play was good," he said as he helped her into her coat. His voice was only slightly husky.

"Wonderful." Hers was overwhelmed by emotion. But if he noticed, Gavin gave no indication. It took all Dori had not to throw her arms around his neck and kiss him. A tiny smile bracketed her mouth, as she reflected that if he'd known what she was thinking, Gavin would have been grateful for her restraint.

The drive back to her house was accomplished in a matter of minutes. He pulled to a stop at the curb, but kept his hand on the steering wheel. "Is Danny with his grandparents tonight?"

Dori had the impression that he didn't ask it conversationally but out of a desire to be alone with her. Her heart pounded painfully. "Y-yes."

He gave her a funny look. "Are you feeling sick again?"

"No, I'm fine." Dori cursed the fact that life had to be so complicated. "Would you like to come in for coffee?" They both knew the invitation was a pretense. When Gavin took her in his arms, she didn't want half the neighborhood watching.

The car engine was still running and Gavin made an elaborate show of checking his watch. "Another time," he said softly, "it's late."

Ten forty-five was not late! If Dori was confused before, it was nothing to the myriad of bewildered emotions that went through her now. "You wanted to say something to me yesterday," she tried again, struggling to sound calm and composed. She forced a smile despite the catch in her voice. "I can't apologize enough for the way I behaved."

"One thing about you, Dori, you're completely unpredictable."

"You did want to tell me something?" she repeated.

"Yes." He paused and she noticed the way his fingers tightened around the steering wheel. "As I said, things are getting a little heavy between us."

"Yes," she whispered tenderly, her heart in her eyes.

"That was something I hadn't planned on."

"I know." Her throat constricted at the strong emotion she felt for him.

"In light of what happened in San Francisco..." He hesitated. "We reached a ten on that last kiss and even you said a ten meant trouble. Lord only knows where we'd progress from there."

"I remember." Who was he trying to kid? They both knew where they were headed and it wasn't the kitchen. She didn't know why he was hedging this way. Everything seemed relatively simple to her.

"Dori," he said hesitantly and cleared the hoarseness from his throat. "I've been thinking that perhaps we've been seeing too much of each other. Maybe it would be best if we cooled things for a while."

No words could have been more unexpected. All this time she'd been waiting to hear a profession of undying love and he'd been trying to tell her he wanted out. To her horror, her eyes filled with stinging tears. Fiercely she blinked them away. Her fingers curled around the door handle in her haste to escape. What a fool she'd been!

"Sure," she managed to stammer without disgracing herself. "Whatever you think is best." The car door swung open and she clambered out in such a frenzied rush that she was fortunate not to trip. "Thank you for the play. As I said before, it was wonderful." Not waiting for any response, she slammed the car door shut and hurried toward the house. The sound of his door opening and closing made her suck in a savage breath and battle for control.

"I thought you said you didn't want any coffee," she said, without turning around to face him. The porch light was sure to reveal her tears and that would embarrass them both.

"Dori, listen, I'm sorry. But I need some time to sort things out. Whatever is going on between us is happening too fast. Give me time to work things out."

From the distance of his voice, Dori guessed he was about halfway up the sidewalk. "I understand." She did, far better than he realized. She'd looked at him with adoring eyes and all the while he'd been trying to think of some way to dump her—or as he'd say, let her down easily. Her eyes blinded by tears, she ripped open her purse and searched hurriedly for the keys. "Don't worry, you've got all the time in the world," she muttered, clenching the house key between stiff fingers.

"A month. All I want is a month." The pause in his voice revealed his uncertainty.

"Take six," she returned impertinently. "Why stop there—make it ten." She wanted to laugh, but the noise that erupted from her throat was a dry, pain-filled sob.

"Dori." His shoe scraped sharply against the porch steps and then there was a tentative moment of silence as he stood there, looking up at her. "Are you crying?"

"Who me?" She laughed, sobbing again. "I'm only a few weeks short of being thirty, Gavin. Women my age don't cry. You don't want to see me again. Fine. I'm mature enough to accept that."

"Turn around and let me see your face."

Her chest heaved with the effort of not sobbing openly. She was such a fool.

"Dori, I didn't mean to hurt you."

"I'm not hurt!" she shouted and leaned her forehead against the screen door. Afraid another sobbing hiccup would escape, she covered her mouth with the palm of her hand. When she was finally able to catch her breath, she turned to face him. "I'm fine, so please don't feel obligated to stick around here. Danny and I'll be just fine."

"Dori, oh, Lord—"

"I'm fine," she insisted and wiped the tears from her face. "See?" Without another word, she turned back to the door, inserted the key and let herself into the house.

"Did you have fun with Mr. Parker last night, Mom?" Danny sat at the kitchen table with Dori who was sipping from a mug of hot coffee. Her mother had phoned earlier to announce that she could drop Danny off on her way to do some errands.

"The play was great." Dori felt frail and vulnerable but managed to give her son a wan smile. Her thoughts were darker and heavier than they'd been since she lost Brad. Danny would have to be told that her relationship with Gavin had come to a standstill, but it wasn't going to be an easy thing to do. "Did you have a good time with Grandma and Grandpa?"

"Yeah, but I'll be glad when you and Mr. Parker decide to get married because I'd rather be a family. Melissa and I could stay alone together and I wouldn't have to have a sitter or go to Grandma's house every time you want to go out."

"Danny, listen." Dori struggled to maintain an unemotional facade, although she felt as if her heart were breaking. "Mr. Parker and I have decided it would be best if we didn't see each other for a while."

"What?" Danny's mouth dropped open in utter disbelief. "But why? I thought you really liked each other. I thought you might even be considering marriage. Melissa was sure…" He let the rest drop as if he'd inadvertently divulged a top secret.

"No." She lowered her gaze and swallowed tightly.

There was no choice but to give Gavin exactly what he'd asked for—time. She hoped and prayed that the budding love he felt for her would be strong enough to bring him back, but she couldn't depend on it. "Gavin isn't ready for that kind of commitment yet and this is something you and I must accept."

"But, Mom—"

"Listen," Dori implored, taking his small hand between her own. "You must promise me that you won't contact Gavin in any way. Sometimes adults need time to think, just like kids do, and we have to respect that. Promise me, Danny. This is important."

He studied her intently, finally nodding. "What about Melissa? Will we be able to see her?"

The two had become good friends and Dori hated to punish them for their parents' problems. "I'm sure some kind of arrangement could be made to have her over on the weekends that Gavin is broadcasting football games." For that matter, Gavin need never know, though she was certain Melissa wouldn't be able to resist telling him.

"You love him, don't you?"

Dori's smile was wistful. "Gavin Parker is a rare man and loving him is easy. But it won't be the end of the world if we never see him again."

Danny's eyes widened incredulously as though he found her words completely shocking. "But Mr. Parker was perfect."

"Yes," she agreed, "he met each requirement on our list, but there are lots of other men who will, too."

"Are you going to start looking for another father for me?" Danny rested his chin in the palms of his hands, his eyes forlorn.

Immediate protests crowded her mind. "Not for a while." Like Gavin, she needed time, but not for the same reasons he did. For her, it would be a waiting game. In a few weeks, she would know if her gamble had paid off. She was a fool to have allowed her heart to become involved; he'd warned her often enough. Now she was suffering the consequences.

In the days that followed, Dori was amazed at her strength of will. It wasn't easy, but when thoughts of Gavin invaded her well-defended mind, she efficiently cast them aside. He didn't make any effort to get in touch with her and she didn't expect him to. Whatever had happened with Deirdre had hurt him so badly that it was possible he would never risk committing himself to another woman. That was his and Melissa's loss...and hers and Danny's.

On Wednesday morning, as Dori stirred hot water into the instant oatmeal, she flipped through the pages of the paper. "Danny," she tossed over her shoulder. "Hurry, or you'll be late for school."

"Okay, Mom." His muffled voice drifted from his bedroom.

Setting his bowl on the table, Dori leaned against the counter and turned to the society page, looking for the Dear Abby column. At first she didn't recognize the people in the picture that dominated the front page of the society section.

Then her glance came to rest on Gavin's smiling face and her heart suddenly dropped to her knees. The oxygen became trapped in her lungs, making it painful to breathe. Some blond-haired beauty was grasping his arm and smiling up at Gavin adoringly. Dori knew the look well. Only a few days before she'd gazed at him in exactly the same doting way. She felt a knife twist in her heart as she read the accompanying article, which described the opening of the opera season with a gala performance of Bizet's *Carmen.* So this was how Gavin was using his time to sort through his feelings for her. It hadn't taken him long to seek out a woman with flawless skin and a perfect body. *Let him,* her mind shouted angrily. Foolish tears burned her eyes and she blinked them away, refusing to give in to the emotion.

"Mom, what's the matter? You look like you want to hit someone."

"I do?" Hurriedly, she folded the paper and stuffed it in the garbage can. "It's nothing. Okay?"

Danny cocked his head and gave her a lopsided look. "Mr. Parker told me that sometimes women can act weird. I guess this is one of those times."

"I'm sick of hearing about Mr. Parker all the time." She jerked open the refrigerator and took out bread for her son's lunch. When he didn't respond, she whirled around. "Did you hear me?"

Danny was paying an inordinate amount of attention to his cereal. "I suppose. Are you going to cry or something?"

"Of course not! Why should I? It's almost Christmas."

His spoon worked furiously, stirring the sugar into the cinnamon-and-raisin-flavored oatmeal. "I don't know, but when your mouth twists up like that, it always means you're real upset."

"Thanks," she returned flippantly.

The remainder of the day was as bad as the morning had been. Nothing went right. She mislaid a file. Her thoughts drifted during an important meeting and when Mr. Sandstorm asked her opinion, Dori hadn't the foggiest idea of what they'd been discussing. Sandy had given her a sympathetic look and salvaged a potentially embarrassing moment by speaking first. As a thank-you Dori bought her friend lunch, though she couldn't really afford it.

The minute she walked into the house, Dori kicked off her shoes and paused to rub her aching arches. Danny was nowhere to be seen and she draped her coat over the back of a kitchen chair, wondering where he'd gone now. He was supposed to stay inside until she got home. She took a package of hamburger out of the refrigerator, but the thought of coming up with a decent meal was almost more than she could face.

As she turned, she noticed the telephone. The receiver was off the hook. The cord stretched around the corner and disappeared into the hall closet. Danny. She crossed to the door and pulled it open.

Danny was sitting cross-legged on the floor and at Dori's intrusion, he glanced up, startled, unable to disguise his sudden look of guilt.

"All right, Daniel Robertson, just who are you talking to?"

Nine

"Oh, hi, Mom," he managed awkwardly, struggling to his feet.

"Who is on the other end of the line?" She repeated her question, but already her mind was whirling with possibilities, all of them unpleasant. If it was Gavin, she was likely to do something stupid, such as grab the receiver and drone in a mechanical-sounding voice that the call had just been disconnected. The memory of his helpful little strategy produced a familiar twinge in her heart. Oh, Lord, she missed Gavin more than she'd ever thought possible. There was no point in trying to fool herself any longer. She was miserable.

"I'm talking to a girl," Danny admitted reluctantly, hot color creeping up his neck at being caught.

"Erica?"

"No." He lowered his gaze and reluctantly handed her the receiver. "It's Melissa."

Dori entered the closet, pushing aside their winter coats, and sat on the floor. For the past few days, she'd been cranky with Danny. She hoped this gesture would show him that she regretted being such a grouch.

Amused at his mother's actions, Danny sat across from her and closed the door. Immediately they were surrounded by a friendly darkness. "Hello, Melissa," Dori murmured into the receiver. "How are you?"

"Fine," the thirteen-year-old answered seriously, "I think."

"Why the 'I think' business? It's nearly Christmas and there's lots of things happening. A young girl like you shouldn't have a care in the world."

"Yes, I know." Melissa sounded depressed, but Dori didn't know how deeply she should delve into the girl's unhappiness. Where Gavin was concerned— and that included his relationship with his daughter— Dori was particularly vulnerable. She loved Gavin and felt great affection for Melissa.

Danny was whispering furiously at her from his end of the closet.

"Excuse me a minute, Melissa. It seems Danny has something extremely important to tell me." She placed her palm over the receiver and glared at her son in the dark. "Yes, Danny."

"Melissa's got a mother-daughter fashion thing at her school and she doesn't have anyone to bring."

Dori nodded knowingly. "Danny says that your school is having a fashion show."

"My home ec class is putting it on. I sewed a jumper and everything. It's almost as pretty as the outfit you helped me buy. The teacher gave me an A on it."

"Congratulations. I'm sure you did a good job to have rated such a high grade." Already Dori knew what was coming and she dreaded having to turn the girl down. But with the way things stood between her and Gavin, Dori couldn't very well offer to go.

"I sewed it superbly," Melissa admitted with a

charming lack of modesty. "It's the best thing I ever made. Better even than the apron, but then I had to take the waistband off four times. I only made one minor mistake on the jumper," she continued, her voice gaining volume and speed with each word. "I sewed the zipper in backward, you know, so the tab was on the inside. I thought it was all right, it still went over my head and everything, but I had to take it out and do it over again. I was mad at myself for being so dumb." She paused to draw in a giant breath, then hurried on. "Will you come and pretend to be my mother? Please, oh, please won't you, Dori? Everyone has a mother coming, except me."

"Oh, Melissa." Dori's shoulders slumped forward as she sagged against the wall. "Honey, I don't know." Her stomach started churning frantically. She hated to refuse the girl, but Gavin was likely to read something unintended into her acceptance.

"Dori, please, I won't ask anything of you ever again. I need a pretend mother for just one night. For the fashion show."

The soft, pleading quality of the girl's voice was Dori's undoing. She played briefly with the idea of suggesting that Melissa ask Lainey, until she recalled the girl's reaction to the blatant blonde. Despite her misgivings, Dori couldn't ignore the yearning in Melissa's request. "I'll do it on two conditions," she agreed cautiously.

"Anything." The young voice rose with excitement.

"First, you mustn't tell any of your friends that I'm your mother. That would be wrong. As much as I wish

I had a daughter like you, Melissa, I can never be your mother.''

"Okay," she agreed with some reluctance, slightly subdued. "What else?"

"I don't want your father to know that I've done this." Gavin would be sure to see more in this simple act of kindness than there was. "Okay, Melissa?"

"That's easy. He won't even need to know because everything's taking place at the school and he never goes there on weekdays. And I promise not to tell him."

"Then I guess all I need to know is the date and time."

"Next Monday at seven-thirty. May I talk to Danny again?"

"Sure." Dori handed the telephone receiver back to her son and got awkwardly to her feet, hitting the top of her head on the rod positioned across the small enclosure. "Ouch," she muttered, as she gingerly opened the door, seeking a safe passage out.

A few minutes later Danny joined her in the kitchen where Dori was frying the hamburger. "That was real nice of you, Mom."

"I'm happy to do it for Melissa. She's a very special young lady." Gavin loved his daughter—that Dori didn't doubt—but she hoped he appreciated her, as well.

"Melissa was real worried about the fashion show. I thought it was tough not having a dad, but I guess it's just as bad without a mom."

And without a husband, Dori thought. "I'm sure it is," she replied smoothly. "Now how about if you set the table?"

"What are we having for dinner?"

Dori looked at the sautéing meat and shrugged. "I don't know yet."

"Aw, Mom, is it another one of *those* meals?"

On Friday morning, Dori overslept. Danny woke her almost twenty minutes after her alarm should have sounded.

"Mom," he murmured, rubbing the sleep from his face. "Aren't we supposed to be up? This isn't Saturday, is it?"

Dori took one look at the silent clock radio, gasped and threw back the covers. "Hurry and get dressed. We're late."

Feeling a little like the rabbit in *Alice in Wonderland*, Dori dashed from one room to the next, exclaiming how late they were. Her shower rivaled Danny's thirty-second baths for a new speed record. She brushed her teeth with one hand and blow-dried her hair with the other. The result was hair that looked as if it had been caught in an egg beater and a toothpaste stain on the front of her blouse.

"Should I buy lunch today?" Danny wanted to know, shoving his arms into a sweatshirt and pulling his head through to gaze at her inquisitively.

"Yes." There was no time to fix it now. "Take a dollar out of my purse."

Danny returned a minute later with her billfold. "All you've got is a ten-dollar bill."

"Oh, great." As she slipped her feet into soft leather pumps, her mind raced frantically. "What about your piggy bank?"

"But, Mom…"

"It's a loan, Danny. I'll pay you back later."

"All right," he agreed with all the charity of an ill-tempered loan shark.

"Hurry now. I'll get the car out of the garage."

Dori was parked in the driveway, revving the cold engine, when Danny ran through the garage. He slammed the door shut and climbed into the car.

"I got the dollar."

"Good." She looked over her shoulder as she backed out of the driveway. Traffic was heavy and driving took all her concentration.

"Mom," Danny said after a few minutes, then cleared his throat. "About that dollar."

"Danny, good grief, I'll pay you back tonight. Now quit worrying about it." She slowed to a full stop at a traffic light.

"But I'm going to need it. It's almost Christmas and I can't afford to be generous."

Dori paused to think over his words before turning to stare at her son. "Did you hear what you just said?"

"Yeah, I want my money back."

"Danny." She gave him an incredulous look. Her son couldn't afford to be generous because it was Christmas? The time of the year when love and human goodness were supposed to be at their peak. A low rumbling sound escaped from Dori's throat. Then she began to giggle. The giggles burst into full laughter until her whole body shook and she had to hold her side to keep from laughing harder. Still engrossed in the pure irony of his statement, Dori reached over and hugged her son. "Thanks," she giggled, "I needed that."

"It's not that funny," Danny objected, but he was

laughing, too. He brushed the hair off his forehead and suddenly sobered, his hand still raised. "Mom, look, it's Mr. Parker. He's in the car right beside us."

Unable to resist, Dori looked over at the Audi stopped next to her. Her laughter fled as she recognized Gavin. He hadn't seen her and Danny, or if he had, he was purposely looking in the opposite direction. Just when she was wondering what, if anything, she could do, Gavin's eyes met hers. Dori's heart gave a wild leap and began to thump madly as the dark, thoughtful eyes looked straight into hers. Stunned, she recognized an aching tenderness in his face. She saw regret, doubts, even pain. She wanted to smile and assure him that she was fine but that she missed him dreadfully. She wanted to ask him how he was doing and about the picture in the paper. Ten other flighty, meaningless thoughts came to her all at once and she didn't have the opportunity to voice even one. A car horn blared impatiently behind her, and Dori glanced up to notice that the traffic light was green and she was holding up a long line of commuters.

"That was Mr. Parker, wasn't it?" Danny said as she stepped on the gas and rushed forward.

"Yes." Her throat felt dry and though earlier there had been laughter Dori now felt the compelling need to cry. Swallowing the urge, she took the next right-hand turn for Danny's school. A quick look in her rearview mirror revealed Gavin traveling forward, as if seeing each other this way was an ordinary, every-day occurrence. Perhaps he did regret their relationship, perhaps she'd read him wrong from the start and it hadn't meant a thing. But Dori couldn't allow herself to believe that. She had to trust her instincts and hold on to her heart. Otherwise it hurt too much.

Saturday and Sunday passed in a blur of vague anticipation. After seeing Gavin on Friday morning, Dori had half expected that he would call her during the weekend. She should have known better than to try to second-guess Gavin Parker. He did things his own way and although it hurt, Dori loved him exactly as he was. When and if he ever admitted to loving her, she would never need to doubt again. That was how Gavin was. She knew with absolute certainty that when he loved, it would be a complete and enduring love, a love to last a lifetime.

The only bright spot in her disappointing weekend was a phone call from Melissa, who wanted to be sure Dori would attend the Mother-Daughter Fashion Show as she'd promised. During the conversation, the girl casually mentioned that Gavin was in L.A. to broadcast a football game.

Monday evening, Dori dressed in her best professional suit, a charcoal gray two-piece with black pinstripes. She wore a white silk blouse and a small red bow tie that added a touch of bright color to the suit. Danny had agreed to submit to the humiliation of having Jody from across the street come to baby-sit. He was vociferous in letting Dori know that this was a sacrifice on his part and he wanted her to tell Melissa all about his unselfishness.

A light drizzle had begun to fall when Dori pulled into the school parking lot. She was surprised by the large number of cars. Dori had assumed Melissa was exaggerating a bit when she'd declared that she would be the only girl there without a mother. This was, after all, a boarding school and there were bound to be several girls whose mothers hadn't been able to attend.

Melissa was standing just inside the doorway of the large auditorium, waiting for Dori. A smile brightened her intense young face the moment she caught Dori's eye. Rushing to her side, Melissa gave Dori an excited hug and handed her a program.

"Is this the world-famous creation, designed by the renowned Melissa Parker?" Dori inquired with a proud smile. The corduroy jumper was a brilliant shade of dark blue with a frilly robin's-egg-blue blouse underneath.

"Do you like it?" Melissa whirled around, holding out the sides of the skirt in Hollywood fashion. Sheer delight created large dimples in each of her round cheeks. "I think it turned out so pretty. I didn't make the blouse, but you probably guessed that already."

"It's wonderful."

Taking her by the arm, Melissa escorted Dori down the middle aisle of folding chairs. "I'm supposed to seat you right here."

"Where are you going?" Dori glanced around her curiously. Only a few mothers were sitting near the front and it looked as though these seats were reserved.

"Everything's almost ready so I have to go backstage, but I'll be back later." She started to move away but abruptly changed her mind. "The choral group is singing first. They really aren't very good, but please applaud."

"I will," Dori promised, doing her utmost to maintain a serious expression. "I take it you're not singing."

"Only if I want to offend Sister Helene."

In spite of herself, Dori chuckled. "Well, break a leg, kid."

Another mother was seated next to Dori a few minutes later and they struck up an easy conversation. It would have been very easy to pretend Melissa was her daughter, but Dori was careful to explain that she was there as a friend of the Parker family. Even at that, Dori felt she was stretching the truth.

The fashion show began with the introduction of the school staff. Then Dori applauded politely at the end of the first series of songs presented by the choral ensemble. Melissa might not have had a finely tuned musical ear, but her assessment of the group wasn't far off. Nonetheless, the applause was enthusiastic.

Following the musical presentation came the fashion show. Dori straightened in her chair as the announcer, a young girl about Melissa's age, stepped forward to the microphone. Obviously nervous, the girl fumbled with her papers and her voice shook as she started to speak.

Melissa in her navy blue jumper was the fourth model. With natural grace, she walked down the middle aisle, turned once, holding out the skirt with one hand, and paused in front of Dori to display the even stitches of her hem. The mothers loved it and laughed outright.

At the end of the fashion show, the headmistress, Sister Helene, approached the front of the room to announce the names of the students who had made the honor roll for the semester.

"Ladies," the soft voice instructed, "when your

daughter's name is read, would you please come forward to stand with her."

When Melissa's name was called out, the girl came to the front of the auditorium and cast a pleading glance at Dori. Her heart pounding, Dori rose from her seat to stand behind Melissa. She noticed that all the mothers with honor-roll daughters came from the first few rows; this was the reason Melissa had escorted Dori to the front. She wished Melissa had said something earlier. But then, it wouldn't have made any difference.

Dori's smile was proud as she placed her hands on Melissa's shoulders and leaned forward to whisper in her ear. "Daughter or not, I'm extremely proud of you."

Twisting her head, Melissa looked up at Dori, her expression somber. "I wish you were my mother."

"I know," Dori murmured quietly, the emotion building until her throat felt swollen with the effort of not crying. Still, she had to brush a stray tear from her cheek and bite her lower lip to keep from sobbing out loud.

The final names were read and there was a round of applause. "What now?" Dori whispered.

"I'm supposed to seat you and bring you a cup of tea and some cookies. Our home ec class made them. They're pretty good...I think. I was doing the sewing...not the cooking." She led Dori to her seat. "I'll be back in a jiffy."

"Fine." Dori crossed her shapely legs and with nothing to do, scanned the program for the fifth time. Her gaze rested on Melissa's name. This child could easily take the place Dori had reserved in her heart for the daughter she'd never had—and never would.

"You enjoyed that little charade, didn't you?" Gavin's voice taunted. Dori turned in shock as he sat down in the vacant chair beside her.

The words ripped through her with the pain of a blunt knife. Her program slipped to the floor and she bent forward to retrieve it. The auditorium seemed to roll beneath her chair and it took Dori a moment to realize it was only her nerves. Fixing a stiff smile on her lips, she straightened, forcing herself to be calm.

"Hello, Gavin," she said with a breathlessness she couldn't control. "What brings you here?"

"My daughter." Heavy emphasis was placed on the possessive pronoun to produce a not-so-subtle reminder that she was an intruder.

"Melissa invited me," Dori said in an attempt to explain her presence. "It's a Mother-Daughter Fashion Show." The minute the words were out, Dori knew she'd said the wrong thing.

"You're not her mother," he replied in a remote, impersonal tone that made her blood run cold.

"No, and I hadn't pretended to be her mother, either."

"That's not the way I saw it. Melissa's name was called and you hurried to the front like every other proud matron."

"What was I supposed to do?" she whispered angrily, her hands clenched in her lap. "Sit there with Melissa giving me pleading looks?"

"Yes," he bit back in a low controlled voice. "Did you think that if you maintained a friendship with my daughter we'd eventually resume our relationship?

That's not the way it's going to happen. I asked for some time and you're not giving it to me. Listen, Dori, this isn't any easier on me." He paused and raked a hand through his hair. "Your coming here tonight makes things damned impossible."

A weary sigh came from deep within Dori. Gavin assumed the worst possible explanation for what she'd done. Perhaps he was looking for a reason to hate her and now he had all the excuse he needed.

"I've fended off a lot of women bent on ruining my independence," he said harshly, "but you're the best. You know I love my daughter. She's my weakest link."

Unable to bear any more of his sarcasm, Dori stood. "You've got it all wrong, Gavin. Melissa is your strongest point. You're arrogant, egotistical and so damned stubborn you can't see what's right in front of your face."

"Dori, what's wrong?" Melissa approached her from behind, carefully holding a cup of hot tea in one hand and a small paper plate of cookies in the other.

Dori took the delicate cup and saucer out of Melissa's shaking fingers. Not knowing exactly what to do with them, she handed the cup to Gavin. If he wanted to play mother, then he could drink the weak tea and eat the stale cookies.

"Daddy…" Melissa choked with surprise and turned stricken eyes to Dori. "I didn't tell him, honest."

"I know," Dori assured her.

"What are you doing here…I didn't tell you about…the tea…this is supposed to be for mothers and…'' The words stumbled over her tongue in her rush to get them out.

"Sit down," Gavin ordered. "Both of you."

As they seated themselves, he dragged his chair around so that he was facing them both. Dori felt like a disobedient child but refused to give in to the sensation. She had done nothing wrong. Her only motive in attending the fashion show had been kindness; she had responded to the pleas of a young girl who desperately wanted a mother so she could be like the other girls. Dori had come for Melissa's sake alone, and the fact that Gavin was the girl's father had almost deterred her from coming at all—despite what he chose to believe.

"I think you'd better tell me what's going on." His eyes challenged Dori in that chilling way she hated.

"I believe I've already explained the circumstances," she inserted dryly. "However, it seems that you've added two and two and come up with five."

"Dad," Melissa demanded with open defense, taking note of Dori's unapologetic tone, "what are you doing here? This isn't for fathers—you're the only man here."

"The notice came from the school about the fashion show," he explained haltingly, glancing around him. "I have every right to come to my daughter's school any time I darn well please."

"But it doesn't give you the right to say those kinds of things to me," Dori stated calmly and drew together the front of her suit jacket. People sitting nearby were beginning to give them unwanted attention.

Gavin's features hardened and a thick brow was raised derisively in her direction. Without looking at his daughter, he instructed, "Melissa, get Dori another cup of tea."

"But, Dad—"

"You heard what I said."

Reluctantly, Melissa rose to her feet. "I'll be back in a couple of minutes." She took a few steps toward the rear of the auditorium, then turned to Dori again. "They have coffee, if you'd rather have that."

"Either one is fine," Dori answered with a smile and a reassuring wink. She probably wouldn't be around to drink it, anyway.

Gavin waited until his daughter was out of earshot. "This whole situation between us has got out of hand."

Dori crossed her arms and leaned back in the hard folding chair, suddenly weary.

"We had a nice thing while it was going, but it's over. You broke the rules," he said accusingly. "Any attempt on your part to drag it out will only be painful for the kids." His voice was tight with impatience. "I'm seeing someone else now," he explained. "Melissa hasn't met her yet, but she will soon."

Dori drew in a ragged breath and found she couldn't release it. It burned in her lungs until she regained her composure enough to slowly exhale. "I believe that." She didn't know how she could remain so calm when every breath was a struggle and every heartbeat caused pain. Deep down, Dori had realized that Gavin would do something like this. "I'm only surprised you waited so long. I scare you to death, Gavin, and you're running as fast as you can in the opposite direction. No doubt you've seen any number of airhead blondes in the past week."

"You think you know me so well." He eyed her coolly. "This time you're wrong. I saw what was happening with us and came to my senses in the nick of time."

Dori marveled at her self-control. Even though the whole world felt as if it were dissolving around her, she sat serenely, an expression of apparent indifference on her face. Whatever Gavin might say, she still tried to believe that eventually he would recognize that he loved her. All she had were her hopes. He was thickheaded enough to deny his love for her all his life. Dori didn't know what made her think she could succeed where so many others had failed.

"If you expected to shock me with your sudden interest in blondes, you haven't. I know you too well."

"You don't know me at all," he answered, though a deep frown marred his brow.

"From the beginning, I've found you very easy to read, Gavin Parker." Inside, Dori was convulsed with pain, but she refused to allow him to glimpse her private agony. "You love me. You may not have admitted it to yourself yet, but you do and someday you'll recognize that. Date all the blondes you like, but when you kiss them, it'll be my lips you taste and when they're in your arms, it's my body you'll long to feel."

"If anyone loves someone around here, it's you." He spoke as though the words were an accusation.

Dori's smile was infinitely sad. "Yes, I'll admit I love you and Melissa."

"I told you not to fall in love with me," he said bitterly. "I warned you from the beginning not to smell orange blossoms, but that's all you women seem to think about."

Dori couldn't deny his words. "Yes, you did, and believe me, I was just as shocked as you when I realized that I could fall in love with someone so pigheaded, irrational and emotionally scarred." She paused to fight the ache in her throat. "I don't know and I don't even want to know what Deirdre did to you. That's in the past, but you're wearing all that emotional pain like a cement shroud."

"I've heard enough." A muscle flexed in his strong jaw.

Letting her gaze fall, Dori tried to blink back the burning tears. "If you've found someone else who can make you happy, then I wish you the very best. I mean that sincerely, but I doubt you'll ever find that elusive contentment. Goodbye, Gavin. I apologize, I truly do, for ruining a promising agreement. With someone less vulnerable than me, it might have worked."

His gaze refused to meet hers. For all the emotion revealed in his eyes, she could have been talking to a man carved in stone. Without a word he was going to allow Dori to leave. Her heart had persisted in hoping that somehow she'd reach him and he'd stop her.

"You're not leaving, are you?" Melissa spoke from behind, setting the china cup on the seat of the beige metal chair. "I brought your tea."

"I can't stay." Impulsively she hugged the girl and brushed back the thick bangs that hung across Melissa's furrowed brow. "Goodbye." Dori's voice quavered with emotion. She wouldn't see Melissa again. Coming this evening had been a terrible mistake.

Melissa clung to her, apparently understanding what had happened. "Dori," she begged, "please...don't leave. I promise..."

"Let her go," Gavin barked, causing several heads to turn.

Instantly, Melissa dropped her hands and took a step in retreat. Dori couldn't have borne another moment without bursting into tears. With quick-paced steps, a forced smile on her face, she hurried out of the auditorium. Once outside, she broke into a half trot, grateful for the cover of darkness. She desperately needed to be alone.

By the time Dori pulled into her garage, the tears were making wet tracks down her face. She turned off the engine and sat with her hands clenching the steering wheel as she fought to control her breathing and stem the flow of emotion.

A glance at her watch assured her that Danny would be in bed and, she hoped, asleep.

The baby-sitter eyed Dori's red face curiously but didn't ask any questions. "There's a phone message for you on the table," the teenager said on her way out the front door.

Dori switched on the kitchen light and smiled absently at the name and number written neatly on the message pad. She reached for the phone and punched out his number, swallowing the painful lump that filled her throat.

He answered on the third ring. "Hi, Tom, it's Dori Robertson, returning your call."

"Hi, Dori," he began awkwardly. "I hope I'm not bothering you."

"No bother." She looked up at the ceiling and gently rubbed her burning eyes. "I had a school function to attend for a friend, but I'm home now."

"How are you?"

Dying, her heart answered. "Splendid," she murmured. "Getting ready to do some Christmas shopping. Danny's managed to hone down his Christmas list to a meager three hundred items."

"Would you like some company? I mean, I understand if you'd rather not, feeling the way I do about Paula."

"I take it you two haven't managed to patch things up?"

"Not yet," he said with an expressive sigh. "About the shopping—I'd appreciate some advice on gifts and such."

"I'd be happy to go with you, Tom."

"I know you've been seeing a lot of that ex-football player."

"I won't be seeing him anymore." She choked down a sob and covered her mouth with her hand to keep from crying.

"How about one night this week, then?"

"Fine," she managed, replacing the receiver a minute later, after a mumbled goodbye. Leaning against the wall, Dori made a sniffling attempt to regain her composure. Crying like this was ridiculous. She'd known from the beginning what she was letting herself in for. It wouldn't do any good to cry about it now.

When she wiped her eyes free of tears, she found Danny standing in the doorway of the kitchen, watching her.

"Oh, Mom," he said softly.

Ten

Danny sat at the kitchen table spreading colored butter frosting over the gingerbread men. His look was thoughtful as he added raisin eyes and three raisin buttons.

The timer on the stove went off and Dori automatically reached for the padded oven mitt.

"You know, Mom, I don't like Mr. Parker anymore. Melissa either. I thought she was all right for a girl, but I was wrong."

"The problem is, Danny, we both love them very much and telling ourselves anything else would be lying." For several days Danny had been brooding and thoughtful. They'd had a long talk after the Mother-Daughter Fashion Show, and Dori had explained that they wouldn't be seeing Gavin or Melissa again. Surprisingly, her son had accepted that without argument.

"I don't love anyone who makes my mom cry," he insisted.

"I'm not crying anymore," she assured him softly, and it was true, she wasn't. There were regrets, but no more tears.

Licking the frosting from his fingers, Danny examined the "new father" requirement list posted on the refrigerator door. "How long do you think it'll be before we start looking again?"

Dori lifted the cut-out cookies from the sheet with a spatula and tilted her head pensively to one side. "Not long." Gradually, her pain-dulled senses were returning to normal. Dating again would probably be the best thing for her, but there was a problem. She wanted only Gavin. Loved only Gavin.

When she finished scraping the cookies from the sheet, Dori noticed that Danny had removed the requirement list, strawberry magnet and all, and taken a pencil from the drawer. Then he'd carried everything to the table. Wiping her floury hands on her apron, she read over his shoulder, as his pencil worked furiously across the bottom of the page. "I'm adding something else," Danny explained needlessly, "I want a new father who won't make my mom cry."

"That's thoughtful, but, Danny, tears can mean several things. There are tears of happiness and tears of frustration, even angry tears. It isn't a bad thing to cry, but sometimes good and necessary." She didn't want to explain that the tears were a measure of her love for Gavin. If she hadn't loved him, it wouldn't have hurt nearly as much when they'd stopped seeing each other.

"Mr. Parker wasn't a very good football player, either," Danny complained.

"He was terrific," Dori countered, "and you know it."

"I threw away all the football cards I had of him, and his autograph."

He said it with a brash air of unconcern as though throwing away the cards had been a trivial thing. But

Dori knew better. She'd found the whole collection of treasures—the cards, the autograph and the program from the Seahawks football game he and Gavin attended—in the bottom of his *Star Wars* garbage can and rescued them. Later, he'd regret discarding those items. He was hurt and angry now, but he'd recover. Next autumn, he'd be pleased when she returned the memorabilia so he could brag to his new junior-high friends that he had Gavin Parker's autograph.

"While the cookies are cooling, why don't you bring in the mail."

"Sure, Mom."

Usually Dori could count on Danny's good behavior during the month of December, but lately he'd been even more thoughtful, loving and considerate. She was almost beginning to worry about him. Not once had he nagged her about Christmas or his presents. Nor had he continued to pursue the new father business. Until today, he'd said nothing.

The phone rang as Danny barged into the kitchen, tossing the mail on the counter. He grabbed the receiver and answered breathlessly.

A couple of minutes later he turned to Dori. "Mom, guess what, it's Jon. He wants to know if I can come over and play. He's real excited because his dad is moving back in and they're going to be a real family again."

"That's wonderful. Tell Jon that I'm very happy for him." Dori wasn't surprised. From the thoughtful way Tom had gone about choosing Christmas presents for his wife and family, Dori realized how deep his love ran. He'd never mentioned why he and his wife had separated, but Dori was pleased to hear that they'd settled their problems. Did she dare hope that Gavin would recognize all the love waiting for him and return to her? No man could kiss and hold her the way he had and then cast her aside without regrets. Paula had her Christmas present and Dori wondered if she would ever have hers.

"Can I go over and play? I'll finish decorating the cookies later."

"Don't worry about it. There are only a few from the last batch and I can do those. Go and have a good time."

"Thanks, Mom." He yanked his coat from the closet and blew her a kiss, something he had taken to doing lately instead of giving her a real kiss. Her son was growing up, and she had to learn to accept that.

"Think nothing of it," she called lightly. "And be home in an hour." The last words were cut off as the back door slammed.

Dori watched Danny's eager escape and sighed. Her son was growing up, maturing. She used to look at him and think of Brad, but now she saw that Danny was becoming himself, a unique and separate person.

"No need to get melancholy," she chided herself aloud, reaching for the stack of mail. At a glance she saw it consisted of bills and a few Christmas cards. She carried them into the living room, slouched onto the sofa and propped her slippered feet on the coffee table. The first envelope had a return address she didn't immediately recognize and curiously she ripped it open. Instead of a card, there was a personal letter written on notebook paper. Unfolding the page, Dori's gaze slid to the bottom, where she discovered Melissa's signature.

Dori's feet dropped to the floor as she straightened. After the first line, she bit her bottom lip and blinked rapidly to clear away the ready tears that sprang to the surface.

Dear Dori,

I wanted to write and thank you for coming to the mother-daughter thing. Dad showing up was a real surprise and I hope you believe me when I tell you that I didn't say anything to him, like I promised. Really, I didn't.

Dad explained that I shouldn't bother you anymore and I won't. That's the hardest part because I really like you. I know Deirdre is my real mother, but I don't think of her as a mother. She's pretty, but I don't think she's really very happy about being a mother. When I think of a mother, I think of someone like you who buys groceries in the Albertson's store and tosses the oranges into the cart like a softball pitcher. Someone who lets me try on her makeup and perfume even if I use too much at first. Mothers are special people, and for the first time in my life I got to see one up really close. Thank you for showing me how I want to love my kids.

I feel bad that things didn't work out with you and my dad. I feel even worse that Dad says I shouldn't ever bother you again. I don't think I'm even supposed to be writing this letter, but Sister Helene said I could. It's only polite to properly thank you. I did promise her I wouldn't sign up for choir next year. Just kidding! Anyway, Dad refuses to let me talk about you or Danny. He doesn't seem to have time for me right now, but that's okay because I'm pretty mad at him anyhow.

I'd like to think of you as my mother, Dori, but I can't because every time I do, I want to cry. You told me once how much you wanted a daughter. I sure wish I could have been yours.

Your almost daughter,
Melissa

Tears clouded Dori's eyes as she refolded the letter and placed it back in the envelope. This was one lesson she hadn't ever counted on learning. This helpless, desolate feeling of hurting to the marrow of her bones, of grieving for a man incapable of commitment. Yet there was no one to blame but herself. He'd warned her not to fall in love with him. The problem was, he hadn't said anything about loving his daughter and Dori did love Melissa. And now, instead of two people facing Christmas with heavy hearts, there were four.

Gavin Parker could take a flying leap into a cow pasture and the next time she saw him—if she ever saw him again—she'd tell him exactly that. How long would it take him to realize how much his women loved him? Let him be angry; she was going to answer this letter. And maybe in a few months, when it wasn't so painful, she'd visit Melissa at the school and they'd spend the day together.

Dori's gaze rested on the gaily trimmed Christmas tree and the few presents gathered about the base. This was supposed to be the happiest time of the year. Only it wasn't. Not for Danny or Dori. Not this year. The stuffed lion Gavin had won for her sat beside the television, and Dori couldn't resist the impulse to go over and pick it up. Hugging it fiercely, she let the soft fur comfort her.

When the surge of emotion subsided, Dori took out stationery and wrote a reply to Melissa. Afterward she felt calmer and even a little cheered. Later that night, after Danny was in bed, she reread it to be certain she'd said everything she wanted to say and decided no letter could ever relay all the love in her heart.

Dearest Melissa,

Thank you for your sweet letter. I felt much better after reading it. I know you didn't tell your father about the fashion show, so please don't think I blame you for that.

I'm going to ask you to do something you may not understand right now. It's important that you not be angry with your father; he needs you now more than ever. He loves you, Melissa, very much, and you must never doubt that. I care about him, too, but you'll have to love him for both of us. Be patient with him.

Later, after the holidays, if Sister Helene thinks it would be all right, I'll come and spend a day with you. Until then, do well in your studies and keep sewing. You show a definite talent for it—especially for stitching hems!

You will always hold a special place in my heart, Melissa, and since I can't be your mother, let me be your friend.

Love,
Dori

Dori was grateful that December was such a busy month. If it had been any other time of the year, she might have fallen prey to even greater doubt and bitterness. Every night of the following week there was an activity she and Danny were expected to attend. She was with family and friends but had never felt more alone. She felt as if a vital part of herself was missing, and there was—her heart. She had given it to Gavin. And now she was caught in this limbo of apathy and indifference. After he'd panicked and run from her love, Dori had thought she could just take up where she'd left off and resume the even pace of her life. Now she was painfully learning that it would be far longer before she found her balance again. But she would, and that was the most important thing.

At the dinner table two days before Christmas, Danny stirred the mashed potatoes with his spoon and cleared his throat as if to make a weighty pronouncement. "Mom, did you know that this is Christmas Eve's eve?"

Dori set her fork aside to give his words serious consideration. "You're right," she said with a thoughtful look. As she remembered, she'd been about his age when she'd made the same discovery.

"And since it's so close to Christmas and all, I thought maybe it would be all right to open one of my presents."

Dori didn't as much as hesitate. "Not until Christmas morning. Waiting is half the fun."

"Aw, Mom, I hate it. Just one gift. Please."

One practiced look silenced him, and he concentrated on slicing his roast beef into bite-sized pieces.

"Are we going to Grandma and Grandpa's again this year?"

They did every year. Dori wondered why Danny asked, when he knew the answer.

"Yes, just like we did last year and the year before that and the year before that and..."

"I get the picture," he mumbled, reaching for his glass of milk. He lifted it to his mouth, then paused, an intense, almost painful look edging its way across his young face. "Do you suppose we'll ever see Mr. Parker and Melissa again?"

"I don't know." A sadness tightened her heart, but she forced a strained smile to her lips. She hoped. Every minute of every hour she hoped, but she dared not say anything to Danny. "Why do you ask?"

"I don't know." He lifted one shoulder in an indifferent shrug. "It just doesn't seem right not seeing them."

"I know." Her throat worked convulsively. "It doesn't seem right for me, either."

Danny pushed his plate aside, his meal only half-eaten. "Can I be excused, Mom? I'm not hungry anymore."

Neither was Dori, for that matter. "Sure," she murmured, laying her knife across her own plate.

Danny carried his dishes to the sink and turned back to Dori. "Do you *have* to work tomorrow?"

Dori wasn't too thrilled at the prospect, either. "Just in the morning. If you like, you can stay home by yourself." Danny was now old enough to be left alone for more than an hour or two. Usually he preferred company, but on Christmas Eve he'd sleep late and then he could watch television until she got home around eleven-thirty.

"Could I really?" He smiled eagerly. "I'd be good and not have anyone over."

"I know."

The following morning Dori had more than one doubt. Twice she phoned Danny from the office. He assured her he was fine, except that he had to keep answering the phone because Grandma had called three times, too. Dori didn't call after that, but when the office closed, she made it to the employee parking lot and out again in record time. On the drive home, she had to restrain herself from speeding. Waiting at a red light, Dori was convinced she'd done the wrong thing in leaving Danny on his own. He wasn't prepared for this type of responsibility. True, he was by himself for an hour after school twice a week, but this was different. He'd been alone in the house for three and a half hours.

The garage door was open for her, and with a sigh of relief she drove inside and parked.

"Danny," she called out, slightly breathless as she walked in the back door. "I'm home. How did everything go?" Hanging her purse in the hall closet, she walked into the living room, faltered and stopped dead. Her heart fell to her knees, rebounded and rocketed into her throat. Gavin was there. There, in her living room. Dressed casually in slacks and a thick sweater, he was staring at her with dark, brooding eyes. Did she dare hope he'd come because he loved her? Her gaze sought Danny, who was perched on the ottoman facing Melissa, who sat in the nearby chair.

"Hi, Mom," Danny looked as confused as Dori felt.

"I told them it was okay if they came inside. That was the right thing to do, wasn't it?"

"Yes, yes, of course." Her fingers refused to co-operate as she fiddled with her coat buttons. She was so happy and so afraid that her knees felt like cooked spaghetti, and she sank weakly into the sofa across from Gavin. "This is a..." Her mind went blank.

"Surprise," Melissa finished for her.

A wonderful surprise, her mind threw back. "Yes."

"They brought us Christmas gifts," Danny explained, pointing to the large stack of gaily wrapped presents under the tree.

"Oh." Dori had the impression that this wasn't really happening, that somehow she'd wake and find this entire scene only a vivid dream. "Thank you. I have yours in the other room."

A hint of a smile touched Gavin's mouth, but his piercing dark eyes studied her like a hawk about to swoop down from the skies to capture its prey. "Were you so sure of me?"

"No, I wasn't sure, but I was desperately hoping."

Their gazes held as he spoke. "Danny and Melissa, why don't you go play a game while I talk to Dori."

"I'm not leaving my mom," Danny declared in a forceful voice and sprang to his feet defensively. He crossed the small room to sit beside his mother.

Utterly surprised by his behavior, Dori stared at him, feeling an odd mixture of pride and disbelief.

A muscle moved in Gavin's rigid jaw when Melissa crossed her arms and looked boldly at her father. "I agree with Danny. We should all hear this."

Dori dropped her eyes to keep Gavin from seeing the laughter sparkling there. The kids were obviously going to stay to the end of this, whether they were welcome or not.

Gavin slid to the edge of his seat and raked his hand through his hair in an uncharacteristic gesture of uncertainty.

"I've been doing a lot of thinking about our agreement," he began on a note of challenge. "Things didn't exactly work out the way I planned them, but—"

"I'm not interested in any more agreements," Dori told him honestly, and immediately regretted interrupting him. Not for anything would she admit that it hadn't worked because she'd done exactly what he'd warned her not to do: fall in love with him.

Another long pause followed as he continued to watch her steadily. "I was hoping, Dori, that you would hear me out before jumping to conclusions." Speaking in front of the children was clearly making him uneasy.

Dori made a limp, apologetic motion with her hand. The living room had never seemed so small, nor Gavin so big. Every nerve in her body was conscious of him and she ached for the feel of his comforting arms. "I'm sorry. I won't interrupt you again."

Gavin ignored her and turned his attention to Danny instead. "Didn't you tell me once that you made out a requirement list for a new father?"

"Yes." Danny nodded his head for emphasis.

"Would you get it for me?"

Danny catapulted from the sofa and into the kitchen. Within seconds he was back thrusting the list at Gavin. "Here, but I don't know why you want to read it. You already know what it says."

"I think Dad might want to apply for the position," Melissa said, her eyes glowing brightly. "Dad and I had a really long talk and he feels bad about what happened and decided—"

"Melissa," he said flatly, "it would be best if I did my own talking."

"Okay, Dad." She leaned back against the cushioned chair and heaved an impatient sigh.

Dori's head was spinning like a satellite gone off its orbit. Her hands felt both clammy and cold and she clasped them in her lap.

Gavin appeared to be studying the list Danny had given him. "I don't know that I've done such a terrific job in the father department, but—"

"Yes, you have, Dad," Melissa inserted. "You've been really good."

Despite herself, Dori found she had to smile at Melissa and her "reallys."

"Melissa, please," Gavin barked and paused to smooth the hair he'd rumpled a few minutes earlier. The muscle in his jaw twitched again. "Dori." He said her name with such emotion that her heart throbbed painfully. "I know I don't deserve someone as wonderful as you, but I'd consider it a great honor if you'd consent to marry me."

The words washed over her like warm, soothing waters and she closed her eyes at the rush of feelings that crowded her heart. "Are you saying you love me?" she whispered, unable to make her voice any stronger.

"Yes," he answered curtly.

"This is for us and not because of the kids?" She knew that Melissa held a powerful hand over her father. From the beginning, both Melissa and Danny had tried to manipulate them.

"I want to marry you because I've learned that I don't want to live without you." His response was honest and direct.

"Then yes, I'll be your wife." Dori's was just as straightforward.

"Okay, let's set the date. The sooner the better."

If he didn't move to take her in his arms soon, she'd embarrass them both by leaping across the room.

"I'm sorry, Mr. Parker, but you can't marry my mom," Danny announced with all the authority of a Supreme Court judge.

"What?" Dori, Melissa and Gavin shouted simultaneously.

Danny eyed all three sternly. "If you read my requirement list for a new father, you'll see that there's another requirement down there now."

Gavin's gaze dropped to the paper clenched in his hand.

"You made my mom cry, Mr. Parker, and you might do it again."

A look of pain flashed across Gavin's face. "I realize that, Danny, and deeply regret any hurt I've caused your mother. If both of you will give me another chance, I promise to make it up to you."

Danny appeared to weigh his words carefully. "Will you make her cry again?"

Frowning thoughtfully, Gavin studied the boy in silence. As she watched them, Dori felt a stirring of love and tenderness for her son and for the man who would become her husband.

"I hope never to cause your mother any pain

again,'' Gavin muttered thickly, ''but I can't promise she won't cry.''

''Mom.'' Danny transferred his attention to Dori. ''What do you think?''

''Danny, come on,'' Melissa said with high-pitched urgency. ''Good grief, this is what we all want! Don't blow it now.''

Danny fixed his eyes on his mother, unswayed by Melissa's plea. ''Well, Mom?''

Dori's gaze met and held with Gavin's and her heart leaped wildly at the tenderness she saw. ''Yes, it's what I want.'' They both stood at the same moment and reached for each other in a spontaneous burst of love and emotion. Gavin caught her in his arms and crushed her against his chest as his hungry mouth came down on hers. With a sigh of longing, Dori received his kiss, glorying in the feel of his arms around her. Coming to her and admitting his love and his need had been difficult for him, and she thanked him with all the love stored in her heart.

Twining her arms around his neck, she held him fiercely. She was vaguely aware of Danny murmuring to Melissa—something about leaving so he didn't have to watch the mushy stuff.

Gavin's arms tightened around her possessively, molding her closer to him while his hand slid up and down her spine, gathering her body as close as possible to his own. ''Dear Lord, I've missed you,'' he whispered hoarsely against her lips, then kissed her again, harder and longer as if he couldn't ever get enough of her.

The sensation was so exquisite that Dori felt tears of happiness spring to her eyes and roll unheeded down her cheeks. "Oh, Gavin, what took you so long?"

Drawing back slightly, Gavin inhaled a shuddering breath. "I don't know. I thought it would be so easy to forget you. There's never been a woman in my life who has haunted me the way you have."

Her eyes shone with joyful tears as she smiled mischievously up at him. "Good." What she didn't tell him was that she'd felt the same things.

"Once I'd been in the sunlight, I couldn't go back to the shadows," Gavin murmured. He buried his face in her hair and breathed in deeply. "I tried," he acknowledged with an ironic laugh. "After Deirdre I didn't want any woman to have this kind of power over me."

"I know."

"Why is it you know me so well?"

Smiling happily, she shook her head. "I guess that comes from loving you so much."

"Everything happened just the way you predicted," he said with a look of chagrin. "No matter who I kissed, it was your lips I tasted. When I held another woman, my heart told me something was wrong, and I longed only for you."

"Oh, Gavin." She spread tiny kisses over his face. Her lips met his eyes, nose, jaw and finally his eager mouth. She didn't need to be told that these lessons had been difficult ones for Gavin. Surrendering his freedom to a woman had been an arduous battle between his will and his heart. But now he would find a new freedom in their love for each other. He had finally come to understand that, and she knew he would love her with all his strength.

Gently the side of his thumb wiped a tear from the highest arch of her cheek. "The worst part was seeing you in the car that morning with Danny." Dori heard the remembered pain that made his voice sound husky. "You looked like sunshine and were laughing as if you hadn't a care in the world. I saw you and felt something so painful I can't even describe it. You had me so tied up in knots, I wasn't worth a damn to anyone and there you were, laughing with Danny as if I meant nothing."

"That's not true," she said, her voice filled with tears. "I was dying inside from wanting you."

"You've got me," he said with an uncharacteristic humbleness. "For as long as you want."

"I love you," Dori whispered fervently, laying her trembling hand on his smoothly shaved cheek. "And I can guarantee you that one lifetime will never be enough."

Cradling her face between both his hands, Gavin gazed into her tear-misted eyes and kissed her with a gentleness that bordered on worship.

"I told you it'd work," Danny whispered contentedly from just inside the kitchen.

"I knew it all along," Melissa agreed with a romantic sigh. "It was obvious from the time we went to the fair. They're perfect together."

"Yeah, your plan worked good," Danny agreed.

"We're not through yet." Her voice dropped slightly as if she were divulging a secret.

"But they're getting married," Danny argued in low tones. "What more could we want?"

Melissa's sigh came close to belligerence. "Honestly, Danny, think about it. Four is such a boring number. By next year there should be five.''

''Five what?''

''People in our family. Now we've got to convince them to have a baby.''

''Hey, good idea,'' Danny said eagerly. ''That'd be great. I'd like a baby brother.''

''They'll have a girl first. The second baby will be a boy for you. Okay?''

''I'd rather have the boy first.''

''Maybe,'' Melissa said, obviously feeling generous.

THE FORGETFUL BRIDE

For Patti Knoll
My witty, charming and talented friend

Prologue

"Not unless we're married."

Ten-year-old Martin Marshall slapped his hands against his thighs in disgust. "I told you she was going to be unreasonable about this."

Caitlin watched as her brother's best friend withdrew a second baseball card from his shirt pocket. If Joseph Rockwell wanted to kiss her, then he was going to have to do it the right way. She might be only eight, but Caitlin knew about these things. Glancing down at the doll held tightly in her arms, she realized instinctively that Barbie wouldn't approve of kissing a boy unless he married you first.

Martin approached her again. "Joe says he'll throw in his Don Drysdale baseball card."

"Not unless we're married," she repeated, smoothing the front of her sundress with a haughty air.

"All right, all right, I'll marry her," Joe muttered as he stalked across the backyard.

"How you gonna do that?" Martin demanded.

"Get your Bible."

For someone who wanted to kiss her so badly, Joseph didn't look very pleased. Caitlin decided to press her luck. "In the fort."

"The fort?" Joe exploded. "No girls are allowed in there and you know it."

"I refuse to get married to a boy who won't allow me into his fort."

"Call it off," Martin demanded. "She's asking too much."

"You don't have to give me the second baseball card," she said. The idea of being the first girl ever to view their precious fort had a certain appeal. For one thing, she'd probably get invited to Betsy McDonald's birthday party.

The boys exchanged glances and started whispering to each other, but Caitlin heard only snatches of their conversation. Martin clearly wasn't thrilled with Joseph's concessions, and he kept shaking his head as though he couldn't believe his friend might actually go through with this. For her part, Caitlin didn't know whether to trust Joseph. He liked playing practical jokes and everyone in the neighborhood knew it.

"It's time to feed my baby," she announced, preparing to leave.

"All right, all right," Joseph said with obvious reluctance. "I'll marry you in the fort. Martin'll say the words, only you can't tell anyone about going inside, understand?"

"If you do," Martin threatened, glaring at his sister, "you'll be sorry."

"I won't tell," Caitlin promised. It would have to be a secret, but that was fine because she liked keeping secrets.

"You ready?" Joseph demanded. Now that the terms were set, he seemed to be in a rush, which rather annoyed Caitlin. The frown on his face didn't please

her, either. A bridegroom should at least *look* happy.
She was about to say so, but decided not to.

"You'll have to change clothes, of course. The suit
you wore on Easter Sunday will do nicely."

"What?" Joseph shrieked. "I'm not wearing any
suit. Listen, Caitlin, you've gone about as far as you
can with this. I get married exactly the way I am or
we call it off."

She sighed, rolling her eyes expressively. "Oh, all
right, but I'll need to get a few things first."

"Just hurry up, would you?"

Martin followed her into the house, letting the
screen door slam behind him. He took his Bible off
the hallway table and rushed back outside.

Caitlin hurried up to her room, where she grabbed
a brush to run through her hair and straightened the
two pink ribbons tied around her pigtails. She always
insisted on pink ribbons because pink was a color for
girls. Boys were supposed to wear blue and brown and
boring colors like that. Boys were okay sometimes,
but mostly they did disgusting things.

Her four dolls accompanied her across the backyard
and into the wooded acre behind. She hated getting
her Mary Janes dusty, but that couldn't be helped.

With a good deal of ceremony, she opened the rick-
ety door and then slowly, the way she'd seen it done
at her older cousin's wedding, Caitlin marched into
the boys' packing-crate-and-cardboard fort.

Pausing inside the narrow entry, she glanced
around. It wasn't anything to brag about. Martin had
made it sound like a palace with marble floors and
crystal chandeliers. She couldn't help feeling disillu-

sioned. If she hadn't been so eager to see the fort, she would have insisted they do this properly, in church.

Her brother stood tall and proud on an upturned apple crate, the Bible clutched to his chest. His face was dutifully somber. Caitlin smiled approvingly. He, at least, was taking this seriously.

"You can't bring those dolls in here," Joseph said loudly.

"I most certainly can. Barbie and Ken and Paula and Jane are our children."

"Our children?"

"Naturally they haven't been born yet, so they're really just a glint in your eye." She'd heard her father say that once and it sounded special. "They're angels for now, but I thought they should be here so you could meet them." She was busily arranging her dolls in a tidy row behind Martin on another apple crate.

Joseph covered his face with his hands and it looked for a moment like he might actually change his mind.

"Are we going to get married or not?" she asked.

"All right, all right." Joseph sighed heavily and pulled her forward, a little more roughly than necessary, in Caitlin's opinion.

The two of them stood in front of Martin, who randomly opened his Bible. He gazed down at the leather-bound book and then at Caitlin and his best friend. He nodded solemnly. "Do you Joseph James Rockwell take Caitlin Rose Marshall for your wife?"

"Lawfully wedded," Caitlin corrected. She remembered this part from a television show.

"Lawfully wedded wife," Martin amended grudgingly.

"I do." Caitlin noticed that he didn't say it with

any real enthusiasm. "I think there's supposed to be something about richer or poorer and sickness and health," Joseph said, smirking at Caitlin as if to say she wasn't the only one who knew the proper words.

Martin nodded and continued. "Do you, Caitlin Rose Marshall, hereby take Joseph James Rockwell in sickness and health and in riches and in poorness?"

"I'll only marry a man who's healthy and rich."

"You can't go putting conditions on this now," Joseph argued. "We already agreed."

"Just say 'I do,'" Martin urged, his voice tight with annoyance. Caitlin suspected that only the seriousness of the occasion prevented him from adding, "You pest."

She wasn't sure if she should go through with this or not. She was old enough to know she liked pretty things and that when she married, her husband would build her a castle at the edge of the forest. He would love her so much, he'd bring home silk ribbons for her hair, and bottles and bottles of expensive perfume. So many that there wouldn't be room for them all on her makeup table.

"Caitlin," Martin said through clenched teeth.

"I do," she answered solemnly.

"I hereby pronounce you married," Martin proclaimed, closing the Bible with a resounding thud. "You may kiss the bride."

Joseph turned to face Caitlin. He was several inches taller than she was. His eyes were a pretty shade of blue that reminded her of the way the sky looked the morning after a bad rainstorm. She liked Joseph's eyes.

"You ready?" he asked.

She nodded, closed her eyes and pressed her lips tightly together as she angled her head to the left. If the truth be known, she wasn't all that opposed to having Joseph kiss her, but she'd never let him know that because...well, because kissing wasn't something ladies talked about.

A long time passed before she felt his mouth touch hers. Actually his lips sort of bounced against hers. Gee, she thought. What a bunch of hullabaloo over nothing.

"Well?" Martin demanded of his friend.

Caitlin opened her eyes to discover Joseph frowning down at her. "It wasn't anything like Pete said it would be," he grumbled.

"Caitlin might be doing it wrong," Martin offered, glaring accusingly at his sister.

"If anyone did anything wrong, it's Joseph." They were making it sound like she'd purposely cheated them. If anyone was being cheated, it was Caitlin, because she couldn't tell Betsy McDonald about going inside their precious fort.

Joseph didn't say anything for a long moment. Then he slowly withdrew his prized baseball card from his shirt pocket. He gazed at it lovingly, then reluctantly held it out to her. "Here," he said, "this is yours now."

"You aren't going to *give* it to her, are you? Not when she flubbed up!" Martin cried. "Kissing a girl wasn't like Pete said, and that's got to be Caitlin's fault. I told you she's not really a girl, anyway. She's a pest."

"A deal's a deal," Joseph said sadly.

"You can keep your silly old baseball card." Head

held high, Caitlin gathered up her dolls in a huff, prepared to make a proper exit.

"You won't tell anyone about us letting you into the fort, will you?" Martin shouted after her.

"No." She'd keep that promise.

But neither of them had said a word about telling everyone in school that she and Joseph Rockwell had gotten married.

One

For the third time that afternoon, Cait indignantly wiped sawdust from the top of her desk. If this remodeling mess got much worse, the particles were going to get into her computer, destroying her vital link with the New York Stock Exchange.

"We'll have to move her out," a gruff male voice said from behind her.

"I beg your pardon," Cait demanded, rising abruptly and whirling toward the doorway. She clapped the dust from her hands, preparing to do battle. So much for this being the season of peace and goodwill. All these men in hard hats strolling through the office, moving things about, was inconvenient enough. But at least she'd been able to close her door to reduce the noise. Now, it seemed, even that would be impossible.

"We're going to have to pull some electrical wires through there," the same brusque voice explained. She couldn't see the man's face, since he stood just outside her doorway, but she had an impression of broad-shouldered height. "We'll have everything back to normal within a week."

"A week!" She wouldn't be able to service her customers, let alone function, without her desk and phone. And just exactly where did they intend to put her? Certainly not in a hallway! She wouldn't stand for it.

The mess this simple remodeling project had created was one thing, but transplanting her entire office as if she were nothing more than a…a tulip bulb was something else again.

"I'm sorry about this, Cait," Paul Jamison said, slipping past the crew foreman to her side.

The wind went out of her argument at the merest hint of his devastating smile. "Don't worry about it," she said, the picture of meekness and tolerance. "Things like this happen when a company grows as quickly as ours."

She glanced across the hallway to her best friend's office, shrugging slightly as if to ask, *Is Paul ever going to notice me?* Lindy shot her a crooked grin and a quick nod that suggested Cait stop being so negative. Her friend's confidence didn't help. Paul was a wonderful district manager and she was fortunate to have the opportunity to work with him. He was both talented and resourceful. The brokerage firm of Webster, Rodale and Missen was an affiliate of the fastest-growing firm in the country. This branch had been open for less than two years and already they were breaking sales records all across the country. Due mainly, Cait believed, to Paul's administrative skills.

Paul was slender, dark-haired and handsome in an urbane, sophisticated way—every woman's dream man. Certainly Cait's. But as far as she could determine, he didn't see her in a similar romantic light. He thought of her as an important team member. One of the staff. At most, a friend.

Cait knew that friendship was often fertile ground for romance, and she hoped for an opportunity to cultivate it. Willingly surrendering her office to an irritating crew of carpenters and electricians was sure to gain her a few points with her boss.

"Where would you like me to set up my desk in the interval?" she asked, smiling warmly at Paul. From habit, she lifted her hand to push back a stray lock of hair, forgetting she'd recently had it cut. That had been another futile attempt to attract Paul's affections—or at least his attention. Her shoulder-length chestnut-brown hair had been trimmed and permed into a pixie style with a halo of soft curls.

The difference from the tightly styled chignon she'd always worn to work was striking, or so everyone said. Everyone, except Paul. The hairdresser had claimed it changed Cait's cooly polished look into one of warmth and enthusiasm. It was exactly the image Cait wanted Paul to have of her.

Unfortunately he didn't seem to detect the slightest difference in her appearance. At least not until Lindy had pointedly commented on the change within earshot of their absentminded employer. Then, and only then, had Paul made a remark about noticing something different; he just hadn't been sure what it was, he'd said.

"I suppose we could move you..." Paul hesitated.

"Your office seems to be the best choice," the foreman said.

Cait resisted the urge to hug the man. He was tall, easily six three, and as solid as Mount Rainier, the majestic mountain she could see from her office window. She hadn't paid much attention to him until this moment and was surprised to note something vaguely familiar about him. She'd assumed he was the foreman, but she wasn't certain. He seemed to be around the office fairly often, although not on a predictable schedule. Every time he did show up, the level of activity rose dramatically.

"Ah...I suppose Cait could move in with me for the time being," Paul agreed. In her daydreams, Cait would play back this moment; her version had Paul looking at her with surprise and wonder, his mouth moving toward hers and—

"Miss?"

Cait broke out of her reverie and glanced toward the foreman—the man who'd suggested she share Paul's office. "Yes?"

"Would you show us exactly what you need moved?"

"Of course," she returned crisply. This romantic heart of hers was always getting her into trouble. She'd look at Paul and her head would start to spin with hopes and fantasies and she'd be lost....

Cait's arms were loaded with files as she followed the carpenters who hauled her desk into a corner of Paul's much larger office. Her computer and phone followed, and within fifteen minutes she was back in business.

She was on the phone, talking with one of her most important clients, when the same man walked back, unannounced, into the room. At first Caitlin assumed he was looking for Paul, who'd stepped out of the office. The foreman—or whatever he was—hesitated, then, scooping up her nameplate, he grinned at her as if he found something highly entertaining. Cait did her best to ignore him, flipping needlessly through the pages of the file.

Not taking the hint, he stepped forward and plunked the nameplate on the edge of her desk. As she glanced up in annoyance, he boldly winked at her.

Cait was not amused. How dare this…this… redneck flirt with her!

She glared at him, hoping he'd have the good manners and good sense to leave—which, of course, he didn't. In fact, he seemed downright stubborn about staying and making her as uncomfortable as possible. Her phone conversation ran its natural course and after making several notations, she replaced the receiver.

"You wanted something?" she demanded, her eyes finding his. Once more she noted his apparent amusement. It didn't make sense.

"No," he answered, grinning. "Sorry to have bothered you."

For the second time, Cait was struck by a twinge of something familiar. He strolled out of her makeshift office as if he owned the building.

Cait waited a few minutes, then approached Lindy. "Did you happen to catch his name?"

"Whose name?"

"The…man who insisted I vacate my office. I don't know who he is. I thought he was the foreman, but…" She crossed her arms and furrowed her brow, trying to remember if she'd heard anyone say his name.

"I have no idea." Lindy pushed back her chair and rolled a pencil between her palms. "He is kinda cute though, don't you think?"

A smile softened Cait's lips. "There's only one man for me and you know it."

"Then why are you asking questions about one of the construction crew?"

"I...don't know. He seems familiar for some reason, and he keeps grinning at me as if he knows something I don't. I hate it when men do that."

"Then ask one of the others what his name is. They'll tell you."

"I can't do that."

"Why not?"

"He might think I'm interested in him."

"And we both know how impossible that would be," Lindy said with mild sarcasm.

"Exactly." Lindy and probably everyone else in the office complex knew how Cait felt about Paul. The district manager himself, however, seemed to be completely oblivious. Other than throwing herself at him, which she'd seriously considered more than once, there was little she could do but be patient. One day when she was least expecting it, Cupid was going to let fly an arrow and hit her lovable boss directly between the eyes.

When it happened—and it would!—Cait planned to be ready.

"You want to go for lunch now?" Lindy asked.

Cait nodded. It was nearly two and she hadn't eaten since breakfast, which had consisted of a banana and a cup of coffee. A West Coast stockbroker's day started before dawn. Cait was generally in the office well before six and didn't stop work until the market closed at one-thirty, Seattle time. Only then did she break for something to eat.

Somewhere in the middle of her turkey on whole wheat, Cait convinced herself she was imagining things when it came to that construction worker. He'd probably been waiting around to ask her where Paul was and then changed his mind. He did say he was sorry for bothering her.

If only he hadn't winked.

He was back the following day, a tool pouch riding on his hip like a six-shooter, hard hat in place. He was issuing orders like a drill sergeant, and Cait found herself gazing after him with reluctant fascination. She'd heard he owned the construction company, and she wasn't surprised.

As she studied him, she noted once again how striking he was. Not because he was extraordinarily handsome, but because he was somehow commanding. He possessed an authority, a presence, that attracted attention wherever he went. Cait was as drawn to it as those around her. She observed how the crew instinctively turned to him for directions and approval.

The more she analyzed him, the more she recognized that he was a man who had an appetite for life. Which meant excitement, adventure and probably women, and that confused her even more because she couldn't recall ever knowing anyone quite like him. Then why did she find him so...familiar?

Cait herself had a quiet nature. She rarely ventured out of the comfortable, compact world she'd built. She had her job, a nice apartment in Seattle's university district, and a few close friends. Excitement to her was growing herbs and participating in nature walks.

The following day while she was studying the construction worker, he'd unexpectedly turned and smiled at something one of his men had said. His smile, she decided, intrigued her most. It was slightly off center and seemed to tease the corners of his mouth. He looked her way more than once and each time she thought she detected a touch of humor, an amused knowledge that lurked just beneath the surface.

"It's driving me crazy," Cait confessed to Lindy over lunch.

"What is?"

"That I can't place him."

Lindy set her elbows on the table, holding her sandwich poised in front of her mouth. She nodded slowly, her eyes distant. "When you figure it out, introduce me, will you? I could go for a guy this sexy."

So Lindy had noticed that earthy sensuality about him, too. Well, of course she had—any woman would.

After lunch, Cait returned to the office to make a few calls. He was there again.

No matter how hard she tried, she couldn't place him. Work became a pretense as she continued to scrutinize him, racking her brain. Then, when she least expected it, he strolled past her and brazenly winked a second time.

As the color clawed up her neck, Cait flashed her attention back to her computer screen.

"His name is Joe," Lindy rushed in to tell her ten minutes later. "I heard one of the men call him that."

"Joe," Cait repeated slowly. She couldn't remember ever knowing anyone named Joe.

"Does that help?"

"No," Cait said, shaking her head regretfully. If she'd ever met this man, she wasn't likely to have overlooked the experience. He wasn't someone a woman easily forgot.

"Ask him," Lindy insisted. "It's ridiculous not to. It's driving you bananas. Then," she added with infuriating logic, "when you find out, you can nonchalantly introduce me."

"I can't just waltz up and start quizzing him," Cait argued. The idea was preposterous. "He'll think I'm trying to pick him up."

"You'll go crazy if you don't."

Cait sighed. "You're right. I'm not going to sleep tonight if I don't settle this."

With Lindy waiting expectantly in her office, Cait approached him. He was talking to another one of the crew and once he'd finished, he turned to her with one of his devastating lazy smiles.

"Hello," she said, and her voice shook slightly. "Do I know you?"

"You mean you've forgotten?" he asked, sounding shocked and insulted.

"Apparently. Though I'll admit you look somewhat familiar."

"I should certainly hope so. We shared something very special a few years back."

"We did?" Cait was more confused than ever.

"Hey, Joe, there's a problem over here," a male voice shouted. "Could you come look at this?"

"I'll be with you in a minute," he answered brusquely over his shoulder. "Sorry, we'll have to talk later."

"But—"

"Say hello to Martin for me, would you?" he asked as he stalked past her and into the room that had once been Cait's office.

Martin, her brother. Cait hadn't a clue what her

brother could possibly have to do with this. Mentally she ran through a list of his teenage friends and came up blank.

Then it hit her. Bull's-eye. Her heart started to pound until it roared like a tropical storm in her ears. Mechanically Cait made her way back to Lindy's office. She sank into a chair beside the desk and stared into space.

"Well?" Lindy pressed. "Don't keep me in suspense."

"Um, it's not that easy to explain."

"You remember him, then?"

She nodded. Oh, Lord, did she ever.

"Good grief, what's wrong? You've gone so pale!"

Cait tried to come up with an explanation that wouldn't sound...ridiculous.

"Tell me," Lindy insisted. "Don't just sit there wearing a silly grin and looking like you're about to faint."

"Um, it goes back a few years."

"All right. Start there."

"Remember how kids sometimes do silly things? Like when you're young and foolish and don't know any better?"

"Me, yes, but not you," Lindy said calmly. "You're perfect. In all the time we've been friends, I haven't seen you do one impulsive thing. Not one. You analyze everything before you act. I can't imagine you ever doing anything silly."

"I did once," Cait corrected, "but I was only eight."

"What could you have possibly done at age eight?"

"I...I got married."

"Married?" Lindy half rose from her chair. "You've got to be kidding."

"I wish I was."

"I'll bet a week's commissions that your husband's name is Joe." Lindy was smiling now, smiling widely.

Cait nodded and tried to smile in return.

"What's there to worry about? Good grief, kids do that sort of thing all the time! It doesn't mean anything."

"But I was a real brat about it. Joe and my brother, Martin, were best friends. Joe wanted to know what it felt like to kiss a girl, and I insisted he marry me first. If that wasn't bad enough, I pressured them into performing the ceremony inside their boys-only fort."

"So, you were a bit of pain—most eight-year-old girls are when it comes to dealing with their brothers. He got what he wanted, didn't he?"

Cait took a deep breath and nodded again.

"What was kissing him like?" Lindy asked in a curiously throaty voice.

"Good heavens, I don't remember," Cait answered shortly, then reconsidered. "I take that back. As I recall, it wasn't so bad, though obviously neither one of us had a clue what we were doing."

"Lindy, you're still here," Paul said as he strolled into the office. He nodded briefly in Cait's direction, but she had the impression he barely saw her. He'd hardly been around in the past couple of days—almost as if he was purposely avoiding her, she mused, but that thought was too painful to consider.

"I was just finishing up," Lindy said, glancing guiltily toward Cait. "We both were."

"Fine, fine, I didn't mean to disturb you. I'll see you two in the morning." With that he was gone.

Cait gazed after him with thinly disguised emotion. She waited until Paul was out of earshot before she spoke. "He's so blind. What do I have to do, hit him over the head?"

"Quit being so negative," Lindy admonished. "You're going to be sharing an office with him for another five days. Do whatever you need to make darn sure he notices you."

"I've tried," Cait murmured, discouraged. And she had. She'd tried every trick known to woman, with little success.

Lindy left the office before her. Cait gathered up some stock reports to read that evening and stacked them neatly inside her leather briefcase. What Lindy had said about her being methodical and careful was true. It was also a source of pride; those traits had served her clients well.

To Cait's dismay, Joe followed her. "So," he said, smiling down at her, apparently oblivious to the other people clustering around the elevator. "Who have you been kissing these days?"

Hot color rose instantly to her face. Did he have to humiliate her in public?

"I could find myself jealous, you know."

"Would you kindly stop," she whispered furiously, glaring at him. Her hand tightened around the handle of her briefcase so hard her fingers ached.

"You figured it out?"

She nodded, her eyes darting to the lighted numbers above the elevator door, praying it would make its descent in record time instead of pausing on each floor.

"The years have been good to you."

"Thank you." *Please hurry,* she urged the elevator.

"I never would've believed Martin's little sister would turn out to be such a beauty."

If he was making fun of her, she didn't appreciate it. She was attractive, she knew that, but she certainly wasn't waiting for anyone to place a tiara on her head. "Thank you," she repeated grudgingly.

He gave an exaggerated sigh. "How are our children doing? What were their names again?" When she didn't answer right away, he added, "Don't tell me you've forgotten."

"Barbie and Ken," she muttered under her breath.

"That's right. I remember now."

If Joe hadn't drawn the attention of her co-workers before, he had now. Cait could have sworn every single person standing by the elevator turned to stare at her. The hope that no one was interested in their conversation was forever lost.

"Just how long do you intend to tease me about this?" she snapped.

"That depends," Joe responded with a chuckle Cait could only describe as sadistic. She gritted her teeth. He might have found the situation amusing, but she derived little enjoyment from being the office laughingstock.

Just then the elevator arrived, and not a moment too soon to suit Cait. The instant the doors slid open, she stepped toward it, determined to get as far away from this irritating man as possible.

He quickly caught up with her and she whirled

around to face him, her back ramrod stiff. "Is this really necessary?" she hissed, painfully conscious of the other people crowding into the elevator ahead of her.

He grinned. "I suppose not. I just wanted to see if I could get a rise out of you. It never worked when we were kids, you know. You were always so prim and proper."

"Look, you didn't like me then and I see no reason for you to—"

"Not *like* you?" he countered loud enough for everyone in the building to hear. "I married you, didn't I?"

Two

Cait's heart seemed to stop. She realized that not only the people on the elevator but everyone left in the office was staring at her with unconcealed interest. The elevator was about to close and she quickly stepped forward, straightening her arms to hold the doors open. She felt like Samson balanced between two marble columns.

"It's not like it sounds," she felt obliged to explain in a loud voice, her gaze pleading.

No one made eye contact with her and, desperate, she turned to glare at Joe, issuing him a silent challenge to retract his words. His eyes were sparkling with mischief. If he did say anything, Cait thought in sudden horror, it was bound to make things even worse.

There didn't seem to be anything to do but tell the truth. "In case anyone has the wrong impression, this man and I are not married," she shouted. "Good grief, I was only eight!"

There was no reaction. It was as if she'd vanished into thin air. Defeated, she dropped her arms and stepped back, freeing the doors, which promptly closed.

Ignoring the other people on the elevator—who

were carefully ignoring her—Cait clenched her hands into hard fists and glared up at Joe. Her face tightened with anger. "That was a rotten thing to do," she whispered hoarsely.

"What? It's true, isn't it?" he whispered back.

"You're being ridiculous to talk as though we're married!"

"We were once. It wounds me that you treat our marriage so lightly."

"I…it wasn't legal." The fact that they were even discussing this was preposterous. "You can't possibly hold me responsible for something that happened so long ago. To play this game now is…is infantile, and I refuse to be part of it."

The elevator finally came to a halt on the ground floor and, eager to make her escape, Cait rushed out. Straightening to keep her dignity intact, she headed through the crowded foyer toward the front doors. Although it was midafternoon, dusk was already settling, casting dark shadows between the towering office buildings.

Cait reached the first intersection and sighed in relief as she glanced around her. Good. No sign of Joseph Rockwell. The light was red and she paused, although others hurried across the street after checking for traffic; Cait always felt obliged to obey the signal.

"What do you think Paul's going to say when he hears about this?" Joe asked behind her.

Cait gave a start, then turned to look at her tormenter. She hadn't thought about Paul's reaction. Her throat seemed to constrict, rendering her speechless, otherwise she would have demanded Joe leave her alone. But he'd raised a question she dared not ignore.

Paul might hear about her former relationship with Joe and might even think there was something between them.

"You're in love with him, aren't you?"

She nodded. At the very mention of Paul's name, her knees went weak. He was everything she wanted in a man and more. She'd been crazy about him for months and now it was all about to be ruined by this irritating, unreasonable ghost from her past.

"Who told you?" Cait snapped. She couldn't imagine Lindy betraying her confidence, but Cait hadn't told anyone else.

"No one had to tell me," Joe explained. "It's written all over you."

Shocked, Cait stared at Joe, her heart sinking. "Do…do you think Paul knows how I feel?"

Joe shrugged. "Maybe."

"But Lindy said…"

The light changed and, clasping her elbow, Joe urged her into the street. "What was it Lindy said?" he prompted when they'd crossed.

Cait glanced up, about to tell him, when she realized exactly what she was doing—conversing with her antagonist. This was the very man who'd gone out of his way to embarrass and humiliate her in front of the entire office staff. Not to mention assorted clients and carpenters.

She stiffened. "Never mind what Lindy said. Now if you'll kindly excuse me…" With her head held high, she marched down the sidewalk. She hadn't gone more than a few feet when the hearty sound of Joe's laughter caught up with her.

"You haven't changed in twenty years, Caitlin Marshall. Not a single bit."

Gritting her teeth, she marched on.

"Do you think Paul's heard?" Cait asked Lindy the instant she had a free moment the following afternoon. The New York Stock Exchange had closed for the day and Cait hadn't seen Paul since morning. It looked like he really *was* avoiding her.

"I wouldn't know," Lindy said as she typed some figures into her computer. "But the word about your childhood marriage has spread like wildfire everywhere else. It's the joke of the day. What did you and Joe do? Make a public announcement before you left the office yesterday afternoon?"

It was so nearly the truth that Cait guiltily looked away. "I didn't say a word," she defended herself. "Joe was the one."

"He told everyone you were married?" A suspicious tilt at the corner of her mouth betrayed Lindy's amusement.

"Not exactly. He started asking about our children in front of everyone."

"There were children?"

Cait resisted the urge to close her eyes and count to ten. "No. I brought my dolls to the wedding. Listen, I don't want to rehash a silly incident that happened years ago. I'm more afraid Paul's going to hear about it and put the wrong connotation on the whole thing. There's absolutely nothing between me and Joseph Rockwell. More than likely Paul won't give the matter a second thought, but I don't want there to be any...doubts between us, if you know what I mean."

"If you're so worried about it, talk to him," Lindy advised without lifting her eyes from the screen. "Honesty is the best policy, you know that."

"Yes, but it could prove to be a bit embarrassing, don't you think?"

"Paul will respect you for telling him the truth before he hears the rumors from someone else. Frankly, Cait, I think you're making a fuss over nothing. It isn't like you've committed a felony, you know."

"I realize that."

"Paul will probably be amused, like everyone else. He's not going to say anything." She looked up quickly, as though she expected Cait to try yet another argument.

Cait didn't. Instead she mulled over her friend's advice, gnawing on her lower lip. "I think you might be right. Paul will respect me for explaining the situation myself, instead of ignoring everything." Telling him the truth could be helpful in other respects, too, now that she thought about it.

If Paul had any feeling for her whatsoever, and oh, how she prayed he did, then he might become just a little jealous of her relationship with Joseph Rockwell. After all, Joe was an attractive man in a rugged outdoor sort of way. He was tall and muscular and, well, good-looking. The kind of good-looking that appealed to women—not Cait, of course, but other women. Hadn't Lindy commented almost immediately on how attractive he was?

"You're right," Cait said, walking resolutely toward the office she was temporarily sharing with Paul. Although she'd felt annoyed, at first, about being shuffled out of her own space, she'd come to think of this inconvenience as a blessing in disguise. However, she had to admit she'd been disappointed thus far. She had assumed she'd be spending a lot of time alone with him. That hadn't happened yet.

The more Cait considered the idea of a heart-to-heart talk with her boss, the more appealing it became. As was her habit, she mentally rehearsed what she wanted to say to him, then gave herself a small pep talk.

"I don't remember that you talked to yourself." The male voice booming behind her startled Cait. "But then there's a great deal I've missed over the years, isn't there, Caitlin?"

Cait was so rattled she nearly stumbled. "What are you doing here?" she demanded. "Why do you insist on following me around? Can't you see I'm busy?" He was the last person she wanted to confront just now.

"Sorry." He raised both hands in a gesture of apology contradicted by his twinkling blue eyes. "How about lunch later?"

He was teasing. He had to be. Besides, it would be insane for her to have anything to do with Joseph Rockwell. Heaven only knew what would happen if she gave him the least bit of encouragement. He'd probably hire a skywriter and announce to the entire city that they'd married as children.

"It shouldn't be that difficult to agree to a luncheon date," he informed her coolly.

"You're serious about this?"

"Of course I'm serious. We have a lot of years to catch up on." His hand rested on his leather pouch, giving him a rakish air of indifference.

"I've got an appointment this afternoon..." She offered the first plausible excuse she could think of; it might be uninspired but it also happened to be true. She'd made plans to eat lunch with Lindy.

"Dinner then. I'm anxious to hear what Martin's been up to."

"Martin," she repeated, stalling for time while she invented another excuse. This wasn't a situation she had much experience with. She did date, but infrequently.

"Listen, bright eyes, no need to look so concerned. This isn't an invitation to the senior prom. It's one friend to another. Strictly platonic."

"You won't mention...our wedding to the waiter. Or anyone else?"

"I promise." As if to offer proof of his intent, he licked the end of his index finger and crossed his heart. "That was Martin's and my secret pledge sign. If either of us broke our word, the other was entitled to come up with a punishment. We both understood it would be a fate worse than death."

"I don't need any broken pledge to torture you, Joseph Rockwell. In two days you've managed to turn my life into..." She paused midsentence as Paul Jamison casually strolled past. He glanced in Cait's direction and smiled benignly.

"Hello, Paul," she called out, weakly raising her right hand. He looked exceptionally handsome this morning in a three-piece dark blue suit. The contrast between him and Joe, who was wearing dust-covered jeans, heavy boots and a tool pouch, was so striking that Cait had to force herself not to stare at her boss. If only Paul had been the one to invite her to dinner...

"If you'll excuse me," she said politely, edging her way around Joe and toward Paul, who'd gone into his office. Their office. The need to talk to him burned within her. Words of explanation began to form themselves in her mind.

Joe caught her by the shoulders, bringing her up short. Cait gasped and raised shocked eyes to his.

"Dinner," he reminded her.

She blinked, hardly knowing what to say. "All right," she mumbled distractedly and recited her address, eager to have him gone.

"Good. I'll pick you up tonight at six." With that he released her and stalked away.

After taking a couple of moments to compose herself, Cait headed toward the office. "Hello, Paul," she said, standing just inside the doorway. "Do you have a moment to talk?"

He glanced up from a file on his desk and grinned warmly. "Of course, Cait. Sit down and make yourself comfortable."

She moved into the room and closed the door behind her. When she looked back to Paul, he'd cocked his eyebrows in surprise. "Problems?" he asked.

"Not exactly." She pulled out the chair opposite his desk and slowly sat down. Now that she had his full attention, she was at a loss. All her prepared explanations and witticisms had flown out of her head. "The rate on municipal bonds has been exceptionally high lately," she commented nervously.

Paul agreed with a quick nod. "They have been for several months now."

"Yes, I know. That's what makes them such excellent value.'' Cait had been selling bonds heavily in the past few weeks.

"You didn't close the door to talk to me about bonds," Paul said softly. "What's troubling you, Cait?"

She laughed uncomfortably, wondering how a man could be so astute in one area and blind in another. If only he would reveal some emotion toward her. Anything. All he did was sit across from her and wait. He was cordial enough, gracious even, but there was no hint of more. Nothing to give Cait any hope that he was starting to care for her.

"It's about Joseph Rockwell."

"The contractor who's handling the remodeling?"

Cait nodded. "I knew him years ago when we were just children." She glanced at Paul, whose face remained blank. "We were neighbors. In fact Joe and my brother, Martin, were best friends. Joe moved out to the suburbs when he and Martin were in the sixth grade and I hadn't heard anything from him since."

"It's a small world, isn't it?" Paul remarked affably enough.

"Joe and Martin were typical young boys," she said, rushing her words a little in her eagerness to have this out in the open. "Full of tomfoolery and pranks."

"Boys will be boys," Paul said without any real enthusiasm.

"Yes, I know. Once—" she forced a light laugh "—they actually involved me in one of their crazy schemes."

"What did they put you up to? Robbing a bank?"

She somehow managed a smile. "Not exactly. Joe—I always called him Joseph back then, because it irritated him. Anyway, Joe and Martin had this friend named Pete who was a year older and he'd spent part of his summer vacation visiting his aunt in Peoria, at least I think it was Peoria… Anyway he came back bragging about having kissed a girl. Naturally Martin and Joe were jealous and as you said, boys will be boys, so they decided that one of them should test it out and see if kissing a girl was everything Pete claimed it was.''

"I take it they decided to make you their guinea pig.''

"Exactly.'' Cait slid to the edge of the chair, delighted that Paul was following this rather convoluted explanation. "I was eight and considered something of a…pest.'' She paused, hoping Paul would make some comment about how impossible that was. When he didn't, she continued, a little disappointed at his restraint. "Apparently I was more of one than I remembered,'' she said, with another forced laugh. "At eight, I didn't think kissing was something nice girls did, at least not without a wedding band on their finger.''

"So you kissed Joseph Rockwell,'' Paul said absently.

"Yes, but there was a tiny bit more than that. I made him marry me.''

Paul's eyebrows shot to the ceiling.

"Now, almost twenty years later, he's getting his revenge by going around telling everyone within earshot that we're actually married. Which of course is ridiculous.''

A couple of strained seconds followed her announcement.

"I'm not sure what to say," Paul murmured.

"Oh, I wasn't expecting you to say anything. I thought it was important to clear the air, that's all."

"I see."

"He's only doing it because…well, because that's Joe. Even when we were kids he enjoyed playing these little games. No one really minded, though, at least not the girls, because he was so cute." She certainly had Paul's attention now.

"I thought you should know," she added, "in case you happened to hear a rumor or something. I didn't want you thinking Joe and I were involved or even considering a relationship. I was fairly certain you wouldn't, but one never knows and I'm a firm believer in being forthright and honest."

Paul blinked. Wanting to fill the awkward silence, Cait chattered on. "Apparently Joe recognized my name when he and his men moved my office in here with yours. He was delighted when I didn't recognize him. In fact, he caused something of a commotion by asking me about our children in front of everyone."

"Children?"

"My dolls," Cait was quick to explain.

"Joe Rockwell's an excellent man. I couldn't fault your taste, Cait."

"The two of us aren't involved," she protested. "Good grief, I haven't seen him in nearly twenty years."

"I see," Paul said slowly. He sounded… disappointed, Cait thought. But she must have misread his tone because there wasn't a single, solitary reason for him to be disappointed. Cait felt foolish now for even trying to explain this fiasco. Paul was so blind when it came to her feelings that there was nothing she could say or do to make him understand.

"I just wanted you to know," she repeated, "in case you heard the rumors and were wondering if there was anything between me and Joseph Rockwell. I wanted to assure you there isn't."

"I see," he said again. "Don't worry about it, Cait. What happened between you and Rockwell isn't going to affect your job."

She stood up to leave, praying she would detect a suggestion of jealousy. A hint of rivalry. Anything to show he cared. There was nothing, so she tried again. "I agreed to have dinner with him, though."

Paul had returned his attention to the papers he'd been reading when she'd interrupted him.

"For old times' sake," she added in a reassuring voice—to fend off any violent display of resentment, she told herself. "I certainly don't have any intention of dating him on a regular basis."

Paul grinned. "Have a good time."

"Yes, I will, thanks." Her heart felt as heavy as a sinking battleship. Without thought of where she was headed or who she would talk to, Cait wandered out of Paul's office, forgetting for a second that she had no office of her own. The area where her desk once sat was cluttered with wire reels, ladders and men. Joe must have left, a fact for which Cait was grateful.

She walked into Lindy's small office across the aisle. Her friend glanced up. "So?" she murmured. "Did you talk to Paul?"

Cait nodded.

"How'd it go?"

"Fine, I guess." She perched on the corner of Lindy's desk, crossing her arms around her waist as her left leg swung rhythmically, keeping time with her discouraged heart. She should be accustomed to disappointment when it came to dealing with Paul, but somehow each rejection inflicted a fresh wound on her already battered ego. "I was hoping Paul might be jealous."

"And he wasn't?"

"Not that I could tell."

"It isn't as though you and Joe have anything to do with each other now," Lindy sensibly pointed out. "Marrying him was a childhood prank. It isn't likely to concern Paul."

"I even mentioned that I was going out to dinner with Joe," Cait said morosely.

"You are? When?" Lindy asked, her eyes lighting up. "Where?"

If only Paul had revealed half as much interest. "Tonight. And I don't know where."

"You are going, aren't you?"

"I guess. I can't see any way of avoiding it. No doubt he'll pester me until I give in. If I ever marry and have daughters, Lindy, I'm going to warn them about boys from the time they're old enough to understand."

"Don't you think you should follow your own advice?" Lindy asked, glancing pointedly in the direction of Paul's office.

"Not if I were to have Paul's children," Cait said, eager to defend her boss. "Our daughter would be so intelligent and perceptive she wouldn't need to be warned."

Lindy's returning smile was distracted. "Listen, I've got a few things to finish up here. Why don't you go over to the deli and grab us a table. I'll meet you there in fifteen minutes."

"Sure," Cait agreed. "Do you want me to order for you?"

"No. I don't know what I want yet."

"Okay, I'll see you in a few minutes."

They often ate at the deli across the street from their office complex. The food was good, the service fast, and generally by three in the afternoon, Cait was famished.

She was so wrapped up in her thoughts, which were muddled and gloomy following her talk with Paul, that she didn't notice how late Lindy was. Her friend rushed into the restaurant more than half an hour after Cait had arrived.

"I'm sorry," she said, sounding flustered and oddly shaken. "I had no idea those last odds and ends would take me so long. Oh, you must be starved. I hope you've ordered." Lindy removed her coat and stuffed it into the booth before sliding onto the red upholstered seat herself.

"Actually, no, I didn't." Cait sighed. "Just tea." Her spirits were at an all-time low. It was becoming painfully clear that Paul didn't harbor a single romantic feeling toward her. She was wasting her time and her emotional energy on him. If only she'd had more experience with the opposite sex. It seemed her whole love life had gone into neutral the moment she'd graduated from college. At the rate matters were developing, she'd still be single by the time she turned thirty—a possibility too dismal to contemplate. She hadn't given much thought to marriage and children, always assuming they'd become part of her life; now she wasn't so sure. Even as a child, she'd pictured her grown-up self with a career *and* a family. Behind the business exterior was a woman traditional enough to hunger for that most special of relationships.

She had to face the fact that marriage would never happen if she continued to love a man who didn't return her feelings. She gave a low groan, then noticed that Lindy was gazing at her in concern.

"Let's order something," Lindy said quickly, reaching for the menu tucked behind the napkin holder. "I'm starved."

"I was thinking I'd skip lunch today," Cait mumbled. She sipped her lukewarm tea and frowned. "Joe will be taking me out to dinner soon. And frankly, I don't have much of an appetite."

"This is all my fault, isn't it?" Lindy asked, looking guilty.

"Of course not. I'm just being practical." If Cait was anything, it was practical—except about Paul. "Go ahead and order."

"You're sure you don't mind?"

Cait gestured nonchalantly. "Heavens, no."

"If you're sure, then I'll have the turkey on whole wheat," Lindy said after a moment. "You know how I like turkey, though you'd think I'd have gotten enough over Thanksgiving."

"I'll just have a refill on my tea," Cait said.

"You're still flying to Minnesota for the holidays, aren't you?" Lindy asked, fidgeting with the menu.

"Mmm-hmm." Cait had purchased her ticket several months earlier. Martin and his family lived near

Minneapolis. When their father had died several years earlier, Cait's mother moved to Minnesota, settling down in a new subdivision not far from Martin, his wife and their four children. Cait tried to visit at least once a year. However, she'd been there in August, stopping off on her way home from a business trip. Usually she made a point of visiting her brother and his family over the Christmas holidays. It was generally a slow week on the stock market, anyway. And if she was going to travel halfway across the country, she wanted to make it worth her while.

"When will you be leaving?" Lindy asked, although Cait was sure she'd already told her friend more than once.

"The twenty-third." For the past few years, Cait had used one week of her vacation at Christmas time, usually starting the weekend before.

But this year Paul was having a Christmas party and Cait didn't want to miss that, so she'd booked her flight closer to the holiday.

The waitress came to take Lindy's order and replenish the hot water for Cait's tea. The instant she moved away from their booth, Lindy launched into a lengthy tirade about how she hated Christmas shopping and how busy the malls were this time of year. Cait stared at her, bewildered. It wasn't like her friend to chat nonstop.

"Lindy," she interrupted, "is something wrong?"

"Wrong? What could possibly be wrong?"

"I don't know. You haven't stopped talking for the last ten minutes."

"I haven't?" There was an abrupt, uncomfortable silence.

Cait decided it was her turn to say something. "I think I'll wear my red velvet dress," she mused.

"To dinner with Joe?"

"No," she said, shaking her head. "To Paul's Christmas party."

Lindy sighed. "But what are you wearing tonight?"

The question took Cait by surprise. She didn't consider this dinner with Joe a real date. He just wanted to talk over old times, which was fine with Cait as long as he behaved himself. Suddenly she glanced up and frowned, then closed her eyes. "Martin's a Methodist minister," she said softly.

"Yes, I know," Lindy reminded her. "I've known that since I first met you, which was what? Three years ago now."

"Four last month."

"So what does Martin's occupation have to do with anything?" Lindy wanted to know.

"Joe Rockwell can't find out," Cait whispered.

"I didn't plan on telling him," Lindy whispered back.

"I've got to make up some other occupation like..."

"Counselor," Lindy suggested. "I'm curious, though. Why can't you tell Joe about Martin?"

"Think about it!"

"I am thinking. I really doubt Joe would care one way or the other."

"He might put some connotation on it. You don't know Joe the way I do. He'd razz me about it all evening, claiming the marriage was valid. You know, because Martin really *is* a minister, and since Martin performed the ceremony, we must really be married—that kind of nonsense.''

''I didn't think of that.''

But then, Lindy didn't seem to be thinking much about anything of late. It was as if she was walking about in a perpetual daydream. Cait couldn't remember Lindy's ever being so scatterbrained. If she didn't know better she'd think there was a man involved.

Three

At ten to six, Cait was blow-drying her hair in a haphazard fashion, regretting that she'd ever had it cut. She was looking forward to this dinner date about as much as a trip to the dentist. All she wanted was to get it over with, come home and bury her head under a pillow while she sorted out how she was going to get Paul to notice her.

Restyling her hair hadn't done the trick. Putting in extra hours at the office hadn't impressed him, either. Cait was beginning to think she could stand on top of his desk naked and not attract his attention.

She walked into her compact living room and smoothed the bulky-knit sweater over her slim hips. She hadn't dressed for the occasion, although the sweater was new and expensive. Gray wool slacks and a powder-blue turtleneck with a silver heart-shaped necklace dangling from her neck were about as dressy as she cared to get with someone like Joe. He'd probably be wearing cowboy boots and jeans, if not his hard hat and tool pouch.

Oh, yes, Cait had recognized his type when she'd first seen him. Joe Rockwell was a man's man. He walked and talked macho. No doubt he drove a truck with tires so high off the ground she'd need a stepladder to climb inside. He was tough and gruff and liked his women meek and submissive. In that case, of course, she had nothing to worry about.

He arrived right on time, which surprised Cait. Being prompt didn't fit the image she had of Joe Rockwell, redneck contractor. She sighed and painted on a smile, then walked slowly to the door.

The smile faded. Joe stood before her, tall and debonair, dressed in a dark gray pin-striped suit. His gray silk tie had *pink* stripes. He was the picture of smooth sophistication. She knew that Joe was the same man she'd seen earlier in dusty work clothes—yet he was different. He was nothing like Paul, of course. But Joseph Rockwell was a devastatingly handsome man. With a devastating charm. Rarely had she seen a man smile the way he did. His eyes twinkled with warmth and life and mischief. It wasn't difficult to imagine Joe with a little boy whose eyes mirrored his. Cait didn't know where that thought came from, but she pushed it aside before it could linger and take root.

"Hello," he said, flashing her that smile.

"Hi." She couldn't stop looking at him.

"May I come in?"

"Oh…of course. I'm sorry," she faltered, stumbling in her haste to step aside. He'd caught her completely off guard. "I was about to change clothes," she said quickly.

"You look fine."

"These old things?" She feigned a laugh. "If you'll excuse me, I'll only be a minute." She poured him a cup of coffee, then dashed into her bedroom, ripping the sweater over her head and closing the door with one foot. Her shoes went flying as she ran to her closet. Jerking aside the orderly row of business jackets and skirts, she pulled clothes off their hangers, considered them, then tossed them on the bed. Nearly everything she owned was more suitable for the office than a dinner date.

The only really special dress she owned was the red velvet one she'd purchased for Paul's Christmas party. The temptation to slip into that was strong but she resisted, wanting to save it for her boss, though heaven knew he probably wouldn't notice.

Deciding on a skirt and blazer, she hopped frantically around her bedroom as she pulled on her panty hose. Next she threw on a rose-colored silk blouse and managed to button it while stepping into her skirt. She tucked the blouse into the waistband and her feet into a pair of medium-heeled pumps. Finally, her velvet blazer and she was ready. Taking a deep breath, she returned to the living room in three minutes flat.

"That was fast," Joe commented, standing by the fireplace, hands clasped behind his back. He was examining a framed photograph that sat on the mantel. "Is this Martin's family?"

"Martin...why, yes, that's Martin, his wife and their children." She hoped he didn't detect the breathless catch in her voice.

"Four children."

"Yes, he and Rebecca decided they wanted a large family." Her heartbeat was slowly returning to normal though Cait still felt light-headed. She had a sneaking suspicion that she was suffering from the effects of unleashed male charm.

She realized with surprise that Joe hadn't once said or done anything to embarrass or fluster her. She'd expected him to arrive with a whole series of remarks designed to disconcert her.

"Timmy's ten, Kurt's eight, Jenny's six and Clay's four." She introduced the freckle-faced youngsters, pointing each one out.

"They're handsome children."

"They are, aren't they?"

Cait experienced a twinge of pride. The main reason she went to Minneapolis every year was Martin's children. They adored her and she was crazy about them. Christmas wouldn't be Christmas without Jenny and Clay snuggling on her lap while their father read them the Nativity story. Christmas was singing carols in front of a crackling wood fire, accompanied by Martin's guitar. It meant stringing popcorn and cranberries for the seven-foot-tall tree that always adorned the living room. It was having the children take turns licking fudge from the sides of the copper kettle, and supervising the decorating of sugar cookies with all four crowded around the kitchen table. Caitlin Marshall might be a dedicated stockbroker with an impressive clientele, but when it came to Martin's children, she was Auntie Cait.

"It's difficult to think of Martin with kids," Joe said, carefully placing the family photo back on the mantel.

"He met Rebecca his first year of college and the rest, as they say, is history."

"What about you?" Joe asked, turning unexpectedly to face her.

"What about me?"

"Why haven't you married?"

"Uh..." Cait wasn't sure how to answer him. She

had a glib reply she usually gave when anyone asked, but somehow she knew Joe wouldn't accept that. "I...I've never really fallen in love."

"What about Paul?"

"Until Paul," she corrected, stunned that she'd forgotten the strong feelings she held for her employer. She'd been so concerned with being honest that she'd overlooked the obvious. "I am deeply in love with Paul," she said defiantly, wanting there to be no misunderstanding.

"There's no need to convince me, Caitlin."

"I'm not trying to convince you of anything. I've been in love with Paul for nearly a year. Once he realizes he loves me too, we'll be married."

Joe's mouth slanted in a wry line and he seemed about to argue with her. Cait waylaid any attempt by glancing pointedly at her watch. "Shouldn't we be leaving?"

After a long moment, Joe said, "Yes, I suppose we should," in a mild, neutral voice.

Cait went to the hall closet for her coat, aware with every step she took that Joe was watching her. She turned back to smile at him, but somehow the smile didn't materialize. His blue eyes met hers, and she found his look disturbing—caressing, somehow, and intimate.

Joe helped her on with her coat and led her to the parking lot, where he'd left his car. Another surprise awaited her. It wasn't a four-wheel-drive truck, but a late sixties black convertible in mint condition.

The restaurant was one of the most respected in Seattle, with a noted chef and a reputation for excellent seafood. Cait chose grilled salmon and Joe ordered Cajun shrimp.

"Do you remember the time Martin and I decided to open our own business?" Joe asked, as they sipped a predinner glass of wine.

Cait did indeed recall that summer. "You might have been a bit more ingenious. A lemonade stand wasn't the world's most creative enterprise."

"Perhaps not, but we were doing a brisk business until an annoying eight-year-old girl ruined everything."

Cait wasn't about to let that comment pass. "You were using moldy lemons and covering the taste with too much sugar. Besides, it's unhealthy to share paper cups."

Joe chuckled, the sound deep and rich. "I should have known then you were nothing but trouble."

"It seems to me that the whole mess was your own fault. You boys wouldn't listen to me. I had to do something before someone got sick on those lemons."

"Carrying a picket sign that read 'Talk to me before you buy this lemonade' was a bit drastic even for you, don't you think?"

"If anything, it brought you more business." Cait said dryly, recalling how her plan had backfired. "All the boys in the neighborhood wanted to see what contaminated lemonade tasted like."

"You were a damn nuisance, Cait. Own up to it." He smiled and Cait sincerely doubted that any woman could argue with him when he smiled full-force.

"I most certainly was not! If anything you two were—"

"Disgusting, I believe, was your favorite word for Martin and me."

"And you did your level best to live up to it," she said, struggling to hold back a smile. She reached for a breadstick and bit into it to disguise her amusement. She'd always enjoyed rankling Martin and Joe, though she'd never have admitted it, especially at the age of eight.

"Picketing our lemonade stand wasn't the worst trick you ever pulled, either," Joe said mischievously.

Cait had trouble swallowing. She should have been prepared for this. If he remembered her complaints about the lemonade stand, he was sure to remember what had happened once Betsy McDonald found out about the kissing incident.

"It wasn't a trick," Cait protested.

"But you told everyone at school that I'd kissed you—even though you'd promised not to."

"Not exactly." There was a small discrepancy that needed clarification. "If you think back you'll remember you said I couldn't tell anyone I'd been inside the fort. You didn't say anything about the kiss."

Joe frowned darkly as if attempting to jog his memory. "How can you remember details like that? All this happened years ago."

"I remember everything," Cait said grandly—a gross exaggeration. She hadn't recognized Joe, after all. But on this one point she was absolutely clear. "You and Martin were far more concerned that I not tell anyone about going inside the fort. You didn't say a word about keeping the kiss a secret."

"But did you have to tell Betsy McDonald? That girl had been making eyes at me for weeks. As soon as she learned I'd kissed you instead of her, she was furious.''

"Betsy was the most popular girl in school. I wanted her for my friend, so I told.''

"And sold me down the river.''

"Would an apology help?'' Confident he was teasing her once again, Cait gave him her most charming smile.

"An apology just might do it.'' Joe grinned back, a grin that brightened his eyes to a deeper, more tantalizing shade of blue. It was with some difficulty that Cait pulled her gaze away from his.

"If Betsy liked you,'' she asked, smoothing the linen napkin across her lap, "then why didn't you kiss her? She'd probably have let you. You wouldn't have had to bribe her with your precious baseball cards, either.''

"You're kidding. If I kissed Betsy McDonald I might as well have signed over my soul,'' Joe said, continuing the joke.

"Even as mere children, men are afraid of commitment,'' Cait said solemnly.

Joe ignored her comment.

"Your memory's not as sharp as you think,'' Cait felt obliged to tell him, enjoying herself more than she'd thought possible.

Once again, Joe overlooked her comment. "I can remember Martin complaining about how you'd line up your dolls in a row and teach them school. Once you even got him to come in as a guest lecturer. Heaven knew what you had to do to get him to play professor to a bunch of dolls.''

"I found a pair of dirty jeans stuffed under the sofa

with something dead in the pocket. Mom would have tanned his hide if she'd found them, so Martin owed me a favor. Then he got all bent out of shape when I collected it. He didn't seem the least bit appreciative that I'd saved him.''

"Good old Martin," Joe said, shaking his head. "I swear he was as big on ceremony as you were. Marrying us was a turning point in his life. From that point on, he started carting a Bible around with him the way some kids do a slingshot. Right in his hip pocket. If he wasn't burying something, he was holding revival meetings. Remember how he got in a pack of trouble at school for writing 'God loves you, ask Martin' on the back wall of the school?"

"I remember."

"I half expected him to become a missionary."

"Martin?" She gave an abrupt laugh. "Never. He likes his conveniences. He doesn't even go camping. Martin's idea of roughing it is doing without valet service."

She expected Joe to chuckle. He did smile at her attempted joke, but that was all. He seemed to be studying her the same way she'd been studying him.

"You surprise me," Joe announced suddenly.

"I do? Am I a disappointment to you?"

"Not in the least. I always thought you'd grow up and have a passel of children yourself. You used to haul those dolls of yours around with you everywhere. If Martin and I were too noisy, you'd shush us, saying the babies were asleep. If we wanted to play in the backyard, we couldn't because you were having a tea party with your dolls. It was enough to drive a ten-year-old boy crazy. But if we ever dared complain, you'd look at us serenely and with the sweetest smile tell us we had to be patient because it was for the children.''

''I did get carried away with all that motherhood business, didn't I?'' Joe's words stirred up uncomfortable memories, the same ones she'd entertained earlier that afternoon. She really did love children. Yet, somehow, without her quite knowing how it had happened, the years had passed and she'd buried the dream. Nowadays she didn't like to think too much about a husband and family—the life that hadn't happened. It haunted her at odd moments.

''I should have known you'd end up in construction,'' she said, switching the subject away from herself.

''How's that?'' Joe asked.

''Wasn't it you who built the fort?''

''Martin helped.''

''Sure, by staying out of the way.'' She grinned. ''I know my brother. He's a marvel with people, but please don't ever give him a hammer.''

Their dinner arrived, and it was as delicious as Cait had expected, although by then she was enjoying herself so much that even a plateful of dry toast would have tasted good. They drank two cups of cappuccino after their meal, and talked and laughed as the hours melted away. Cait couldn't remember the last time she'd laughed so much.

When at last she happened to glance at her watch, she was shocked to realize it was well past ten. ''I had no idea it was so late!'' she said. ''I should probably get home.'' She had to be up by five.

Joe took care of the bill and collected her coat.

When they walked outside, the December night was clear and chilly, with a multitude of stars twinkling brightly above.

"Are you cold?" he asked as they waited for the valet to deliver the car.

"Not at all." Nevertheless, he placed his arm around her shoulders, drawing her close.

Cait didn't protest. It felt natural for this man to hold her close.

His car arrived and they drove back to her apartment building in silence. When he pulled into the parking lot, she considered inviting him inside for coffee, then decided against it. They'd already drunk enough coffee, and besides, they both had to work the following morning. But more important, Joe might read something else into the invitation. He was an old friend. Nothing more. And she wanted to keep it that way.

She turned to him and smiled softly. "I had a lovely time. Thank you so much."

"You're welcome, Cait. We'll do it again."

Cait was astonished to realize how appealing another evening with Joseph Rockwell was. She'd underestimated him.

Or had she?

"There's something else I'd like to try again," he was saying, his eyes filled with devilry.

"Try again?"

He slid his arm behind her and for a breathless moment they looked at each other. "I don't know if I've got a chance without trading a few baseball cards, though."

Cait swallowed. "You want to kiss me?"

He nodded. His eyes seemed to grow darker, more

intense. "For old times' sake." His hand caressed the curve of her neck, his thumb moving slowly toward the scented hollow of her throat.

"Well, sure. For old times' sake." She was amazed at the way her heart was reacting to the thought of Joe holding her...kissing her.

His mouth began a slow descent toward hers, his warm breath nuzzling her skin.

"Just remember," she whispered when his mouth was about to settle over hers. Her hands gripped his lapels. "Old times'..."

"I'll remember," he said as his lips came down on hers.

She sighed and slid her hands up his solid chest to link her fingers at the base of his neck. The kiss was slow and thorough. When it was over, Cait's hands were clenching his collar.

Joe's fingers were in her hair, tangled in the short, soft curls, cradling the back of her head.

A sweet rush of joy coursed through her veins. Cait felt a bubbling excitement, a burst of warmth, unlike anything she'd ever known before.

Then he kissed her a second time...

"Just remember..." she repeated when he pulled his mouth from hers and buried it in the delicate curve of her neck.

He drew in several ragged breaths before asking, "What is it I'm supposed to remember?"

"Yes, oh, please, remember."

He lifted his head and rested his hands lightly on her shoulders, his face only inches from hers. "What's so important you don't want me to forget?" he whispered.

It wasn't Joe who was supposed to remember; it was Cait. She didn't realize she'd spoken out loud. She blinked, uncertain, then tilted her head to gaze down at her hands, anywhere but at him. "Oh...that I'm in love with Paul."

There was a moment of silence. An awkward moment. "Right," he answered shortly. "You're in love with Paul." His arms fell away and he released her.

Cait hesitated, uneasy. "Thanks again for a wonderful dinner." Her hand closed around the door handle. She was eager now to make her escape.

"Any time," he said flippantly. His own hands gripped the steering wheel.

"I'll see you soon."

"Soon," he repeated. She climbed out of the car, not giving Joe a chance to come around and open the door for her. She was aware of him sitting in the car, waiting until she'd unlocked the lobby door and stepped inside. She hurried down the first-floor hall and into her apartment, turning on the lights so he'd know she'd made it safely home.

Then she slowly removed her coat and carefully hung it in the closet. When she peeked out the window, she noticed that Joe had already left.

Lindy was at her desk working when Cait arrived the next morning. Cait smiled at her as she hurried past, but didn't stop to indulge in conversation.

Cait could feel Lindy's gaze trailing after her and she knew her friend was disappointed that she hadn't told her about the dinner date with Joe Rockwell.

Cait didn't want to talk about it. She was afraid that if she said anything to Lindy, she wouldn't be able to avoid mentioning the kiss, which was a subject she wanted to avoid at all costs. She wouldn't be able to delay her friend's questions forever, but Cait wanted to put them off until at least the end of the day. Longer, if possible.

What a fool she'd been to let Joe kiss her. It had seemed so right at the time, a natural conclusion to a delightful evening.

The fact that she'd let him do it without even making a token protest still confused her. If Paul was to hear of it, he might think she really *was* interested in Joe. Which, of course, she wasn't.

Her boss was a man of principle and integrity—and altogether a frustrating person to fall in love with. Judging by his reaction to her dinner with Joe, he seemed immune to jealousy. Now if only she could discover a way of letting him know how she felt…and spark his interest in the process!

The morning was hectic. Out of the corner of her eye, Cait saw Joe arrive. Although she was speaking to an important client on the phone, she stared after him as he approached the burly foreman. She watched Joe remove a blueprint from a long, narrow tube and roll it open so two other men could study it. There seemed to be some discussion, then the foreman nodded and Joe left, without so much as glancing in Cait's direction.

That stung.

At least he could have waved hello. But if he wanted to ignore her, well, fine. She'd do the same.

The market closed on the up side, the Dow Jones industrial average at 2600 points after brisk trading. The day's work was over.

As Cait had predicted, Lindy sought her out almost immediately.

"So how'd your dinner date go?"

"It was fun."

"Where'd he take you? Sam's Bar and Grill the way you thought?"

"Actually, no," she said, clearing her throat, feeling more than a little foolish for having suggested such a thing. "He took me to Henry's." She announced it louder than necessary, since Paul was strolling into the office just then. But for all the notice he gave her, she might as well have been fresh paint drying on the company wall.

"Henry's," Lindy echoed. "He took you to Henry's? Why, that's one of the best restaurants in town. It must have cost him a small fortune."

"I wouldn't know. My menu didn't list any prices."

"You're joking. No one's ever taken me anyplace so fancy. What did you order?"

"Grilled salmon." She continued to study Paul for some clue that he was listening in on her and Lindy's conversation. He was seated at his desk, reading a report on short-term partnerships as a tax advantage. Cait had read it earlier in the week and had recommended it to him.

"Was it wonderful?" Lindy pressed.

It took Cait a moment to realize her friend was quizzing her about the dinner. "Excellent. The best fish I've had in years."

"What did you do afterward?"

Cait looked back at her friend. "What makes you think we did anything? We had dinner, talked, and then he drove me home. Nothing more happened. Understand? Nothing.''

''If you say so,'' Lindy said, eyeing her suspiciously. ''But you're certainly defensive about it.''

''I just want you to know that nothing happened. Joseph Rockwell is an old friend. That's all.''

Paul glanced up from the report, but his gaze connected with Lindy's before slowly progressing to Cait.

''Hello, Paul,'' Cait greeted him cheerfully. ''Are Lindy and I disturbing you? We'd be happy to go into the hallway if you'd like.''

''No, no, you're fine. Don't worry about it.'' He glanced past them to the doorway and got to his feet. ''Hello, Rockwell.''

''Am I interrupting a meeting?'' Joe asked, stepping into the office as if it didn't really matter whether he was or not. His hard hat was back in place, along with the dusty jeans and the tool pouch. And yet Cait had no difficulty remembering last night's sophisticated dinner companion when she looked at him.

''No, no,'' Paul answered, ''we were just chatting. Come on in. Problems?''

''Not really. But there's something I'd like you to take a look at in the other room.''

''I'll be right there.''

Joe threw Cait a cool smile as he strolled past. ''Hello, Cait.''

''Joe.'' Her heart was pounding hard, and that was ridiculous. It must have been due to embarrassment, she told herself. Joe was a friend, a boy from the old neighborhood; just because she'd allowed him to kiss her, it didn't mean there was—or ever would be—

anything romantic between them. The sooner she made him understand this, the better.

"Joe and Cait went out to dinner last night," Lindy said pointedly to Paul. "He took her to Henry's."

"How nice," Paul commented, clearly more interested in troubleshooting with Joe than discussing Cait's dating history.

"We had a good time, didn't we?" Joe asked Cait.

"Yes, very nice," she responded stiffly.

Joe waited until Paul was out of the room before he stepped back and dropped a kiss on her cheek. Then he announced loudly enough for everyone in the vicinity to hear, "You were incredible last night."

Four

"I thought you said nothing happened," Lindy said, looking intently at a red-faced Cait.

"Nothing did happen." Cait was furious enough to kick Joe Rockwell in the shins the way he deserved. How dared he say something so...so embarrassing in front of Lindy! And probably within earshot of Paul!

"But why would he say something like that?"

"How should I know?" Cait snapped. "One little kiss and he makes it sound like—"

"He kissed you?" Lindy asked sharply, her eyes narrowing. "You just got done telling me there's nothing between the two of you."

"Good grief, the kiss didn't mean anything. It was for old times' sake. Just a platonic little kiss." All right, she was exaggerating a bit, but it couldn't be helped.

While Cait was speaking, she gathered her things and shoved them in her briefcase. Then she slammed the lid closed and reached for her coat, thrusting her arms into the sleeves, her movements abrupt and ungraceful.

"Have a nice weekend," she said tightly, not completely understanding why she felt so annoyed with

Lindy. "I'll see you Monday." She marched through the office, but paused in front of Joe.

"You wanted something, sweetheart?' he asked in a cajoling voice.

"You're despicable!"

Joe looked downright disappointed. "Not low and disgusting?"

"That, too."

He grinned ear to ear just the way she knew he would. "I'm glad to hear it."

Cait bit back an angry retort. It wouldn't do any good to engage in a verbal battle with Joe Rockwell. He'd have a comeback for any insult she could hurl. Seething, Cait marched to the elevator and jabbed the button impatiently.

"I'll be by later tonight, darling," Joe called to her just as the doors were closing, effectively cutting off any protest from her.

He was joking. He had to be joking. No man in his right mind could possibly expect her to invite him into her home after this latest stunt. Not even the impertinent Joe Rockwell.

Once home, Cait took a long, soothing shower, dried her hair and changed into jeans and a sweater. Friday nights were generally quiet ones for her. She was munching on pretzels and surveying the bleak contents of her refrigerator when there was a knock on the door.

It couldn't possibly be Joe, she told herself.

It was Joe, balancing a large pizza on the palm of one hand and clutching a bottle of red wine in the other.

Cait stared at him, too dumbfounded at his audacity to speak.

"I come bearing gifts," he said, presenting the pizza to her with more than a little ceremony.

"Listen here, you...you fool, it's going to take a whole lot more than pizza to make up for that stunt you pulled this afternoon."

"Come on, Cait, lighten up a little."

"Lighten up! You...you..."

"I believe the word you're looking for is fool."

"You have your nerve." She dug her fists into her hips, knowing she should slam the door in his face. She would have, too, but the pizza smelled *so* good it was difficult to maintain her indignation.

"Okay, I'll admit it," Joe said, his deep blue eyes revealing genuine contrition. "I got carried away. You're right, I am an idiot. All I can do is ask your forgiveness." He lifted the lid of the pizza box and Cait was confronted by the thickest, most mouth-watering masterpiece she'd ever seen. The top was crowded with no less than ten tempting toppings, all covered with a thick layer of hot melted cheese.

"Do you accept my humble apology?" Joe pressed, waving the pizza under her nose.

"Are there any anchovies on that thing?"

"Only on half."

"You're forgiven." She took him by the elbow and dragged him inside her apartment.

Cait led the way into the kitchen. She got two plates from the cupboard and collected knives, forks and napkins as she mentally reviewed his crimes. "I couldn't believe you actually said that," she mumbled, shaking her head. She set the kitchen table, neatly positioning the napkins after shoving the day's mail to one side. "The least you could do is tell me why you found it necessary to say that in front of Paul. Lindy had already started grilling me. Can you imagine what she and Paul must think now?" She retrieved two wineglasses from the cupboard and set them by the plates. "I've never been more embarrassed in my life."

"Never?" he prompted, opening and closing her kitchen drawers until he located a corkscrew.

"Never," she repeated. "And don't think a pizza's going to ensure lasting peace."

"I wouldn't dream of it."

"It's a start, but you're going to owe me a good long time for this prank, Joseph Rockwell."

"I'll be good," he promised, his eyes twinkling. He agilely removed the cork, tested the wine and then filled both glasses.

Cait jerked out a wicker-back chair and threw herself down. "Did Paul say anything after I left?"

"About what?" Joe slid out a chair and joined her.

Cait had already dished up a thick slice for each of them, fastidiously using a knife to disconnect the strings of melted cheese that stretched from the box to their plates.

"About me, of course," she growled.

Joe handed her a glass of wine. "Not really."

Cait paused and lifted her eyes to his. "Not really? What does that mean?"

"Only that he didn't say much about you."

Joe was taunting her, dangling bits and pieces of information, waiting for her reaction. She should have known better than to trust him, but she was so anxious to find out what Paul had said that she ignored her pride. "Tell me everything he said," she demanded, "word for word."

Joe had a mouthful of pizza and Cait was left to wait several moments until he swallowed. "I seem to recall he said something about your explaining that the two of us go back a long way."

Cait straightened, too curious to hide her interest. "Did he look concerned? Jealous?"

"Paul? No, if anything, he looked bored."

"Bored," Cait repeated. Her shoulders sagged with defeat. "I swear that man wouldn't notice me if I pranced around his office naked."

"That's a clever idea, and one that just might work. Maybe you should practice around the house first, get the hang of it. I'd be willing to help you out if you're really serious about this." He sounded utterly nonchalant, as though she'd suggested subscribing to cable television. "This is what friends are for. Do you need help undressing?"

Cait took a sip from her wine to hide a smile. Joe hadn't changed in twenty years. He was still witty and fun-loving and a terrible tease. "Very funny."

"Hey, I wasn't kidding. I'll pretend I'm Paul and—"

"You promised you were going to be good."

He wiggled his eyebrows suggestively. "I will be. Just you wait."

Cait could feel the tide of color flow into her cheeks. She quickly lowered her eyes to her plate. "Joe, cut it out. You're making me blush and I hate to blush. My face looks like a ripe tomato." She lifted her slice of pizza and bit into it, chewing thoughtfully. "I don't understand you. Every time I think I have you figured out you do something to surprise me.''

"Like what?''

"Like yesterday. You invited me to dinner, but I never dreamed you'd take me someplace as elegant as Henry's. You were the perfect gentleman all evening and then today, you were so...''

"Low and disgusting.''

"Exactly.'' She nodded righteously. "One minute you're the picture of charm and culture and the next you're badgering me with your wisecracks.''

"I'm a tease, remember?''

"The problem is that I can't deal with you when I don't know what to expect.''

"That's my charm.'' He reached for a second piece of pizza. "Women are said to adore the unexpected in a man.''

"Not this woman,'' she informed him promptly. "I need to know where I stand with you.''

"A little to the left.''

"Joe, please, I'm not joking. I can't have you pulling stunts like you did today. I've lived a good, clean life for the past twenty-eight years. Two days with you has ruined my reputation with the company. I can't walk into the office and hold my head up any longer. I hear people whispering and I know they're talking about me.''

"Us,'' he corrected. "They're talking about us.''

"That's even worse. If they want to talk about me and a man, I'd rather it was Paul. Just how much longer is this remodeling project going to take, anyway?'' As far as Cait was concerned, the sooner Joe and his renegade crew were out of her office, the sooner her life would settle back to normal.

"Not too much longer."

"At the rate you're progressing, Webster, Rodale and Missen will have offices on the moon."

"Before the end of the year, I promise."

"Yes, but just how reliable are your promises?"

"I'm being good, aren't I?"

"I suppose," she conceded ungraciously, jerking a stack of mail away from Joe as he started to sort through it.

"What's this?" Joe asked, rescuing a single piece of paper before it fluttered to the floor.

"A Christmas list. I'm going shopping tomorrow."

"I should have known you'd be organized about that, too." He sounded vaguely insulting.

"I've been organized all my life. It isn't likely to change now."

"That's why I want you to lighten up a little." He continued studying her list. "What time are you going?"

"The stores open at eight and I plan to be there then."

"I suppose you've written down everything you need to buy so you won't forget anything."

"Of course."

"Sounds sensible." His remark surprised her. He scanned her list, then yelped, "Hey, I'm not on here!" He withdrew a pen from his shirt pocket and added his own name. "Do you want me to give you a few suggestions on what I'd like?"

"I already know what I'm getting you."

Joe arched his brows. "You do? And please don't say 'nothing.'"

"No, but it'll be something appropriate—like a muzzle."

"Oh, Caitlin, darling, you injure me." He gave her one of his devilishly handsome smiles, and Cait could feel herself weakening. Just what she didn't want! She had every right to be angry with Joe. If he hadn't brought that pizza, she'd have slammed the door in his face. Wouldn't she? Sure, she would! But she'd always been susceptible to Italian food. Her only other fault was Paul. She did love him. No one seemed to believe that, but she'd known almost from the moment they'd met that she was destined to spend the rest of her life loving Paul Jamison. Only she'd rather do it as his wife than his employee!

"Have you finished your shopping?" she asked idly, making small talk with Joe since he seemed determined to hang around.

"I haven't started. I have good intentions every year, you know, like I'll get a head start on finding the perfect gifts for my nieces and nephews, but they never work out. Usually panic sets in Christmas Eve and I tear around the stores like mad and buy everything in sight. Last year I forgot wrapping paper. My mother saved the day."

"I doubt it'd do any good to suggest you get organized."

"I haven't got the time."

"What are you doing right now? Write out your list, stick to it and make the time to go shopping."

"My darling Cait, is this an invitation for me to join you tomorrow?"

"Uh…" Cait hadn't intended it to be, but she supposed she couldn't object as long as he behaved himself. "You're welcome on one condition."

"Name it."

"No jokes, no stunts like you pulled today and absolutely no teasing. If you announce to a single person that we're married, I'm walking away from you and that's a promise."

"You've got it." He raised his hand, then ceremoniously crossed his heart.

"Lick your fingertips first," Cait demanded. The instant the words were out of her mouth, she realized how ridiculous she sounded, as if they were eight and ten all over again. "Forget I said that."

His eyes were twinkling as he stood to deliver his plate to the sink. "I swear it's a shame you're so in love with Paul," he told her. "If I'm not careful, I could fall for you myself." With that, he kissed her on the cheek and let himself out the door.

Pressing her fingers to her cheek, Cait drew in a deep, shuddering breath and held it until she heard the door close. Then and only then did it seep out in ragged bursts, as if she'd forgotten how to breathe normally.

"Oh, Joe," she whispered. The last thing she wanted was for Joe to fall in love with her. Not that he wasn't handsome and sweet and wonderful. He was. He always had been. He just wasn't for her. Their personalities were poles apart. Joe was unpredictable, always doing the unexpected, whereas Cait's life ran like clockwork.

She liked Joe. She almost wished she didn't, but she couldn't help herself. However, a steady diet of his pranks would soon drive her into the nearest asylum.

Standing, Cait closed the pizza box and tucked the uneaten portion into the top shelf of her refrigerator. She was putting the dirty plates in her dishwasher when the phone rang. She quickly washed her hands and reached for it.

"Hello."

"Cait, it's Paul."

Cait was so startled that the receiver slipped out of her hand. Grabbing for it, she nearly stumbled over the open dishwasher door, knocking her shin against the sharp edge. She yelped and swallowed a cry as she jerked the dangling phone cord toward her.

"Sorry, sorry," she cried, once she'd rescued the telephone receiver. "Paul? Are you still there?"

"Yes, I'm here. Is this a bad time? I could call back later if this is inconvenient. You don't have company, do you? I wouldn't want to interrupt a party or anything."

"Oh, no, now is perfect. I didn't realize you had my home number...but obviously you do. After all, we've been working together for nearly a year now." Eleven months and four days, not that she was counting or anything. "Naturally my number would be in the personnel file."

He hesitated and Cait bent over to rub her shin where it had collided with the dishwasher door. She was sure to have an ugly bruise, but a bruised leg was a small price to pay. Paul had phoned her!

"The reason I'm calling..."

"Yes, Paul," she prompted when he didn't immediately continue.

The silence lengthened before he blurted out, "I just wanted to thank you for passing on that article on the tax advantages of limited partnerships. It was thoughtful of you and I appreciate it."

"Any time. I read quite a lot in that area, you know. There are several recent articles on the same subject. If you'd like, I could bring them in next week."

"Sure. That would be fine. Thanks again, Cait. Goodbye."

The line was disconnected before Cait could say anything else and she was left holding the receiver. A smile came, slow and confident, and with a small cry of triumph, she tossed the telephone receiver into the air, caught it behind her back and replaced it with a flourish.

Cait was dressed and waiting for Joe early the next morning. "Joe," she cried, throwing open her apartment door, "I could just kiss you."

He was dressed in faded jeans and a hip-length bronze-colored leather jacket. "Hey, I'm not stopping you," he said, opening his arms.

Cait ignored the invitation. "Paul phoned me last night." She didn't even try to contain her excitement; she felt like leaping and skipping and singing out loud.

"Paul did?" Joe sounded surprised.

"Yes. It was shortly after you left. He thanked me for giving him an interesting article I found in one of the business journals and—this is the good part—he asked if I was alone...as if it really mattered to him."

"If you were alone?" Joe repeated, and frowned. "What's that got to do with anything?"

"Don't you understand?" For all his intelligence Joe could be pretty obtuse, sometimes. "He wanted to know if *you* were here with me. I makes sense, doesn't it? Paul's jealous, only he doesn't realize it yet. Oh, Joe, I can't remember ever being this happy. Not in years and years and years."

"Because Paul Jamison phoned?"

"Don't sound so skeptical. It's exactly the break I've been looking for all these months. Paul's finally noticed me and it's all thanks to you."

"At least you're willing to give credit where credit is due." But he still didn't seem particularly thrilled.

"It's just so incredible," she continued. "I don't think I slept a wink last night. There was something in his voice that I've never heard before. Something...deep and personal. I don't know how to explain it. For the first time in a whole year, Paul knows I'm alive!"

"Are we going Christmas shopping or not?" Joe demanded brusquely. "Damn it all, Cait, I never expected you to go soft over a stupid phone call."

"But this wasn't just any call," she reminded him. She reached for her purse and her coat in one sweeping motion. "This call was from *Paul*."

"You sound like a silly schoolgirl." Joe frowned, but Cait wasn't about to let his short temper destroy her mood. Paul had phoned her at home and she was sure that this was the beginning of a *real* relationship. Next he'd ask her out for lunch, and then...

They left her apartment and walked down the hall, Cait grinning all the way. Standing just outside the front doors was a huge truck with gigantic wheels. Just the type of vehicle she'd expected him to drive the night he'd taken her to Henry's.

"This is your truck?" she asked when they were outside. She was unable to keep the laughter out of her voice.

"Is there something wrong with it?"

"Not a single thing, but Joe, honestly, you are so predictable."

"That's not what you said yesterday."

She grinned as he opened the truck door, set down a stool for her and helped her climb into the cab. The seat was cluttered, but so wide she was able to shove everything to one side. When she'd made room for herself, she fastened the seat belt, snapping it jauntily in place. She was so happy, the whole world seemed delightful this morning.

"Will you quit smiling before someone suggests you've been overdosing on vitamins?" Joe grumbled.

"My, aren't we testy this morning."

"Where to?" he asked, starting the engine.

"Any of the big shopping malls will do. You decide. Do you have your list all made out?"

Joe patted his heart. "It's in my shirt pocket."

"Good."

"Have you decided what you're going to buy for whom?"

His smile was slightly off kilter. "Not exactly. I thought I'd follow you around and buy whatever you did. Do you know what you're getting your mother? Mine's damn difficult to buy for. Last year I ended up getting her cat food. She's got five cats of her own and God only knows how many strays she's feeding."

"At least your idea was practical."

"Well, there's that, and the fact that by the time I started my Christmas shopping the only store open was a supermarket."

Cait laughed. "Honestly, Joe!"

"Hey, I was desperate and before you get all righteous on me, Mom thought the cat food and the two rib roasts were great gifts."

"I'm sure she did," Cait returned, grinning. She found herself doing a lot of that when she was with Joe. Imagine buying his mother rib roasts for Christmas!

"Give me some ideas, would you? Mom's a hard case."

"To be honest, I'm not all that imaginative myself. I buy my mother the same thing every year."

"What is it?"

"Long-distance phone coupons. That way she can phone her sister in Dubuque and her high-school friend in Olathe, Kansas. Of course she calls me every now and again, too."

"Okay, that takes care of Mom. What about Martin? What are you buying him?"

"A bronze eagle." She'd decided on that gift last summer when she'd attended Sunday services at Martin's church. In the opening part of his sermon, Martin had used eagles to illustrate a point of faith.

"An eagle," Joe repeated. "Any special reason?"

"Y-yes," she said, not wanting to explain. "It's a long story, but I happen to be partial to eagles myself."

"Any other hints you'd care to pass on?"

"Buy wrapping paper in the after-Christmas sales.

It's about half the price and it stores easily under the bed.''

"Great idea. I'll have to remember that for next year.''

Joe chose Northgate, the shopping mall closest to Cait's apartment. The parking lot was already beginning to fill up and it was only a few minutes after eight.

Joe managed to park fairly close to the entrance and came around to help Cait out of the truck. This time he didn't bother with the step stool, but gripped her around the waist to lift her down. "What did you mean when you said I was so predictable?'' he asked, giving her a reproachful look.

With her hands resting on his shoulders and her feet dangling in midair, she felt vulnerable and small. "Nothing. It was just that I assumed you drove one of those Sherman-tank trucks, and I was right. I just hadn't seen it before.''

"The kind of truck I drive bothers you?'' His brow furrowed in a scowl.

"Not at all. What's the matter with you today, Joe? You're so touchy.''

"I am not touchy,'' he snapped.

"Fine. Would you mind putting me down then?'' His large hands were squeezing her waist almost painfully, though she doubted he was aware of it. She couldn't imagine what had angered him. Unless it was the fact that Paul had called her—which didn't make sense. Maybe, like most men, he just hated shopping.

He lowered her slowly to the asphalt and released her with seeming reluctance. "I need a coffee break,'' he announced grimly.

"But we just arrived."

Joe forcefully expelled his breath. "It doesn't matter. I need something to calm my nerves."

If he needed a caffeine fix so early in the day, Cait wondered how he'd manage during the next few hours. The stores became quickly crowded this time of year, especially on a Saturday. By ten it would be nearly impossible to get from one aisle to the next.

By twelve, she knew: Joe disliked Christmas shopping every bit as much as she'd expected.

"I've had it," Joe complained after making three separate trips back to the truck to deposit their spoils.

"Me, too," Cait agreed laughingly. "This place is turning into a madhouse."

"How about some lunch?" Joe suggested. "Some place far away from here. Like Tibet."

Cait laughed again and tucked her arm in his. "That sounds like a great idea."

Outside, they noticed several cars circling the lot looking for a parking space and three of them rushed to fill the one Joe vacated. Two cars nearly collided in their eagerness. One man leapt out of his and shook an angry fist at the other driver.

"So much for peace and goodwill," Joe commented. "I swear Christmas brings out the worst in everyone."

"And the best," Cait reminded him.

"To be honest, I don't know what crammed shopping malls and fighting the crowds and all this commercialism have to do with Christmas in the first place," he grumbled. A car cut in front of him, and Joe blared his horn.

"Quite a lot when you think about it," Cait said

softly. "Imagine the streets of Bethlehem, the crowds and the noise..." The Christmas before, fresh from a shopping expedition, Cait had asked herself the same question. Christmas seemed so commercial. The crowds had been unbearable. First at Northgate, where she did most of her shopping and then at the airport. Sea-Tac had been filled with activity and noise, everyone in a hurry to get someplace or another. There seemed to be little peace or good cheer and a whole lot of selfish concern and rudeness. Then, in the tranquility of church on Christmas Eve, everything had come into perspective for Cait. There had been crowds and rudeness that first Christmas, too, she reasoned. Yet in the midst of that confusion had come joy and peace and love. For most people, it was still the same. Christmas gifts and decorations and dinners were, after all, expressions of the love you felt for your family and friends. And if the preparations sometimes got a bit chaotic, well, that no longer bothered Cait.

"Where should we go to eat?" Joe asked, breaking into her thoughts. They were barely moving, stuck in heavy traffic.

She looked over at him and smiled serenely. "Any place will do. There're several excellent restaurants close by. You choose, only let it be my treat this time."

"We'll talk about who pays later. Right now, I'm more concerned with getting out of this traffic sometime within my life span."

Still smiling, Cait said, "I don't think it'll take much longer."

He returned her smile. "I don't, either." His eyes held hers for what seemed an eternity—until someone behind them honked irritably. Joe glanced up and saw that traffic ahead of them had started to move. He immediately stepped on the gas.

Cait didn't know what Joe had found so fascinating about her unless it was her unruly hair. She hadn't combed it since leaving the house; it was probably a mass of tight, disorderly curls. She'd been so concerned with finding the right gift for her nephews and niece that she hadn't given it a thought.

"What's wrong?" she asked, feeling self-conscious.

"What makes you think anything's wrong?"

"The way you were looking at me a few minutes ago."

"Oh, that," he said easing, into a restaurant parking lot. "I don't think I've ever fully appreciated how lovely you are," he answered in a calm, matter-of-fact voice.

Cait blushed and looked away. "I'm sure you're mistaken. I'm really not all that pretty. I sometimes wondered if Paul would have noticed me sooner if I was a little more attractive."

"Trust me, Bright Eyes," he said, turning off the engine. "You're pretty enough."

"For what?"

"For this." And he leaned across the seat and captured her mouth with his.

Five

"I...wish you hadn't done that," Cait whispered, slowly opening her eyes in an effort to pull herself back to reality.

As far as kisses went, Joe's were good. Very good. He kissed better than just about anyone she'd ever kissed before—but that didn't alter the fact that she was in love with Paul.

"You're right," he muttered, opening the door and climbing out of the cab. "I shouldn't have done that." He walked around to her side and yanked the door open with more force than necessary.

Cait frowned, wondering at his strange mood. One minute he was holding her in his arms, kissing her tenderly; the next he was short-tempered and irritable.

"I'm hungry," he barked, lifting her abruptly down onto the pavement. "I sometimes do irrational things when I haven't eaten."

"I see." The next time she went anywhere with Joseph Rockwell, she'd have to be certain he ate a good meal first.

The restaurant was crowded and Joe gave the receptionist their names to add to the growing waiting list. Sitting on the last empty chair in the foyer, Cait set her large black leather purse on her lap and started rooting through it.

"What are you looking for? Uranium?" Joe teased, watching her.

"Crackers," she answered, shifting the bulky bag and handing him several items to hold while she continued digging.

"You're looking for crackers? Whatever for?"

She glanced up long enough to give him a look that questioned his intelligence. "For obvious reasons. If you're irrational when you're hungry, you might do something stupid while we're here. Frankly, I don't want you to embarrass me." She returned to the task with renewed vigor. "I can just see you standing on top of the table tap-dancing."

"That's one way to gain the waiter's attention. Thanks for suggesting it."

"Aha!" Triumphantly Cait pulled two miniature bread sticks wrapped in cellophane from the bottom of her purse. "Eat," she instructed. "Before you're overcome by some other craziness."

"You mean before I kiss you again," he said in a low voice, bending his head toward hers.

She leaned back quickly, not giving him any chance of following through on that. "Exactly. Or waltz with the waitress or any of the other loony things you do."

"You have to admit I've been good all morning."

"With one minor slip," she reminded him, pressing the bread sticks into his hand. "Now eat."

Before Joe had a chance to open the package, the hostess approached then with two menus tucked under her arm. "Mr. and Mrs. Rockwell. Your table is ready."

"Mr. and Mrs. Rockwell," Cait muttered under her breath, glaring at Joe. She should have known she couldn't trust him.

"Excuse me, miss," Cait said, standing abruptly and raising her index finger. "His name is Rockwell, mine is Marshall," she explained patiently. She was not about to let Joe continue his silly games. "We're just friends here for lunch." Her narrowed eyes caught Joe's, which looked as innocent as freshly fallen snow. He shrugged as though to say any misunderstanding hadn't been *his* fault.

"I see," the hostess replied. "I'm sorry for the confusion."

"No problem." Cait hadn't wanted to make a big issue of this, but on the other hand she didn't want Joe to think he was going to get away with it, either.

The woman led them to a linen-covered table in the middle of the room. Joe held out Cait's chair for her and then whispered something to the hostess who immediately cast Cait a sympathetic glance. Joe's own gaze rested momentarily on Cait before he pulled out his chair and sat across from her.

"All right, what did you say to her?" she hissed.

The menu seemed to command his complete interest for a couple of minutes. "What makes you think I said anything?"

"I heard you whispering and then she gave me this pathetic look like she wanted to hug me and tell me everything was going to be all right."

"Then you know."

"Joe, don't play games with me," Cait warned.

"All right, if you must know, I explained that you'd suffered a head injury and developed amnesia."

"Amnesia," she repeated loudly enough to attract the attention of the diners at the next table. Gritting her teeth, Cait snatched up her menu, gripping it tightly enough to curl the edges. It didn't do any good to argue with Joe. The man was impossible. Every time she tried to reason with him, he did something to make her regret it.

"How else was I supposed to explain the fact you'd forgotten our marriage?" he asked reasonably.

"I did not forget our marriage," she informed him from between clenched teeth, reviewing the menu and quickly making her selection. "Good grief, it wasn't even legal."

She realized that the waitress was standing by their table, pen and pad in hand. The woman's ready smile faded as she looked from Cait to Joe and back again. Her mouth tightened as if she strongly suspected they really were involved in something illegal.

"Uh…" Cait hedged, feeling like even more of an idiot. The urge to explain was overwhelming, but every time she tried, she only made matters worse. "I'll have the club sandwich," she said, glaring across the table at Joe.

"That sounds good. I'll have the same," he said, closing his menu.

The woman scribbled down their order, then hurried away, pausing to glance over her shoulder as if she wanted to be able to identify them later in a police lineup.

"Now look what you've done," Cait whispered heatedly once the waitress was far enough away from their table not to overhear.

"Me?"

Maybe she was being unreasonable, but Joe was the one who'd started this nonsense in the first place. No one had ever gotten a rise out of her the way Joe did. No one could rattle her so effectively. And worse, she let him.

This shopping trip was a good example, and so was the pizza that led up to it. No woman in her right mind should have allowed Joe into her apartment after what he'd said to her in front of Lindy. Not only had she invited him inside her home, she'd agreed to let him accompany her Christmas shopping. She ought to have her head examined!

"What's wrong?" Joe asked, tearing open the package of bread sticks. Rather pointless in Cait's opinion, since their lunch would be served any minute.

"What's wrong?" she cried, dumbfounded that he had to ask. "You mean other than the hostess believing I've suffered a head injury and the waitress thinking that we're drug dealers or something equally disgusting?"

"Here." He handed her one of the miniature breadsticks. "Eat this and you'll feel better."

Cait sincerely doubted that, but she took it, anyway, muttering under her breath.

"Relax," he urged.

"Relax," she mocked. "How can I possibly relax when you're doing and saying things I find excruciatingly embarrassing?"

"I'm sorry, Cait. Really, I am." To his credit, he did look contrite. "But you're so easy to fluster and I can't seem to stop myself."

Their sandwiches arrived, thick with slices of turkey, ham and a variety of cheeses. Cait was reluctant to admit how much better she felt after she'd eaten. Joe's spirits had apparently improved, as well.

"So," he said, his hands resting on his abdomen. "What do you have planned for the rest of the afternoon?"

Cait hadn't given it much thought. "I suppose I should wrap the gifts I bought this morning." But the thought didn't particularly excite her. Good grief, after the adventures she'd had with Joe, it wasn't any wonder.

"You mean you actually wrap gifts before Christmas Eve?" Joe asked. "Doesn't that take all the fun out of it? I mean, for me it's a game just to see if I can get the presents bought."

She grinned, trying to imagine herself in such a disorganized race to the deadline. Definitely not her style.

"How about a movie?" he suggested out of the blue. "I have the feeling you don't get out enough."

"A movie?" Cait ignored the comment about her social life, mainly because he was right. She rarely took the time to go to a show.

"We're both exhausted from fighting the crowds," Joe added. "There's a six-cinema theater next to the restaurant. I'll even let you choose."

"I suppose you'd object to a love story?"

"We can see one if you insist, only..."

"Only what?"

"Only promise me you won't ever expect a man to say the things those guys on the screen do."

"I beg your pardon?"

"You heard me. Women hear actors say this incredible drivel and then they're disappointed when real men don't."

"Real men like you, I suppose?"

"Right." He looked smug, then suddenly he frowned. "Does Paul like romances?"

Cait hadn't a clue, since she'd never gone on a date with Paul and the subject wasn't one they'd ever discussed at the office. "I imagine he does," she said, dabbing her mouth with her napkin. "He isn't the type of man to be intimidated by such things."

Joe's deep blue eyes widened with surprise and a touch of respect. "Ouch. So Martin's little sister reveals her claws."

"I don't have claws. I just happen to have strong opinions on certain subjects." She reached for her purse while she was speaking and removed her wallet.

"What are you doing now?" Joe demanded.

"Paying for lunch." She sorted through the bills and withdrew a twenty. "It's my turn and I insist on paying…" She hesitated when she saw Joe's deepening frown. "Or don't real men allow women friends to buy their lunch?"

"Sure, go ahead," he returned flippantly.

It was all Cait could do to hide a smile. She guessed that her gesture in paying for their sandwiches would somehow be seen as compromising his male pride.

Apparently she was right. As they were walking toward the cashier, Joe stepped up his pace, grabbed the check from her hand and slapped some money on the counter. He glared at her as if he expected a drawn-out public argument. After the fuss they'd already caused in the restaurant, Cait was darned if she was going to let that happen.

"Joe," she argued, the minute they were out the door. "What was that all about?"

"All right, you win. Tell me my views are outdated, but when a woman goes out with me I pick up the tab, no matter how liberated she is."

"But this isn't a real date. We're only friends, and even that's—"

"I don't give a damn. Consider it an apology for the embarrassment I caused you earlier."

"You're a chauvinist, aren't you?"

"I'm not! I just have certain…standards."

"So I see." His attitude shouldn't have come as any big surprise. Just as Cait had told him earlier, he was shockingly predictable.

Hand at her elbow, Joe led the way across the car-filled lot toward the sprawling theater complex. The movies appealed to a wide audience. There was a Disney classic showing, along with a horror flick and a couple of adventure movies and last, but not least, a well-publicized love story.

As they stood in line, Cait caught Joe's gaze lingering on the poster for one of the adventure films, yet another story about a law-and-order cop with renegade ideas.

"I suppose you're more interested in seeing that than the romance."

"I already promised you could choose the show, and I'm a man of my word. If, however, you were to pick another movie—" he buried his hands in his pockets as he grinned at her appealingly "—I wouldn't complain."

"I'm willing to pick another movie, but on one condition."

"Name it." His eyes lit up.

"I pay."

"Those claws of yours are out again."

She raised her hands and flexed her fingers in a catlike motion. "It's your decision."

"What about popcorn?"

"You can buy that if you insist."

"All right," he said, "you've got yourself a deal."

When it was Cait's turn at the ticket window, she purchased two for the Disney classic.

"Disney?" Joe repeated, shocked when Cait handed him his ticket.

"It seemed like a good compromise," she answered.

For a moment it looked as if he was going to argue with her, then a slow grin spread across his face. "Disney," he said again. "You're right, it does sound like fun. Only I hope we're not the only ones there over the age of ten."

They sat toward the back of the theater, sharing a large bucket of buttered popcorn. The theater was crowded and several kids seemed to be taking turns running up and down the aisles. Joe needn't have worried; there were plenty of adults in attendance, but of course most of them were accompanying children.

The lights dimmed and Cait reached for a handful of popcorn, relaxing in her seat. "I love this movie."

"How many times have you seen it?"

"Five or six. But it's been several years now."

"Me, too." Joe relaxed beside her, crossing his long legs and leaning back.

The credits started to roll, but the noise level hadn't decreased much. "Will the kids bother you?" Joe wanted to know.

"Heavens, no. I love kids."

"You do?" The fact that he was so surprised seemed vaguely insulting and Cait stiffened.

"We've already had this discussion," she responded, licking the salt from her fingertips.

"We did? When?"

"The other day. You commented on how much I used to enjoy playing with my dolls and how you'd expected me to be married with a house full of children." His words had troubled her then, because "a house full of children" was exactly what Cait would have liked, and she seemed a long way from realizing her dream.

"Ah, yes, I remember our conversation about that now." He scooped up a large handful of popcorn. "You'd be a very good mother, you know."

That Joe would say this was enough to bring an unexpected rush of tears to her eyes. She blinked them back, surprised that she'd get weepy over something so silly.

The previews were over and the audience settled down as the movie started. Cait focused her attention on the screen, munching popcorn every now and then, reaching blindly for the bucket. Their hands collided more than once and almost before she was aware of it, their fingers were entwined. It was a peaceful sort of feeling, being linked to Joe this way. There was a *rightness* about it that she didn't want to explore just yet. He hadn't really changed; he was still lovable and funny and fun. For that matter, she hadn't changed very much, either....

The movie was as good as Cait remembered, better, even—perhaps because Joe was there to share it with her. She half expected him to make the occasional wisecrack, but he seemed to respect the artistic value of the classic animation and, judging by his whole-hearted laughter, he enjoyed the story.

When the show was over, he released Cait's hand. Hurriedly she gathered her purse and coat. As they walked out of the noisy, crowded theater, it seemed only natural to hold hands again.

Joe opened the truck, lifted down the step stool and helped her inside. Dusk came early these days, and bright, cheery lights were ablaze on every street. A vacant lot across the street was now filled with Christmas trees. A row of red lights was strung between two posts, sagging in the middle, and a portable tape player sent forth saccharine versions of better-known Christmas carols.

"Have you bought your tree yet?" Joe asked, nodding in the direction of the lot after he'd climbed into the driver's seat and started the engine.

"No. I don't usually put one up since I spend the holidays with Martin and his family."

"Ah."

"What about you? Or is that something else you save for Christmas Eve?" she joked. It warmed her a little to imagine Joe staying up past midnight to decorate a Christmas tree for his nieces and nephews.

"Finding time to do the shopping is bad enough."

"Your construction projects keep you that busy?" She hadn't given much thought to Joe's business. She knew from little remarks Paul had made that Joe was very successful. It wasn't logical that she should feel pride in his accomplishments, but she did.

"Owning a business isn't like being in a nine-to-five job. I'm on call twenty-four hours a day, but I wouldn't have it any other way. I love what I do.''

''I'm happy for you, Joe. I really am.''

''Happy enough to decorate my Christmas tree with me?''

''When?''

''Next weekend.''

''I'd like to,'' she told him, touched by the invitation, ''but I'll have left for Minnesota by then.''

''That's all right,'' Joe said, grinning at her. ''Maybe next time.''

She turned, frowning, to hide her blush.

They remained silent as he concentrated on easing the truck into the heavy late-afternoon traffic.

''I enjoyed the movie,'' she said some time later, resisting the urge to rest her head on his shoulder. The impulse to do that arose from her exhaustion, she told herself. Nothing else!

''So did I,'' he said softly. ''Only next time, I'll be the one to pay. Understand?''

Next time. There it was again. She suspected Joe was beginning to take their relationship, such as it was, far too seriously. Already he was suggesting they'd be seeing each other soon, matter-of-factly discussing dates as if they were long-time companions. Almost as if they were married...

She was mulling over this realization when Joe pulled into the parking area in front of her building. He climbed out and began to gather her packages, bundling them in his arms. She managed to scramble down by herself, not giving him a chance to help her, then she led the way into the building and unlocked her door.

Cait stood just inside the doorway and turned slightly to take a couple of the larger packages from Joe's arms.

"I had a great time," she told him briskly.

"Me, too." He nudged her, forcing her to enter the living room. He followed close behind and unloaded her remaining things onto the sofa. His presence seemed to reach out and fill every corner of the room.

Neither of them spoke for several minutes, but Cait sensed Joe wanted her to invite him to stay for coffee. The idea was tempting but dangerous. She mustn't let him think there might ever be anything romantic between them. Not when she was in love with Paul. For the first time in nearly a year, Paul was actually beginning to notice her. She refused to ruin everything now by becoming involved with Joe.

"Thank you for…today," she said, returning to the door, intending to open it for him. Instead, Joe caught her by the wrist and pulled her against him. She was in his arms before she could voice a protest.

"I'm going to kiss you," he told her, his voice rough yet oddly tender.

"You are?" She'd never been more aware of a man, of his hard, muscular body against hers, his clean, masculine scent. Her own body reacted in a chaotic scramble of mixed sensations. Above all, though, it felt *good* to be in his arms. She wasn't sure why and dared not examine the feeling.

Slowly, leisurely, he lowered his head. She made a soft weak sound as his mouth touched hers.

Cait sighed, forgetting for a moment that she meant to free herself before his kiss deepened. Before things went any further…

Joe must have sensed her resolve because his hands slid down her spine in a gentle caress, drawing her even closer. His mouth began a sensuous journey along her jaw, and down her throat—

"Joe!" She moaned his name, uncertain of what she wanted to say.

"Hmm?"

"Are you hungry again?" She wondered desperately if there were any more bread sticks in the bottom of her purse. Maybe that would convince him to stop.

"Very hungry," he told her, his voice low and solemn. "I've never been hungrier."

"But you had lunch and then you ate nearly all the popcorn."

He hesitated, then slowly raised his head. "Cait, are we talking about the same things here? Oh, hell, what does it matter? The only thing that matters is this." He covered her parted lips with his.

Cait felt her knees go weak and sagged against him, her fingers gripping his jacket as though she expected to collapse any moment. Which was becoming a distinct possibility as he continued to kiss her....

"Joe, no more, please." But she was the one clinging to him. She had to do something, and fast, before her ability to reason was lost entirely.

He drew an unsteady breath and muttered something she couldn't decipher as his lips grazed the delicate line of her jaw.

"We...need to talk," she announced, keeping her eyes tightly closed. If she didn't look at Joe, then she could concentrate on what she had to do.

"All right," he agreed.

"I'll make a pot of coffee."

With a heavy sigh, Joe abruptly released her. Cait half fell against the sofa arm, requiring its support while she collected herself enough to walk into the kitchen. She unconsciously reached up and brushed her lips, as if she wasn't completely sure even now that he'd taken her in his arms and kissed her.

He hadn't been joking this time, or teasing. The kisses they'd shared were serious kisses. The type a man gives a woman he's strongly attracted to. A woman he's interested in developing a relationship with. Cait found herself shaking, unable to move.

"You want me to make that coffee?" he suggested.

She nodded and sank down on the couch. She could scarcely stand, let alone prepare a pot of coffee.

Joe returned a few minutes later, carrying two steaming mugs. Carefully he handed her one, then sat across from her on the blue velvet ottoman.

"You wanted to talk?"

Cait nodded. "Yes." Her throat felt thick, clogged with confused emotion, and forming coherent words suddenly seemed beyond her means. She tried gesturing with her free hand, but that only served to frustrate Joe.

"Cait," he asked, "what's wrong?"

"Paul." The name came out in an eerie squeak.

"What about him?"

"He phoned me."

"Yes, I know. You already told me that."

"Don't you understand?" she cried, her throat unexpectedly clearing. "Paul is finally showing some interest in me and now you're kissing me and telling anyone who'll listen that the two of us are married and you're doing ridiculous things like…" She paused to draw in a deep breath. "Joe, oh please, Joe, don't fall in love with me."

"Fall in love with you?" he echoed incredulously. "Caitlin, you can't be serious. It won't happen. No chance."

Six

"No chance?" Cait repeated, convinced she'd misunderstood him. She blinked a couple of times as if that would correct her hearing. Either Joe was underestimating her intelligence, or he was more of a…a cad than she'd realized.

"You have nothing to worry about." He sipped coffee, his gaze steady, and emotionless. "I'm not falling in love with you."

"In other words you make a habit of kissing unsuspecting women."

"It isn't a habit," he answered thoughtfully. "It's more of a pastime."

"You certainly seem to be making a habit of it with me." Her anger was quickly gaining momentum and she was at odds to understand why she found his casual attitude so offensive. He was telling her exactly what she wanted to hear. But she hadn't expected her ego to take such a beating in the process. The fact that he wasn't the least bit tempted to fall in love with her should have pleased her.

It didn't.

It was as if their brief kisses were little more than a pleasant interlude for him. Something to occupy his time and keep him from growing bored with her company.

"This may come as something of a shock to you," Joe continued indifferently, "but a man doesn't have to be in love with a woman to kiss her."

"I know that," Cait snapped, fighting to hold back her temper, which was threatening to break free at any moment. "But you don't have to be so...so casual about it, either. If I wasn't involved with Paul, I might have taken you seriously."

"I didn't know you were involved with Paul," he returned with mild sarcasm. He leaned forward and rested his elbows on his knees, his pose infuriatingly relaxed. "If that was true I'd never have taken you out. The way I see it, the involvement is all on your part. Am I wrong?"

"No," she admitted reluctantly. How like a man to talk about semantics in the middle of an argument!

"So," he said, leaning back again and crossing his legs. "Are you enjoying the kisses? I take it I've improved from the first go-around."

"You honestly want me to rate you?" she sputtered.

"Obviously I'm much better than I was as a kid, otherwise you wouldn't be so worried." He took another drink of his coffee, smiling pleasantly all the while.

"Believe me, I'm not worried."

He arched his brows. "Really?"

"No doubt you expect me to fall at your feet, overcome by your masculine charm. Well, if that's what you're waiting for, you have one hell of a long wait!"

His grin was slightly off center, as if he was picturing her arrayed at his feet—and enjoying the sight.

"I think the problem here is that *you* might be falling in love with *me* and just don't know it."

"Falling in love with you and not know it?" she repeated with a loud disbelieving snort. "You've gone completely out of your mind. There's no chance of that."

"Why not? Plenty of women have told me I'm a handsome son of a gun. Plus, I'm said to possess a certain amount of charm. Heaven knows, I'm generous enough and rather—"

"Who told you that? Your mother?" She made it sound like the most ludicrous thing she'd heard in years.

"You might be surprised to learn that I do have admirers."

Why this news should add fuel to the fire of her temper was beyond Cait, but she was so furious with him she could barely sit still. "I don't doubt it, but if I fall in love with a man you can believe it won't be just because he's 'a handsome son of a gun,'" she quoted sarcastically. "Look at Paul— He's the type of man I'm attracted to. What's on the inside matters more than outward appearances."

"Then why are you so worried about falling in love with me?"

"I'm not worried! You've got it the wrong way around. The only reason I mentioned anything was because I thought *you* were beginning to take our times together much too seriously."

"I already explained that wasn't a problem."

"So I heard." Cait set her coffee aside. Joe was upsetting her so much that her hand was shaking hard enough to spill it.

"Well," Joe murmured, glancing at her. "You never did answer my question."

"Which one?" she asked irritably.

"About how I rated as a kisser."

"You weren't serious!"

"On the contrary." He set his own coffee down and raised himself off the ottoman far enough to clasp her by the waist and pull her into his lap.

Caught off balance, Cait fell onto his thighs, too astonished to struggle.

"Let's try it again," he whispered in a rough undertone.

"Ah…" A frightening excitement took hold of Cait. Her mind commanded her to leap away from this man, but some emotion, far stronger than common sense or prudence, urged the opposite.

Before she could form a protest, Joe bent toward her and covered her mouth with his. She'd hold herself stiff in his arms, that was what she'd do, teach him the lesson he deserved. How dared he assume she'd automatically fall in love with him. How dared he insinuate he was some…some Greek god women adored. But the instant his lips met hers, Cait trembled with a mixture of shock and profound pleasure.

Everything within her longed to cry out at the unfairness of it all. It shouldn't be this good with Joe. They were friends, nothing more. This was the kind of response she expected when Paul kissed her. If he ever did.

She meant to pull away, but instead, Cait moaned softly. It felt so incredibly wonderful. So incredibly right. At that moment, there didn't seem to be anything to worry about—except the likelihood of dissolving in his arms then and there.

Suddenly Joe broke the contact. Her instinctive disappointment, even more than the unexpectedness of the action, sent her eyes flying open. Her own dark eyes met his blue ones, which now seemed almost aquamarine.

"So, how do I rate?" he murmured thickly, as though he was having trouble speaking himself.

"Good." A one-word reply was all she could manage, although she was furious with him for asking.

"Just good?"

She nodded forcefully.

"I thought we were better than that."

"We?"

"Naturally I'm only as good as my partner."

"Th-then how do you rate me?" She had to ask. Like a fool she handed him the ax and laid her neck on the chopping board. Joe was sure to use the opportunity to trample all over her ego, to turn the whole bewildering experience into a joke. She couldn't take that right now. She dropped her gaze, waiting for him to devastate her.

"Much improved."

She cocked one brow in surprise. She had no idea what to say next.

They were both silent. Then he said softly, "You know, Cait, we're getting better at this. Much, much better." He pressed his forehead to hers. "If we're not careful, you just might fall in love with me, after all."

"Where were you all day Saturday?" Lindy asked early Monday morning, walking into Cait's office. The renovations to it had just been completed late Friday and Cait had moved everything back into her office first thing this morning. ''I must have tried calling you ten times.''

''I told you I was going Christmas shopping. In fact, I bought some decorations for my office.''

Lindy nodded. ''But all day?'' Her eyes narrowed suspiciously as she set down her briefcase and leaned against Cait's desk, crossing her arms. ''You didn't happen to be with Joe Rockwell, did you?''

Cait could feel a telltale shade of pink creep up her neck. She lowered her gaze to the list of current Dow Jones stock prices and took a moment to compose herself. She couldn't admit the truth. ''I said I was shopping,'' she said somewhat defensively. Then, in an effort to change the topic, she reached for a thick folder with Paul's name inked across the top and said, ''You wouldn't happen to know what Paul's schedule is for the day, would you?''

''N-no, I haven't seen him yet. Why do you ask?''

Cait flashed her friend a bright smile. ''He phoned me Friday night. Oh, Lindy, I was so excited I nearly fell all over myself.'' She dropped her voice as she glanced around to make sure none of the others could hear her. ''I honestly think he intends to ask me out.''

''Did he say so?''

''Not exactly.'' Cait frowned. Lindy wasn't revealing any of the enthusiasm she expected.

''Then why did he phone?''

Cait rolled her chair away from the desk and glanced around once again. ''I think he might be jealous,'' she whispered.

''Really?'' Lindy's eyes widened.

"Don't look so surprised." Cait, however, was much too excited recounting Paul's phone call to be offended by Lindy's attitude.

"What makes you think Paul would be jealous?" Lindy asked next.

"Maybe I'm magnifying everything in my own mind because it's what I so badly want to believe. But he did phone…"

"What did he say?" Lindy pressed, sounding more curious now. "It seems to me he must have had a reason."

"Oh, he did. He mentioned something about appreciating an article I'd given him, but we both know that was just an excuse. What clued me in to his jealousy was the way he kept asking if I was alone."

"But that could have several connotations, don't you think?" Lindy suggested.

"Yes, I know, but it made sense that he'd want to know if Joe was at the apartment or not."

"And was he?"

"Of course not," Cait said righteously. She didn't feel guilty about hiding the fact that he'd been there earlier, or that they'd spent nearly all of Saturday together. "I'm sure Joe's ridiculous remark when I left the office Friday is what convinced Paul to phone me. If I wasn't so furious with Joe, I might even be grateful."

"What's that?" Lindy asked abruptly, pointing to the thick folder in front of Cait. Her lips had thinned slightly as if she was confused or annoyed—about what, Cait couldn't figure out.

"This, my friend," she began, holding up the

folder, "is the key to my future with our dedicated manager."

Lindy didn't immediately respond and looked more puzzled then before. "How do you mean?"

Cait couldn't get over the feeling that things weren't quite right with her best friend; she seemed to be holding something back. But Cait realized Lindy would tell her when she was ready. Lindy always hated being pushed or prodded.

"The folder?" Lindy prompted when Cait didn't answer.

Cait flipped it open. "I spent all day Sunday reading through old business journals looking for additional articles that might interest Paul. I must have gone back five years. I copied the articles I consider the most valuable and added a brief analysis of my own. I was hoping to give it to him sometime today. That's why I was asking if you knew his schedule."

"Unfortunately I don't," Lindy murmured. She straightened, reached for her briefcase and made a show of checking her watch. Then she looked up to smile reassuringly at Cait. "I'd better get to work. I'll come by later to help you put up your decorations, okay?"

"Thanks," Cait said, then added, "Wish me luck with Paul."

"You know I do," Lindy mumbled on her way out the door.

Mondays were generally slow for the stock market, slow, that is, unless there was a crisis. World events and financial reports had a significant impact on the market. However, as the day progressed, everything ran smoothly.

Cait glanced up every now and again, half expecting to see Joe lounging in her doorway. His men had started early that morning, but by noon, Joe hadn't arrived.

Not until much later did she realize it was Paul she should be anticipating, not Joe. Paul was the romantic interest of her life and it irritated her that Joe seemed to preoccupy her thoughts.

As it happened, Paul did stroll past her office shortly after the New York market closed. Grabbing the folder, Cait raced toward his office, not hesitating for an instant. This was her golden opportunity and she was taking hold of it with both hands.

"Good afternoon, Paul," she said cordially as she stood in his doorway, clutching the folder. "Do you have a moment or would you rather I came back later?"

He looked tired, as if the day had already been a grueling one. It was all Cait could do not to offer to massage away the stress and worry that complicated his life. Her heart swelled with a renewed wave of love. For a wild, impetuous moment, it was true, she'd suffered her doubts. Any woman would have when a man like Joe took her in his arms. He might be arrogant in the extreme and one of the worst pranksters she'd ever met, but despite all that, he had a certain charm. But now that she was with Paul, Cait remembered sharply who it was she really loved.

"I don't want to be a bother," she added softly.

He offered her a listless smile. "Come in, Cait. Now is fine." He gestured toward a chair.

She hurried into the office, trying to keep the bounce out of her step. Knowing she'd be spending a few extra minutes alone with Paul, Cait had taken special care with her appearance that morning.

He glanced up and smiled at her again, but this time Cait thought she could see a glimmer of appreciation in his eyes. "What can I do for you? I hope you're pleased with your office." He frowned slightly.

For a second, she forgot what she was doing in Paul's office and stared at him blankly until his own gaze fell to the folder. "The office looks great," she said quickly. "Um, the reason I'm here..." She faltered, then gulped in a quick breath and continued, "I went through some of the business journals I have at home and found several I felt would interest you." She extended the folder to him, like a ceremonial offering.

He took it from her and opened it gingerly. "Gracious," he said, flipping through the pages and scanning her written comments, "you must have spent hours on this."

"It was...nothing." She'd willingly have done a good deal more to gain his appreciation and eventually his love.

"I won't have a chance to look at this for a few days," he said.

"Oh, please, there's no rush. You happened to mention you got some useful insights from the previous article I gave you. So I thought I'd share a few others that seem relevant to what's happening with the market now."

"It's very thoughtful of you."

"I was happy to do it. More than happy," she amended with her most brilliant smile. When he didn't say anything more, Cait rose reluctantly to her feet.

"You must be swamped after being in meetings most of the day, so I'll leave you for now."

She was almost at the door when he spoke. "Actually I only dropped into the office to collect a few things before heading out again. I've got an important date this evening."

Cait felt as if the floor had suddenly disappeared and she was plummeting through empty space. "Date?" she repeated before she could stop herself. It was a struggle to keep smiling.

Paul's grin was downright boyish. "Yes, I'm meeting her for dinner."

"In that case, have a good time."

"Thanks, I will," he returned confidently, his eyes alight with excitement. "Oh, and by the way," he added, indicating the folder she'd worked so hard on, "thanks for all the effort you put into this."

"You're...welcome."

By the time Cait returned to her office she felt numb. Paul had an important date. It wasn't as though she'd expected him to live the life of a hermit, but before today, he'd never mentioned going out with anyone. She might have suspected he'd thrown out the information hoping to make her jealous if it hadn't been for one thing. He seemed genuinely thrilled about this date. Besides, Paul wasn't the kind of man to resort to pretense.

"Cait, my goodness," Lindy said, strolling into her office a while later, "what's wrong? You look dreadful."

Cait swallowed against the lump in her throat and managed a shaky smile. "I talked to Paul and gave him the research I'd done."

"He didn't appreciate it?" Lindy picked up the wreath that lay on Cait's desk and pinned it to the door.

"I'm sure he did," she replied. "What he doesn't appreciate is me. I might as well be invisible to that man." She pushed the hair away from her forehead and braced both elbows on her desk, feeling totally disheartened. Unless she acted quickly, she was going to lose Paul to some faceless, nameless woman.

"You've been invisible to him before. What's different about this time?" She fastened a silver bell to the window as Cait abstractedly fingered her three ceramic Wise Men.

"Paul's got a date, and from the way he said it, this isn't with just any woman, either. Whoever she is must be important, otherwise he wouldn't have mentioned her. He looked like a little kid who's been given the keys to a candy store."

The information seemed to surprise Lindy as much as it had Cait. She was quiet for a few minutes before she asked quietly, "What are you going to do about it?"

"Heavens, I don't know," Cait cried, hiding her face in her hands. She'd once jokingly suggested to Joe that she parade around naked in an effort to gain Paul's attention. Of course she'd been exaggerating, but some form of drastic action was obviously needed. If only she knew what.

Lindy mumbled an excuse and left. It wasn't until Cait looked up that she realized her friend was gone. She sighed wearily. She'd arrived at work this morning with such bright expectations, and now everything had gone wrong. She felt more depressed than she'd been in a long time. She knew the best remedy would be to force herself into some physical activity. Anything. The worst possible thing she could do was sit home alone and mope. Maybe she should plan to buy herself a Christmas tree and some ornaments. Her spirits couldn't help being at least a little improved by that; it would get her out of the house, if nothing else. And then she'd have something to entertain herself with, instead of brooding about this unexpected turn of events. Getting out of the house had an added advantage. If Joe phoned, she wouldn't be there to answer.

No sooner had that thought passed through her mind when a large form filled her doorway.

Joe.

A bright orange hard hat was pushed back on his head, the way movie cowboys wore their Stetsons. His boots were dusty and his tool pouch rode low on his hip, completing the gunslinger image. Even the way he stood with his thumbs tucked in his belt suggested he was expecting a showdown.

"Hi, beautiful," he drawled, giving her that lazy, intimate smile of his. The one designed, Cait swore, just to unnerve her. But it wasn't going to work, not in her present state of mind.

"Don't you have anyone else to pester?" she snapped.

"My, my," Joe said, shaking his head in mock chagrin. Disregarding her lack of welcome, he strode into the office and threw himself down in the chair beside her desk. "You're in a rare mood."

"You would be too after the day I've had. Listen, Joe, as you can see, I'm poor company. Go flirt with the receptionist if you're looking to make someone miserable.''

"Those claws are certainly sharp this afternoon." He ran his hands down the front of his shirt, pretending to inspect the damage inflicted. "What's wrong?" Some of the teasing light faded from his eyes as he studied her.

She sent him a look meant to blister his ego, but as always Joe seemed invincible against her practiced glares.

"How do you know I'm not here to invest fifty thousand dollars?" he demanded, making himself at home by reaching across her desk for a pen. He rolled it casually between his palms.

Cait wasn't about to fall for this little game. "Are you here to invest money?"

"Not exactly. I wanted to ask you to—"

"Then come back when you are." She grabbed a stack of papers and slapped them down on her desk. But being rude, even to Joe, went against her nature. She was battling tears and the growing need to explain her behavior, apologize for it, when he slowly rose to his feet. He tossed the pen carelessly onto her desk.

"Have it your way. If asking you to join me to look for a Christmas tree is such a terrible crime, then—"

"You're going to buy a Christmas tree?"

"That's what I just said." He flung the words over his shoulder on his way out the door.

In that moment, Cait felt as though the whole world was tumbling down around her shoulders. She felt like such a shrew. He'd come here wanting to include her in his Christmas preparations and she'd driven him away with a spiteful tongue and a haughty attitude.

Cait wasn't a woman easily given to tears, but she struggled with them now. Her lower lip started to quiver. She might have been eight years old all over again—this was like the day she found out she wasn't invited to Betsy McDonald's birthday party. Only now it was Paul doing the excluding. He and this important woman of his were going out to have the time of their lives while she stayed home in her lonely apartment, suffering from a serious bout of self-pity.

Gathering up her things, Cait thrust the papers into her briefcase with uncharacteristic negligence. She put on her coat, buttoned it quickly and wrapped the scarf around her neck as though it was a hangman's noose.

Joe was talking to the foreman of the crew who'd been unobtrusively working around the office all day. He hesitated when he saw her, halting the conversation. Cait's eyes briefly met his and although she tried to disguise how regretful she felt, she obviously did a poor job of it. He took a step toward her, but she raised her chin a notch, too proud to admit her feelings.

She had to walk directly past Joe on her way to the elevator and forced herself to look anywhere but at him.

The stocky foreman clearly wanted to resume the discussion, but Joe ignored him and stared at Cait instead, with narrowed, assessing eyes. She could feel his questioning concern as profoundly as if he'd touched her. When she could bear it no longer, she turned to face him, her lower lip quivering uncontrollably.

"Cait," he called out.

She raced for the elevator, fearing she'd burst into tears before she could make her grand exit. She didn't bother to respond, knowing that if she said anything she'd make an even greater fool of herself than usual. She wasn't even sure what had prompted her to say the atrocious things to Joe that she had. He wasn't the one who'd upset her, yet she'd unfairly taken her frustrations out on him.

She should have known it would be impossible to make a clean getaway. She almost ran through the office, past the reception desk, toward the elevator.

"Aren't you going to answer me?" Joe demanded, following on her heels like a Mississippi hound.

"No." She concentrated on the lighted numbers above the elevator, which moved with painstaking slowness. Three more floors and she could make good her escape.

"What's so insulting about inviting you to go Christmas-tree shopping?" he asked.

Close to weeping, she waved her free hand, hoping he'd understand that she was incapable of explaining just then. Her throat was clogged up and it hurt to breathe, let alone talk. Her eyes filled with tears, and everything started to blur.

"Tell me," he commanded a second time.

Cait gulped at the tightness in her throat. "Y-you wouldn't understand." Why, oh why, wouldn't that elevator hurry?

"Try me."

It was either give in and explain, or stand there and argue. The first choice was easier; frankly, Cait hadn't the energy to fight with him. Sighing deeply, she began, "It—it all started when I made up this folder of business articles for Paul…"

"I might have known Paul had something to do with this," Joe muttered under his breath.

"I spent hours putting it together for him, adding little comments, and...and... I don't know what I expected but it wasn't..."

"What happened? What did Paul do?"

Cait rubbed her eyes with the back of her hand. "If you're going to interrupt me, then I can't see any reason to explain."

"Boss?" the foreman called out, sounding impatient.

Just then the elevator arrived and the doors opened, revealing half a dozen men and women. They stared out at Cait and Joe while he blocked the entrance, gripping her by the elbow.

"Joseph," she hissed, "let me go!" Recognizing her advantage, she called out, "This man refuses to release my arm." If she expected a knight in shining armor to leap to her rescue, Cait was to be sorely disappointed. It was as if no one had heard her.

"Don't worry, folks, we're married." Joe charmed them with another of his lazy, lopsided grins.

"Boss?" the foreman pleaded again.

"Take the rest of the day off," Joe shouted. "Tell the crew to go out and buy Christmas gifts for their wives."

"You want me to do what?" the foreman shouted back. Joe moved into the elevator with Cait.

"You heard me."

"Let me make sure I understand you right. You want the men to go Christmas shopping for their wives? I thought you just said we're on a tight schedule?"

"That's right," Joe said loudly as the elevator doors closed.

Cait had never felt more conspicuous in her life. Every eye was focused on her and Joe, and it was all she could do to keep her head held high.

When the tension became intolerable, Cait turned to face her fellow passengers. "We are not married," she announced.

"Yes, we are," Joe insisted. "She's simply forgotten."

"I did not forget our marriage and don't you dare tell them that cock-and-bull story about amnesia."

"But, darling—"

"Stop it right now, Joseph Rockwell! No one believes you. These people can take one look at us and determine that I'm the one who's telling the truth."

The elevator finally stopped on the ground floor, a fact for which Cait was deeply grateful. The doors glided open and two women stepped out first, but not before pausing to get a good appreciative look at Joe.

"Does she do this often?" one of the men asked, directing his question to Joe, his amusement obvious.

"Unfortunately, yes," he answered, chuckling as he tucked his hand under Cait's elbow and led her into the foyer. She tried to jerk her arm away, but he wouldn't allow it. "You see, I married a forgetful bride."

Seven

Pacing the carpet in the living room, Cait nervously smoothed the front of her red satin dress, her heart pumping a mile a second while she waited impatiently for Joe to arrive. She'd spent hours preparing for this Christmas party, which was being held in Paul's home. Her stomach was in knots and had been for hours.

She, the mysterious woman Paul was dating, would surely be there. Cait would have her first opportunity to size up the competition. Cait had studied her reflection countless times, trying to be objective about her chances with Paul based on looks alone. The dress was gorgeous. Her hair flawless. Everything else was as perfect as she could make it.

The doorbell sounded and Cait hurried across the room, throwing open the door. "You know what you are, Joseph Rockwell?"

"Late?" he suggested.

Cait pretended not to hear him. "A bully," she furnished. "A badgering bully, no less. I'm sorry I ever agreed to let you take me to Paul's party. I don't know what I was thinking of."

"No doubt you were hoping to corner me under the mistletoe," he remarked, with a wink that implied he wouldn't be difficult to persuade.

"First you practically kidnap me into going Christmas-tree shopping with you," she raged on. "Then—"

"Come on, Cait, admit it, you had fun." He lounged indolently on her sofa while she got her coat and purse.

She hesitated, her mouth twitching with a smile. "Who'd ever believe that a man who bought his mother a rib roast and a case of cat food for Christmas last year would be so particular about a silly tree?" Joe had dragged her to no less than four lots, searching for the perfect tree.

"I took you to dinner afterward, didn't I?" he reminded her.

Cait nodded. She had to admit it: Joe had gone out of his way to help her forget her troubles. Although she'd made the tree-shopping expedition sound like a chore, he'd turned the evening into an enjoyable and, yes, a memorable one.

His good mood had been infectious and after a while she'd completely forgotten Paul was out with another woman—someone so special that his enthusiasm about her had overcome his normal restraint.

"I've changed my mind," Cait decided suddenly, clasping her hands over her stomach, which was in turmoil. "I don't want to go to this Christmas party, after all." The evening was already doomed. She couldn't possibly have a good time watching the man she loved entertain the woman *he* loved. Cait couldn't think of a single reason to expose herself to that kind of misery.

"Not go to the party?" Joe repeated. "But I thought

you'd arranged your flight schedule just so you could.''

"I did, but that was before.'' Cait stubbornly squared her shoulders and elevated her chin just enough to convince Joe she meant business. He might be able to bully her into going shopping with him for a Christmas tree, but this was something entirely different. ''*She'll* be there,'' Cait added as an explanation.

"She?'' Joe repeated slowly, burying his hands in his suit pockets. He was devilishly handsome in his dark blue suit and no doubt knew it. He was no less comfortable in tailored slacks than he was in dirty jeans.

A lock of thick hair slanted across his forehead; Cait managed—it was an effort—to resist brushing it back. An effort not because it disrupted his polished appearance, but because she had the strangest desire to run her fingers through his hair. Why she would think such a thing now was beyond her. She'd long since stopped trying to figure out her feelings for Joe. He was a friend and a confidant even if, at odd moments, he behaved like a lunatic. Just remembering some of the comments he'd made to embarrass her was enough to bring color to her cheeks.

"I'd think you'd want to meet her,'' Joe challenged. "That way you can size her up.''

"I don't even want to know what she looks like,'' Cait countered sharply. She didn't need to. Cait already knew everything she cared to about Paul's hot date. "She's beautiful.''

"So are you.''

Cait gave a short, derisive laugh. She wasn't discounting her own homespun appeal. She was reasonably attractive, and never more so than this evening. Catching a glimpse of herself in the mirror, she was pleased to note how nice her hair looked, with the froth of curls circling her head. But she wasn't going to kid herself, either. Her allure wasn't extraordinary by any stretch of the imagination. Her eyes were a nice warm shade of brown, though, and her nose was kind of cute. Perky, Lindy had once called it. But none of that mattered. Measuring herself against Paul's sure-to-be-gorgeous, nameless date was like comparing bulky sweat socks with a silk stocking. She'd already spent hours picturing her as a classic beauty... tall...sophisticated.

"I've never taken you for a coward," Joe said in a flat tone as he headed toward the door.

Apparently he wasn't even going to argue with her. Cait almost wished he would, just so she could show him how strong her will was. Nothing he could say or do would convince her to attend this party. Besides, her feet hurt. She was wearing new heels and hadn't broken them in yet, and if she did go to the party, she'd probably be limping for days afterward.

"I'm not a coward," she insisted, schooling her face to remain as emotionless as possible. "All I'm doing is exercising a little common sense. Why depress myself over the holidays? This is the last time I'll see Paul before Christmas. I leave for Minnesota in the morning."

"Yes, I know." Joe frowned as he said it, hesitating before he opened her door. "You're sure about this?"

"Positive." She was mildly surprised Joe wasn't

putting up more of a fuss. From past experience, she'd expected a full-scale verbal battle.

"The choice is yours of course," he granted, shrugging. "But if it was me, I know I'd spend the whole time I was away regretting it." He studied her when he'd finished, then smiled in a way Cait could only describe as crafty.

She groaned inwardly. If there was one thing that drove her crazy about Joe it was the way he made the most outrageous statements. Then every once in a while he'd say something so wise it caused her to doubt her own conclusions and beliefs. This was one of those times. He was right: if she didn't go to Paul's, she'd regret it. Since she was leaving the following day for Minnesota, she wouldn't be able to ask anyone about the party, either.

"Are you coming or not?" he demanded.

Grumbling under her breath, Cait let him help her on with her coat. "I'm coming, but I don't like it. Not one darn bit."

"You're going to do just fine."

"They probably said that to Joan of Arc."

Cait clutched the punch glass in both hands, as though terrified someone might try to take it back. Standing next to the fireplace, with its garlanded mantel and cheerful blaze, she hadn't moved since they'd arrived a half hour earlier.

"Is *she* here yet?" she whispered to Lindy when her friend strolled past carrying in a tray of canapés.

"Who?"

"Paul's woman friend," Cait said pointedly. Both Joe and Lindy were beginning to exasperate her. "I've been standing here for the past thirty minutes hoping to catch a glimpse of her.''

Lindy looked away. ''I...I don't know if she's here or not.''

''Stay with me, for heaven's sake,'' Cait requested, feeling shaky inside and out. Joe had deserted her almost as soon as they'd arrived. Oh, he'd stuck around long enough to bring her a cup of punch, but then he'd drifted away, leaving Cait to deal with the situation on her own. This was the very man who'd insisted she attend this Christmas party, claiming he'd be right by her side the entire evening in case she needed him.

''I'm helping Paul with the hors d'oeuvres,'' Lindy explained, ''otherwise I'd be happy to stay and chat.''

''See if you can find Joe for me, would you?'' She'd do it herself, but her feet were killing her.

''Sure.''

Once Lindy was gone, Cait scanned the crowded living room. Many of the guests were business associates and clients Paul had worked with over the years. Naturally everyone from the office was there, as well.

''You wanted to see me?'' Joe asked, reaching her side.

''Thank you very much,'' she hissed, doing her best to sound sarcastic and keep a smile on her face at the same time.

''You're welcome.'' He leaned one elbow on the fireplace mantel and grinned boyishly at her. ''Might I ask what you're thanking me for?''

''Don't play games with me, Joe. Not now, please.'' She shifted her weight from one foot to the other, drawing his attention to her shoes.

''Your feet hurt?'' he asked, frowning.

"Walking across hot coals would be less painful than these stupid high heels."

"Then why did you wear them?"

"Because they go with the dress. Listen, would you mind very much if we got off the subject of my shoes and discussed the matter at hand?"

"Which is?"

Joe was being as obtuse as Lindy had been. Surely he was doing it deliberately, just to get a rise out of her. Well, it was working.

"Did you see her?" she asked with exaggerated patience.

"Not yet," he whispered back as though they were exchanging top-secret information. "She doesn't seem to have arrived."

"Have you talked to Paul?"

"No. Have you?"

"Not really." Paul had greeted them at the door, but other than that, Cait hadn't had a chance to do anything but watch him mingle with his guests. The day at the office hadn't been any help, either. Paul had breezed in and out without giving Cait more than a friendly wave. Since they hadn't exchanged a single word, it was impossible for her to determine how his date had gone.

It must have been a busy day for Lindy, as well, because Cait hadn't had a chance to talk to her, either. They'd met on their way out the door late in the afternoon and Lindy had hurried past, muttering that she'd see Cait at Paul's party.

"I think I'll go help Lindy with the hors d'oeuvres," Cait said now. "Do you want me to get you anything?"

"Nothing, thanks." He was grinning as he strolled away, leaving Cait to wonder what he found so amusing.

Cait limped into the kitchen, leaving the polished wooden door swinging in her wake. She stopped abruptly when she encountered Paul and Lindy in the middle of a heated discussion.

"Oh, sorry," Cait apologized automatically.

Paul's gaze darted to Cait's. "No problem," he said pointedly. "I was just leaving." He stalked past her, shoving the door open with the palm of his hand. Once again the door swung back and forth.

"What was that all about?" Cait wanted to know.

Lindy continued transferring the small cheese-dotted crackers from the cookie sheet onto the serving platter. "Nothing."

"It sounded as if you and Paul were arguing."

Lindy straightened and bit her lip. She avoided looking at Cait, concentrating on her task as if it was of vital importance to properly arrange the crackers on the plate.

"You were arguing, weren't you?" Cait pressed.

"Yes."

As far as she knew, Lindy and Paul had always gotten along. The fact that they were at odds with each other surprised her. "About what?"

"I—I gave Paul my two-week notice this afternoon."

Cait was so shocked, she pulled out a kitchen chair and sank down on it. "You did what?" Removing her high heels, she massaged her pinched toes.

"You heard me."

"But why? Good grief, Lindy, you never said a

word to anyone. Not even me. The least you could have done was talk to me about it first.'' No wonder Paul was angry. If Lindy left, it would mean bringing in someone new when the office was short-staffed. With Cait and a number of other people away for the holidays, the place would be a madhouse.

''Did you receive an offer you couldn't refuse?'' Cait hadn't had any idea her friend was unhappy at Webster, Rodale and Missen. That didn't shock her nearly as much as Lindy's remaining tight-lipped about it all.

''It wasn't exactly an offer—but it was something like that,'' Lindy replied vaguely. With that, she set aside the cookie sheet, smiled at Cait and then carried the platter into the living room.

For the past couple of weeks Cait had noticed that something was troubling her friend. It hadn't been anything she could readily name. Just that Lindy hadn't been her usual high-spirited self. Cait had meant to ask her about it, but she'd been so busy herself, so involved with her own problems, that she'd never brought it up.

She was still sitting there rubbing her feet when Joe sauntered into the kitchen, nibbling on a cheese cracker. ''I thought I'd find you in here.'' He pulled out the chair across from her and sat down.

''Has she arrived yet?''

''Apparently so.''

Cait dropped her foot and frantically worked the shoe back and forth until she'd managed to squeeze her toes inside. Then she forced her other foot into its shoe. ''Well, for heaven's sake, why didn't you say something sooner?'' she chastised. She straightened, ran her hands down the satin skirt and drew a shaky breath. "How do I look?"

"Like your feet hurt."

She sent him a scalding look. "Thank you very much," she muttered sarcastically. Hobbling to the door, she opened it a crack and peeked out, hoping to catch sight of the mystery woman. From what she could see, there weren't any new arrivals.

"What does she look like?" Cait demanded and whirled around to discover Joe standing directly behind her. She nearly collided with him and gave a small cry of surprise. Joe caught her by the shoulders to keep her from stumbling. Eager to question him about Paul's date, she didn't take the time to analyze why her heartrate soared when his hands made contact with her bare skin.

"What does she look like?" Cait demanded again.

"I don't know," Joe returned flippantly.

"What do you mean you don't know? You just said she'd arrived."

"Unfortunately she doesn't have a tattoo across her forehead announcing that she's the woman Paul's dating."

"Then how do you know she's here?" If Joe was playing games with her, she'd make damn sure he'd regret it. Her love for Paul was no joking matter.

"It's more a feeling I have."

"You had me stuff my feet back into these shoes for a stupid feeling?" It was all she could do not to slap him silly. "You are no friend of mine, Joseph Rockwell. No friend whatsoever." Having said that, she limped back into the living room.

Obviously unscathed by her remark, Joe strolled out

of the kitchen behind her. He walked over to the tray of canapés and helped himself to three or four while Cait did her best to ignore him.

Since the punch bowl was close by, she poured herself a second glass. The taste was sweet and cold, but Cait noticed that she felt a bit light-headed afterward. Potent drinks didn't sit well on an empty stomach, so she scooped up a handful of mixed nuts.

"I remember a time when you used to line up all the Spanish peanuts and eat those first," Joe said from behind her. "Then it was the hazelnuts, followed by the—"

"Almonds." Leave it to him to bring up her foolish past. "I haven't done that since I was—"

"Twenty," he guessed.

"Twenty-five," she corrected.

Joe laughed, and despite her aching feet and the certainty that she should never have come to this party, Cait laughed, too.

Refilling her punch glass, she downed it all in a single drink. Once more, it tasted cool and refreshing.

"Cait," Joe warned, "how much punch have you had?"

"Not enough." She filled the crystal cup a third time—or was it the fourth?—squared her shoulders and gulped it down. When she'd finished, she wiped the back of her hand across her mouth and smiled bravely.

"Are you purposely trying to get drunk?" he demanded.

"No." She reached for another handful of nuts. "All I'm looking for is a little courage."

"Courage?"

"Yes," she said with a sigh. "The way I figure it…" She paused, smiling giddily, then twisted around in a full circle. "There *is* some mistletoe here, isn't there?"

"I think so," Joe said, frowning. "What makes you ask?"

"I'm going to kiss Paul," she announced proudly. "All I have to do is wait until he strolls past. Then I'll grab him by the hand, wish him a merry Christmas and give him a kiss he won't soon forget." If the fantasy fulfilled itself, Paul would then realize he'd met the woman of his dreams, and then and there propose marriage….

"What is kissing Paul supposed to prove?"

She returned to reality. "Well, this is where you come in. I want you to look around and watch the faces of the other women. If any one of them shows signs of jealousy, then we'll know who it is."

"I'm not sure this plan of yours will work."

"It's better than trusting those feelings of yours," she countered.

She spied the mistletoe hanging from the archway between the formal dining room and the living room. Slouched against the wall, hands tucked behind her back, Cait waited patiently for Paul to stroll past.

Ten minutes passed or maybe it was fifteen—Cait couldn't tell. Yawning, she covered her mouth. "I think we should leave," Joe suggested as he casually walked by. "You're ready to drop on your feet."

"I haven't kissed Paul yet," she reminded him.

"He seems to be involved in a lengthy discussion. This could take a while."

"I'm in no hurry." Her throat felt unusually dry.

She would have preferred something nonalcoholic, but the only drink nearby was the punch.

"Cait," Joe warned when he saw her helping herself to yet another glass.

"Don't worry, I know what I'm doing."

"So did the captain of the *Titanic*."

"Don't get cute with me, Joseph Rockwell. I'm in no mood to deal with someone amusing." Finding herself hilariously funny, she smothered a round of giggles.

"Oh, no," Joe groaned. "I was afraid of this."

"Afraid of what?"

"You're drunk!"

She gave him a sour look. "That's ridiculous. All I had is four little, bitty glasses of punch." To prove she knew exactly what she was doing, she held up three fingers, recognized her mistake and promptly corrected herself. At least she tried to do it promptly, figuring out how many fingers equaled four seemed to take an inordinate amount of time. She finally held up two from each hand.

Expelling her breath, she leaned back against the wall and closed her eyes. That was her second mistake. The world took a sharp and unexpected nosedive. Snapping open her eyes, Cait looked to Joe as the anchor that would keep her afloat. He must have read the panic in her expression because he walked over to her and slowly shook his head.

"That does it, Miss Singapore Sling. I'm getting you out of here."

"But I haven't been under the mistletoe yet."

"If you want anyone to kiss you, it'll be me."

The offer sounded tempting, but it was her stubborn

boss Cait wanted to kiss, not Joe. "I'd rather dance with you."

"Unfortunately there isn't any music at the moment."

"You need music to dance?" It sounded like the saddest thing she'd ever heard, and her bottom lip started to tremble at the tragedy of it all. "Oh, dear, Joe," she whispered, placing both hands on the sides of her head. "I think you might be right. The liquor seems to be affecting me...."

"It's that bad, is it?"

"Uh, yes... The whole room's just started to pitch and heave. We're not having an earthquake, are we?"

"No." His hand was on her forearm, guiding her toward the front door.

"Wait," she said dramatically, raising her index finger. "I have a coat."

"I know. Wait here and I'll get it for you." He seemed worried about leaving her. Cait smiled at him, trying to reassure him she'd be perfectly fine, but she seemed unable to keep her balance. He urged her against the wall, stepped back a couple of paces as though he expected her to slip sideways, then hurriedly located her coat.

"What's wrong?" he asked when he returned.

"What makes you think anything's wrong?"

"Other than the fact that you're crying?"

"My feet hurt."

Joe rolled his eyes. "Why did you wear those stupid shoes in the first place?"

"I already told you," she whimpered. "Don't be mad at me." She held out her arms to him, needing his comfort. "Would you carry me to the car?"

Joe hesitated. "You want me to carry you?" He sounded as though it was a task of Herculean proportions.

"I can't walk." She'd taken the shoes off, and it would take God's own army to get them back on. She couldn't very well traipse outside in her stocking feet.

"If I carry you, we'd better find another way out of the house."

"All right." She agreed just to prove what an amicable person she actually was. When she was a child, she'd been a pest, but she wasn't anymore and she wanted to be sure Joe understood that.

Grasping Cait's hand, he led her into the kitchen.

"Don't you think we should make our farewells?" she asked. It seemed the polite thing to do.

"No," he answered sharply. "With the mood you're in you're likely to throw yourself in Paul's arms and demand that he make mad passionate love to you there on the spot."

Cait's face went fire-engine red. "That's ridiculous."

Joe mumbled something she couldn't hear while he lifted her hand and slipped one arm, then the other, into the satin-lined sleeves of her full-length coat.

When he'd finished, Cait climbed on top of the kitchen chair, stretching out her arms to him. Joe stared at her as though she'd suddenly turned into a werewolf.

"What are you doing now?" he demanded in an exasperated voice.

"You're going to carry me, aren't you?"

"I was considering it."

"I want a piggyback ride. You gave Betsy Mc-Donald a piggyback ride once and not me."

"Cait," Joe groaned. He jerked his fingers through his hair, and offered her his hand, wanting her to climb down from the chair. "Get down before you fall. Good Lord, I swear you'd try the patience of a saint."

"I want you to carry me piggyback," she insisted. "Oh, please, Joe. My toes hurt so bad."

Once again her hero grumbled under his breath. She couldn't make out everything he said, but what she did hear was enough to curl her hair. With obvious reluctance, he walked to the chair, and giving a sigh of pure bliss, Cait wrapped her arms around his neck and hugged his lean hips with her legs. She laid her head on his shoulder and sighed again.

Still grumbling, Joe moved toward the back door.

Just then the kitchen door opened and Paul and Lindy walked in. Lindy gasped. Paul just stared.

"It's all right," Cait was quick to assure them. "Really it is. I was waiting under the mistletoe and you—"

"She downed four glasses of punch nonstop," Joe inserted before Cait could admit she'd been waiting there for Paul.

"Do you need any help?" Paul asked.

"None, thanks," Joe returned. "There's nothing to worry about."

"But…" Lindy looked concerned.

"She ain't heavy," Joe teased. "She's my wife."

The phone rang, waking Cait from a sound sleep. Her head began throbbing in time to the painful noise and she groped for the telephone receiver.

"Hello," she barked, instantly regretting that she'd spoken loudly.

"How are you feeling?" Joe asked.

"About like you'd expect," she whispered, keeping her eyes closed and gently massaging one temple. It felt as though tiny men had taken up residence in her head and were pounding away, hoping to attract her attention.

"What time does your flight leave?" he asked.

"It's okay. I'm not scheduled to leave until afternoon."

"It is afternoon."

Her eyes flew open. "What?"

"Do you still need me to take you to the airport?"

"Yes...please." She tossed aside the covers and reached for her clock, stunned to realize Joe was right. "I'm already packed. I'll be dressed by the time you arrive. Oh, thank goodness you phoned."

Cait didn't have time to listen to the pounding of the tiny men in her head. She showered and dressed in record time, swallowed a cup of coffee and a couple of aspirin, and was just shrugging into her coat when Joe arrived at the door.

She let him in, despite the suspiciously wide grin he wore.

"What's so amusing?"

"What makes you think I'm amused?" He strolled into the room, hands behind his back, as if he owned the place.

"Joe, we don't have time for your little games. Come on, or I'm going to miss my plane. What's with you, anyway?"

"Nothing." He circled her living room, still wearing that silly grin. "I don't suppose you realize it, but liquor has a peculiar effect on you."

Cait stiffened. "It does?" She remembered most of the party with great clarity. Good thing Joe had taken her home when he had.

"Liquor loosens your tongue."

"So?" She picked up two shopping bags filled with wrapped packages, leaving the lone suitcase for him. "Did I say anything of interest?"

"Oh my, yes."

"Joe," she groaned, glancing quickly at her watch. They needed to get moving if she was to catch her flight. "Discount whatever I said—I'm sure I didn't mean it. If I insulted you, I apologize. If I told any family secrets, kindly forget I mentioned them."

He strolled to her side and tucked his finger under her chin. "This was a secret all right," he informed her in a lazy drawl.

"Are you sure it's true?"

"Relatively sure."

"What did I do? Declare undying love for you? Because if I did—"

"No, no, nothing like that."

"Just how long do you intend to torment me like this?" She was rapidly losing interest in his little game.

"Not much longer." He looked exceptionally pleased with himself. "So Martin's a minister now. Funny you never thought to mention that before."

"Ah…" Cait set aside the two bags and lowered herself to the sofa. So he'd found out. Worse, she'd been the one to tell him.

"That may well have some interesting ramifications, my dear. Have you ever stopped to think about them?"

Eight

"This is exactly why I didn't tell you about Martin," Cait informed Joe as he tossed her suitcase into the back seat of his car. She checked her watch again and groaned. They had barely an hour and a half before her flight was scheduled to leave. Cait was never late. Never—at least not when it was her own fault.

"It seems to me," Joe continued, his face deadpan, "there could very well be some legal grounds to our marriage."

Joe was saying that just to annoy her, and unfortunately it was working. "I've never heard anything more ridiculous in my life."

"Think about it, Cait," he said, ignoring her protest. "We could be celebrating our anniversary this spring. How many years is it now? Eighteen? My, how the years fly."

"Listen, Joe, I don't find this amusing." Again she glanced at her watch. If only she hadn't slept so late. Never again would she sample Christmas punch. Briefly she wondered what else she'd said to Joe, then decided it was better not to know.

"I heard a news report of a three-car pileup on the freeway, so we'd better take the side streets."

"Just hurry," Cait urged in an anxious voice.

"I'll do the best I can," Joe said, "but worrying about it isn't going to get us there any faster."

She glared at him. She couldn't help it. He wasn't the one who'd been planning this trip for months. If she missed this flight, her nephews and niece wouldn't have their Christmas presents from their Auntie Cait. Nor would she share in the family traditions that were so much a part of her Christmas. It was vital she get to the airport on time.

Everyone else had apparently heard about the accident on the freeway, too, and the downtown area was crowded with the overflow. Cait and Joe were delayed at every intersection and twice were forced to sit through two changes of the traffic signal.

Cait was growing more panicky by the moment. She just had to make this flight. But it almost seemed that she'd get to the airport faster if she simply jumped out of the car and ran there.

Joe stopped for another red light, but when the signal turned green, they still couldn't move—a delivery truck in front of them had stalled. Furious, Cait rolled down the window and stuck out her head. "Listen here, buster, get this show on the road," she shouted at the top of her lungs.

Her head was pounding and she prayed the aspirin would soon take affect.

"Quite the Christmas spirit," Joe muttered dryly under his breath.

"I can't help it. I have to catch this plane."

"You'll be there in plenty of time."

"At this rate we won't make it to Sea-Tac Airport before Easter!"

"Relax, will you?" Joe suggested gently. He turned

on the radio and a medley of Christmas carols filled the air. Normally the music would have had a calming effect on Cait, but she was suffering from a hangover, depression and severe anxiety, all at the same time. Her fingernails found their way into her mouth.

Suddenly she straightened. "Darn! I forgot to give you your Christmas gift. I left it at home."

"Don't worry about it."

"I didn't get you a gag gift the way I said." Actually she was pleased with the book she'd managed to find—an attractive coffee-table volume about the history of baseball.

Cait waited for Joe to mention *her* gift. Surely he'd bought her one. At least she fervently hoped he had, otherwise she'd feel like a fool. Though, admittedly, that was a feeling she'd grown accustomed to in the past few weeks.

"I think we might be able to get back on the freeway here," Joe said, as he made a sharp lefthand turn. They crossed the overpass, and from their vantage point, Cait could see that the freeway was unclogged and running smoothly.

"Thank God," she whispered, relaxing against the back of the thickly cushioned seat as Joe drove quickly ahead.

Her chauffeur chuckled. "I seem to remember you lecturing me—"

"I never lecture," she said testily. "I may have a strong opinion on certain subjects, but let me assure you, I never lecture."

"You were right, though. The streets of Bethlehem must have been crowded and bustling with activity at the time of that first Christmas. I can see it all now, can't you? A rug dealer is held up by a shepherd driving his flock through the middle of town.''

Cait smiled for the first time that morning, because she could easily picture the scene Joe was describing.

"Then some furious woman, impatient to make it to the local camel merchant on time, sticks her nose in the middle of everything and shouts at the rug dealer to get his show on the road.'' He paused to chuckle at his own wit. "I'm convinced she wouldn't have been so testy except that she was suffering from one whopper of a hangover.''

"Very funny,'' Cait grumbled, smiling despite herself.

He took the exit for the airport and Cait was gratified to note that her flight wasn't scheduled to leave for another thirty minutes. She was cutting it close, closer than she ever had before, but she'd confirmed her ticket two days earlier and had already been assigned her seat.

Joe pulled up at the drop-off point for her airline and gave her suitcase to a skycap while Cait rummaged around in her purse for her ticket.

"I suppose this is goodbye for now,'' he said with an endearingly crooked grin that sent her pulses racing.

"I'll be back in less than two weeks,'' she reminded him, trying to keep her tone light and casual.

"You'll phone once you arrive?''

She nodded. For all her earlier panic, Cait now felt oddly unwilling to part company with Joe. She should be rushing through the airport to her gate assignment, but she lingered, her heart overflowing with emotions she couldn't name.

"Have a safe trip," he said quietly.

"I will. Thanks so much...for everything."

"You're welcome." His expression sobered and the ever-ready mirth drained from his eyes. Cait wasn't sure who moved first. All she knew was that she was in Joe's arms, his thumb caressing the softness of her cheek as they gazed hungrily into each other's eyes.

Slowly he leaned forward to kiss her. Cait's eyes drifted shut as his mouth met hers.

Joe's kiss was heart-stoppingly tender. The noise and activity around them seemed to fade into the distance. Cait could feel herself dissolving. She moaned and arched closer, not wanting to leave the protective haven of his arms. Joe shuddered and hugged her tight, as if he, too, found it difficult to part.

"Merry Christmas, love," he whispered, releasing her with a reluctance that made her heart sing.

"Merry Christmas," she echoed, but she didn't move.

Joe gave her the gentlest of nudges. "You'd better hurry, Cait."

"Oh, right," she said, momentarily forgetting why she was at the airport. Reaching for the bags filled with gaily wrapped Christmas packages, she took two steps backward. "I'll phone when I arrive."

"Do. I'll be waiting to hear from you." He thrust his hands into his pockets and Cait had the distinct impression he did it to stop himself from reaching out for her again. The thought was a romantic one, a certainty straight from her heart.

Her heart... Her heart was full of feeling for Joe. More than she'd ever realized. He'd dominated her life these past few weeks—taking her to dinner, bribing his way back into her good graces with a pizza, taking her on a Christmas shopping expedition, escorting her to Paul's party. Joe had become her whole world. Joe, not Paul. Joe.

Given no other choice, Cait abruptly turned and hurried into the airport, through the security check and down the concourse to the proper gate.

The flight had already been called and only a handful of passengers had yet to board. Several were making lingering farewells to loved ones.

Cait dashed to the ticket counter to check in. A young soldier stood just ahead of her. "But you don't understand," the tall marine was saying to the airline employee. "I booked this flight over a month ago. I've got to be on that plane!"

"I couldn't be more sorry," the woman apologized, her dark eyes filled with regret. "This sort of thing happens, especially during holidays, but your ticket's for standby. I wish I could do something for you, but there isn't a single seat available."

"But I haven't seen my family in over a year. My Uncle Harvey is driving from Duluth to visit. He was in the marines, too. My mom's been baking for three weeks. Don't you see? I can't disappoint them now!"

Cait watched as the ticket agent rechecked her computer. "If I could magically create a seat for you, I would," she said sympathetically. "But there just isn't one."

"But when I bought the ticket, the woman told me I wouldn't have a problem getting on the flight. She said there're always no-shows. She sounded so sure."

"I couldn't be more sorry," the agent repeated, looking past the young marine to Cait.

"All right," he said, forcefully expelling his breath. "When's the next flight with available space? Any flight within a hundred miles of Minneapolis. I'll walk the rest of the way if I have to."

Once again, the woman consulted her computer. "We have space available the evening of the twenty-sixth."

"The twenty-sixth!" the young man shouted. "But that's after Christmas and eats up nearly all my leave. I'd be home less than a week."

"May I help you?" the airline employee said to Cait. She looked almost as unhappy as the marine, but apparently there wasn't anything she could do to help him.

Cait stepped forward and handed the woman her ticket. The soldier gazed at it longingly, then moved dejectedly from the counter and lowered himself into one of the molded plastic chairs.

Cait hesitated, remembering how she'd stuck her head out the window of Joe's truck that morning and shouted impatiently at the truck driver who was holding up traffic. A conversation she'd had with Joe earlier returned to haunt her. She'd argued that Christmas was a time filled with love and good cheer, the one time of year that brought out the very best in everyone. And sometimes, Joe had insisted, the very worst.

"Since you already have your seat assignment, you may board the flight now."

Cait grabbed the ticket with both hands, the urge to hurry nearly overwhelming her. Yet she hesitated.

"Excuse me," Cait said, drawing a breath and making her decision. She approached the soldier. He seemed impossibly young now that she had a good look at him. No more than eighteen, maybe nineteen. He'd probably joined the service right out of high school. His hair was cropped close to his head and his combat boots were so shiny Cait could see her reflection in them.

The marine glanced up at her, his face heavy with defeat. "Yes?"

"Did I hear you say you needed a ticket for this plane?"

"I have a ticket, ma'am. But it's standby and there aren't any seats."

"Here," she said, giving him her ticket. "Take mine."

The way his face lit up was enough to blot out her own disappointment at missing Christmas with Martin and her sister-in-law. The kids. Her mother... "My family's in Minneapolis, too, but I was there this summer."

"Ma'am, I can't let you do this."

"Don't cheat me out of the pleasure."

The last call for their flight was announced. The marine stood, his eyes wide with disbelief. "I insist," Cait said, her throat growing thick. "Here," she handed him the two bags full of gifts for her nephews and nieces. "There'll be a man waiting on the other end. A tall minister—he'll have on a collar. Give him these. I'll phone so he'll know to look for you."

"But, ma'am—"

"We don't have time to argue. Just do it."

"Thank you...I can't believe you're doing this." He reached inside his jacket and gave her his ticket. "Here. At least you'll be able to get a refund."

Cait smiled and nodded. Impulsively the marine

hugged her, then swinging his duffel bag over his shoulder, he picked up the two bags of gifts and jogged down the ramp.

Cait waited for a couple of minutes, then wiped the tears from her eyes. She wasn't completely sure why she was crying. She'd never felt better in her life.

It was around six when she awoke. The apartment was dark and silent. Sighing, she picked up the phone, dragged it onto the bed with her and punched out Joe's number.

He answered on the first ring, as if he'd been waiting for her call. "How was the flight?" he asked immediately.

"I wouldn't know. I wasn't on it."

"You missed the plane!" he shouted incredulously. "But you were there in plenty of time."

"I know. It's a long story, but basically, I gave my seat to someone who needed it more than I did." She smiled dreamily, remembering how the young marine's face had lit up. "I'll tell you about it sometime."

"Where are you now?"

"Home."

He exhaled sharply, then said, "I'll be over in fifteen minutes."

Actually it took him twelve. By then Cait had brewed a pot of coffee and made herself a peanut-butter-and-jelly sandwich. She hadn't eaten all day and was starved. She'd just finished the sandwich when Joe arrived.

"What about your luggage?" Joe asked, looking concerned. He didn't give her a chance to respond.

"Exactly what do you mean, you gave your seat away?"

Cait explained as best she could. Even now she found herself surprised by her actions. Cait rarely behaved spontaneously. But something about that young soldier had reached deep within her heart and she'd reacted instinctively.

"The airline is sending my suitcase back to Seattle on the next available flight, so there's no need to worry," Cait explained. "I talked to Martin, who was quick to tell me the Lord would reward my generosity."

"Are you going to catch a later flight, then?" Joe asked. He helped himself to a cup of coffee and pulled out the chair across from hers.

"There aren't any seats," Cait said. She leaned back, yawning, and covered her mouth. Why she should be so tired after sleeping away most of the afternoon was beyond her. "Besides, the office is short-staffed. Lindy gave Paul her notice and a trainee is coming in, which makes everything even more difficult. They can use me."

Joe frowned. "Giving up your vacation is one way to impress Paul."

Words of explanation crowded on the end of her tongue. She realized Joe wasn't insulting her; he was only stating a fact. What he didn't understand was that Cait hadn't thought of Paul once the entire day. Her staying or leaving had absolutely nothing to do with him.

If she'd been thinking of anyone, it was Joe. She knew now that giving up her seat to the marine hadn't been entirely unselfish. When Joe kissed her goodbye, her heart had started telegraphing messages she had yet to fully decode. The plain and honest truth was that she hadn't wanted to leave him. It was as if she really did belong to him....

That perception had been with her from the moment they'd parted at the airport. It had followed her in the taxi on the ride back to the apartment. Joe was the last person she thought of when she'd fallen asleep, and the first person she remembered when she awoke.

It was the most amazing thing.

"What are you going to do for Christmas?" Joe asked, still frowning into his coffee cup. For someone who'd seemed downright regretful that she was flying halfway across the country, he didn't seem all that pleased to be sharing her company now.

"I...haven't decided yet. I suppose I'll spend a quiet day by myself." She'd wake up late, indulge in a lazy scented bath, find something sinful for breakfast. Ice cream, maybe. Then she'd paint her toenails and settle down with a good book. The day would be lonely, true, but certainly not wasted.

"It'll be anything but quiet," Joe challenged.

"Oh?"

"You'll be spending it with me and my family."

"This is the first time Joe has ever brought a girl to join us for Christmas," Virginia Rockwell said as she set a large tray of freshly baked cinnamon rolls in the center of the huge kitchen table. She wiped her hands clean on the apron that was secured around her thick waist.

Cait felt she should explain. She was a little uncomfortable arriving unannounced with Joe this way. "Joe and I are just friends."

Mrs. Rockwell shook her head, which set the white curls bobbing. "I saw my son's eyes when he brought you into the house." She grinned knowingly. "I remember you from the old neighborhood, with your starched dresses and the pigtails with those bright pink ribbons. You were a pretty girl then and you're even prettier now."

"The starched dresses were me all right," Cait confirmed. She'd been the only girl for blocks around who always wore dresses to school.

Joe's mother chuckled again. "I remember the sensation you caused in the neighborhood when you revealed that Joe had kissed you." She chuckled, her eyes shining. "His father and I got quite a kick out of that. I still remember how furious Joe was when he learned his secret was out."

"I only told one person," Cait protested. But Betsy had told plenty of others, and the news had spread with alarming speed. However, Cait figured she'd since paid for her sins tenfold. Joe had made sure of that in the past few weeks.

"It's so good to see you again, Caitlin. When we've got a minute I want you to sit down and tell me all about your mother. We lost contact years ago, but I always thought she was a darling."

"I think so, too," Cait agreed, carrying a platter of scrambled eggs to the table. She did miss being with her family, but Joe's mother made it almost as good as being home. "I know that's how Mom feels about you, too. She'll want to thank you for being kind enough to invite me into your home for Christmas."

"I wouldn't have it any other way."

"I know." She glanced into the other room where Joe was sitting with his brother and sister-in-law. Her heart throbbed at the sight of him with his family. But these newfound feelings for Joe left her at a complete loss. What she'd told Mrs. Rockwell was true. Joe was her friend. The very best friend she'd ever had. She was grateful for everything he'd done for her since they'd chanced upon each other, just weeks ago, really. But their friendship was developing into something much stronger. If only she didn't feel so...so ardent about Paul. If only she didn't feel so confused!

Joe laughed at something one of his nephews said and Cait couldn't help smiling. She loved the sound of his laughter. It was vigorous and robust and lively—just like his personality.

"Joe says you're working as a stockbroker right here in Seattle."

"Yes. I've been with Webster, Rodale and Missen for over a year now. My degree was in accounting but—"

"Accounting?" Mrs. Rockwell nodded approvingly. "My Joe has his own accountant now. Good thing, too. His books were in a terrible mess. He's a builder, not a pencil pusher, that boy."

"Are you telling tales on me, Mom?" Joe asked as he sauntered into the kitchen. He picked up a piece of bacon and bit off the end. "When are we going to open the gifts? The kids are getting restless."

"The kids, nothing. You're the one who's eager to tear into those packages," his mother admonished. "We'll open them after breakfast, the way we do every Christmas."

Joe winked at Cait and disappeared into the living room once more.

Mrs. Rockwell watched her son affectionately. "Last year he shows up on my doorstep bright and early Christmas morning needing gift wrap. Then, once he's got all his presents wrapped, he walks into my kitchen—" her face crinkled in a wide grin "—and he sticks all those presents in my refrigerator." She chuckled at the memory. "For his brother, he bought two canned hams and three gallons of ice cream. For me it was canned cat food and a couple of rib roasts."

Breakfast was a bustling affair, with Joe's younger brother, his wife and their children gathered around the table. Joe sat next to Cait and held her hand while his mother offered the blessing. Although she wasn't home with her own family, Cait felt she had a good deal for which to be thankful.

Conversation was pleasant and relaxed, but foremost on the children's minds was opening the gifts. The table was cleared and the dishes washed in record time.

Cait sat beside Joe, holding a cup of coffee, as the oldest grandchild gave out the presents. Christmas music played softly in the background as the children tore into their packages. The youngest, a two-year-old girl, was more interested in the box than in the gift itself.

When Joe came to the square package Cait had given him, he shook it enthusiastically.

"Be careful, it might break," she warned, knowing there was no chance of that happening.

Carefully he removed the bows, then slowly unwrapped his gift. Cait watched expectantly as he lifted the book from the layers of bright paper. "A book on baseball?"

Cait nodded, smiling. "As I recall, you used to collect baseball cards."

"I ended up trading away my two favorites."

"I'm sure it was for a very good reason."

"Of course."

Their eyes held until it became apparent that everyone in the room was watching them. Cait glanced self-consciously away.

Joe cleared his throat. "This is a great gift, Cait. Thank you, very much."

"You're welcome very much."

He leaned over and kissed her as if it was the most natural thing in the world. It felt right, their kiss. If anything Cait was sorry to stop at one.

"Surely you have something for Cait," Virginia Rockwell prompted her son.

"Of course I do."

"He's probably keeping it in the refrigerator," Cait suggested, to the delight of Joe's family.

"Oh, ye of little faith," he said, removing a box from his shirt pocket.

"I recognize that paper," Sally, Joe's sister-in-law, murmured to Cait. "It's from Stanley's."

Cait's eyes widened at the name of an expensive local jewelry store. "Joe?"

"Go ahead and open it," he urged.

Cait did as he suggested, hands fumbling in her eagerness. She slipped off the ribbon and peeled away the gold textured wrap to reveal a white jeweler's box. It contained a second box, a small black velvet one, which she opened very slowly, She gasped at the lovely cameo brooch inside.

"Oh, Joe," she whispered. It was a lovely piece carved in onyx and overlaid with ivory. She'd longed for a cameo, a really nice one, for years and wondered how Joe could possibly have known.

"You gonna kiss Uncle Joe?" his nephew asked, "'cause if you are, I'm hiding my eyes."

"Of course she's going to kiss me," Joe answered for her. "Only she can do it later when there aren't so many curious people watching her." He glanced swiftly at his mother. "Just the way Mom used to thank Dad for her Christmas gift. Isn't that right, Mom?"

"I'm sure Cait...will," Virginia answered, clearly flustered. She patted her hand against the side of her head as though she feared the pins had fallen from her hair, her gaze skirting around the room.

Cait didn't blame the older woman for being embarrassed, but one look at the cameo and she was willing to forgive him anything.

The day flew past. After the gifts were opened—with everyone exclaiming in surprised delight over the gifts Joe had bought, with Cait's help—the family gathered around the piano. Mrs. Rockwell played as they sang a variety of Christmas carols, their voices loud and cheerful. Joe's father had died several years earlier, but often throughout the day he was mentioned with affection and love. Cait hadn't known Joe's father well. She barely remembered his mother, but the family obviously felt Andrew Rockwell's presence far more than his absence on this festive day.

Joe drove Cait back to her apartment late that night.

Mrs. Rockwell had insisted on sending a plate of cookies and candy home with her, and Cait swore it was enough goodies to last her a month of Sundays. Now she felt sleepy and warm; leaning her head against the seat, she closed her eyes.

"We're here," Joe whispered close to her ear.

Reluctantly Cait opened her eyes and sighed. "I had such a wonderful day. Thank you, Joe." She couldn't quite stifle a yawn as she reached for the door handle, thinking longingly of bed.

"That's it?" He sounded disappointed.

"What do you mean, that's it?"

"I seem to remember a certain promise you made this morning."

Cait frowned, not sure she understood what he meant. "When?"

"When we were opening the gifts," he reminded her.

"Oh," Cait said, straightening. "You mean when I opened your gift to me and saw the brooch."

Joe nodded with slow, exaggerated emphasis. "Right. Now do you remember?"

"Of course." The kiss. He planned to claim the kiss she'd promised him. She brushed her mouth quickly over his and grinned. "There."

"If that's the best you can do, you should have kissed me in front of Charlie."

"You're faulting my kissing ability?"

"Charlie's dog gives better kisses than that."

Cait felt more than a little insulted. "Is this a challenge, Joseph Rockwell?"

"Yes," he returned archly. "You're darn right it is."

"All right, then you're on." She set the plate of cookies aside, slid over on the wide seat and slipped her arms around Joe's neck. Next she wove her fingers into his thick hair.

"This is more like it," Joe murmured contentedly.

Cait paused. She wasn't entirely sure why. Perhaps it was because she'd suddenly lost all interest in making fun out of something that had always been so wonderful between them.

Joe's eyes met hers, and the laughter and fun seemed to empty out of them. Slowly he expelled his breath and brushed his lips along her jaw. The warmth of his breath was exciting as his mouth skimmed toward her temple. His arms closed around her waist and pulled her tight against him.

Impatiently he began to kiss her, introducing her to a world of warm, thrilling sensations. His moist mouth then explored the curve of her neck. It felt so good that Cait closed her eyes and experienced a curious weightlessness she'd never known—a heightened awareness of physical longing.

"Oh, Cait..." He broke away from her, his breathing labored and heavy. She knew instinctively that he wanted to say more, but he changed his mind and buried his face in her hair, exhaling sharply.

"How am I doing?" she whispered once she found her voice.

"Just fine."

"Are you ready to retract your statement?"

He hesitated. "I don't know. Convince me again." So she did, her kiss moist and gentle, her heart fluttering hard against her ribs.

"Is that good enough?" she asked when she'd recovered her breath.

Joe nodded, as though he didn't quite trust his own voice. "Excellent."

"I had a wonderful day," she whispered. "I can't thank you enough for including me."

Joe shook his head lightly as though there was so much more he wanted to say to her and couldn't. Cait slipped out of the car and walked into her building, turning on the lights when she reached her apartment. She slowly put away her things, wanting to wrap this feeling around her like a warm quilt. Minutes later, she glanced out her window to see Joe still sitting in his car, his hands gripping the steering wheel and his head bent over. It looked to Cait as though he was battling with himself to keep from following her inside. And she would have welcomed him if he had.

Nine

Cait stared at the computer screen for several minutes, blind to the information in front of her. Deep in thought, she released a long, slow breath.

Paul had seemed grateful to see her when she'd shown up at the office that morning. The week between Christmas and New Year's could be a harried one. Lindy had looked surprised, then quickly retreated into her own office after exchanging a brief good-morning and little else. Her friend's behavior continued to baffle Cait, but she couldn't concentrate on Lindy's problems just now, or even on her work.

No matter what she did, Cait couldn't stop thinking about Joe and the kisses they'd exchanged Christmas evening. Nor could she forget his tortured look as he'd sat in his car after she'd gone into her apartment. Even now she wasn't certain why she hadn't immediately run back outside. And by the time she'd decided to do that, he was gone.

Cait was so absorbed in her musings that she barely heard the knock at her office door. Guiltily she glanced up to find Paul standing just inside her doorway, his hands in his pockets, his eyes weary.

"Paul!" Cait waited for her heart to trip into double time the way it usually did whenever she was anywhere near him. It didn't, which was a relief but no longer much of a surprise.

"Hello, Cait." His smile was uneven, his face tight. He seemed ill at ease and struggling to disguise it. "Have you got a moment?"

"Sure. Come on in." She stood and motioned toward her client chair. "This is a pleasant surprise. What can I do for you?"

"Nothing much," he said vaguely, sitting down. "Uh, I just wanted you to know how pleased I am that you're here. I'm sorry you canceled your vacation, but I appreciate your coming in today. Especially in light of the fact that Lindy will be leaving." His mouth thinned briefly.

No one, other than Joe and Martin, was aware of the real reason Cait wasn't in Minnesota the way she'd planned. Nor had she suggested to Paul that she'd changed her plans to help him out because they'd be short-staffed; apparently he'd drawn his own conclusions.

"So Lindy's decided to follow through with her resignation?"

Paul nodded, then frowned anew. "Nothing I say will change her mind. That woman's got a stubborn streak as wide as a…" He shrugged, apparently unable to come up with an appropriate comparison.

"The construction project's nearly finished," Cait offered, making small talk rather than joining in his criticism of Lindy. Absently she stood up and wandered around her office, stopping to straighten the large Christmas wreath on her door, the one she and Lindy had put up earlier in the month. Lindy was her friend and she wasn't about to agree with Paul, or argue with him, for that matter. Actually she should have been pleased that Paul had sought her out this way, but she felt curiously indifferent. And she did have several things that needed to be done.

"Yes, I'm delighted with the way everything's turned out," Paul said, "Joe Rockwell's done a fine job. His reputation is excellent and I imagine he'll be one of the big-time contractors in the area within the next few years."

Cait nodded casually, hoping she'd concealed the thrill of excitement that had surged through her at the mention of Joe's name. She didn't need Paul to tell her Joe's future was bright; she could see that for herself. At Christmas, his mother had boasted freely about his success. Joe had recently received a contract for a large government project—his most important to date—and she was exceptionally proud of him. He might have trouble keeping his books straight, but he left his customers satisfied. If he worked as hard at satisfying them as he did at finding the right Christmas tree, Cait could well believe that he was gaining a reputation for excellence.

"Well, listen," Paul said, drawing in a deep breath, "I won't keep you." His eyes were clouded as he stood and headed toward the door. He hesitated, turning back to face her. "I don't suppose you'd be free for dinner tonight, would you?"

"Dinner," Cait repeated as though she'd never heard the word before. Paul was inviting her to dinner? After all these months? Now, when she least expected it? Now, when it no longer mattered? After all the times she'd ached to the bottom of her heart for some attention from him, he was finally asking her out on a date? Now?

"That is, if you're free."

"Uh…yes, sure…that would be nice."

"Great. How about if I pick you up around five-thirty? Unless that's too early for you?"

"Five-thirty will be fine."

"I'll see you then."

"Thanks, Paul." Cait felt numb. There wasn't any other way to describe it. It was as if her dreams were finally beginning to play themselves out—too late. Paul, whom she'd loved from afar for so long, wanted to take her to dinner. She should be dancing around the office with glee, or at least feeling something other than this peculiar dull sensation in the pit of her stomach. If this was such a significant, exciting, hoped-for event, why didn't she feel any of the exhilaration she'd expected?

After taking a moment to collect her thoughts, Cait walked down the hallway to Lindy's office and found her friend on the phone. Lindy glanced up, smiled feebly in Cait's direction, then abruptly dropped her gaze as if the call demanded her full attention.

Cait waited a couple of minutes, then decided to return later when Lindy wasn't so busy. She needed to talk to her friend, needed her counsel. Lindy had always encouraged Cait in her dreams of a relationship with Paul. When she was discouraged, it was Lindy who cheered her sagging spirits. Yes, it was definitely time for a talk. She'd try to get Lindy to confide in her, too. Cait valued Lindy's friendship; true, she couldn't help being hurt that the person she considered one of her best friends would give notice to leave the firm without so much as discussing it with her. But Lindy must have had her reasons. And maybe she, too, needed some support just about now.

Hearing her own phone ring, Cait hurried back to her office. She was busy for the remainder of the day. The New York Stock Exchange was due to close in a matter of minutes when Joe happened by.

"Hi," Cait greeted, her smile wide and welcoming. Her gaze connected with Joe's and he returned her smile. Her heart reacted automatically, leaping with sheer happiness.

"Hi, yourself." He sauntered into her office and threw himself down in the same chair Paul had taken earlier, stretching out his long legs in front of him and folding his hands over his stomach. "So how's the world of finance this fine day?"

"About as well as always."

"Then we're in deep trouble," he joked.

His smile was infectious. It always had been, but Cait had initially resisted him. Her defenses had weakened long before, though, and she responded readily with a smile of her own.

"You done for the day?"

"Just about." She checked the time. In another five minutes, New York would be closing down. There were several items she needed to clear from her desk, but nothing pressing. "Why?"

"Why?" It was little short of astonishing how far Joe's eyebrows could reach, Cait noted, all but disappearing into his hairline.

"Can't a man ask a simple question?" Joe asked.

"Of course." The banter between them was like a well-rehearsed play. Never had Cait been more at ease with a man—or had more fun with a man. Or with anyone, really. "What I want to know is whether 'simple' refers to the question or to the man asking it."

"Ouch," Joe said, grinning broadly. "Those claws are sharp this afternoon."

"Actually today's been good." Or at least it had since he'd arrived.

"I'm glad to hear it. How about dinner?" He jumped to his feet and pretended to waltz around her office, playing a violin. "You and me. Wine and moonlight and music. Romance and roses." He wiggled his eyebrows at her suggestively. "You work too hard. You always have. I want you to enjoy life a little more. It would be good for both of us."

Joe didn't need to give her an incentive to go out with him. Cait's heart soared at the mere idea. Joe made her laugh, made her feel good about herself and the world. Of course, he possessed a remarkable talent for driving her crazy, too. But she supposed a little craziness was good for the spirit.

"Only promise me you won't wear those high heels of yours," he chided, pressing his hand to the small of her back. "I've suffered excruciating back pains ever since Paul's Christmas party."

Paul's name seemed to leap out and grab Cait by the throat. "Paul," she repeated, sagging against the back of her chair. "Oh, dear."

"I know you consider him a dear," Joe teased. "What has your stalwart employer done this time?"

"He asked me out to dinner," Cait admitted, frowning. "Out of the blue this morning he popped into my office and invited me to dinner as if we'd been dating for months. I was so stunned, I didn't know what to think."

"What did you tell him?" Joe seemed to consider the whole thing a huge joke. "Wait—" he held up his hand "—you don't need to answer that. I already know. You sprang at the offer."

"I didn't exactly spring," she contended, somewhat offended by Joe's attitude. The least he could do was show a little concern. She'd spent Christmas with him, and according to his own mother this was the first time he'd ever brought a woman home for the holiday. Furthermore, despite his insisting to all and sundry that they were married, he certainly didn't seem to mind her seeing another man.

"I'll bet you nearly went into shock." A smile trembled at the edges of his mouth as if he was picturing her reaction to Paul's invitation and finding it all terribly amusing.

"I did not go into shock," she defended herself heatedly. She'd been taken by surprise, that was all.

"Listen," he said walking toward the door, "have a great time. I'll catch you later." With that he was gone.

Cait couldn't believe it. Her mouth dropped open and she paced frantically, clenching and unclenching her fists. It took her a full minute to recover enough to run after him.

Joe was talking to his foreman, the same stocky man he'd been with the day he followed Cait into the elevator.

"Excuse me," she said, interrupting their conversation, "but when you're finished I'd like a few words with you, Joe.'' Her back was ramrod stiff and she kept flexing her hands as though preparing for a fight.

Joe glanced at his watch. "It might be a while."

"Then might I have a few minutes of your time now?"

The foreman stepped away, his step cocky. "You want me to dismiss the crew again, boss? I can tell them to go out and buy a New Year's present for their wives, if you like."

The man was rewarded with a look that was hot enough to barbecue spareribs. "That won't be necessary, thanks, anyway, Harry."

"You're welcome, boss. We only serve to please."

"Then please me by kindly shutting up."

Harry chuckled and returned to another section of the office.

"You wanted something?" Joe demanded of Cait.

Boy, did she. "Is that all you're going to say?"

"About what?"

"About my going to dinner with Paul? I expected you to be…I don't know, upset or something."

"Why should I be upset? Is he going to have his way with you? I sincerely doubt it, but if you're worried, invite me along and I'll be more than happy to protect your honor."

"What's the matter with you?" she demanded, not bothering to disguise her fury and disappointment. She stared at Joe, waiting for him to mock her again, but once more he surprised her. His gaze sobered.

"You honestly expect me to be jealous?"

"Not jealous exactly," she corrected, although he wasn't far from the truth. "Concerned."

"I'm not. Paul's a good man."

"I know, but—"

"You've been in love with him for months—"

"I think it was more of an infatuation."

"True. But he's finally asked you out, and you've accepted."

"Yes, but—"

"We know each other well, Cait. We were married, remember?"

"I'm not likely to forget it." Especially when Joe took pains to point it out at every opportunity. "Shouldn't that mean...something?" Cait couldn't believe she'd said that. For weeks she'd suffered acute mortification every time Joe mentioned the childhood stunt. Now she was using it to suit her own purposes.

Joe reached out and took hold of her shoulders. "As a matter of fact, our marriage does mean a good deal."

Hearing Joe admit as much was gratifying.

"I want only the best for you," he continued. "It's what you deserve. All I can say is that I'd be more than pleased if everything works out between you and Paul. Now if you'll excuse me, I need to talk over some matters with Harry."

"Oh, right, sure, go ahead." She couldn't seem to get the words out fast enough. When she'd called Martin to explain why she wouldn't be in Minnesota for Christmas, he'd claimed that God would reward her sacrifice. If Paul's invitation to dinner was God's reward, she wanted her airline ticket back.

The numb feeling returned as Cait walked back to her office. She didn't know what to think. She'd believed...she'd hoped she and Joe shared something very special. Clearly their times together meant something entirely different to him than they had to her.

Otherwise he wouldn't behave so casually about her going out with Paul. And he certainly wouldn't seem so pleased about it!

That was what hurt Cait the most, and yes, she was hurt. It had taken her several minutes to identify her feelings, but now she did.

More by accident than design, Cait walked into Lindy's office. Her friend had already put on her coat and was carrying her briefcase, ready to leave the office.

"Paul asked me out to dinner," Cait blurted out.

"He did?" Lindy's eyes widened with surprise. But she didn't turn it into a joke, the way Joe had.

Cait nodded. "He just strolled in as if it was something he did every day and asked me out."

"Are you happy about it?"

"I don't know," Cait answered honestly. "I suppose I should be pleased. It's what I'd prayed would happen for months."

"Then what's the problem?" Lindy asked.

"Joe doesn't seem to care. He said he hopes everything works out the way I want it to."

"Which is?" Lindy pressed.

Cait had to think about that a moment, her heart in her throat. "Honest to heaven, Lindy, I don't know anymore."

"I understand the salmon here is superb," Paul was saying, reading over the Boathouse menu. It was a well-known restaurant on Lake Union.

Cait scanned the list of entrées, which featured fresh seafood, then chose the grilled salmon—the same dish she'd ordered that night with Joe. Tonight, though, she wasn't sure why she was even bothering. She wasn't hungry, and Paul was going to be wasting good money while she made a pretense of enjoying her meal.

"I understand you've been seeing a lot of Joe Rockwell," he said conversationally.

That Paul should mention Joe's name right now was ironic. Cait hadn't stopped thinking about him from the moment he'd dropped into her office earlier that afternoon. Their conversation had left a bitter taste in her mouth. She'd sincerely believed their relationship was developing into something...special. Yet Joe had gone out of his way to give her the opposite impression.

"Cait?" Paul stared at her.

"I'm sorry, what were you saying?"

"Simply that you and Joe Rockwell have been seeing a lot of each other recently."

"Uh, yes. As you know, we were childhood friends," she murmured. "Actually Joe and my older brother were best friends. Then Joe's family moved to the suburbs and our families lost contact."

"Yes, I remember you mentioned that."

The waitress came for their order, and Paul requested a bottle of white wine. Then he chatted amicably for several minutes, mentioning subjects of shared interest from the office.

Cait listened attentively, nodding from time to time or adding the occasional comment. Now that she had his undivided attention, Cait wondered what it was about Paul that she'd found so extraordinary. He was attractive, but not nearly as dynamic or exciting as she found Joe. True, Paul possessed a certain charm, but compared to Joe, he was subdued and perhaps even a little dull. Cait couldn't imagine her stalwart boss carrying her piggyback out the back door because her high heels were too tight. Nor could she see Paul bantering with her the way Joe did.

The waitress delivered the wine bottle, opened it and poured them each a glass, after Paul had given his approval. Their dinners followed shortly afterward. After taking a bite or two of her delicious salmon, Cait noticed that Paul hadn't touched his meal. If anything, he seemed restless.

He rolled the stem of the wineglass between his fingers, watching the wine swirl inside. Then he suddenly blurted out, "What do you think of Lindy's leaving the firm?"

Cait was taken aback by the fervor in his voice when he mentioned Lindy's name. "Frankly I was shocked," Cait said. "Lindy and I have been good friends for a couple of years now." There'd been a time when the two had done nearly everything together. The summer before, they'd vacationed in Mexico and returned to Seattle with enough handwoven baskets and bulky blankets to set up shop themselves.

"Lindy's resigning came as a surprise to you, then?"

"Yes, this whole thing caught me completely unaware. Lindy didn't even mention the other job offer to me. I always thought we were good friends."

"Lindy *is* your friend," Paul said with enough conviction to persuade the patrons at the nearby tables. "You wouldn't believe what a good friend she is."

"I...know that." But friends sometimes had surprises up their sleeves. Lindy was a good example of that, and apparently so was Joe.

"I find Lindy an exceptional woman," Paul commented, watching Cait closely.

"She's probably one of the best stockbrokers in the business," Cait said, taking a sip of her wine.

"My...admiration for her goes beyond her keen business mind."

"Oh, mine, too," Cait was quick to agree. Lindy was the kind of friend who would traipse through the blazing sun of Mexico looking for a conch shell because she knew Cait really wanted to take one home with her. And Lindy had listened to countless hours of Cait's bemoaning her sorry fate of unrequited love for Paul.

"She's a wonderful woman."

Joe was wonderful, too, Cait thought. So wonderful her heart ached at his indifference when she'd announced she would be dining with Paul.

"Lindy's the kind of woman a man could treasure all his life," Paul went on.

"I couldn't agree with you more," Cait said. Now, if only Joe would realize what a treasure *she* was. He'd married her once—well, sort of—and surely the thought of spending their lives together had crossed his mind in the past few weeks.

Paul hesitated as though he were at a loss for words. "I don't suppose you've given any thought to the reason Lindy made this unexpected decision to resign?"

Frankly Cait hadn't. Her mind and her heart had been so full of Joe that deciphering her friend's actions had somehow escaped her. "She received a better offer, didn't she?" Which was understandable. Lindy would be an asset to any firm.

It was then that Cait understood. Paul hadn't asked

her to dinner out of any desire to develop a romantic relationship with her. He saw her as a means of discovering what had prompted Lindy to resign. This new awareness came as a relief, a burden lifted from her shoulders. Paul wasn't interested in her. He never had been and probably never would be. A few weeks ago, that realization would have been a crushing defeat, but all Cait experienced now was an overwhelming sense of gratitude.

"I'm sure if you talk to Lindy, she might reconsider," Cait suggested.

"I've tried, trust me. But there's a problem."

"Oh?" Now that Cait had sampled the salmon, she discovered it to be truly delicious. She hadn't realized how hungry she was.

"Cait, look at me," Paul said, raising his voice slightly. His face was pinched, his eyes intense. "Damn, but you've made this nearly impossible."

She looked up at him, her face puzzled. "What is it, Paul?"

"You have no idea, do you? I swear you've got to be the most obtuse woman in the world." He pushed aside his plate and briefly closed his eyes, shaking his head. "I'm in love with Lindy. I have been for weeks…months. But for the life of me I couldn't get her to notice me. I swear I did everything but turn cartwheels in her office. It finally dawned on me why she wasn't responding."

"Me?" Cait asked in a feeble, mouselike squeak.

"Exactly. She didn't want to betray your friendship. Then one afternoon—I think it was the day you first recognized Joe—we, Lindy and I, were in my office alone together and— Oh hell, I don't know how it happened, but Lindy was looking something up for me and she stumbled over one of the cords the construction crew was using. Fortunately I was able to catch her before she fell to the floor. I know it wasn't her fault, but I was so angry, afraid she might have been hurt. Lindy was just as angry with me for being angry with her, and it seemed the only way to shut her up was to kiss her. That was the beginning and I swear to you everything exploded in our faces at that moment.''

Cait swallowed, fascinated by the story. "Go on."

"I tried for days to get her to agree to go out with me. But she kept refusing until I demanded to know why."

"She told you...how I felt about you?" The thought was mortifying.

"Of course not. Lindy's too good a friend to divulge your confidence. Besides, she didn't need to tell me. I've known all along. Good grief, Cait, what did I have to do to discourage you? Hire a skywriter?"

"I don't think anything that drastic was necessary," she muttered, humiliated to the very marrow of her bones.

"I repeatedly told Lindy I wasn't attracted to you, but she wouldn't listen. Finally she told me if I'd talk to you, explain everything myself, she'd agree to go out with me."

"The phone call," Cait said on a stroke of genius. "That was the reason you called me, wasn't it? You wanted to talk about Lindy, not that business article."

"Yes." He looked deeply grateful for her insight, late though it was.

"Well, for heaven's sake, why didn't you?"

"Believe me, I've kicked myself a dozen times since. I wish I knew. At the time, it seemed so heartless to have such a frank discussion over the phone. Again and again, I promised myself I'd say something. Lord knows I dropped enough hints, but you weren't exactly receptive."

She winced. "But why is Lindy resigning?"

"Isn't it obvious?" Paul demanded. "It was becoming increasingly difficult for us to work together. She didn't want to betray her best friend, but at the same time…"

"But at the same time you two were falling in love."

"Exactly. I can't lose her, Cait. I don't want to hurt your feelings, and believe me, it's nothing personal— you're a trustworthy employee and a decent person— but I'm simply not attracted to you."

Paul didn't seem to be the only one. Other than treating their relationship like one big joke, Joe hadn't ever claimed any romantic feelings for her, either.

"I had to do something before I lost Lindy."

"I couldn't agree more."

"You're not angry with her, are you?"

"Good heavens, no," Cait said, offering him a brave smile.

"We both thought something was developing between you and Joe Rockwell. You seemed to be seeing quite a bit of each other, and then at the Christmas party—"

"Don't remind me," Cait said with a low groan.

Paul's face creased in a spontaneous smile. "Joe certainly has a wit about him, doesn't he?"

Cait gave a resigned nod.

Now that Paul had cleared the air, he seemed to develop an appetite. He reached for his dinner and ate heartily. By contrast, Cait's salmon had lost its appeal. She stared down at her plate, wondering how she could possibly make it through the rest of the evening.

She did, though, quite nicely. Paul didn't even seem to notice that anything was amiss. It wasn't that Cait was distressed by his confession. If anything, she was relieved at this turn of events and delighted that Lindy had fallen in love. Paul was obviously crazy about her; she'd never seen him more animated than when he was discussing Lindy. It still amazed Cait that she'd been so unperceptive about Lindy's real feelings. Not to mention Paul's...

Paul dropped her off at her building and saw her to the front door. "I can't thank you enough," he said, his voice warm. Impulsively he hugged her, then hurried back to his sports car.

Although she was certainly guilty of being obtuse, Cait knew exactly where Paul was headed. No doubt Lindy would be waiting for him, eager to hear the details of their conversation. Cait planned to talk to her friend herself first thing in the morning.

Cait's apartment was dark and lonely. So lonely the silence seemed to echo off the walls. She hung up her coat before turning on the lights, her thoughts as dark as the room had been.

She made herself a cup of tea. Then she sat on the sofa, tucking her feet beneath her as she stared unseeingly at the walls, assessing her options. They seemed terribly limited.

Paul was in love with Lindy. And Joe...Cait had no idea where she stood with him. For all she knew—

Her thoughts were interrupted by the phone. She answered on the second ring.

"Cait?" It was Joe and he seemed surprised to find her back so early. "When did you get in?"

"A few minutes ago."

"You don't sound right. Is something wrong?"

"My goodness," she said, breaking into sobs. "What could possibly be wrong?"

Ten

The flow of emotion took Cait by storm. She'd had no intention of crying; in fact, the thought hadn't even entered her mind. One moment she was sitting there, contemplating the evening's revelations, and the next she was sobbing hysterically into the phone.

"Cait?"

"Oh," she wailed. "This is all your fault in the first place." Cait didn't know what made her say that. The words had slipped out before she'd realized it.

"What happened?"

"Nothing. I...I can't talk to you now. I'm going to bed." With that, she gently replaced the receiver. Part of her hoped Joe would call back, but the telephone remained stubbornly silent. She stared at it for several minutes. Apparently Joe didn't care if he talked to her or not.

The tears continued to flow. They remained a mystery to Cait. She wasn't a woman given to bouts of crying, but now that she'd started she couldn't seem to stop.

She changed out of her dress and into a pair of sweats, pausing halfway through to wash her face.

Sniffling and hiccuping, she sat on the end of her bed and dragged a shuddering breath through her lungs. Crying like this made absolutely no sense whatsoever.

Paul was in love with Lindy. At one time, the news would have devastated her, but not now. Cait felt a tingling happiness that her best friend had found a man to love. And the infatuation she'd held for Paul couldn't compare with the strength of her love for Joe.

Love.

There, she'd admitted it. She was in love with Joe. The man who told restaurant employees that she was suffering from amnesia. The man who walked into elevators and announced to total strangers that they were married. Yet this was the same man who hadn't revealed a minute's concern about her dating Paul Jamison.

Joe was also the man who'd gently held her hand through a children's movie. The man who made a practice of kissing her senseless. The man who'd held her in his arms Christmas night as though he never intended to let her go.

Joseph Rockwell was a fun-loving jokester who took delight in teasing her. He was also tender and thoughtful and loving—the man who'd captured her heart only to drop it carelessly.

Her doorbell chimed and she didn't need to look in the peephole to know it was Joe. But she felt panicky all of a sudden, too confused and vulnerable to see him now.

She walked slowly to the door and opened it a crack.

"What the hell is going on?" Joe demanded, not waiting for an invitation to march inside.

Cait wiped her eyes on her sleeve and shut the door. "Nothing."

"Did Paul try anything?"

She rolled her eyes. "Of course not."

"Then why are you crying?" He stood in the middle of her living room, fists planted on his hips as if he'd welcome the opportunity to punch out her boss.

If Cait knew why it was necessary to cry nonstop like this, she would have answered him. She opened her mouth, hoping some intelligent reason would emerge, but the only thing that came out was a low-pitched squeak. Joe was gazing at her in complete confusion. "I...Paul's in love."

"With you?" His voice rose half an octave with disbelief.

"Don't make it sound like such an impossibility," she said crossly. "I'm reasonably attractive, you know." If she was expecting Joe to list her myriad charms, Cait was disappointed.

Instead, his frown darkened. "So what's Paul being in love got to do with anything?"

"Absolutely nothing. I wished him and Lindy the very best."

"So it is Lindy?" Joe murmured as though he'd known it all along.

"You didn't honestly think it was me, did you?"

"Hell, how was I supposed to know? I *thought* it was Lindy, but it was you he was taking to dinner. Frankly it didn't make a whole lot of sense to me."

"Which is something else," Cait grumbled, standing so close to him, their faces were only inches apart. Her hands were planted on her hips, her pose mirroring his. They resembled a pair of gunslingers ready for a shootout, Cait thought absently. "I want to know one thing. Every time I turn around, you're telling anyone and everyone who'll listen that we're married. But when it really matters you—"

"When did it really matter?"

Cait ignored the question, thinking the answer was obvious. "You casually turn me over to Paul as if you couldn't wait to be rid of me. Obviously you couldn't have cared less."

"I cared," he shouted.

"Oh, right," she shouted back, "but if that was the case, you certainly didn't bother to show it!"

"What was I supposed to do, challenge him to a duel?"

He was being ridiculous, Cait decided, and she refused to take the bait. The more they talked, the more unreasonable they were both becoming.

"I thought dating Paul was what you wanted," he complained. "You talked about it long enough. Paul this and Paul that. He'd walk past and you'd all but swoon."

"That's not the least bit true." Maybe it had been at one time, but not now and not for weeks. "If you'd taken the trouble to ask me, you might have learned the truth."

"You mean you don't love Paul?"

Cait rolled her eyes again. "Bingo."

"It isn't like you to be so sarcastic."

"It isn't like you to be so...awful."

He seemed to mull that over for a moment. "If we're going to be throwing out accusations," he said tightly, "then maybe you should take a look at yourself."

"What exactly do you mean by that?" As usual, no one could get a reaction out of Cait more effectively than Joe. "Never mind," she answered, walking to the door. "This discussion isn't getting us anywhere. All we seem capable of doing is hurling insults at each other."

"I disagree," Joe answered calmly. "I think it's time we cleared the air."

She took a deep breath, feeling physically and emotionally deflated.

"Joe, it'll have to wait. I'm in no condition to be rational right now and I don't want either of us saying things we'll regret." She held open her door for him. "Please?"

He seemed about to argue with her, then he sighed and dropped a quick kiss on her mouth. Wide-eyed, she watched him leave.

Lindy was waiting in Cait's office early the following morning, holding two plastic cups of freshly brewed coffee. Her eyes were wide and expectant as Cait entered the office. They stared at each other for several moments.

"Are you angry with me?" Lindy whispered. She handed Cait one of the cups in an apparent peace offering.

"Of course not," Cait murmured. She put down her briefcase and accepted the cup, which she placed carefully on her desk. Then she gave Lindy a reassuring hug, and the two of them sat down for their much postponed talk.

"Why didn't you tell me?" Cait burst out.

"I wanted to," Lindy said earnestly. "I had to stop

myself a hundred times. The worst part of it was the guilt—knowing you were in love with Paul, and loving him myself.''

Cait wasn't sure how she would have reacted to the truth, but she preferred to think she would've understood, and wished Lindy well. It wasn't as though Lindy had stolen Paul away from her.

"I don't think I realized how I felt," Lindy continued, "until one afternoon when I tripped over a stupid cord and fell into Paul's arms. From there, everything sort of snowballed.''

"Paul told me.''

"He…told you about that afternoon?''

Cait grinned and nodded. "I found the story wildly romantic.''

"You don't mind?'' Lindy watched her closely as if half-afraid of Cait's reaction even now.

"I think it's wonderful.''

Lindy's smile was filled with warmth and excitement. "I never knew being in love could be so delightful, but at the same time cause so much pain.''

"Amen to that,'' Cait stated emphatically.

Her words shot like live bullets into the room. If Cait could have reached out and pulled them back, she would have.

"Is it Joe Rockwell?'' Lindy asked quietly.

Cait nodded, then shook her head. "See how much he's confused me?'' She made a sound that was half sob, half giggle. "That man infuriates me so much I want to scream. Or cry.'' Cait had always thought of herself as a sane and sensible person. She lived a quiet life, worked hard at her job, enjoyed traveling and crossword puzzles. Then she'd bumped into Joe. Suddenly she found herself demanding piggyback rides, talking to strangers in elevators and seeking out phantom women at Christmas parties while downing spiked punch like it was soda pop.

"But then at other times?" Lindy prompted.

"At other times I love him so much I hurt all the way through. I love everything about him. Even those loony stunts of his. In fact, I usually laugh as hard as everyone else does. Even if I don't always want him to know it."

"So what's going to happen with you two?" Lindy asked. She took a sip of coffee and as she did so, Cait caught a flash of diamond.

"Lindy?" Cait demanded, jumping out of her seat. "What's that on your finger?"

Lindy's face broke into a smile so wide Cait was nearly blinded. "You noticed."

"Of course I did."

"It's from Paul. After he had dinner with you, he stopped over at my apartment. We talked for the longest time and then after a while he asked me to marry him. At first I didn't know what to say. It seems so soon. We…we hardly know each other."

"Good grief, you've worked together for months."

"I know," Lindy said with a shy smile. "That was what Paul told me. It didn't take him long to convince me. He had the ring all picked out. Isn't it beautiful?"

"Oh, Lindy." The diamond was a lovely solitaire set in a wide band of gold. The style and shape were perfect for Lindy's long, elegant finger.

"I didn't know if I should wear it until you and I had talked, but I couldn't make myself take it off this morning."

"Of course you should wear it!" The fact that Paul had been carting it around when he'd had dinner with her didn't exactly flatter her ego, but she was so thrilled for Lindy that seemed a minor concern.

Lindy splayed her fingers out in front of her to better show off the ring. "When he slipped it on my finger, I swear it was the most romantic moment of my life. Before I knew it, tears were streaming down my face. I still don't understand why I felt like crying. I think Paul was as surprised as I was."

There must have been something in the air that reduced susceptible females to tears, Cait decided. Whatever it was had certainly affected her.

"Now you've sidetracked me," Lindy said, looking up from her diamond, her gaze dreamy and warm. "You were telling me about you and Joe."

"I was?"

"Yes, you were," Lindy insisted.

"There's nothing to tell. If there was you'd be the first person to hear. I know," she admitted before her friend could bring up the point, "we have seen a lot of each other recently, but I don't think it meant anything to him. When he found out Paul had invited me to dinner, he seemed downright delighted."

"I'm sure it was all an act."

Cait wished she could believe that. Oh, how she wished it.

"You're in love with him?" Lindy asked softly, hesitantly.

Cait nodded and lowered her eyes. It hurt to think about Joe. Everything was a game to him—one big joke. Lindy had been right about one thing, though.

Love was the most wonderful experience of her life. And the most painful.

The New York Stock Exchange had closed and Cait was punching some figures into her computer when Joe strode into her office and closed the door.

"Feel free to come in," she muttered, continuing her work. Her heart was pounding but she dared not let him know the effect he had on her.

"I will make myself at home, thank you," he answered cheerfully, ignoring her sarcasm. He pulled out a chair and sat down expansively, resting one ankle on the opposite knee and relaxing as if he was in a movie theater, waiting for the main feature to begin.

"If you're here to discuss business, might I suggest investing in blue-chip stocks? They're always a safe bet." Cait went on typing, doing her best to ignore Joe—which was nearly impossible, although she gave an Oscar-winning performance, if she did say so herself.

"I'm here to talk business all right," Joe said, "but it has nothing to do with the stock market."

"What business could the two of us possibly have?" she asked, her voice deliberately ironic.

"I want to continue the discussion we were having last night."

"Perhaps you do, but unfortunately that was last night and this is now." How confident she sounded, Cait thought, mildly pleased with herself. "I can do without hearing you list my no doubt numerous flaws."

"It's your being my wife I want to discuss."

"Your wife?" She wished he'd quit throwing the

subject at her as if it meant something to him. Something other than a joke.

"Yes, my wife." He gave a short laugh. "Believe me, it isn't your flaws I'm here to discuss."

Despite everything, Cait's heart raced. She reached for a stack of papers and switched them from one basket to another. Her entire filing system was probably in jeopardy, but she had to do something with her hands before she stood up and reached out to Joe. She did stand then, but it was to remove a large silver bell strung from a red velvet ribbon hanging in her office window.

"Paul and Lindy are getting married," he supplied next.

"Yes, I know. Lindy and I had a long talk this morning." She took the wreath off her door next.

"I take it the two of you are friends again?"

"We were never not friends," Cait answered stiffly, stuffing the wreath, the bell and the three ceramic Wise Men into the bottom drawer of her filing cabinet. Hard as she tried not to, she could feel her defenses crumbling. "Lindy's asked me to be her maid of honor and I've agreed."

"Will you return the favor?"

It took a moment for the implication to sink in, and even then Cait wasn't sure she should follow the trail Joe seemed to be forging through this conversation. She leaned forward and rested her hands on the edge of the desk.

"I'm destined to be an old maid," she said flippantly, although she couldn't help feeling a sliver of real hope.

"You'll never be that."

Cait was hoping he'd say her beauty would make her irresistible, or that her warmth and wit and intelligence was sure to attract a dozen suitors. Instead he said the very thing she could have predicted. "We're already married, so you don't need to worry about being a spinster."

Cait released a sigh of impatience. "I wish you'd give up on that, Joe. It's growing increasingly old."

"As I recall, we celebrated our eighteenth wedding anniversary not long ago."

"Don't be ridiculous. All right," she said, straightening abruptly. If he wanted to play games, then she'd respond in kind. "Since we're married, I want a family."

"Hey, sweetheart," he cried, tossing his arms in the air, "that's music to my ears. I'm willing."

Cait prepared to leave the office, if not the building. "Somehow I knew you would be."

"Two or three," he interjected, then chuckled and added, "I suppose we should name the first two Barbie and Ken."

Cait sent him a scalding look that made him chuckle even louder.

"If you prefer, we'll leave the names open to negotiation," he said.

"Of all the colossal nerve..." Cait muttered, moving to the window and gazing out.

"If you want daughters, I've got no objection, but from what I understand that's not left up to us."

Cait turned around, folding her arms across her chest. "Correct me if I'm wrong," she said coldly, certain he'd delight in doing so. "But you did just ask me to marry you. Could you confirm that?"

"All I'm looking to do is make legal what's already been done."

Cait frowned. Was he serious, or wasn't he? He was talking about marriage, about joining their lives as if he were planning a bid on a construction project.

"When Paul asked Lindy to marry him, he had a diamond ring with him."

"I was going to buy you a ring," Joe said emphatically. "I still am. But I thought you'd want to pick it out yourself. If you wanted a diamond, why didn't you say so? I'll buy you the whole store if that'll make you happy."

"One ring will suffice, thank you."

"Pick out two or three. I understand diamonds are an excellent investment."

Cait frowned. "Not so fast," she said, holding out her arm. It was vital she maintain some distance between them. If Joe kissed her or started talking about having children again, they might never get the facts clear.

"Not so fast?" he repeated incredulously. "Honey, I've been waiting eighteen years to discuss this. You're not going to ruin everything now, are you?" He advanced a couple of steps toward her.

"I'm not agreeing to anything until you explain yourself." For every step he took toward her, Cait retreated two.

"About what?" Joe was frowning, which wasn't a good sign.

"Paul."

His eyelids slammed shut, then slowly raised. "I don't understand why that man's name has to come into every conversation you and I have."

Cait decided it was better to ignore that comment. "You haven't even told me you love me."

"I love you." He actually sounded annoyed, as if she'd insisted on having the obvious reiterated.

"You might say it with a little more feeling," Cait suggested.

"If you want feeling, come here and let me kiss you."

"No."

"Why not?" By now they'd completely circled her desk. "We're talking serious things here. Trust me, sweetheart, a man doesn't bring up marriage and babies with just any woman. I love you. I've loved you for years, only I didn't know it."

"Then why did you let Paul take me out to dinner?"

"You mean I could have stopped you?"

"Of course. I didn't want to go out with him! I was sick about having to turn down your offer for dinner, and you didn't even seem to care that I was going out with another man. And as far as you were concerned, he was your main competition."

"I wasn't worried."

"That wasn't the impression I got later."

"All right, all right," Joe said, rifling his fingers through his hair. "I didn't think Paul was interested in you. I saw him and Lindy together one night at the office and the electricity between them was so thick it could have lit up Seattle."

"You knew about Lindy and Paul?"

Joe shrugged. "Let me put it this way. I had a sneaking suspicion. But when you started talking about Paul as though you were in love with him, I got worried.''

''You should have been.'' Which was a bold-faced lie.

Somehow without her being quite sure how it happened, Joe maneuvered himself so only a few inches separated them.

''Are you ever going to kiss me?'' he demanded.

Meekly Cait nodded and walked into his arms like a child opening the gate and skipping up the walkway to home. This was the place she belonged. With Joe. This was home and she need never doubt his love again.

With a sigh that seemed to come from the deepest part of him, Joe swept her close. For a breathless moment they looked into each other's eyes. He was about to kiss her when there was a knock at her door.

Harry, Joe's foreman, walked in without waiting for a response. ''I don't suppose you've seen Joe—'' He stopped abruptly. ''Oh, sorry,'' he said, flustered and eager to make his escape.

''No problem,'' Cait assured him. ''We're married. We have been for years and years.''

Joe was chuckling as his mouth settled over hers, and in a single kiss he wiped out all the doubts and misgivings, replacing them with promises and thrills.

Epilogue

The robust sound of organ music filled the Seattle church as Cait slowly stepped down the center aisle, her feet moving in time to the traditional music. As the maid of honor, Lindy stood to one side of the altar while Joe and his brother, who was serving as the best man, waited on the other.

Cait's brother, Martin, stood directly ahead of her. He smiled at Cait as the assembly rose and she came down the aisle, her heart overflowing with happiness.

Cait and Joe had planned this day for months. If there'd been any lingering doubts that Joe really loved her, they were long gone. He wasn't the type of man who expressed his love with flowery words and gifts. But Cait had known that from the first. He'd insisted on building their home before the wedding and they'd spent countless hours going over the plans. Cait was helping him with his accounting and would be taking over the task full-time as soon as they started their family. Which would be soon, very soon. The way Cait figured it, she'd be pregnant by next Christmas.

But before they began their real life together, they'd enjoy a perfect honeymoon in New Zealand. He'd wanted to surprise her with the trip, but Cait had needed a passport. They'd only be gone two weeks, which was all the time Joe could afford to take, since he had several large projects coming up.

As the organ concluded the "Wedding March," Cait handed her bouquet to Lindy and placed her hands in Joe's. He smiled down on her as if he'd never seen a more beautiful woman in his life. From the look on his face, Cait knew he could hardly keep from kissing her right then and there.

"Dearly beloved," Martin said, stepping forward, "we are gathered here today in the sight of God and man to celebrate the love of Joseph James Rockwell and Caitlin Rose Marshall."

Cait's eyes locked with Joe's. She did love him, so much her heart felt close to bursting. After all these months of waiting for this moment, Cait was sure she'd be so nervous her voice would falter. That didn't happen. She'd never felt more confident of anything than her feelings for Joe and his for her. Cait's voice rang out strong and clear, as did Joe's.

As they exchanged the rings, Cait could hear her mother and Joe's weeping softly in the background. But these were tears of shared happiness. The two women had renewed their friendship and were excited about the prospect of grandchildren.

Cait waited for the moment when Martin would tell Joe he could kiss his bride. Instead he closed his Bible, reverently set it aside, and said, "Joseph James Rockwell, do you have the baseball cards with you?"

"I do."

Cait looked at them as if they'd both lost their minds. Joe reached inside his tuxedo jacket and produced two flashy baseball cards.

"You may give them to your bride."

With a dramatic flourish, Joe did as Martin instructed. Cait stared down at the two cards and grinned broadly.

"You may now kiss the bride," Martin declared. Joe was more than happy to comply.

From *USA TODAY* bestselling author

EMILIE RICHARDS

comes the story of a woman who has played life
by the book, and now the rules have changed.

Faith Bronson, daughter of a prominent Virginia senator and wife
of a charismatic lobbyist, finds her privileged life shattered when
her marriage ends abruptly. Only just beginning to face the lie
she has lived, she finds sanctuary with her two children in a
run-down row house in exclusive Georgetown. This historic
house harbors deep secrets of its own, secrets that force Faith
to confront the deceit that has long defined her.

PROSPECT STREET

"Richards adds to the territory
staked out by such authors as
Barbara Delinsky and Kristin Hannah....
Richards' writing is unpretentious and
effective and her characters burst with
vitality and authenticity."

—*Publishers Weekly*

*Available the first week of June 2003
wherever paperbacks are sold!*

MIRA®

Bestselling Author

Jeanette Baker

When Kellie Delaney's twin brother dies in a tragic accident in London, her initial grief quickly turns to shock and then to rage when she discovers the truth: Connor had been working undercover for British Special Forces and his death was no accident. Armed with little more than her anger and her desire to exact justice and revenge, Kellie travels to a sleepy Irish town to track down Tom Whelan, the man she is convinced is responsible for her loss. Instead, she meets a man who is the antithesis of a killer. And the more she learns about him the more she falls under his spell, finally suspecting that Tom Whelan could be her ally—not her foe. But who, then, is responsible for the death of Connor Delaney? Who is tracking Kellie's every movement? Who wants her silenced?

The Delaney Woman

"...thoughtful exposition and flawless writing..."
—*Publishers Weekly* on *Blood Roses*

Available the first week of June 2003 wherever paperbacks are sold!

New York Times **Bestselling Author**

LISA JACKSON

A TWIST OF FATE

When Kane Webster buys First Puget Bank, he knows he is buying trouble. Someone is embezzling funds, and the evidence points to Erin O'Toole. Kane is determined to see her incriminated—until he meets her. He didn't expect to feel such an intense attraction to Erin—or to fall in love with her.

After her divorce, Erin has no desire to get involved with anyone—especially not her new boss. But she can't resist Kane Webster. Before she can help it, she's swept into a passionate affair with a man she barely knows…a man she already loves. But when she discovers Kane's suspicions, she must decide—can she stay with a man who suspects her of criminal intent?

"A natural talent!" —*Literary Times*

Available the first week of June 2003 wherever paperbacks are sold!